GIANT DAYS™

VOLUME TWELVE

BOOM! BOX™

BOOM! BOX™

GIANT DAYS Volume Twelve, February 2020. Published by BOOM! Box, a division of Boom Entertainment, Inc. Giant Days is ™ & © 2020 John Allison. Originally published in single magazine form as GIANT DAYS No. 45-48. ™ & © 2018-2019 John Allison. All rights reserved. BOOM! Box™ and the BOOM! Box logo are trademarks of Boom Entertainment, Inc., registered in various countries and categories. All characters, events, and institutions depicted herein are fictional. Any similarity between any of the names, characters, persons, events, and/or institutions in this publication to actual names, characters, and persons, whether living or dead, events, and/or institutions is unintended and purely coincidental. BOOM! Box does not read or accept unsolicited submissions of ideas, stories, or artwork.

BOOM! Studios, 5670 Wilshire Boulevard, Suite 400, Los Angeles, CA 90036-5679. Printed in China. First Printing.

ISBN: 978-1-68415-484-5, eISBN: 978-1-64144-642-6

GIANT DAYS™

CREATED + WRITTEN BY
JOHN ALLISON

ART BY
MAX SARIN &
JOHN ALLISON
(CHAPTER 48)

COLORS BY
WHITNEY COGAR

LETTERS BY
JIM CAMPBELL

COVER BY
MAX SARIN

SERIES DESIGNER
GRACE PARK

COLLECTION DESIGNER
CHELSEA ROBERTS

EDITOR
SOPHIE PHILIPS-ROBERTS

SENIOR EDITOR
SHANNON WATTERS

CHAPTER
FORTY-FIVE

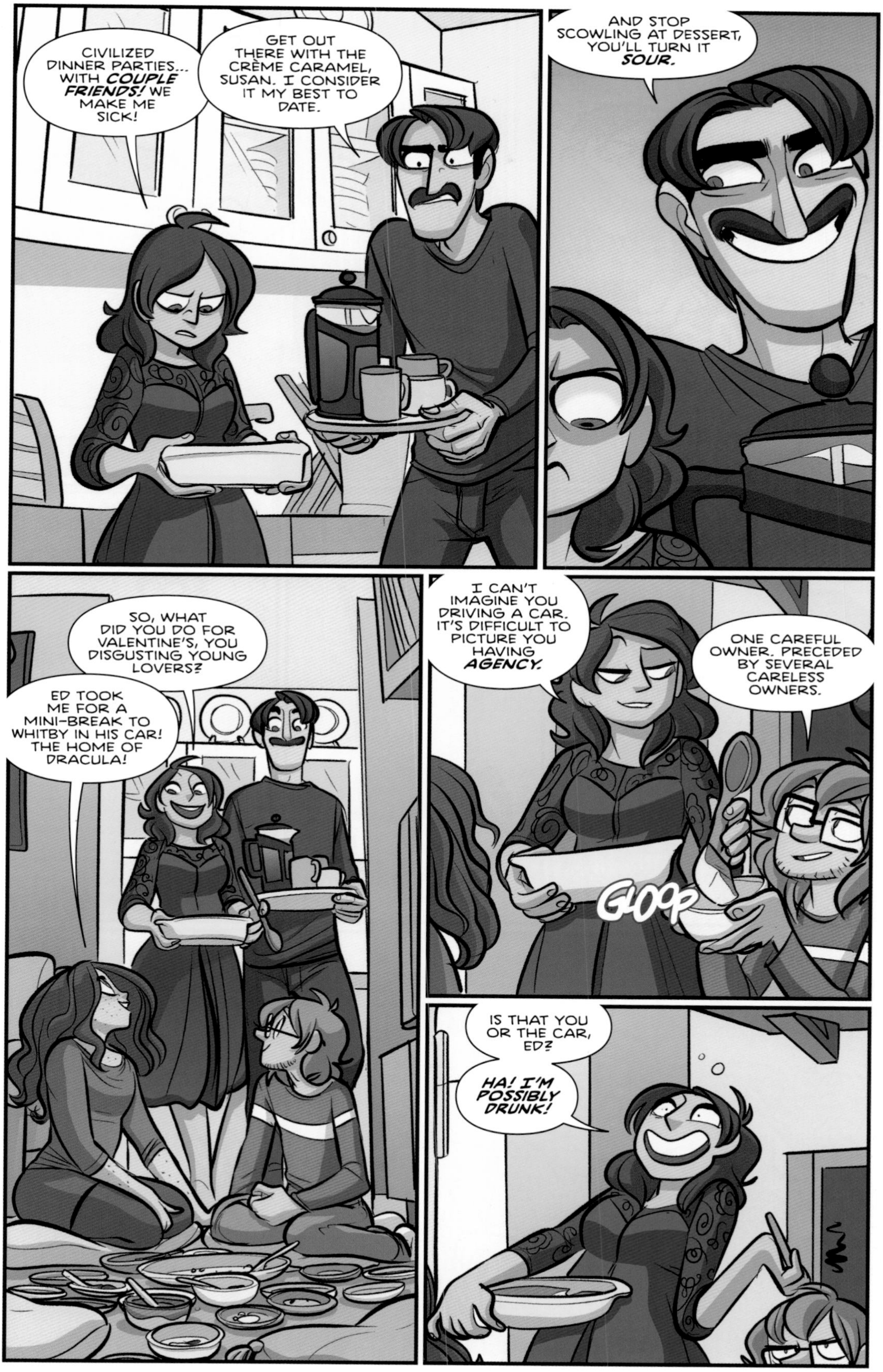

CIVILIZED DINNER PARTIES... WITH COUPLE FRIENDS! WE MAKE ME SICK!
GET OUT THERE WITH THE CRÈME CARAMEL, SUSAN. I CONSIDER IT MY BEST TO DATE.
AND STOP SCOWLING AT DESSERT, YOU'LL TURN IT SOUR.
SO, WHAT DID YOU DO FOR VALENTINE'S, YOU DISGUSTING YOUNG LOVERS?
ED TOOK ME FOR A MINI-BREAK TO WHITBY IN HIS CAR! THE HOME OF DRACULA!
I CAN'T IMAGINE YOU DRIVING A CAR. IT'S DIFFICULT TO PICTURE YOU HAVING AGENCY.
ONE CAREFUL OWNER. PRECEDED BY SEVERAL CARELESS OWNERS.
GLOOP
IS THAT YOU OR THE CAR, ED?
HA! I'M POSSIBLY DRUNK!

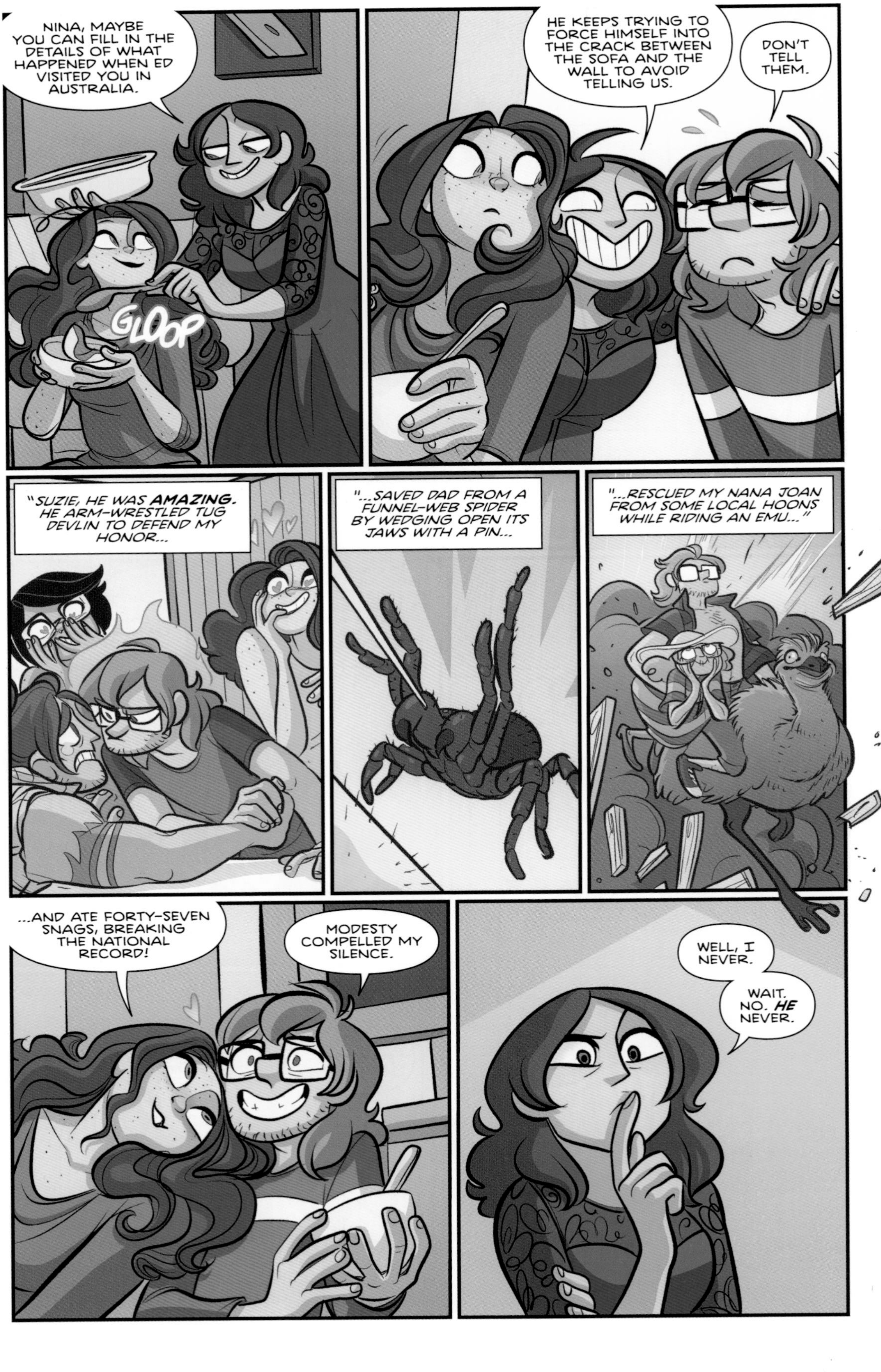
NINA, MAYBE YOU CAN FILL IN THE DETAILS OF WHAT HAPPENED WHEN ED VISITED YOU IN AUSTRALIA.
GLOOP
HE KEEPS TRYING TO FORCE HIMSELF INTO THE CRACK BETWEEN THE SOFA AND THE WALL TO AVOID TELLING US.
DON'T TELL THEM.
"SUZIE, HE WAS AMAZING. HE ARM-WRESTLED TUG DEVLIN TO DEFEND MY HONOR...
"...SAVED DAD FROM A FUNNEL-WEB SPIDER BY WEDGING OPEN ITS JAWS WITH A PIN...
"...RESCUED MY NANA JOAN FROM SOME LOCAL HOONS WHILE RIDING AN EMU..."
...AND ATE FORTY-SEVEN SNAGS, BREAKING THE NATIONAL RECORD!
MODESTY COMPELLED MY SILENCE.
WELL, I NEVER.
WAIT. NO. HE NEVER.

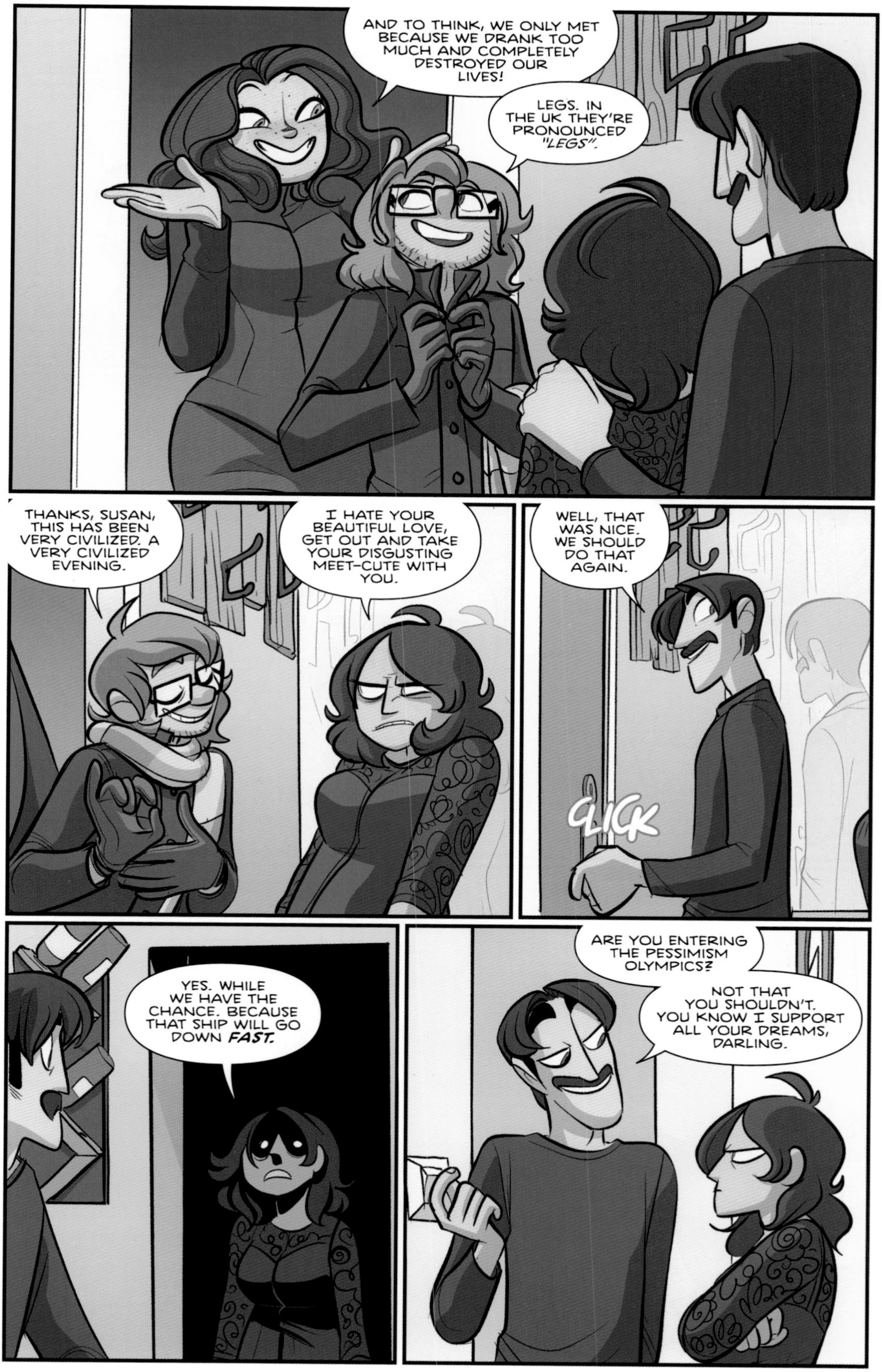
AND TO THINK, WE ONLY MET BECAUSE WE DRANK TOO MUCH AND COMPLETELY DESTROYED OUR LIVES!
LEGS. IN THE UK THEY'RE PRONOUNCED "LEGS".
THANKS, SUSAN, THIS HAS BEEN VERY CIVILIZED. A VERY CIVILIZED EVENING.
I HATE YOUR BEAUTIFUL LOVE, GET OUT AND TAKE YOUR DISGUSTING MEET-CUTE WITH YOU.
WELL, THAT WAS NICE. WE SHOULD DO THAT AGAIN.
CLICK
YES. WHILE WE HAVE THE CHANCE. BECAUSE THAT SHIP WILL GO DOWN FAST.
ARE YOU ENTERING THE PESSIMISM OLYMPICS?
NOT THAT YOU SHOULDN'T. YOU KNOW I SUPPORT ALL YOUR DREAMS, DARLING.

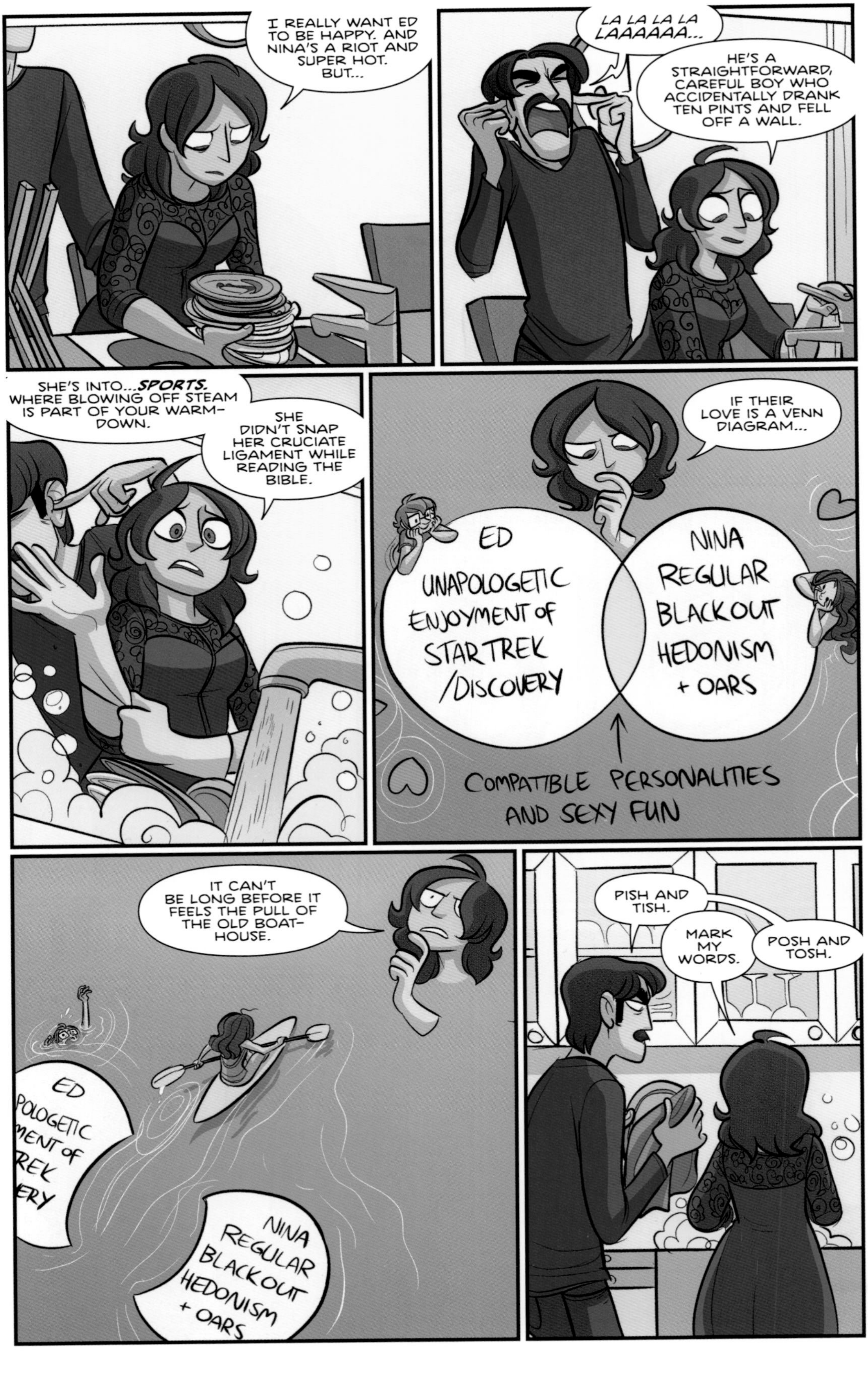
I REALLY WANT ED TO BE HAPPY. AND NINA'S A RIOT AND SUPER HOT. BUT...
LA LA LA LA LAAAAAA...
HE'S A STRAIGHTFORWARD, CAREFUL BOY WHO ACCIDENTALLY DRANK TEN PINTS AND FELL OFF A WALL.
SHE'S INTO... SPORTS. WHERE BLOWING OFF STEAM IS PART OF YOUR WARM-DOWN.
SHE DIDN'T SNAP HER CRUCIATE LIGAMENT WHILE READING THE BIBLE.
IF THEIR LOVE IS A VENN DIAGRAM...
ED
UNAPOLOGETIC ENJOYMENT OF STAR TREK /DISCOVERY
NINA
REGULAR BLACKOUT HEDONISM + OARS
COMPATIBLE PERSONALITIES AND SEXY FUN
IT CAN'T BE LONG BEFORE IT FEELS THE PULL OF THE OLD BOAT-HOUSE.
ED
POLOGETIC
MENT OF
REK
ERY
NINA
REGULAR
BLACKOUT
HEDONISM
+ OARS
PISH AND TISH.
MARK MY WORDS.
POSH AND TOSH.

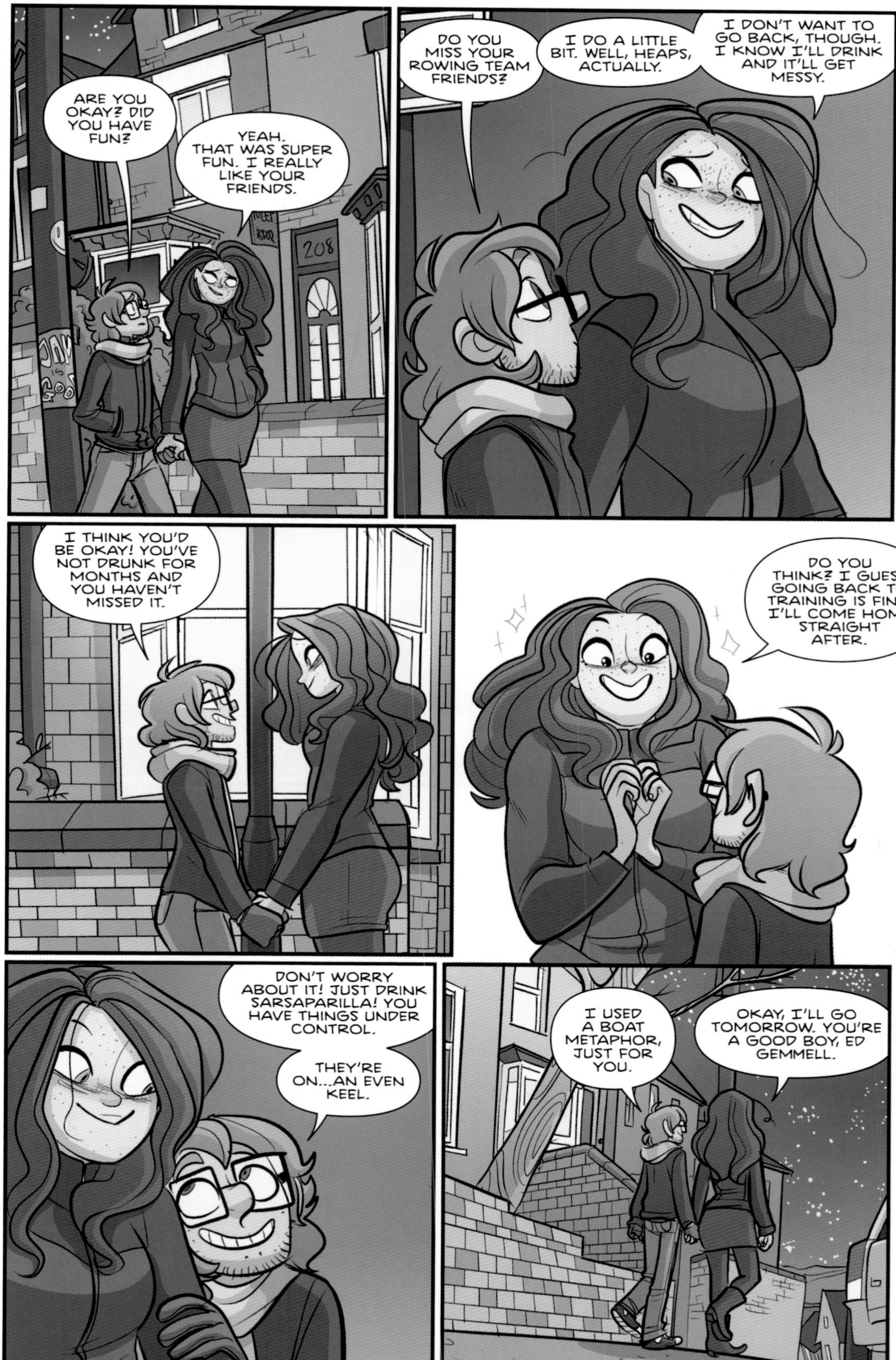
ARE YOU OKAY? DID YOU HAVE FUN?
YEAH. THAT WAS SUPER FUN. I REALLY LIKE YOUR FRIENDS.
208
DO YOU MISS YOUR ROWING TEAM FRIENDS?
I DO A LITTLE BIT. WELL, HEAPS, ACTUALLY.
I DON'T WANT TO GO BACK, THOUGH. I KNOW I'LL DRINK AND IT'LL GET MESSY.
I THINK YOU'D BE OKAY! YOU'VE NOT DRUNK FOR MONTHS AND YOU HAVEN'T MISSED IT.
DO YOU THINK? I GUESS GOING BACK TO TRAINING IS FINE. I'LL COME HOME STRAIGHT AFTER.
DON'T WORRY ABOUT IT! JUST DRINK SARSAPARILLA! YOU HAVE THINGS UNDER CONTROL.
THEY'RE ON...AN EVEN KEEL.
I USED A BOAT METAPHOR, JUST FOR YOU.
OKAY, I'LL GO TOMORROW. YOU'RE A GOOD BOY, ED GEMMELL.

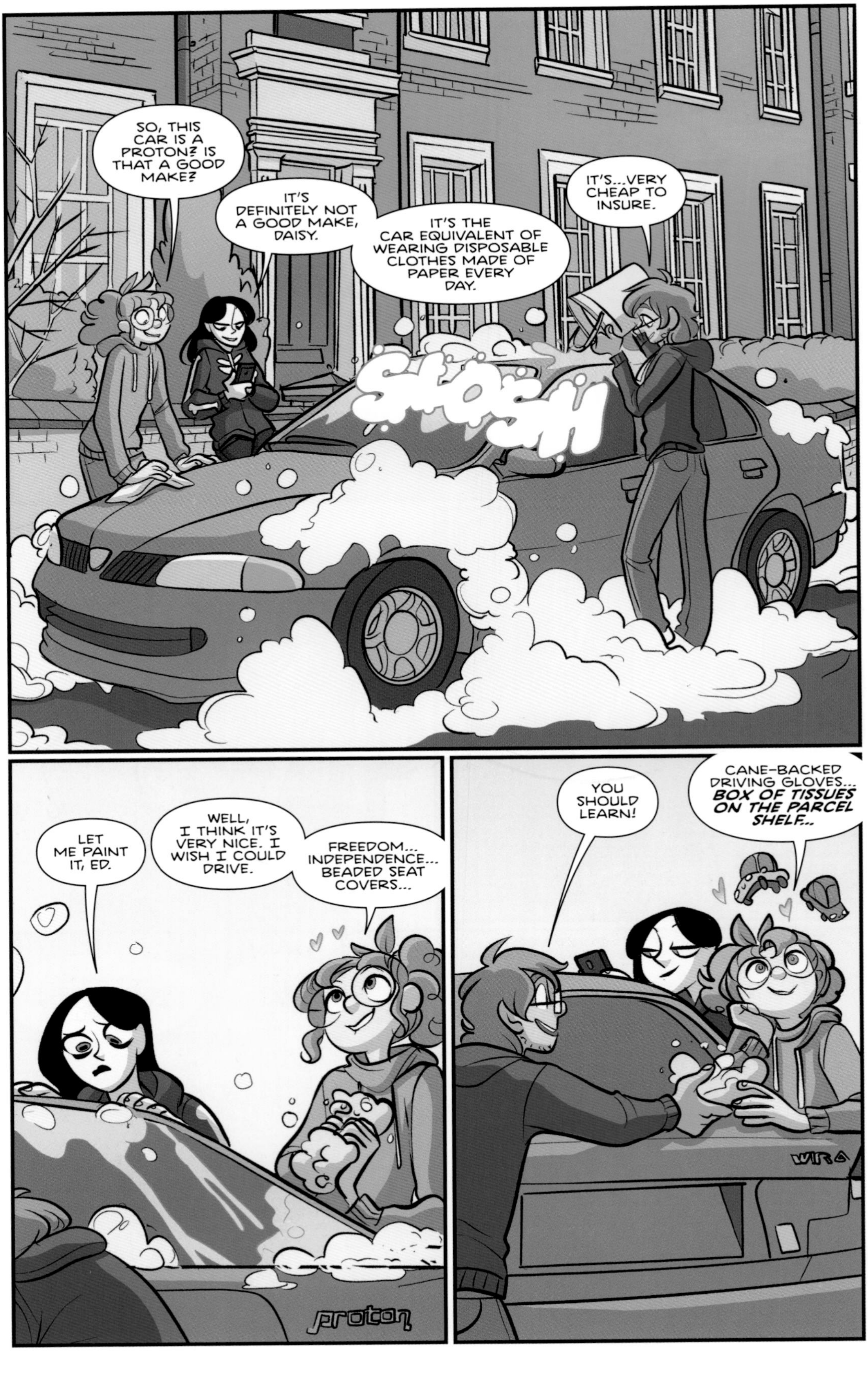
SO, THIS CAR IS A PROTON? IS THAT A GOOD MAKE?
IT'S DEFINITELY NOT A GOOD MAKE, DAISY.
IT'S THE CAR EQUIVALENT OF WEARING DISPOSABLE CLOTHES MADE OF PAPER EVERY DAY.
IT'S...VERY CHEAP TO INSURE.
SHOSH
LET ME PAINT IT, ED.
WELL, I THINK IT'S VERY NICE. I WISH I COULD DRIVE.
FREEDOM... INDEPENDENCE... BEADED SEAT COVERS...
proton
YOU SHOULD LEARN!
CANE-BACKED DRIVING GLOVES... ***BOX OF TISSUES ON THE PARCEL SHELF...***
WIRA

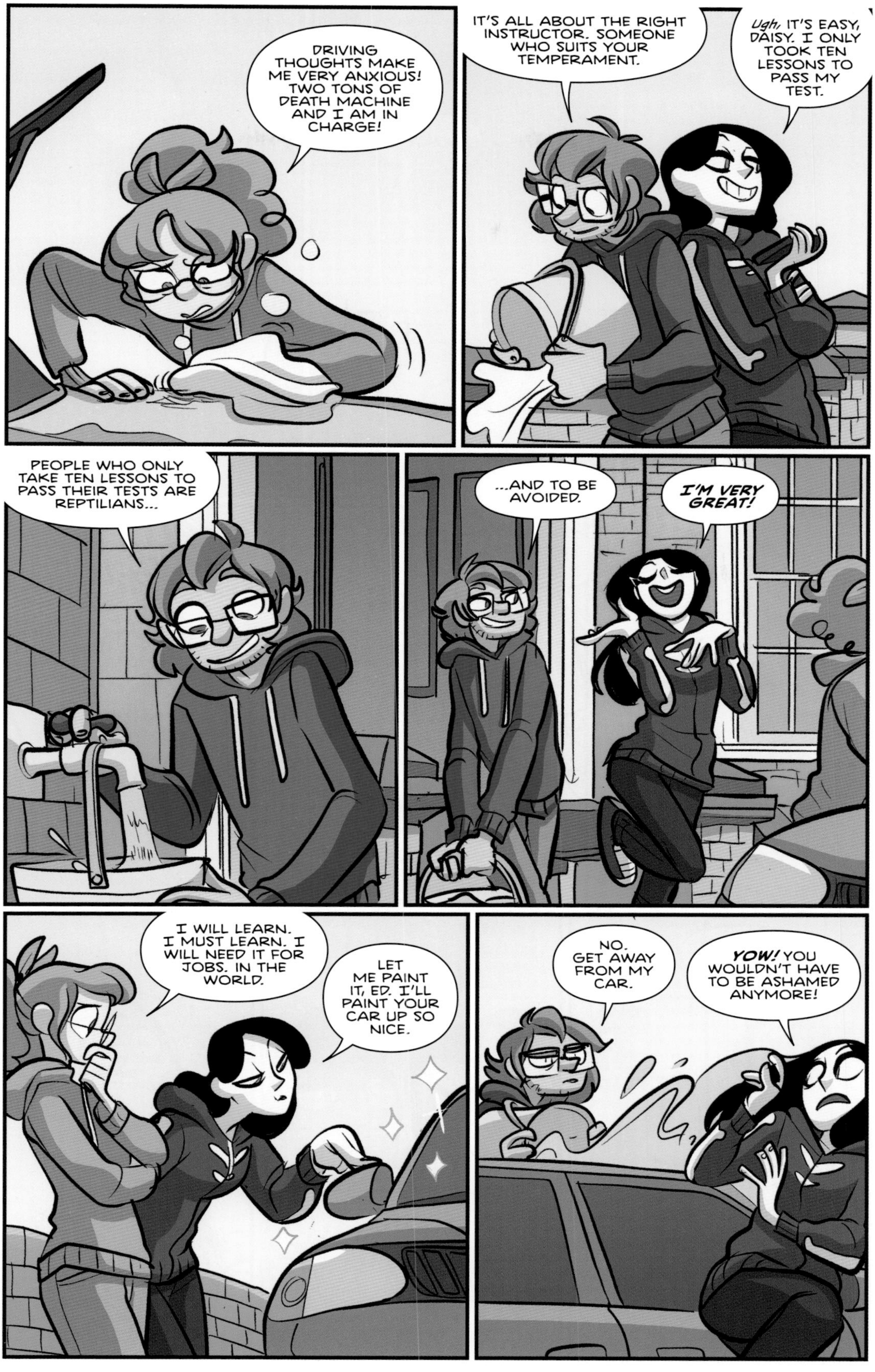
DRIVING THOUGHTS MAKE ME VERY ANXIOUS! TWO TONS OF DEATH MACHINE AND I AM IN CHARGE!
IT'S ALL ABOUT THE RIGHT INSTRUCTOR. SOMEONE WHO SUITS YOUR TEMPERAMENT.
Ugh, IT'S EASY, DAISY. I ONLY TOOK TEN LESSONS TO PASS MY TEST.
PEOPLE WHO ONLY TAKE TEN LESSONS TO PASS THEIR TESTS ARE REPTILIANS...
...AND TO BE AVOIDED.
I'M VERY GREAT!
I WILL LEARN. I MUST LEARN. I WILL NEED IT FOR JOBS. IN THE WORLD.
LET ME PAINT IT, ED. I'LL PAINT YOUR CAR UP SO NICE.
NO. GET AWAY FROM MY CAR.
YOW! YOU WOULDN'T HAVE TO BE ASHAMED ANYMORE!

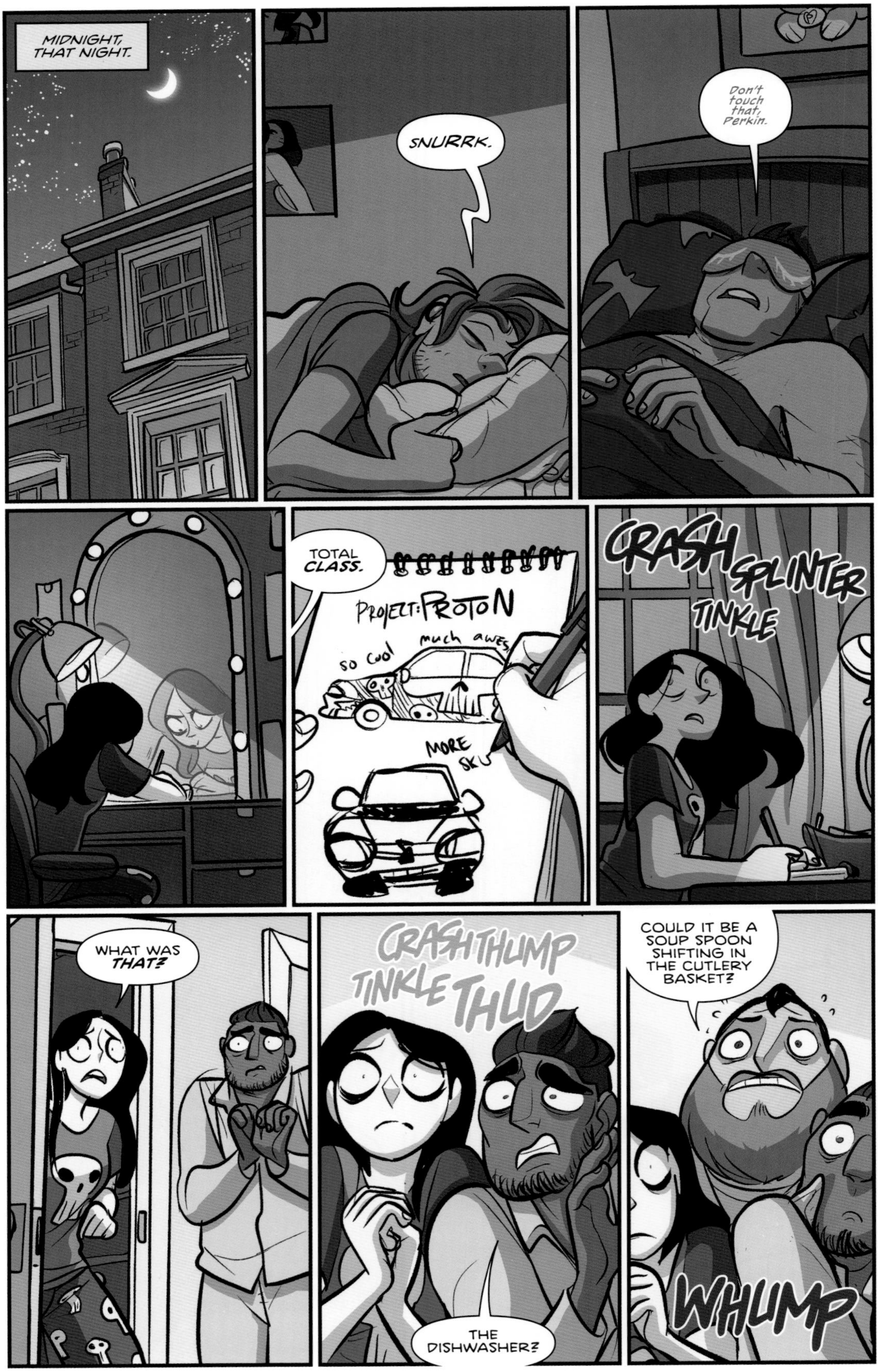
MIDNIGHT, THAT NIGHT.
SNURRK.
Don't touch that, Perkin.
TOTAL CLASS.
PROJECT: PROTON
so cool
much awes
MORE SKU
CRASH SPLINTER TINKLE
WHAT WAS THAT?
CRASH THUMP TINKLE THUD
THE DISHWASHER?
COULD IT BE A SOUP SPOON SHIFTING IN THE CUTLERY BASKET?
WHUMP

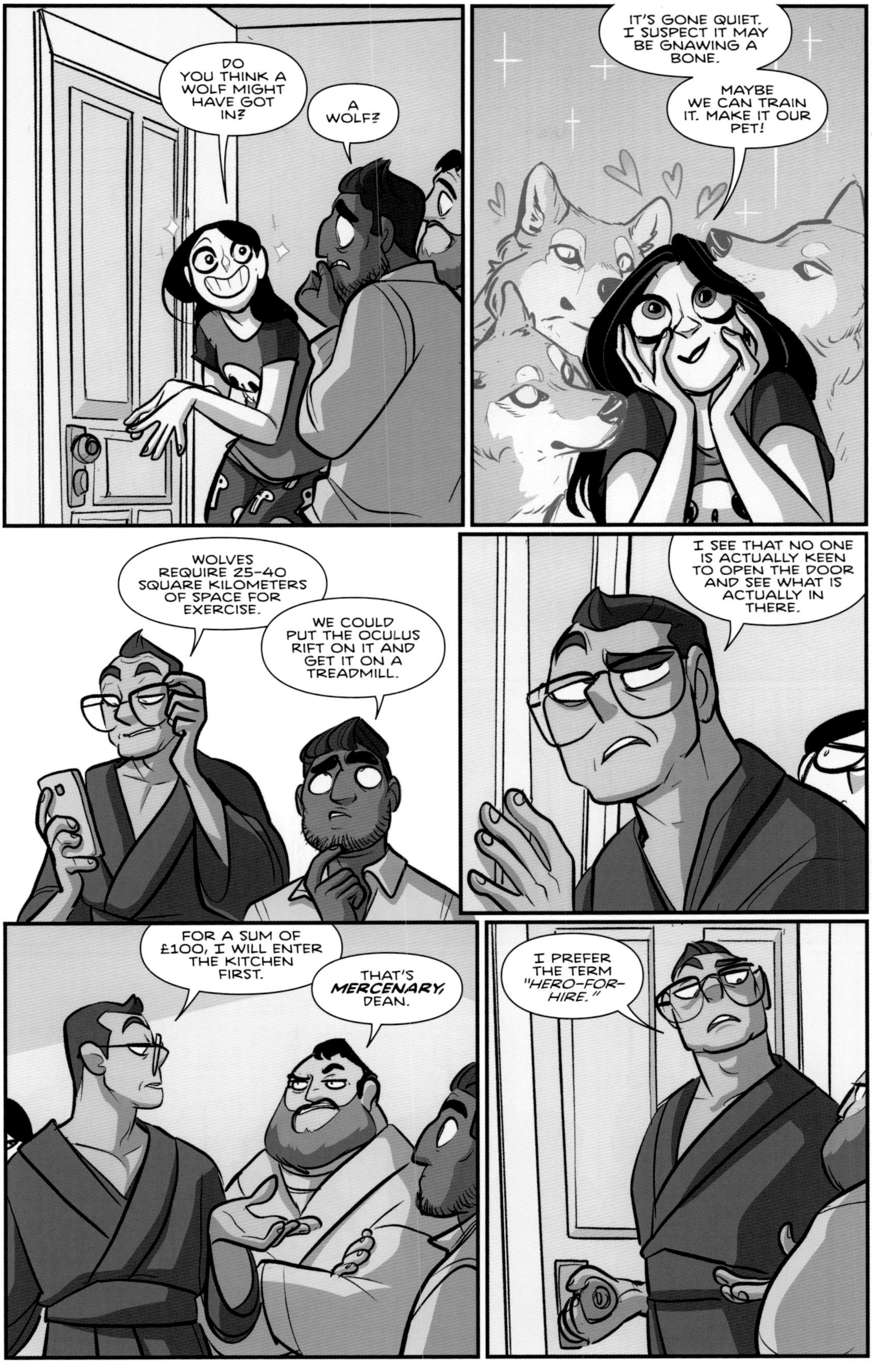
DO YOU THINK A WOLF MIGHT HAVE GOT IN?
A WOLF?
IT'S GONE QUIET. I SUSPECT IT MAY BE GNAWING A BONE.
MAYBE WE CAN TRAIN IT. MAKE IT OUR PET!
WOLVES REQUIRE 25-40 SQUARE KILOMETERS OF SPACE FOR EXERCISE.
WE COULD PUT THE OCULUS RIFT ON IT AND GET IT ON A TREADMILL.
I SEE THAT NO ONE IS ACTUALLY KEEN TO OPEN THE DOOR AND SEE WHAT IS ACTUALLY IN THERE.
FOR A SUM OF £100, I WILL ENTER THE KITCHEN FIRST.
THAT'S ***MERCENARY,*** DEAN.
I PREFER THE TERM *"HERO-FOR-HIRE."*

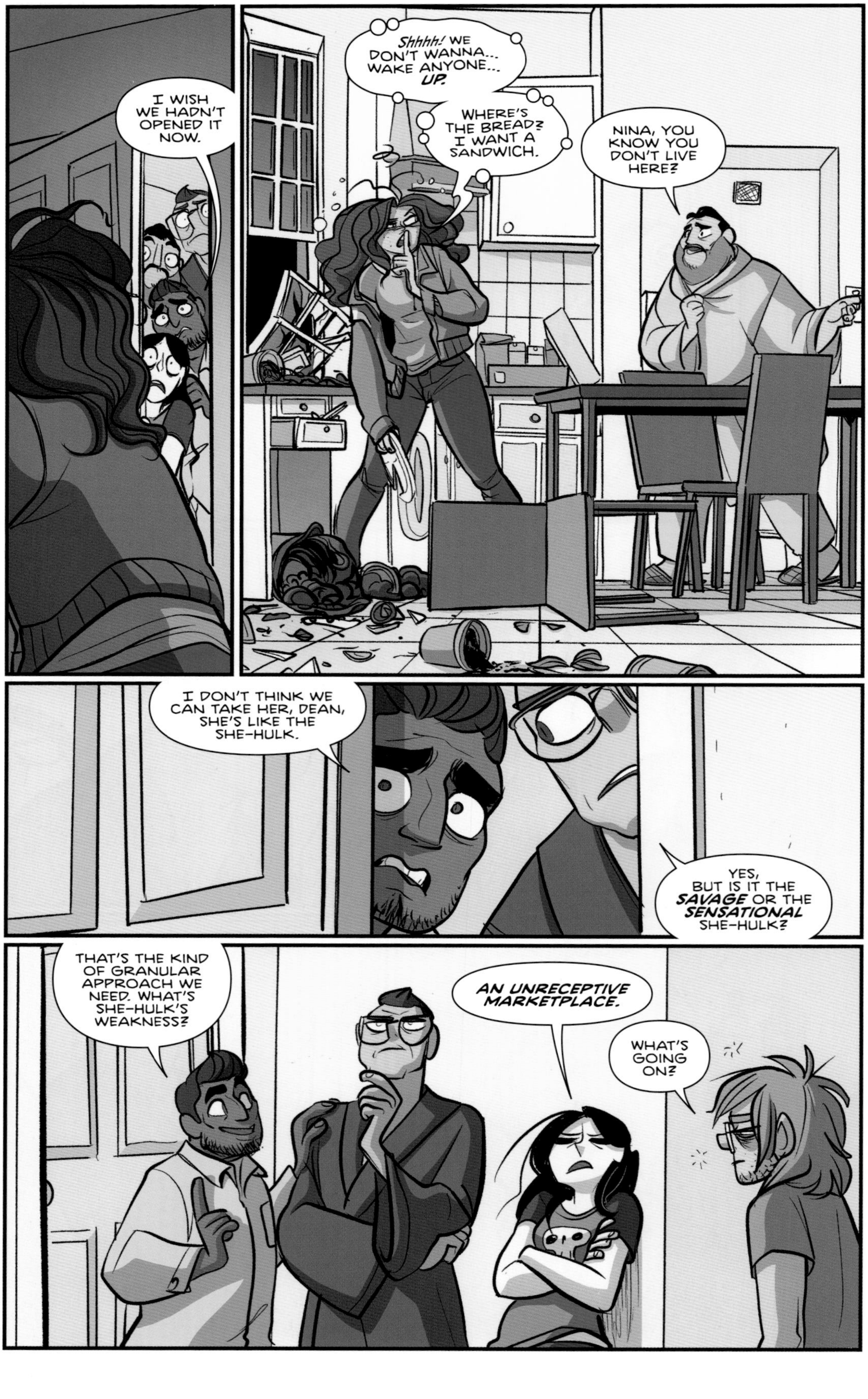
I WISH WE HADN'T OPENED IT NOW.
Shhhh! WE DON'T WANNA... WAKE ANYONE... UP.
WHERE'S THE BREAD? I WANT A SANDWICH.
NINA, YOU KNOW YOU DON'T LIVE HERE?
I DON'T THINK WE CAN TAKE HER, DEAN, SHE'S LIKE THE SHE-HULK.
YES, BUT IS IT THE SAVAGE OR THE SENSATIONAL SHE-HULK?
THAT'S THE KIND OF GRANULAR APPROACH WE NEED. WHAT'S SHE-HULK'S WEAKNESS?
AN UNRECEPTIVE MARKETPLACE.
WHAT'S GOING ON?

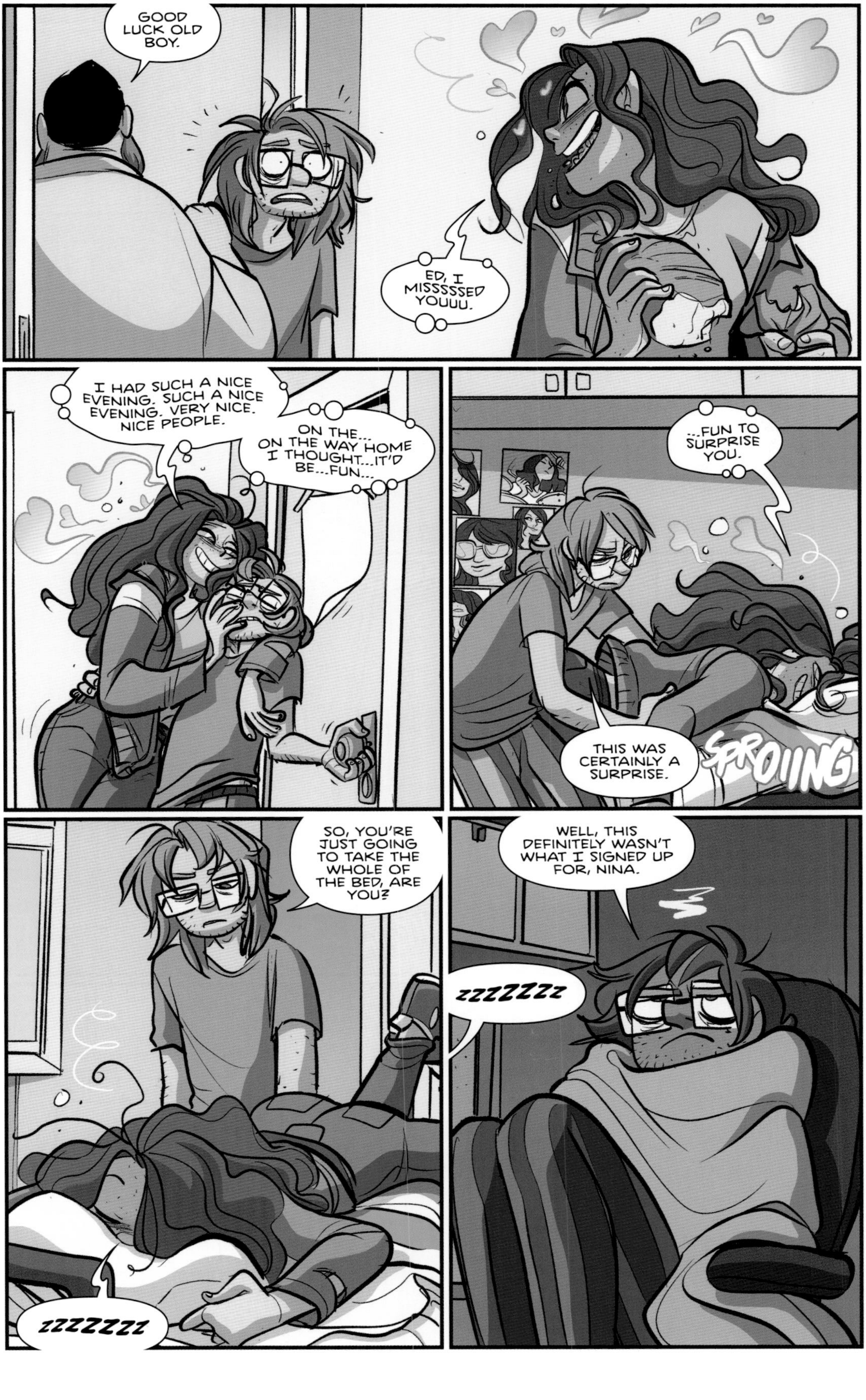
GOOD LUCK OLD BOY.
ED, I MISSSSSED YOUUU.
I HAD SUCH A NICE EVENING. SUCH A NICE EVENING. VERY NICE. NICE PEOPLE.
ON THE... ON THE WAY HOME I THOUGHT...IT'D BE...FUN...
...FUN TO SURPRISE YOU.
THIS WAS CERTAINLY A SURPRISE.
SPROIING!
SO, YOU'RE JUST GOING TO TAKE THE WHOLE OF THE BED, ARE YOU?
ZZZZZZZ
WELL, THIS DEFINITELY WASN'T WHAT I SIGNED UP FOR, NINA.
ZZZZZZZ

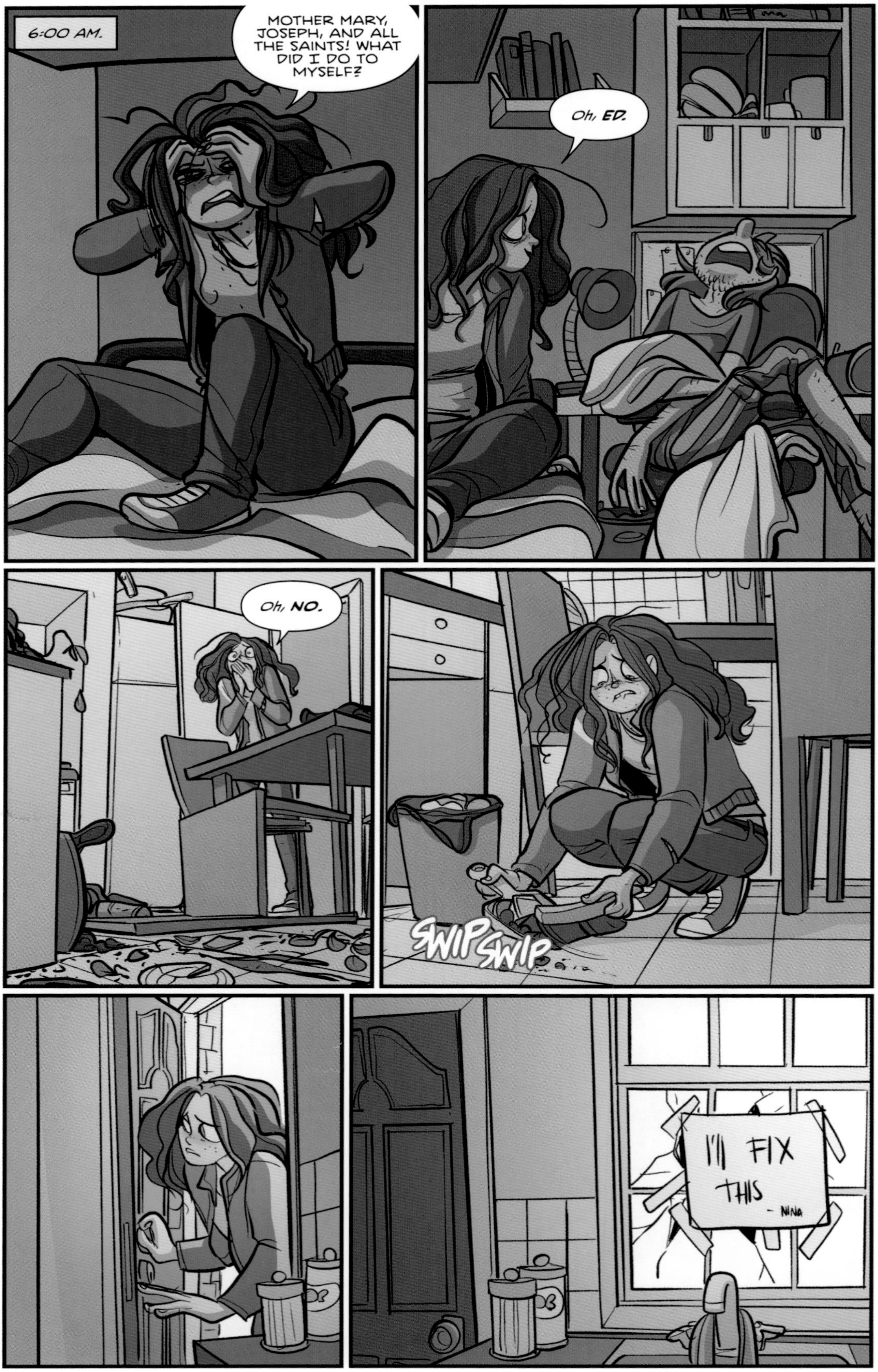
6:00 AM.
MOTHER MARY, JOSEPH, AND ALL THE SAINTS! WHAT DID I DO TO MYSELF?
Oh, ED.
Oh, NO.
SWIP SWIP
I'll FIX THIS
- NINA

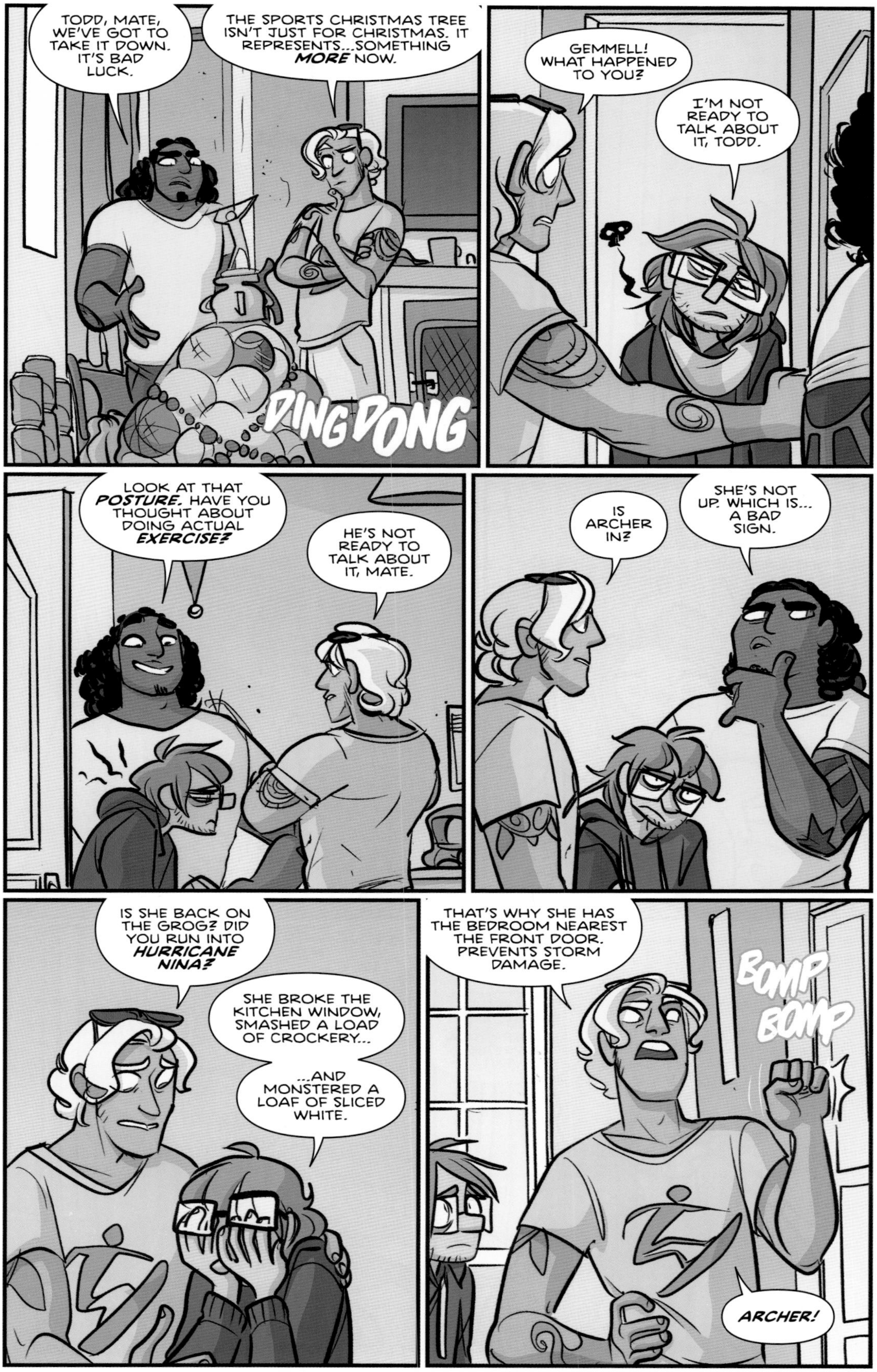
TODD, MATE, WE'VE GOT TO TAKE IT DOWN. IT'S BAD LUCK.
THE SPORTS CHRISTMAS TREE ISN'T JUST FOR CHRISTMAS. IT REPRESENTS...SOMETHING MORE NOW.
DING DONG
GEMMELL! WHAT HAPPENED TO YOU?
I'M NOT READY TO TALK ABOUT IT, TODD.
LOOK AT THAT POSTURE. HAVE YOU THOUGHT ABOUT DOING ACTUAL EXERCISE?
HE'S NOT READY TO TALK ABOUT IT, MATE.
IS ARCHER IN?
SHE'S NOT UP. WHICH IS... A BAD SIGN.
IS SHE BACK ON THE GROG? DID YOU RUN INTO HURRICANE NINA?
SHE BROKE THE KITCHEN WINDOW, SMASHED A LOAD OF CROCKERY...
...AND MONSTERED A LOAF OF SLICED WHITE.
THAT'S WHY SHE HAS THE BEDROOM NEAREST THE FRONT DOOR. PREVENTS STORM DAMAGE.
BOMP BOMP
ARCHER!

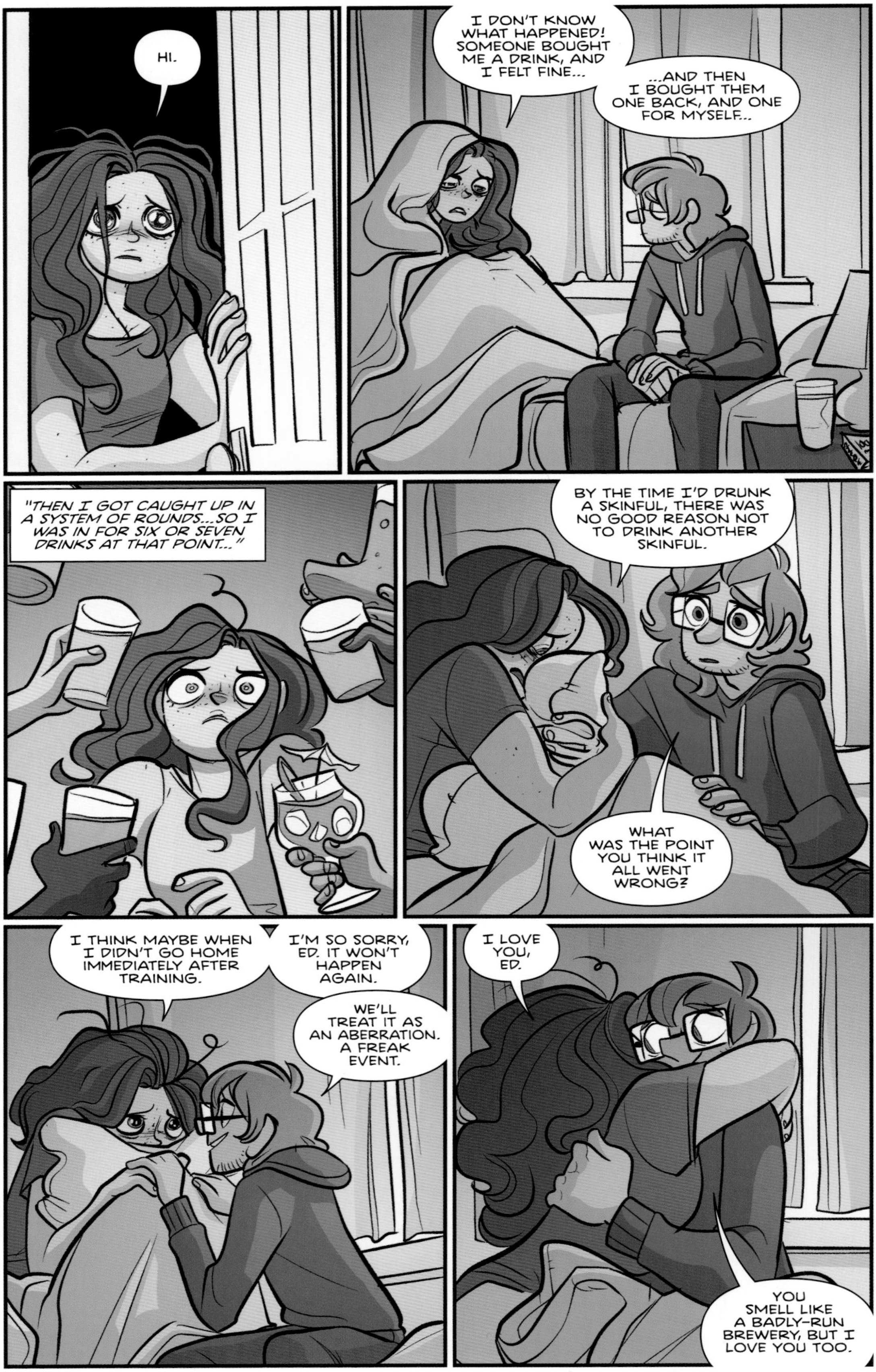
HI.
I DON'T KNOW WHAT HAPPENED! SOMEONE BOUGHT ME A DRINK, AND I FELT FINE...
...AND THEN I BOUGHT THEM ONE BACK, AND ONE FOR MYSELF...
"THEN I GOT CAUGHT UP IN A SYSTEM OF ROUNDS...SO I WAS IN FOR SIX OR SEVEN DRINKS AT THAT POINT..."
BY THE TIME I'D DRUNK A SKINFUL, THERE WAS NO GOOD REASON NOT TO DRINK ANOTHER SKINFUL.
WHAT WAS THE POINT YOU THINK IT ALL WENT WRONG?
I THINK MAYBE WHEN I DIDN'T GO HOME IMMEDIATELY AFTER TRAINING.
I'M SO SORRY, ED. IT WON'T HAPPEN AGAIN.
WE'LL TREAT IT AS AN ABERRATION. A FREAK EVENT.
I LOVE YOU, ED.
YOU SMELL LIKE A BADLY-RUN BREWERY, BUT I LOVE YOU TOO.

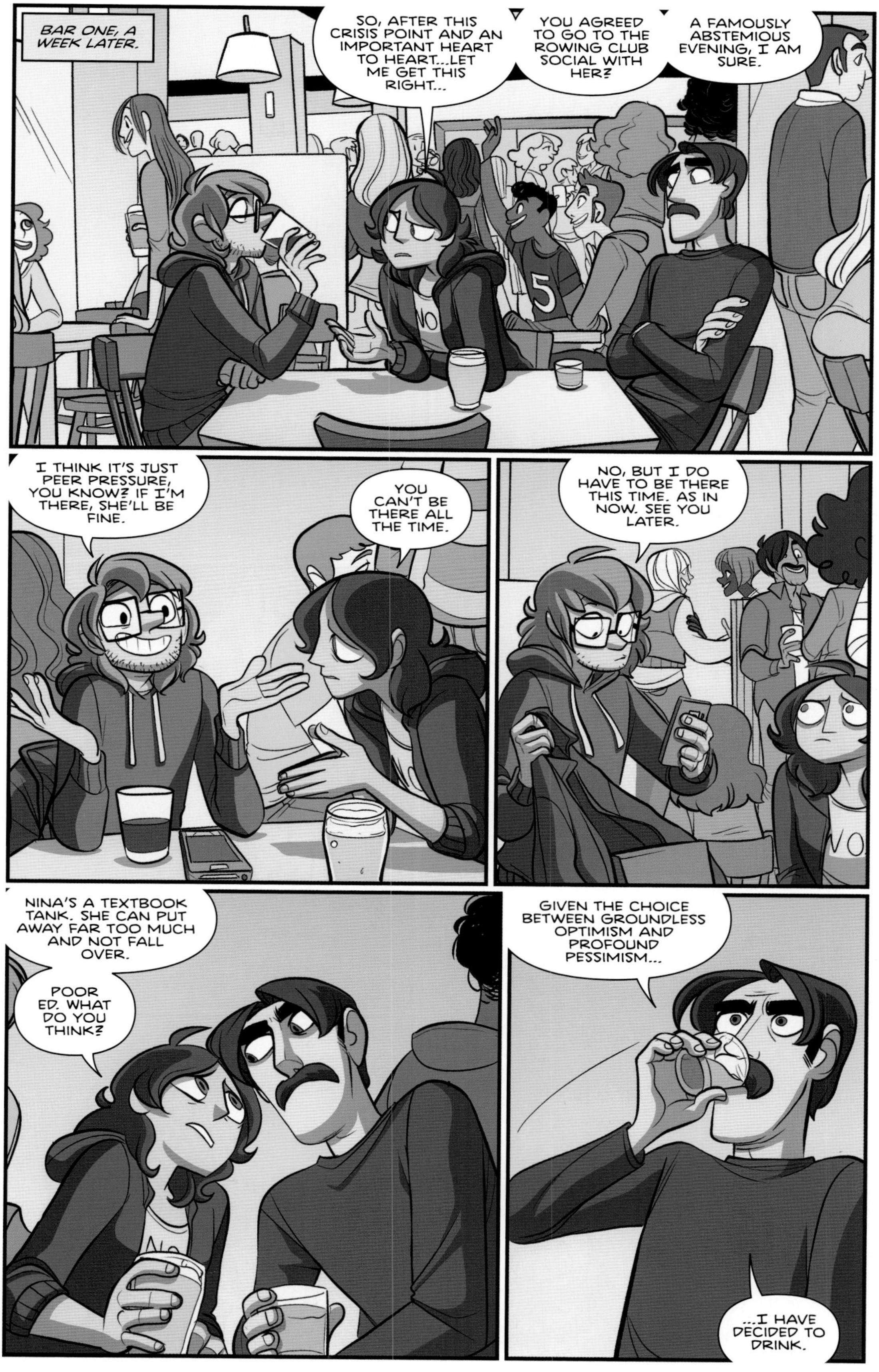
BAR ONE, A WEEK LATER.
SO, AFTER THIS CRISIS POINT AND AN IMPORTANT HEART TO HEART...LET ME GET THIS RIGHT...
YOU AGREED TO GO TO THE ROWING CLUB SOCIAL WITH HER?
A FAMOUSLY ABSTEMIOUS EVENING, I AM SURE.
I THINK IT'S JUST PEER PRESSURE, YOU KNOW? IF I'M THERE, SHE'LL BE FINE.
YOU CAN'T BE THERE ALL THE TIME.
NO, BUT I DO HAVE TO BE THERE THIS TIME. AS IN NOW. SEE YOU LATER.
NINA'S A TEXTBOOK TANK. SHE CAN PUT AWAY FAR TOO MUCH AND NOT FALL OVER.
POOR ED. WHAT DO YOU THINK?
GIVEN THE CHOICE BETWEEN GROUNDLESS OPTIMISM AND PROFOUND PESSIMISM...
...I HAVE DECIDED TO DRINK.

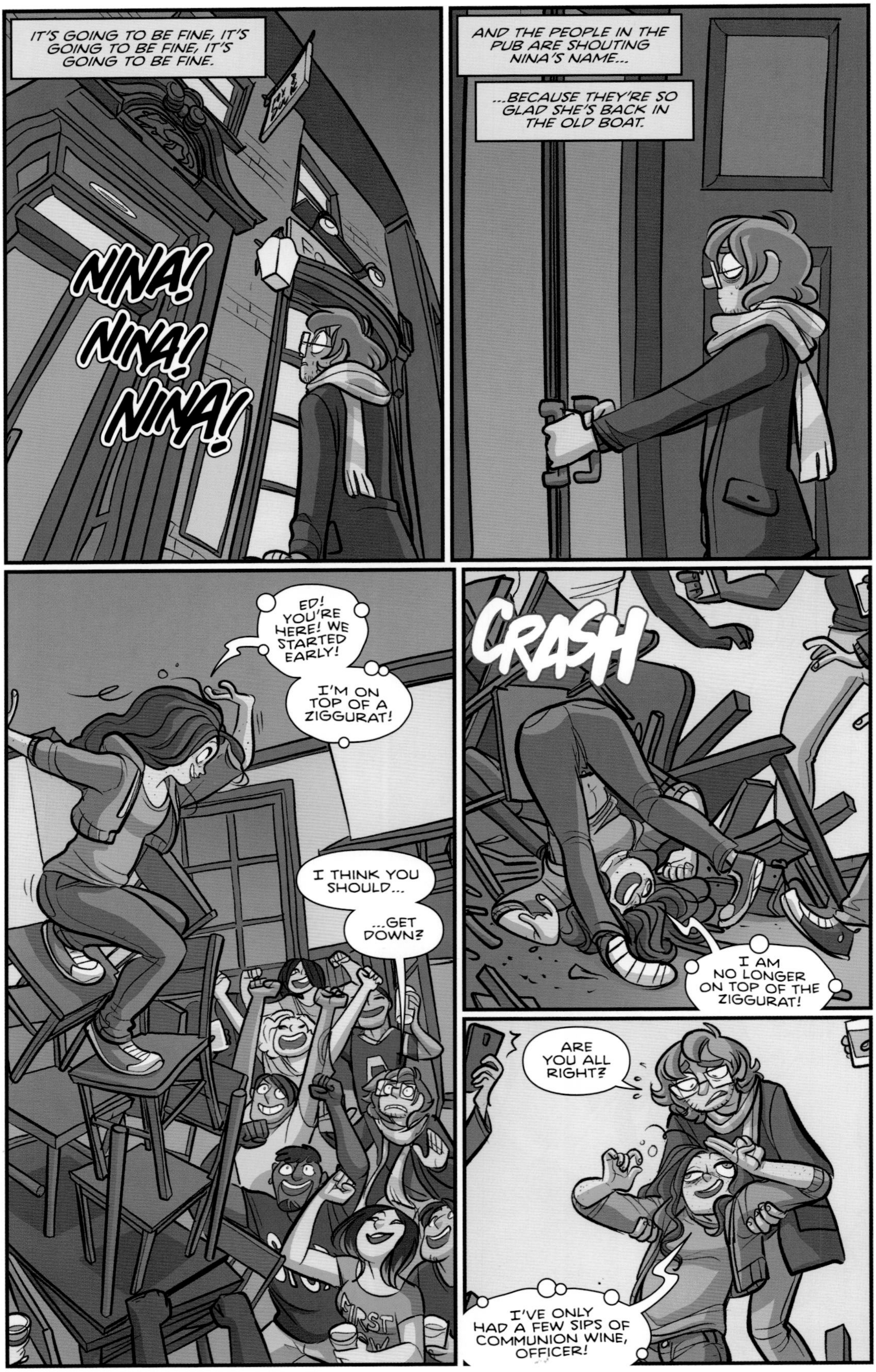
IT'S GOING TO BE FINE, IT'S GOING TO BE FINE, IT'S GOING TO BE FINE.
NINA! NINA! NINA!
AND THE PEOPLE IN THE PUB ARE SHOUTING NINA'S NAME...
...BECAUSE THEY'RE SO GLAD SHE'S BACK IN THE OLD BOAT.
ED! YOU'RE HERE! WE STARTED EARLY!
I'M ON TOP OF A ZIGGURAT!
I THINK YOU SHOULD...
...GET DOWN?
CRASH
I AM NO LONGER ON TOP OF THE ZIGGURAT!
ARE YOU ALL RIGHT?
I'VE ONLY HAD A FEW SIPS OF COMMUNION WINE, OFFICER!

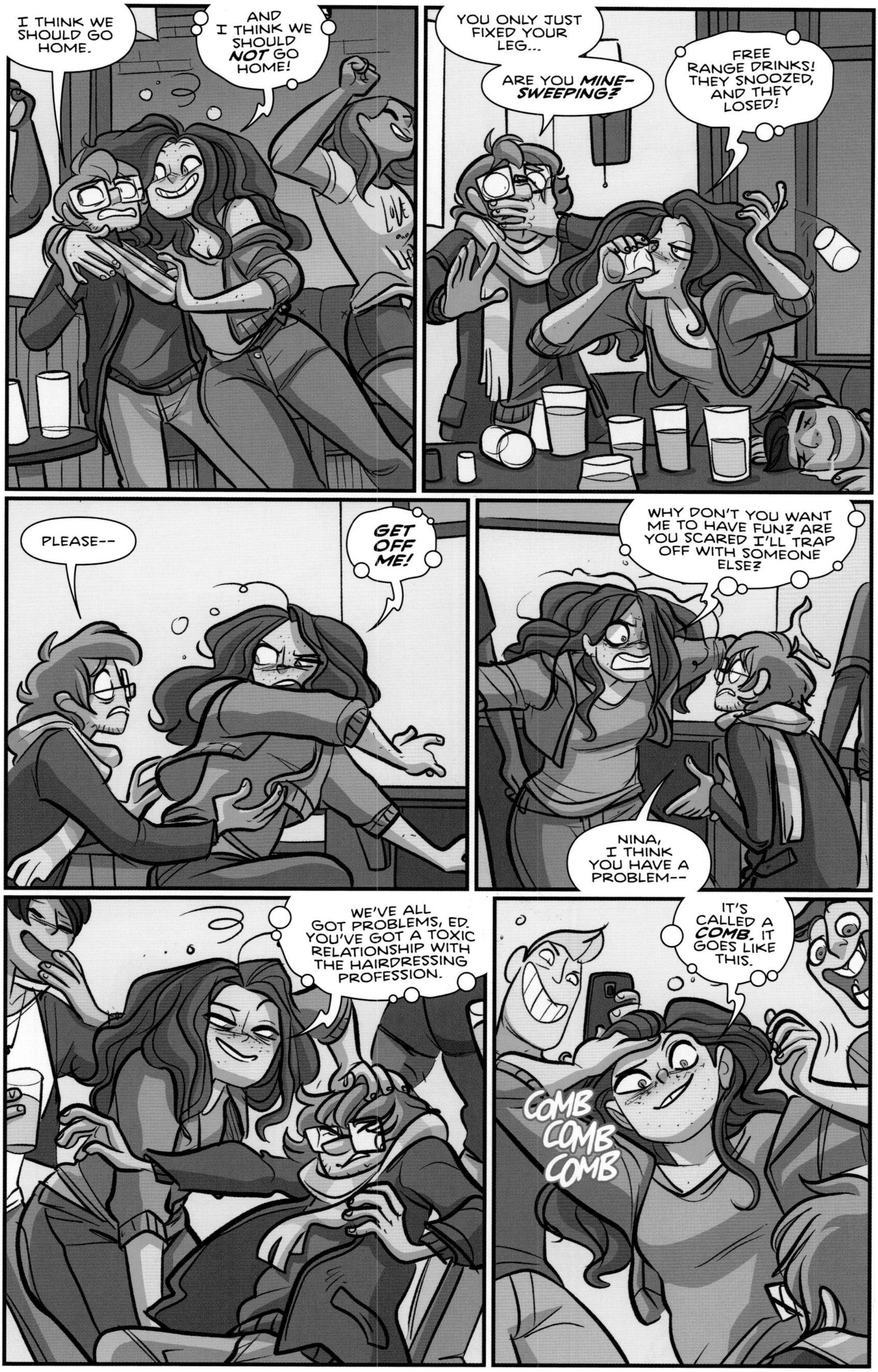
I THINK WE SHOULD GO HOME.
AND I THINK WE SHOULD NOT GO HOME!
YOU ONLY JUST FIXED YOUR LEG...
ARE YOU MINE-SWEEPING?
FREE RANGE DRINKS! THEY SNOOZED, AND THEY LOSED!
PLEASE--
GET OFF ME!
WHY DON'T YOU WANT ME TO HAVE FUN? ARE YOU SCARED I'LL TRAP OFF WITH SOMEONE ELSE?
NINA, I THINK YOU HAVE A PROBLEM--
WE'VE ALL GOT PROBLEMS, ED. YOU'VE GOT A TOXIC RELATIONSHIP WITH THE HAIRDRESSING PROFESSION.
IT'S CALLED A COMB. IT GOES LIKE THIS.
COMB COMB COMB

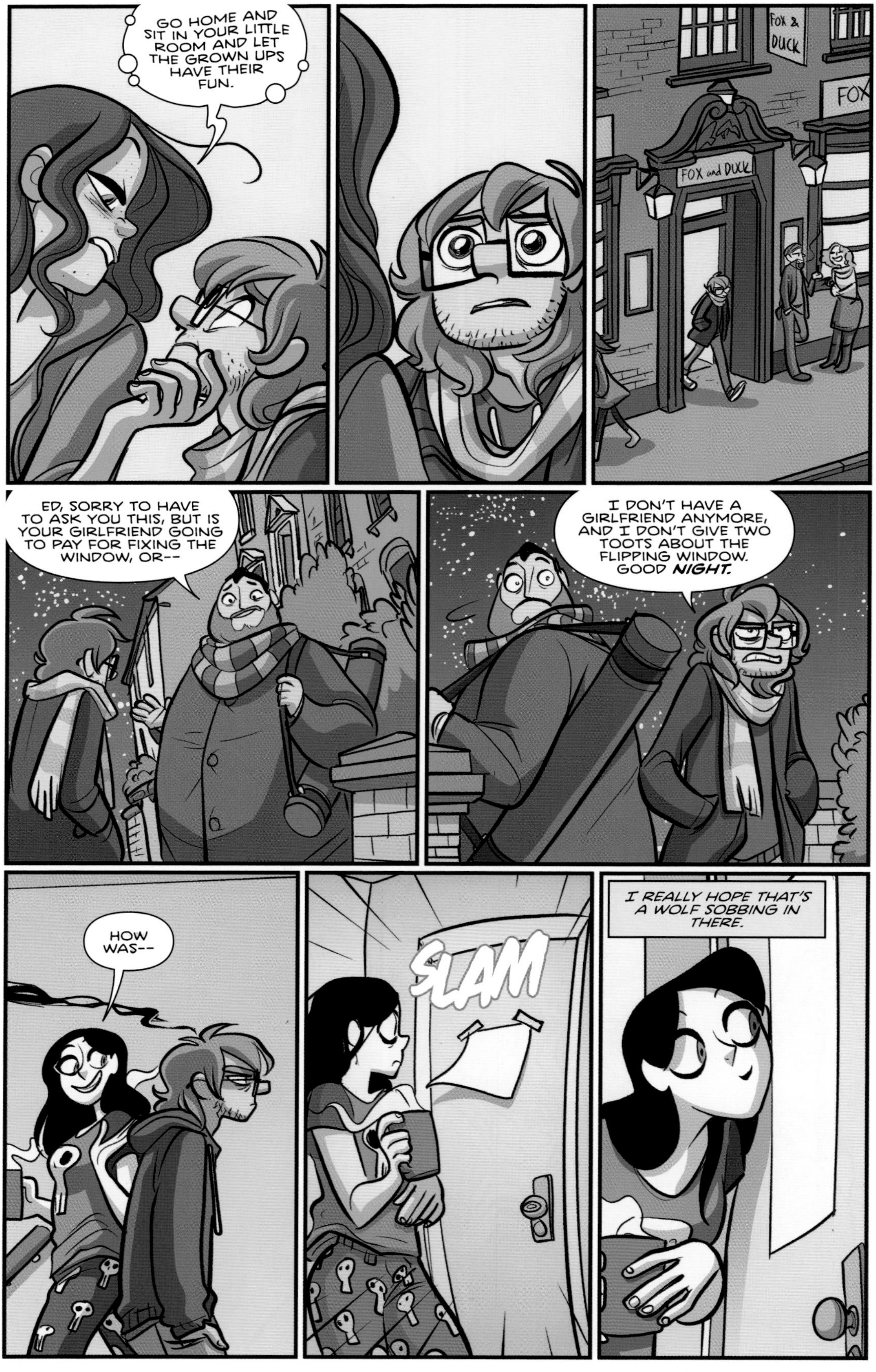
GO HOME AND SIT IN YOUR LITTLE ROOM AND LET THE GROWN UPS HAVE THEIR FUN.
FOX & DUCK
FOX and DUCK
FOX
ED, SORRY TO HAVE TO ASK YOU THIS, BUT IS YOUR GIRLFRIEND GOING TO PAY FOR FIXING THE WINDOW, OR--
I DON'T HAVE A GIRLFRIEND ANYMORE, AND I DON'T GIVE TWO TOOTS ABOUT THE FLIPPING WINDOW. GOOD NIGHT.
HOW WAS--
SLAM
I REALLY HOPE THAT'S A WOLF SOBBING IN THERE.

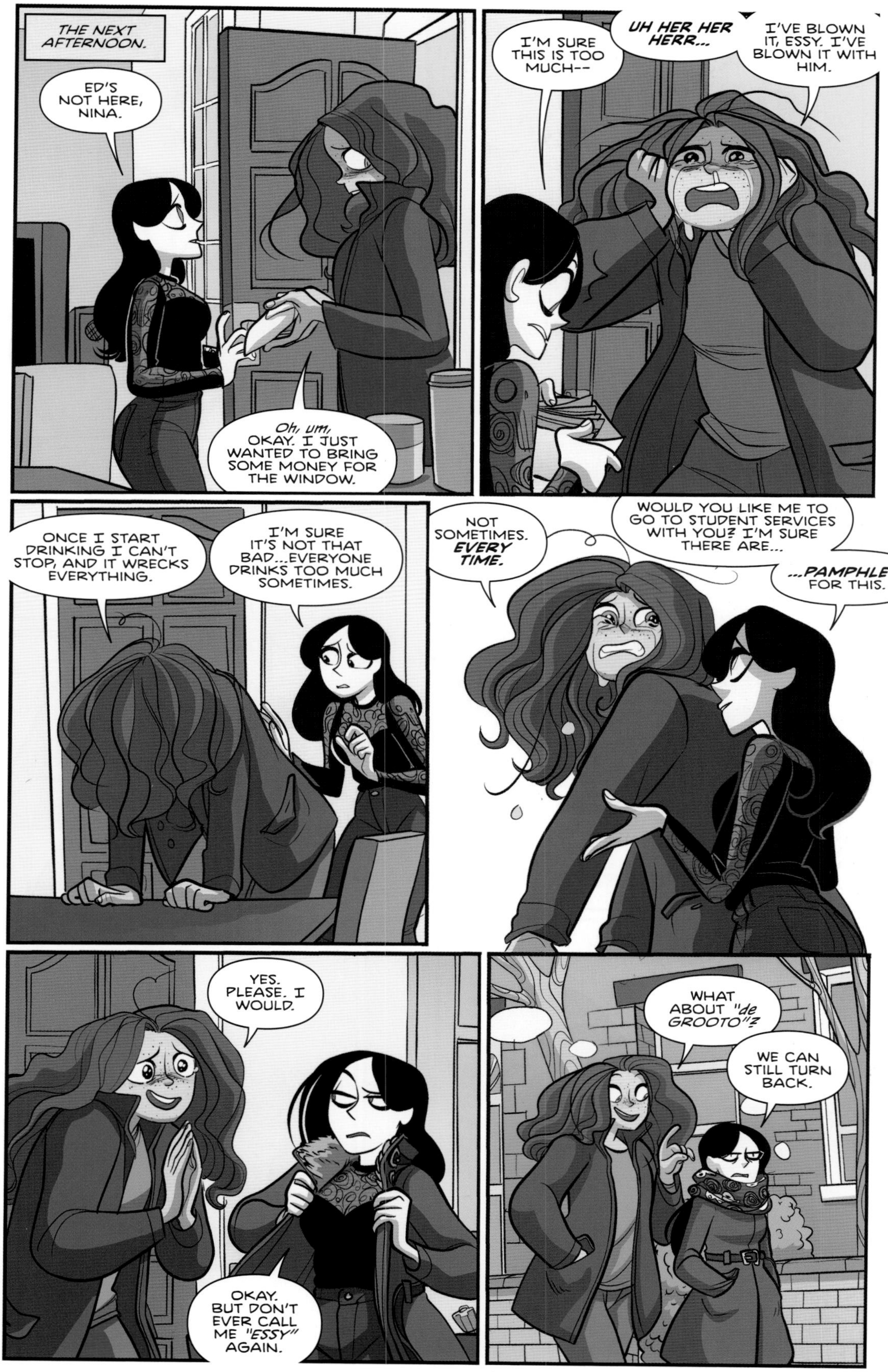
THE NEXT AFTERNOON.
ED'S NOT HERE, NINA.
Oh, um, OKAY. I JUST WANTED TO BRING SOME MONEY FOR THE WINDOW.
I'M SURE THIS IS TOO MUCH--
UH HER HER HERR...
I'VE BLOWN IT, ESSY. I'VE BLOWN IT WITH HIM.
ONCE I START DRINKING I CAN'T STOP, AND IT WRECKS EVERYTHING.
I'M SURE IT'S NOT THAT BAD...EVERYONE DRINKS TOO MUCH SOMETIMES.
NOT SOMETIMES. EVERY TIME.
WOULD YOU LIKE ME TO GO TO STUDENT SERVICES WITH YOU? I'M SURE THERE ARE...
...PAMPHLETS FOR THIS.
YES. PLEASE. I WOULD.
OKAY. BUT DON'T EVER CALL ME "ESSY" AGAIN.
WHAT ABOUT "de GROOTO"?
WE CAN STILL TURN BACK.

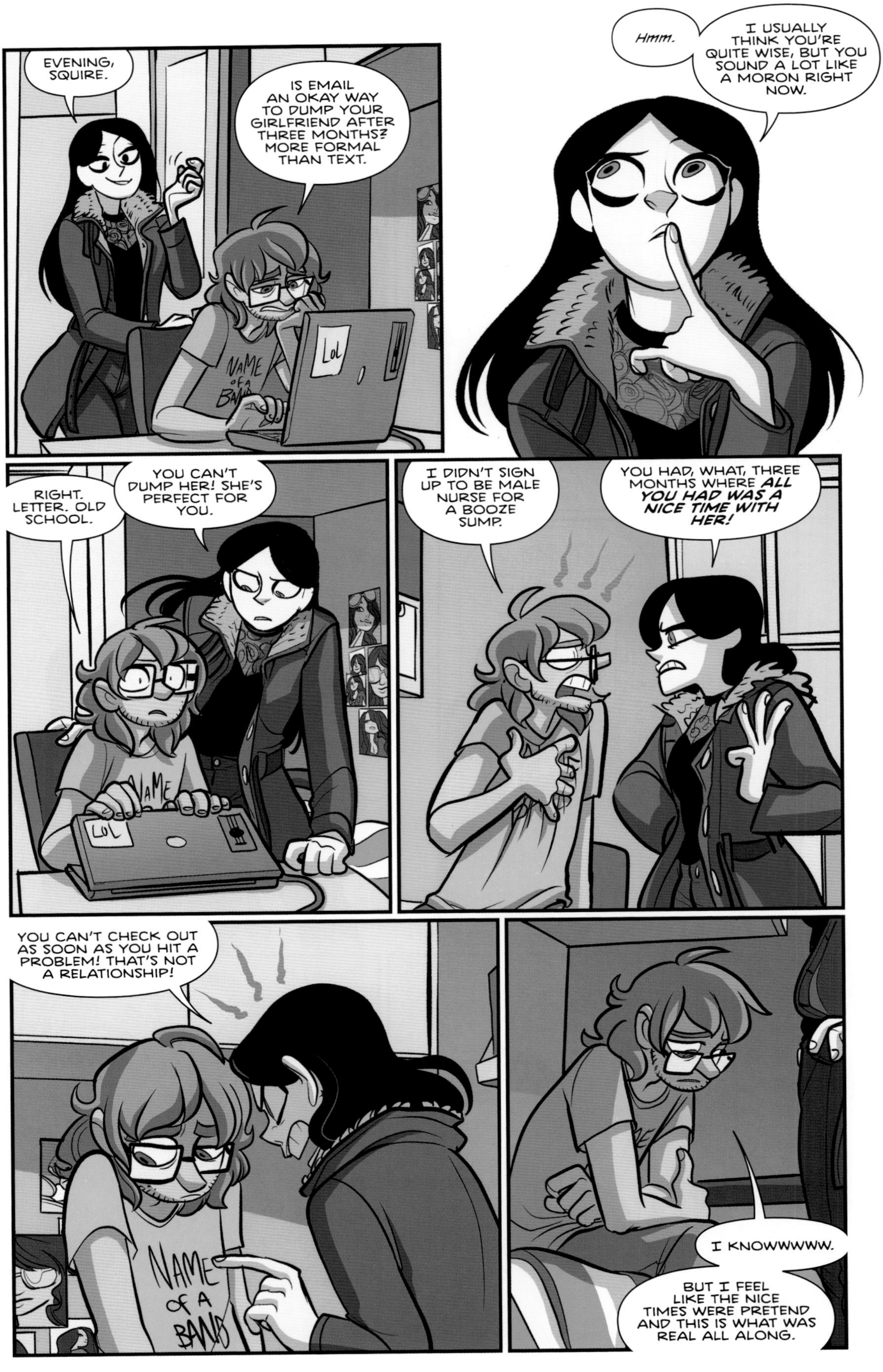
EVENING, SQUIRE.
IS EMAIL AN OKAY WAY TO DUMP YOUR GIRLFRIEND AFTER THREE MONTHS? MORE FORMAL THAN TEXT.
LOL
NAME of a BAND
Hmm.
I USUALLY THINK YOU'RE QUITE WISE, BUT YOU SOUND A LOT LIKE A MORON RIGHT NOW.
RIGHT. LETTER. OLD SCHOOL.
YOU CAN'T DUMP HER! SHE'S PERFECT FOR YOU.
LOL
I DIDN'T SIGN UP TO BE MALE NURSE FOR A BOOZE SUMP.
YOU HAD, WHAT, THREE MONTHS WHERE *ALL YOU HAD WAS A NICE TIME WITH HER!*
YOU CAN'T CHECK OUT AS SOON AS YOU HIT A PROBLEM! THAT'S NOT A RELATIONSHIP!
NAME of a BAND
I KNOWWWWW.
BUT I FEEL LIKE THE NICE TIMES WERE PRETEND AND THIS IS WHAT WAS REAL ALL ALONG.

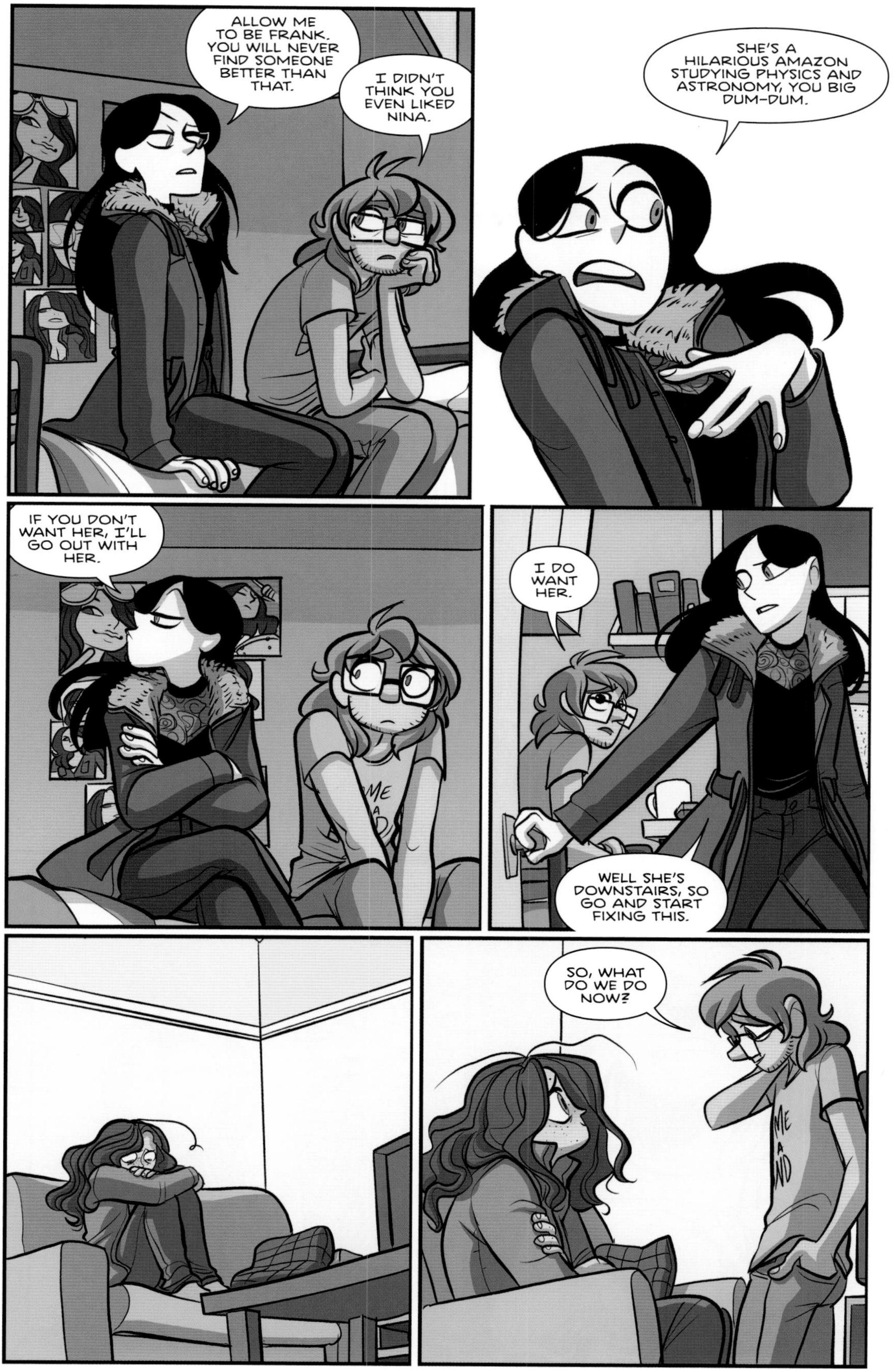
ALLOW ME TO BE FRANK. YOU WILL NEVER FIND SOMEONE BETTER THAN THAT.
I DIDN'T THINK YOU EVEN LIKED NINA.
SHE'S A HILARIOUS AMAZON STUDYING PHYSICS AND ASTRONOMY, YOU BIG DUM-DUM.
IF YOU DON'T WANT HER, I'LL GO OUT WITH HER.
I DO WANT HER.
WELL SHE'S DOWNSTAIRS, SO GO AND START FIXING THIS.
SO, WHAT DO WE DO NOW?

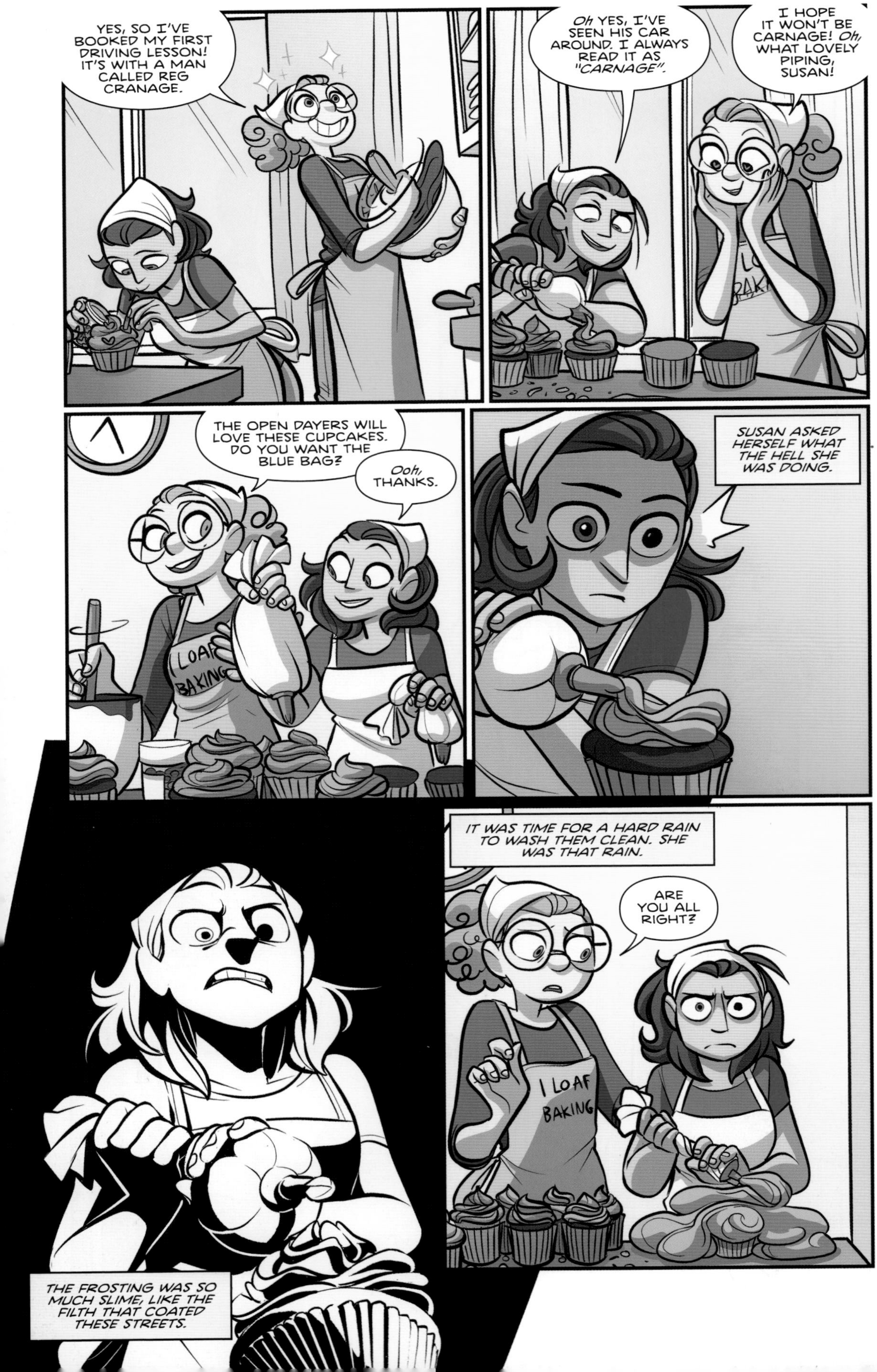
YES, SO I'VE BOOKED MY FIRST DRIVING LESSON! IT'S WITH A MAN CALLED REG CRANAGE.
Oh YES, I'VE SEEN HIS CAR AROUND. I ALWAYS READ IT AS *"CARNAGE"*.
I HOPE IT WON'T BE CARNAGE! *Oh*, WHAT LOVELY PIPING, SUSAN!
THE OPEN DAYERS WILL LOVE THESE CUPCAKES. DO YOU WANT THE BLUE BAG?
Ooh, THANKS.
SUSAN ASKED HERSELF WHAT THE HELL SHE WAS DOING.
IT WAS TIME FOR A HARD RAIN TO WASH THEM CLEAN. SHE WAS THAT RAIN.
ARE YOU ALL RIGHT?
THE FROSTING WAS SO MUCH SLIME, LIKE THE FILTH THAT COATED THESE STREETS.

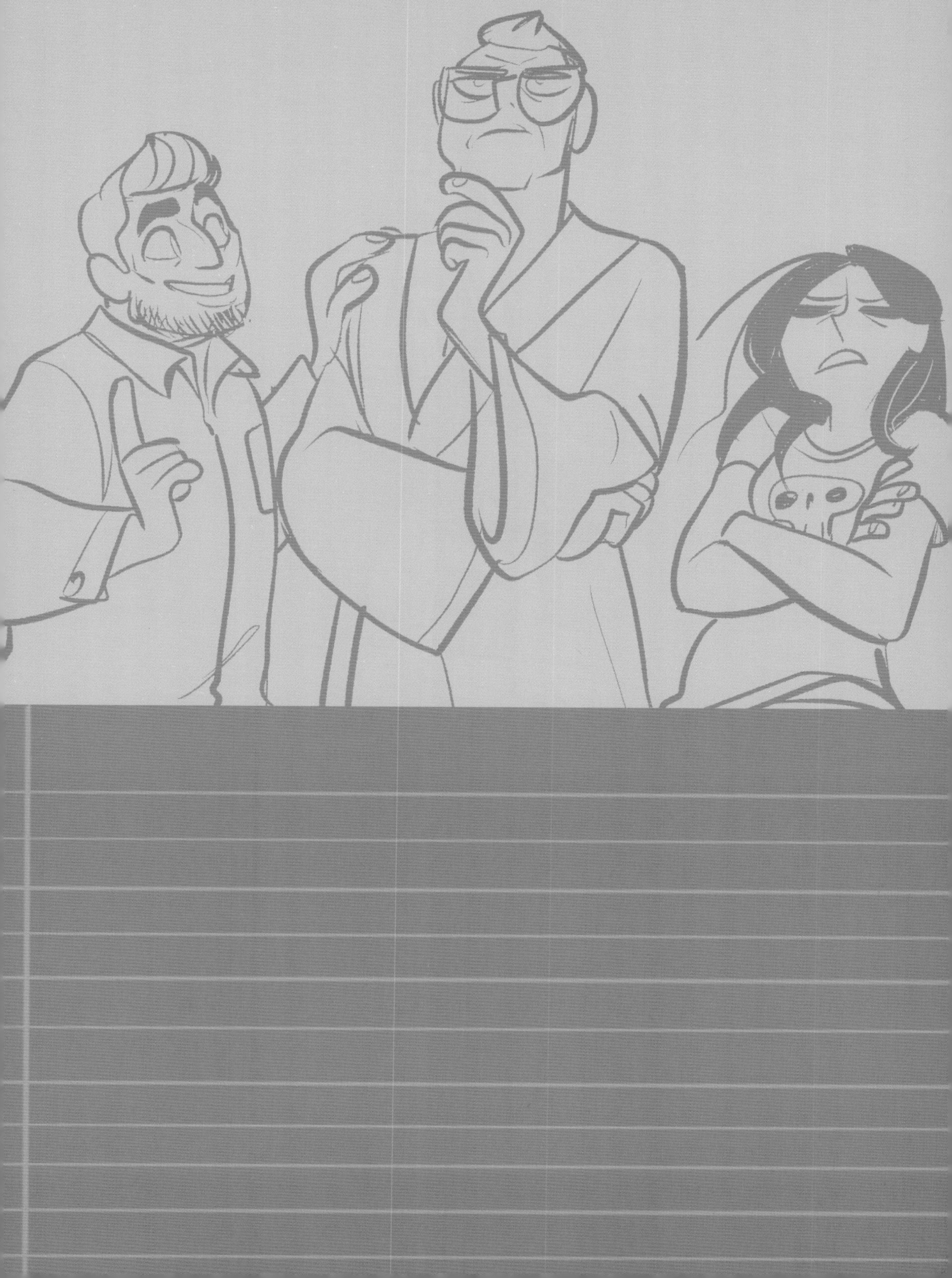

CHAPTER
FORTY-SIX

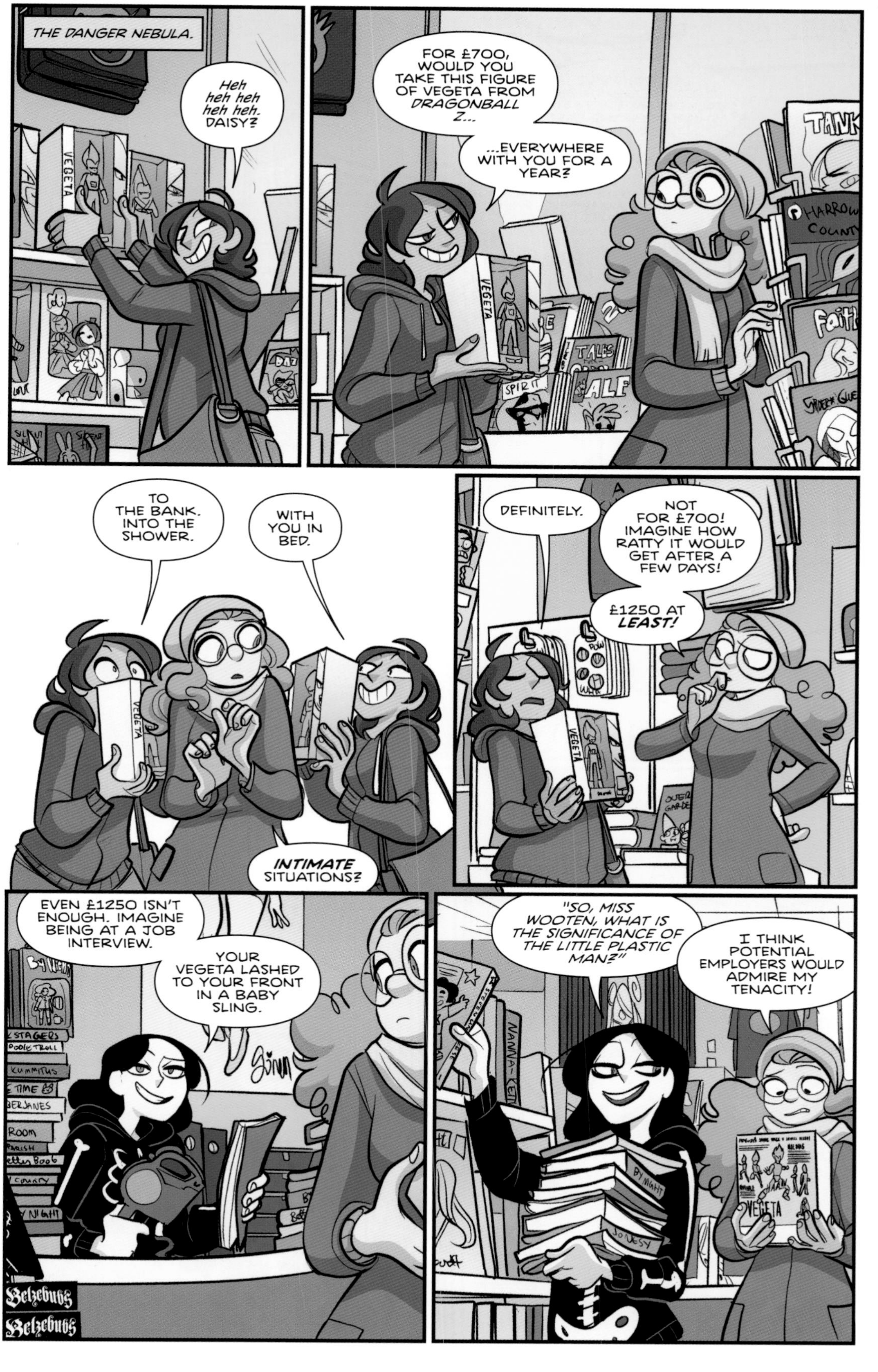
THE DANGER NEBULA.
Heh heh heh heh heh. DAISY?
FOR £700, WOULD YOU TAKE THIS FIGURE OF VEGETA FROM DRAGONBALL Z...
...EVERYWHERE WITH YOU FOR A YEAR?
TO THE BANK. INTO THE SHOWER.
WITH YOU IN BED.
INTIMATE SITUATIONS?
DEFINITELY.
NOT FOR £700! IMAGINE HOW RATTY IT WOULD GET AFTER A FEW DAYS!
£1250 AT LEAST!
EVEN £1250 ISN'T ENOUGH. IMAGINE BEING AT A JOB INTERVIEW.
YOUR VEGETA LASHED TO YOUR FRONT IN A BABY SLING.
"SO, MISS WOOTEN, WHAT IS THE SIGNIFICANCE OF THE LITTLE PLASTIC MAN?"
I THINK POTENTIAL EMPLOYERS WOULD ADMIRE MY TENACITY!

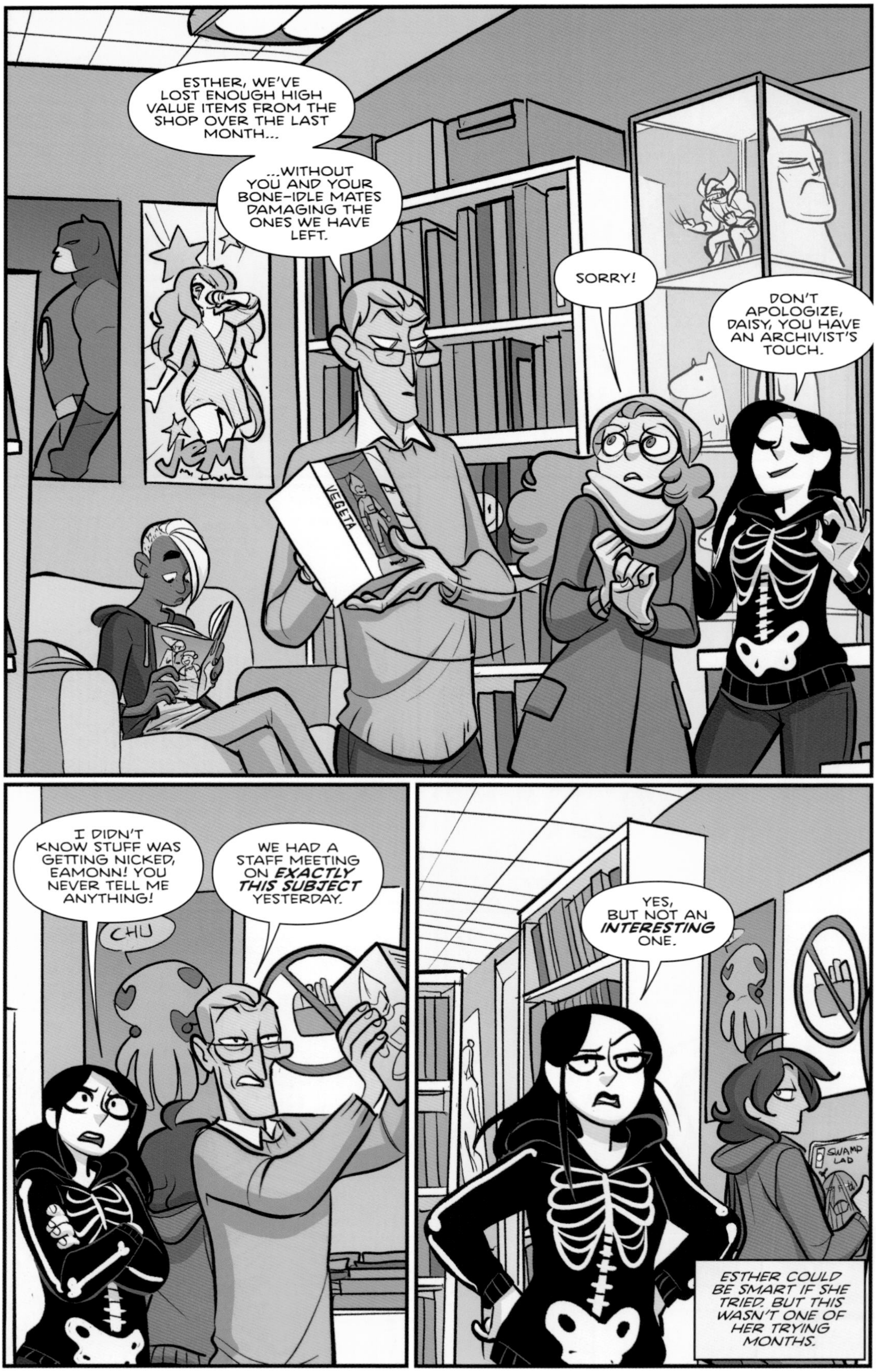

ESTHER, WE'VE LOST ENOUGH HIGH VALUE ITEMS FROM THE SHOP OVER THE LAST MONTH...
...WITHOUT YOU AND YOUR BONE-IDLE MATES DAMAGING THE ONES WE HAVE LEFT.
SORRY!
DON'T APOLOGIZE, DAISY, YOU HAVE AN ARCHIVIST'S TOUCH.
JEM
VEGETA
I DIDN'T KNOW STUFF WAS GETTING NICKED, EAMONN! YOU NEVER TELL ME ANYTHING!
CHU
WE HAD A STAFF MEETING ON ***EXACTLY THIS SUBJECT*** YESTERDAY.
YES, BUT NOT AN ***INTERESTING*** ONE.
SWAMP LAD
ESTHER COULD BE SMART IF SHE TRIED. BUT THIS WASN'T ONE OF HER TRYING MONTHS.

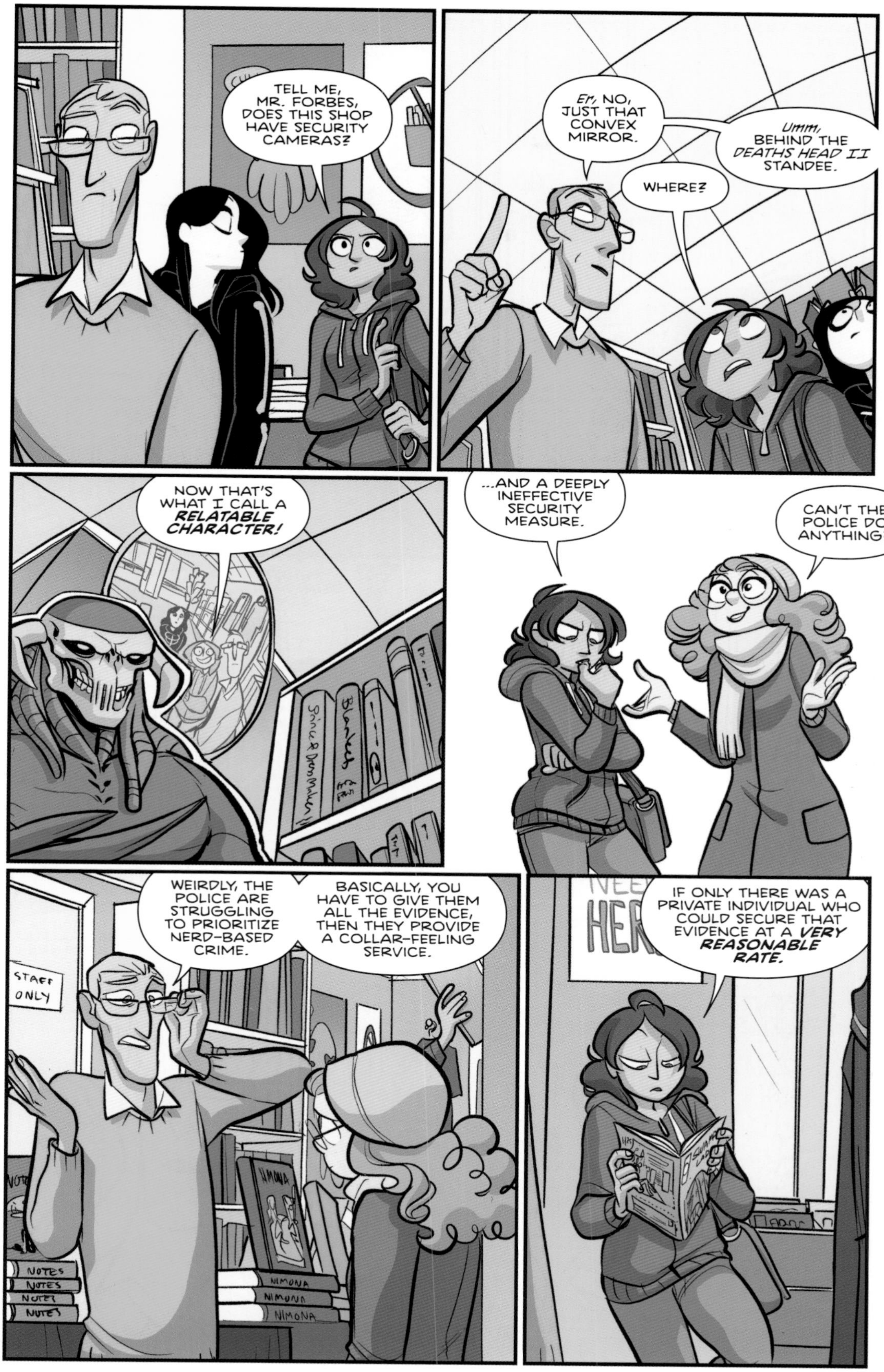
TELL ME, MR. FORBES, DOES THIS SHOP HAVE SECURITY CAMERAS?
ER, NO, JUST THAT CONVEX MIRROR.
WHERE?
UMM, BEHIND THE DEATHS HEAD II STANDEE.
NOW THAT'S WHAT I CALL A RELATABLE CHARACTER!
...AND A DEEPLY INEFFECTIVE SECURITY MEASURE.
CAN'T THE POLICE DO ANYTHING?
WEIRDLY, THE POLICE ARE STRUGGLING TO PRIORITIZE NERD-BASED CRIME.
BASICALLY, YOU HAVE TO GIVE THEM ALL THE EVIDENCE, THEN THEY PROVIDE A COLLAR-FEELING SERVICE.
STAFF ONLY
NIMONA
NOTES
IF ONLY THERE WAS A PRIVATE INDIVIDUAL WHO COULD SECURE THAT EVIDENCE AT A VERY REASONABLE RATE.

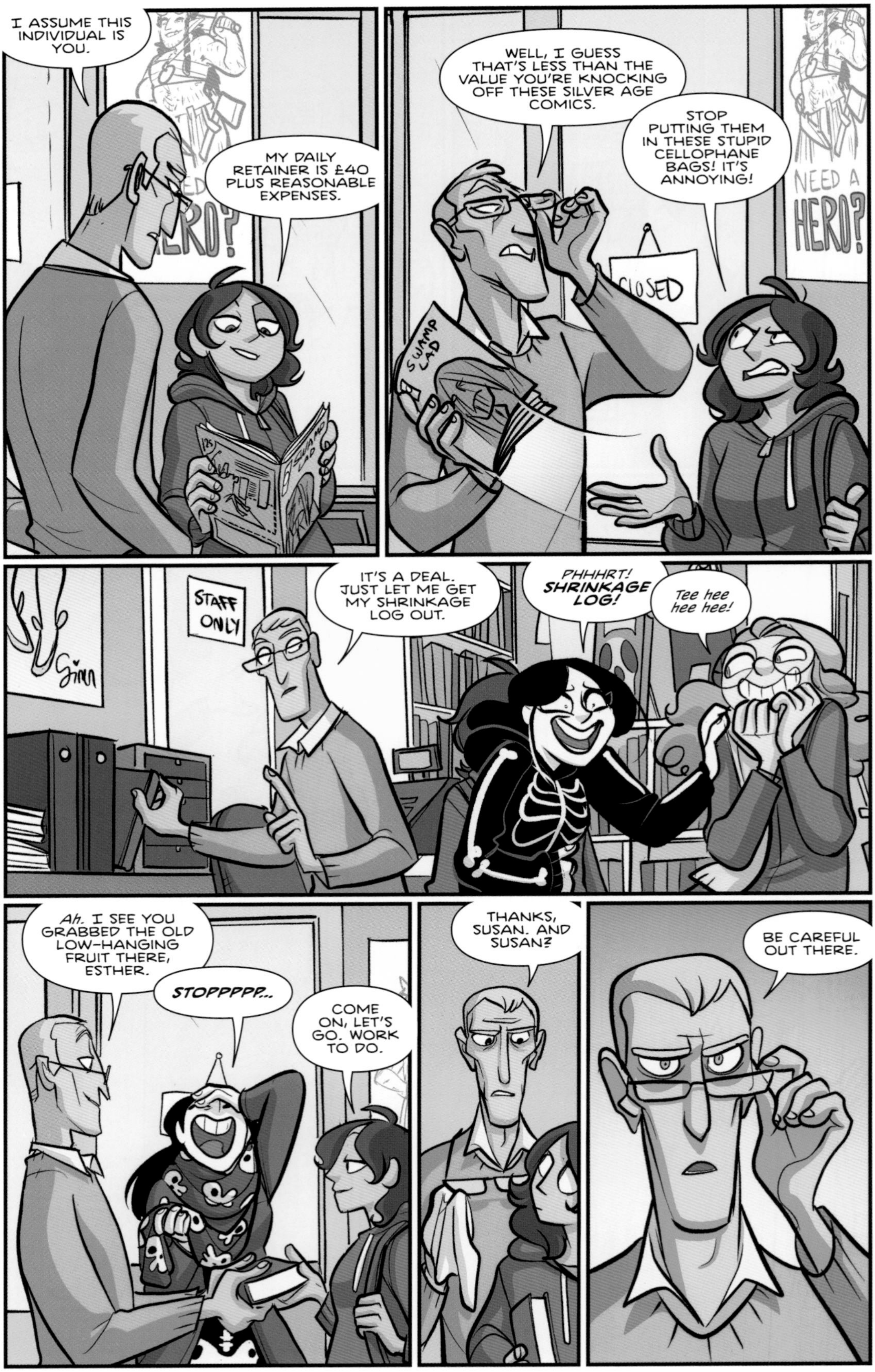
I ASSUME THIS INDIVIDUAL IS YOU.
NEED A HERO?
MY DAILY RETAINER IS £40 PLUS REASONABLE EXPENSES.
WELL, I GUESS THAT'S LESS THAN THE VALUE YOU'RE KNOCKING OFF THESE SILVER AGE COMICS.
STOP PUTTING THEM IN THESE STUPID CELLOPHANE BAGS! IT'S ANNOYING!
NEED A HERO?
CLOSED
SWAMP LAD
STAFF ONLY
IT'S A DEAL. JUST LET ME GET MY SHRINKAGE LOG OUT.
PHHHRT! SHRINKAGE LOG!
Tee hee hee hee!
Ah. I SEE YOU GRABBED THE OLD LOW-HANGING FRUIT THERE, ESTHER.
STOPPPPP...
COME ON, LET'S GO. WORK TO DO.
THANKS, SUSAN. AND SUSAN?
BE CAREFUL OUT THERE.

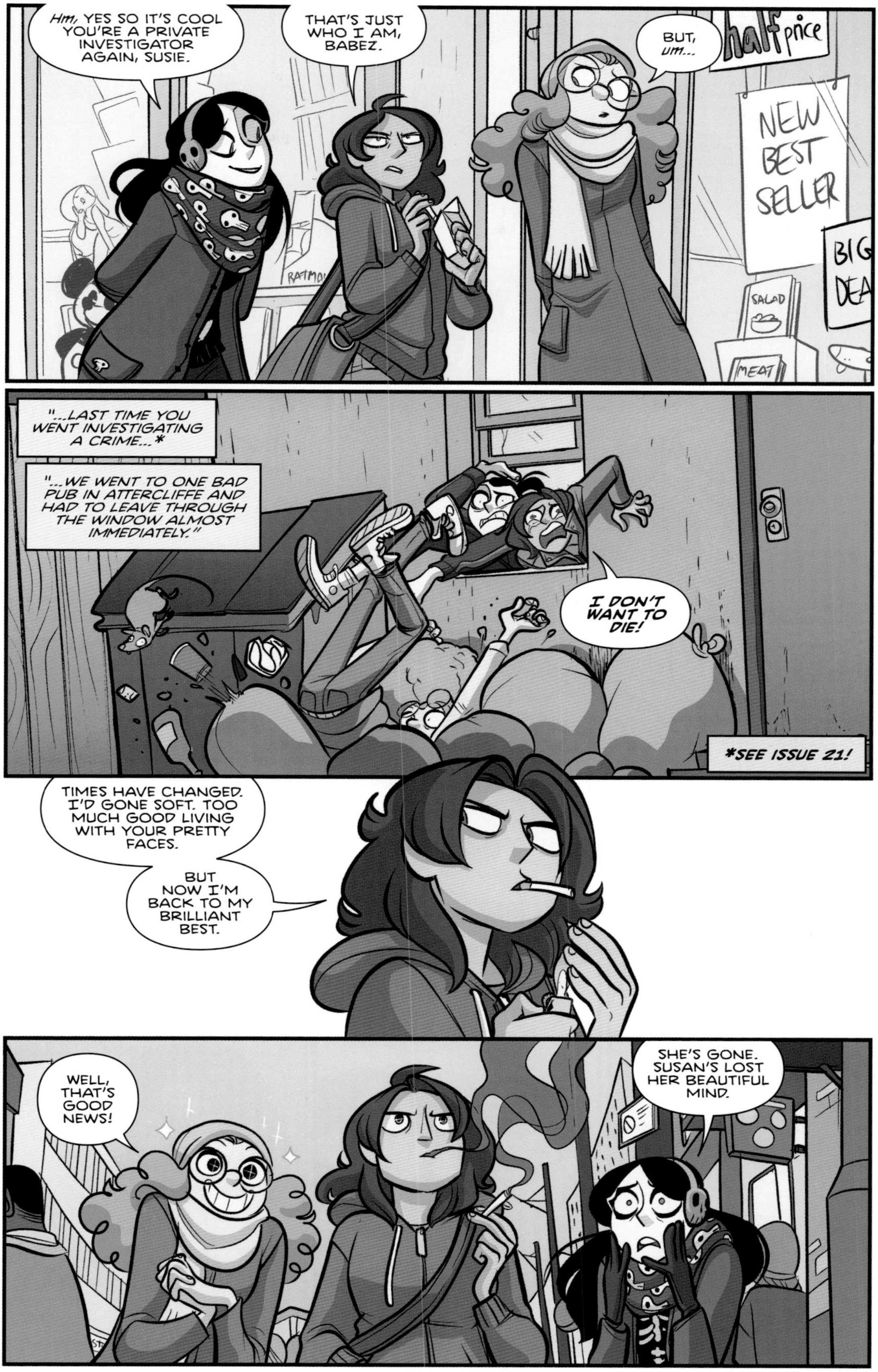
HM, YES SO IT'S COOL YOU'RE A PRIVATE INVESTIGATOR AGAIN, SUSIE.
THAT'S JUST WHO I AM, BABEZ.
BUT, UM...
half price
NEW BEST SELLER
SALAD
MEAT
"...LAST TIME YOU WENT INVESTIGATING A CRIME...*
"...WE WENT TO ONE BAD PUB IN ATTERCLIFFE AND HAD TO LEAVE THROUGH THE WINDOW ALMOST IMMEDIATELY."
I DON'T WANT TO DIE!
*SEE ISSUE 21!
TIMES HAVE CHANGED. I'D GONE SOFT. TOO MUCH GOOD LIVING WITH YOUR PRETTY FACES.
BUT NOW I'M BACK TO MY BRILLIANT BEST.
WELL, THAT'S GOOD NEWS!
SHE'S GONE. SUSAN'S LOST HER BEAUTIFUL MIND.

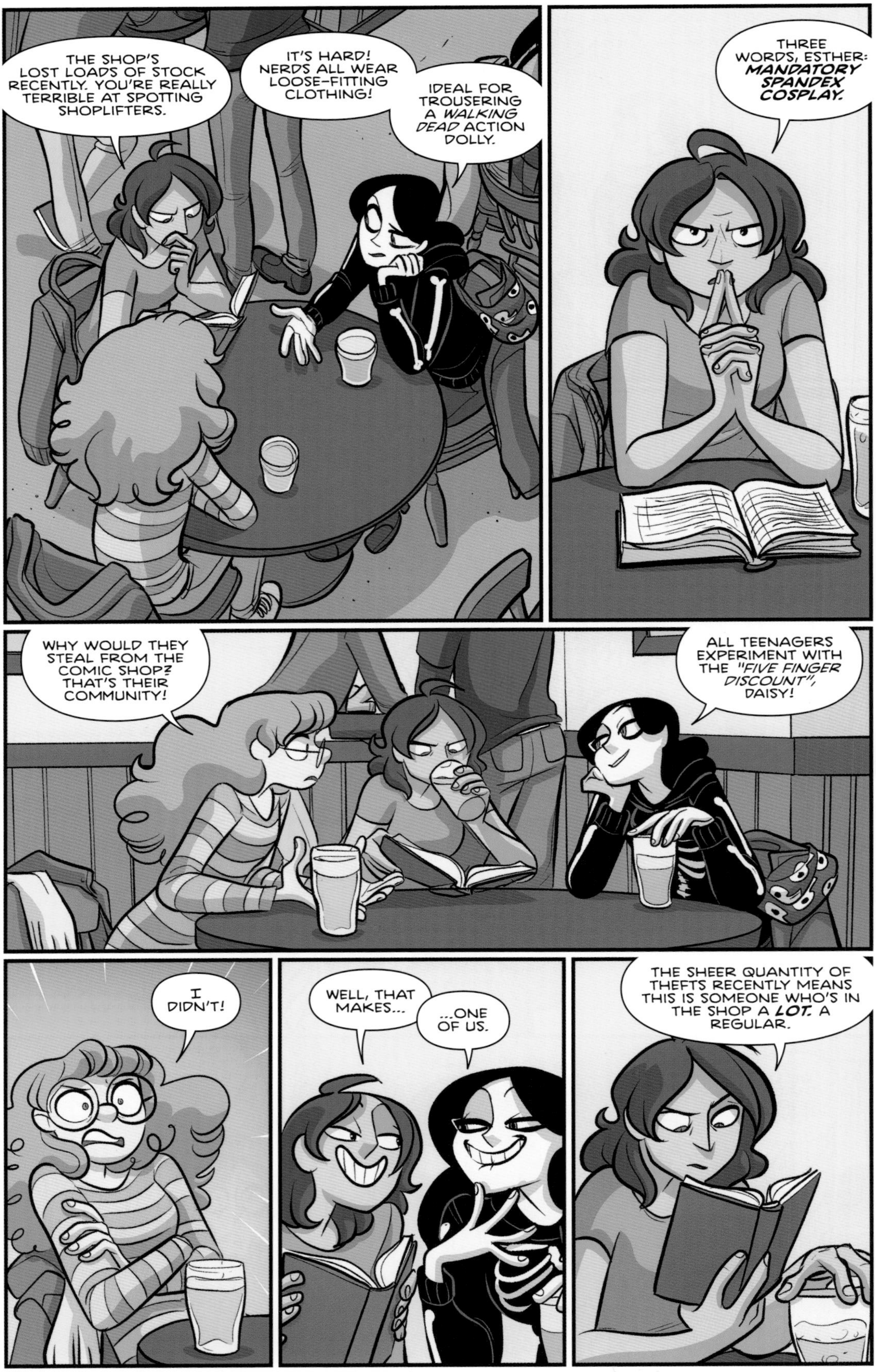
THE SHOP'S LOST LOADS OF STOCK RECENTLY. YOU'RE REALLY TERRIBLE AT SPOTTING SHOPLIFTERS.
IT'S HARD! NERDS ALL WEAR LOOSE-FITTING CLOTHING!
IDEAL FOR TROUSERING A *WALKING DEAD* ACTION DOLLY.
THREE WORDS, ESTHER: ***MANDATORY SPANDEX COSPLAY.***
WHY WOULD THEY STEAL FROM THE COMIC SHOP? THAT'S THEIR COMMUNITY!
ALL TEENAGERS EXPERIMENT WITH THE *"FIVE FINGER DISCOUNT"*, DAISY!
I DIDN'T!
WELL, THAT MAKES...
...ONE OF US.
THE SHEER QUANTITY OF THEFTS RECENTLY MEANS THIS IS SOMEONE WHO'S IN THE SHOP A ***LOT.*** A REGULAR.

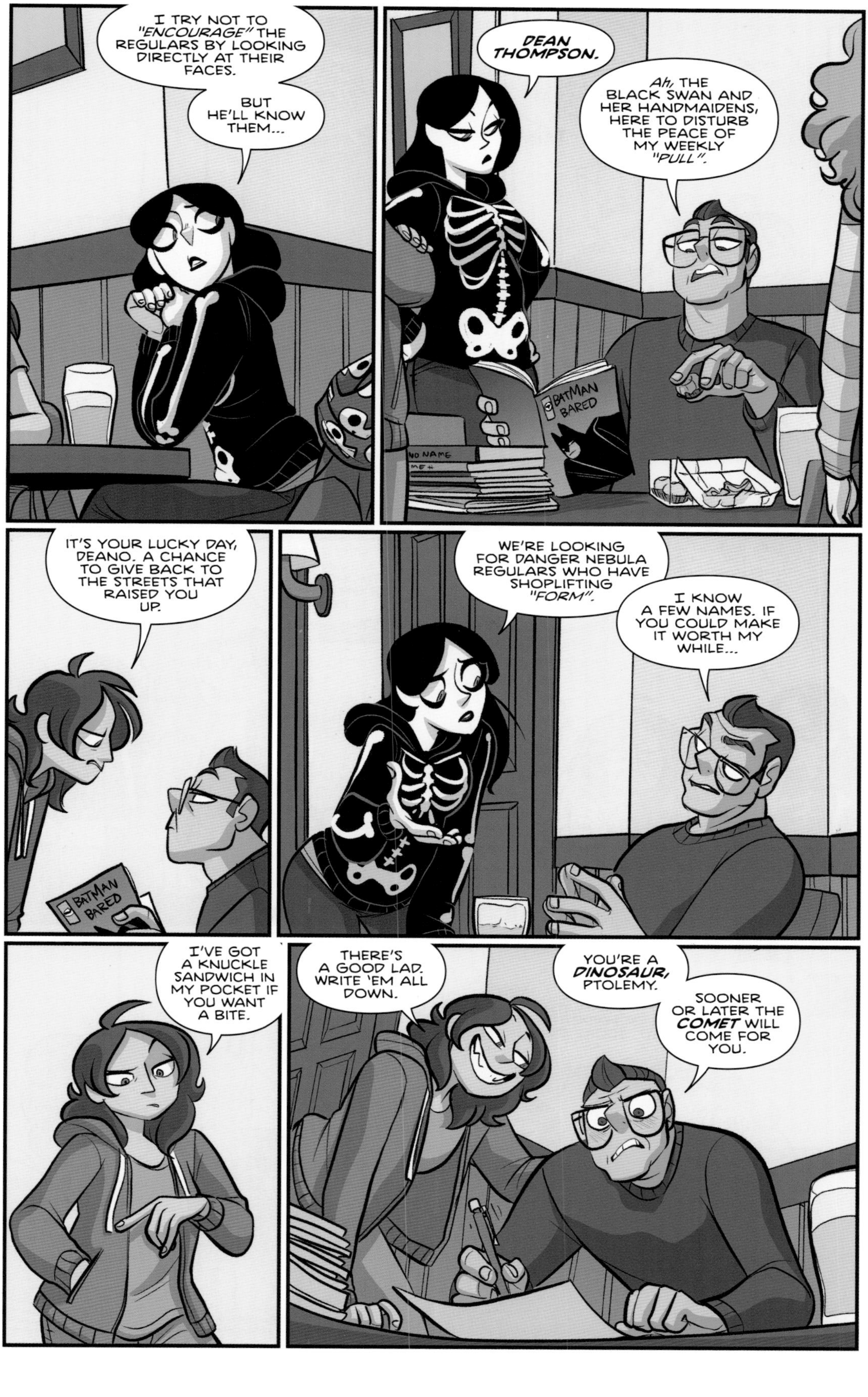
I TRY NOT TO "ENCOURAGE" THE REGULARS BY LOOKING DIRECTLY AT THEIR FACES.
BUT HE'LL KNOW THEM...
DEAN THOMPSON.
AH, THE BLACK SWAN AND HER HANDMAIDENS, HERE TO DISTURB THE PEACE OF MY WEEKLY "PULL".
BATMAN BARED
NO NAME
MEH
IT'S YOUR LUCKY DAY, DEANO. A CHANCE TO GIVE BACK TO THE STREETS THAT RAISED YOU UP.
BATMAN BARED
WE'RE LOOKING FOR DANGER NEBULA REGULARS WHO HAVE SHOPLIFTING "FORM".
I KNOW A FEW NAMES. IF YOU COULD MAKE IT WORTH MY WHILE...
I'VE GOT A KNUCKLE SANDWICH IN MY POCKET IF YOU WANT A BITE.
THERE'S A GOOD LAD. WRITE 'EM ALL DOWN.
YOU'RE A DINOSAUR, PTOLEMY.
SOONER OR LATER THE COMET WILL COME FOR YOU.

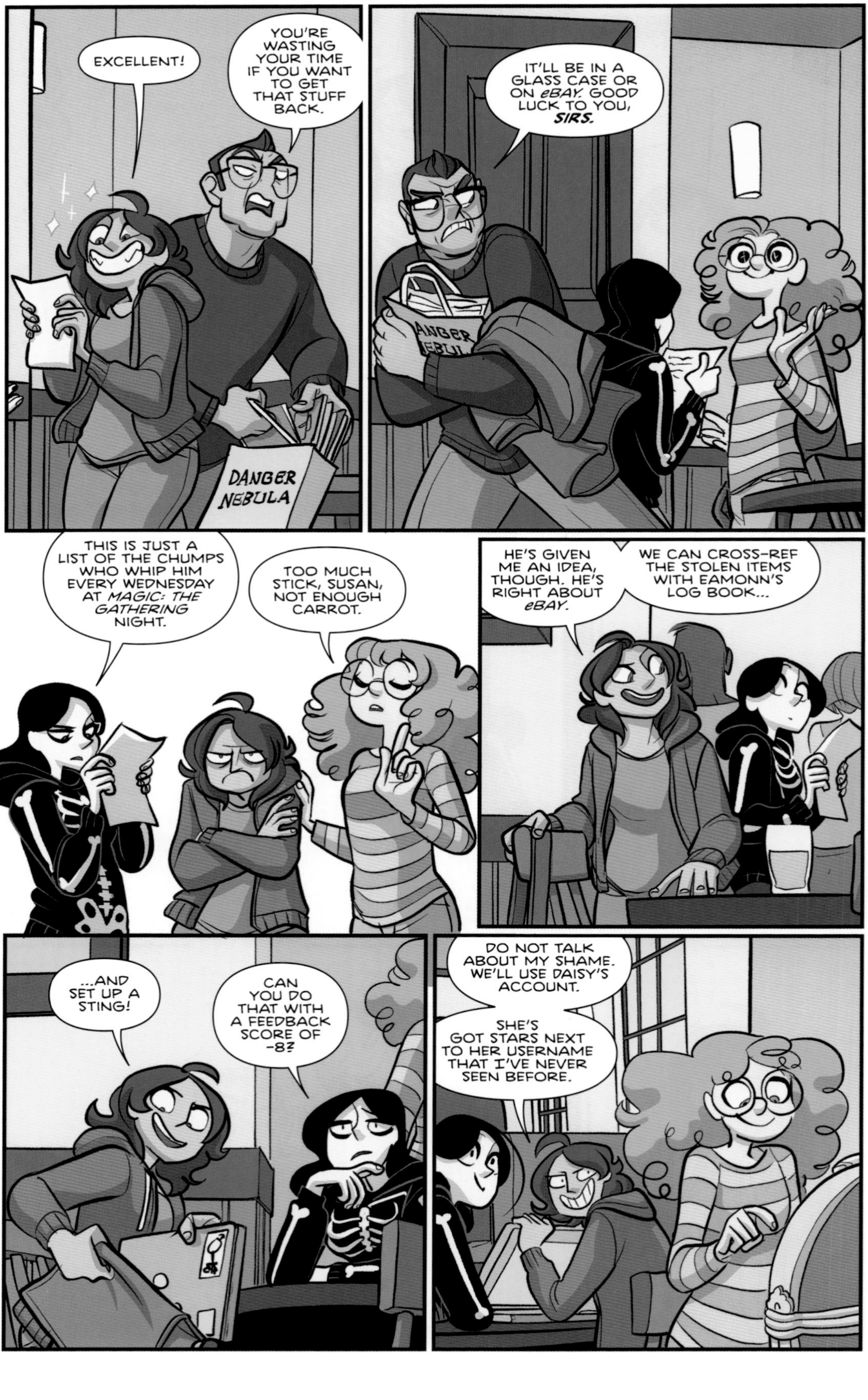
EXCELLENT!
YOU'RE WASTING YOUR TIME IF YOU WANT TO GET THAT STUFF BACK.
DANGER NEBULA
IT'LL BE IN A GLASS CASE OR ON *eBAY.* GOOD LUCK TO YOU, ***SIRS.***
THIS IS JUST A LIST OF THE CHUMPS WHO WHIP HIM EVERY WEDNESDAY AT *MAGIC: THE GATHERING* NIGHT.
TOO MUCH STICK, SUSAN, NOT ENOUGH CARROT.
HE'S GIVEN ME AN IDEA, THOUGH. HE'S RIGHT ABOUT *eBAY.*
WE CAN CROSS-REF THE STOLEN ITEMS WITH EAMONN'S LOG BOOK...
...AND SET UP A STING!
CAN YOU DO THAT WITH A FEEDBACK SCORE OF -8?
DO NOT TALK ABOUT MY SHAME. WE'LL USE DAISY'S ACCOUNT.
SHE'S GOT STARS NEXT TO HER USERNAME THAT I'VE NEVER SEEN BEFORE.

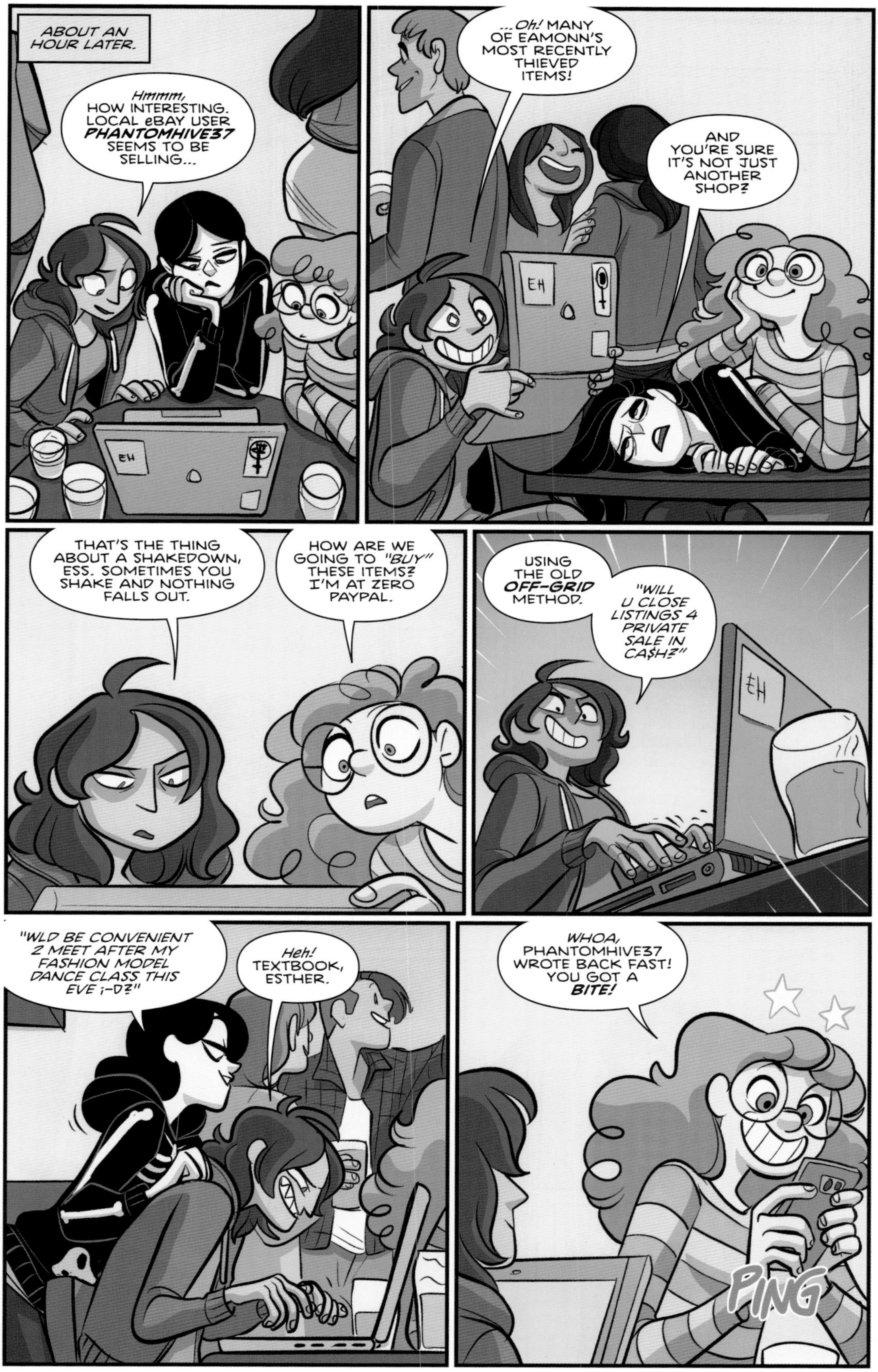
ABOUT AN HOUR LATER.
Hmmm, HOW INTERESTING. LOCAL eBAY USER PHANTOMHIVE37 SEEMS TO BE SELLING...
...Oh! MANY OF EAMONN'S MOST RECENTLY THIEVED ITEMS!
AND YOU'RE SURE IT'S NOT JUST ANOTHER SHOP?
THAT'S THE THING ABOUT A SHAKEDOWN, ESS. SOMETIMES YOU SHAKE AND NOTHING FALLS OUT.
HOW ARE WE GOING TO "BUY" THESE ITEMS? I'M AT ZERO PAYPAL.
USING THE OLD OFF-GRID METHOD.
"WILL U CLOSE LISTINGS 4 PRIVATE SALE IN CA$H?"
"WLD BE CONVENIENT 2 MEET AFTER MY FASHION MODEL DANCE CLASS THIS EVE ;-D?"
Heh! TEXTBOOK, ESTHER.
WHOA, PHANTOMHIVE37 WROTE BACK FAST! YOU GOT A BITE!
PING

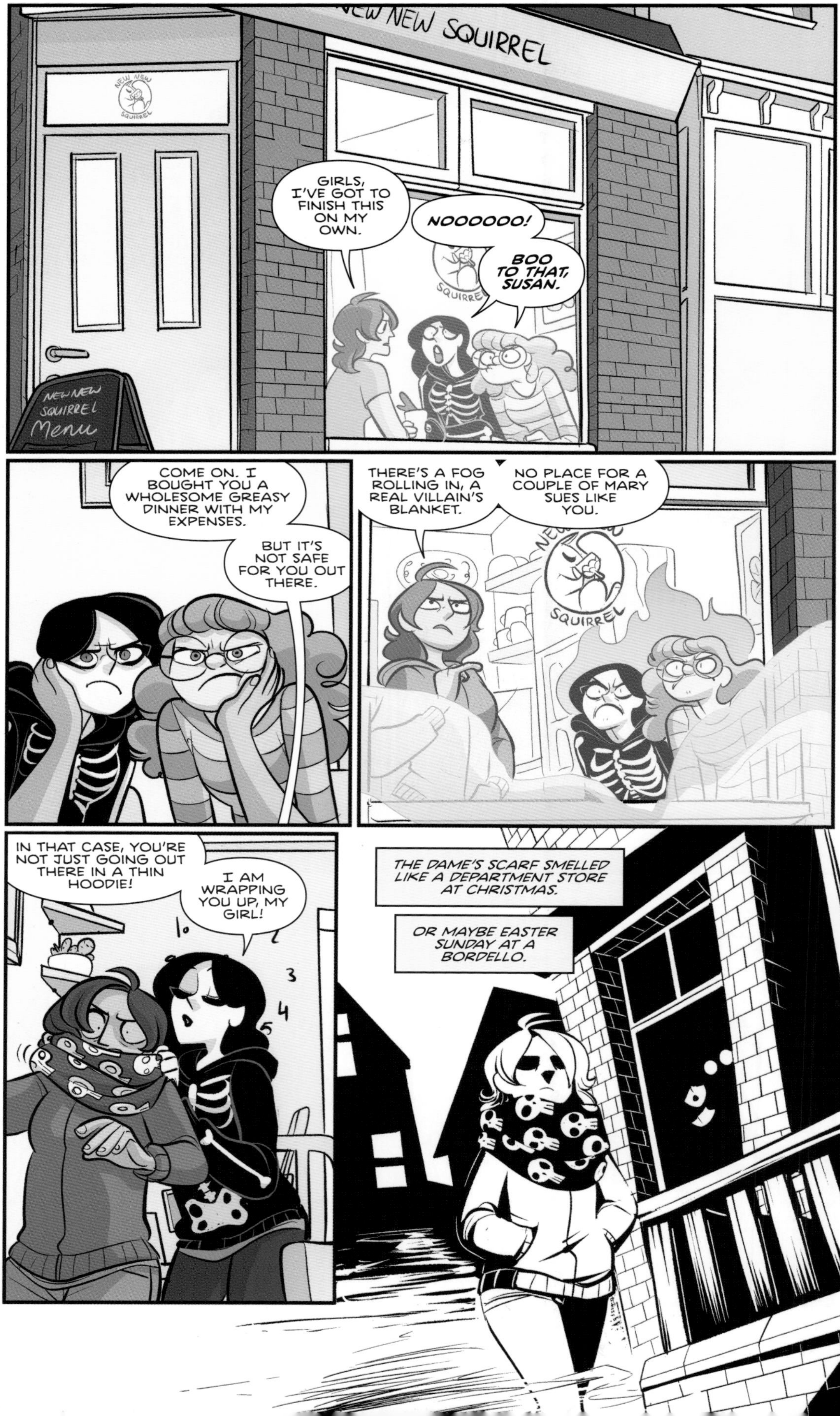
NEW NEW SQUIRREL
NEW NEW SQUIRREL
GIRLS, I'VE GOT TO FINISH THIS ON MY OWN.
NOOOOOO!
BOO TO THAT, SUSAN.
SQUIRREL
NEW NEW SQUIRREL Menu
COME ON. I BOUGHT YOU A WHOLESOME GREASY DINNER WITH MY EXPENSES.
BUT IT'S NOT SAFE FOR YOU OUT THERE.
THERE'S A FOG ROLLING IN, A REAL VILLAIN'S BLANKET.
NO PLACE FOR A COUPLE OF MARY SUES LIKE YOU.
SQUIRREL
IN THAT CASE, YOU'RE NOT JUST GOING OUT THERE IN A THIN HOODIE!
I AM WRAPPING YOU UP, MY GIRL!
1
2
3
4
5
THE DAME'S SCARF SMELLED LIKE A DEPARTMENT STORE AT CHRISTMAS.
OR MAYBE EASTER SUNDAY AT A BORDELLO.

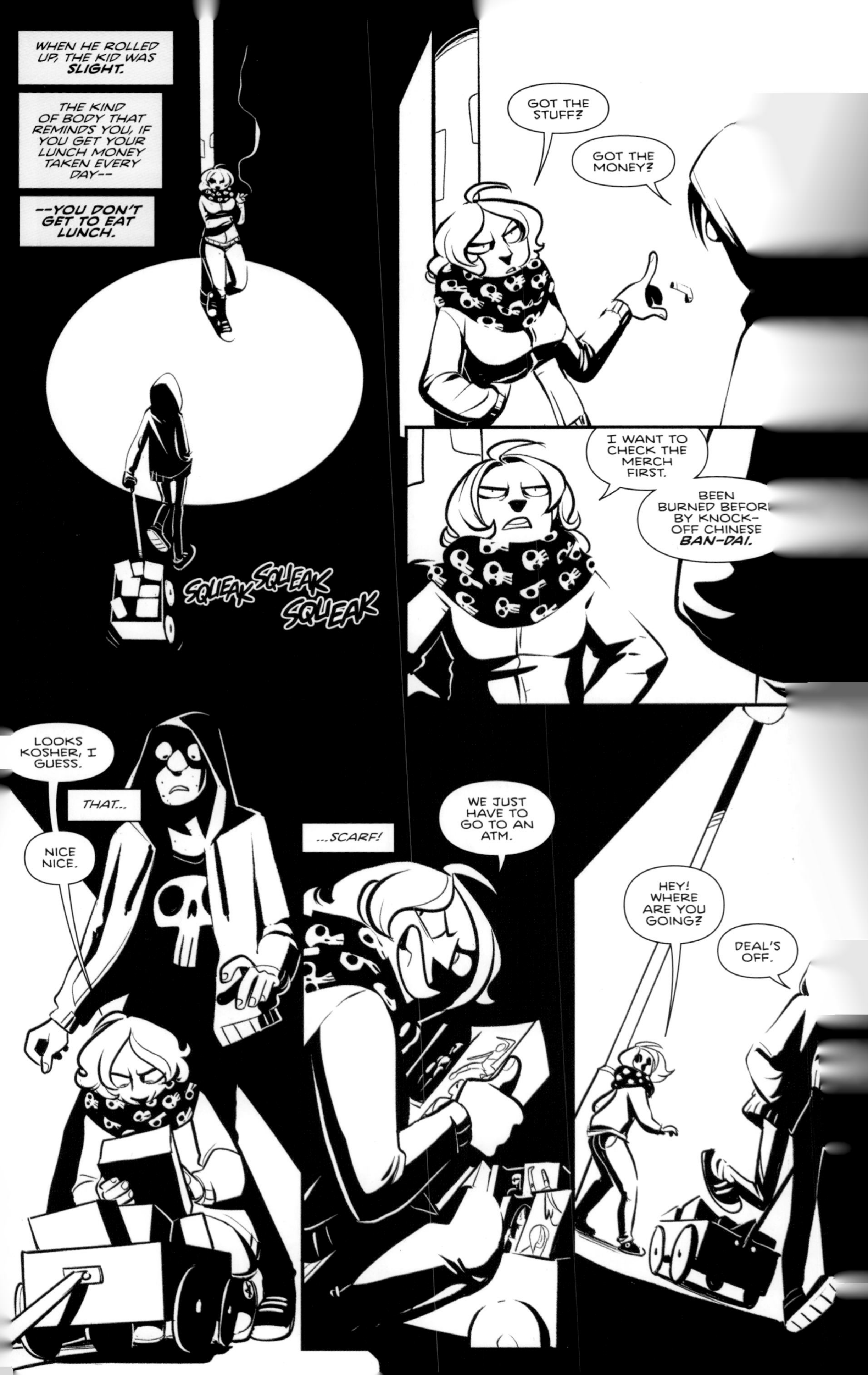
WHEN HE ROLLED UP, THE KID WAS SLIGHT.
THE KIND OF BODY THAT REMINDS YOU, IF YOU GET YOUR LUNCH MONEY TAKEN EVERY DAY--
--YOU DON'T GET TO EAT LUNCH.
SQUEAK SQUEAK SQUEAK
GOT THE STUFF?
GOT THE MONEY?
I WANT TO CHECK THE MERCH FIRST.
BEEN BURNED BEFORE BY KNOCK-OFF CHINESE BAN-DAI.
LOOKS KOSHER, I GUESS.
THAT...
NICE NICE.
...SCARF!
WE JUST HAVE TO GO TO AN ATM.
HEY! WHERE ARE YOU GOING?
DEAL'S OFF.

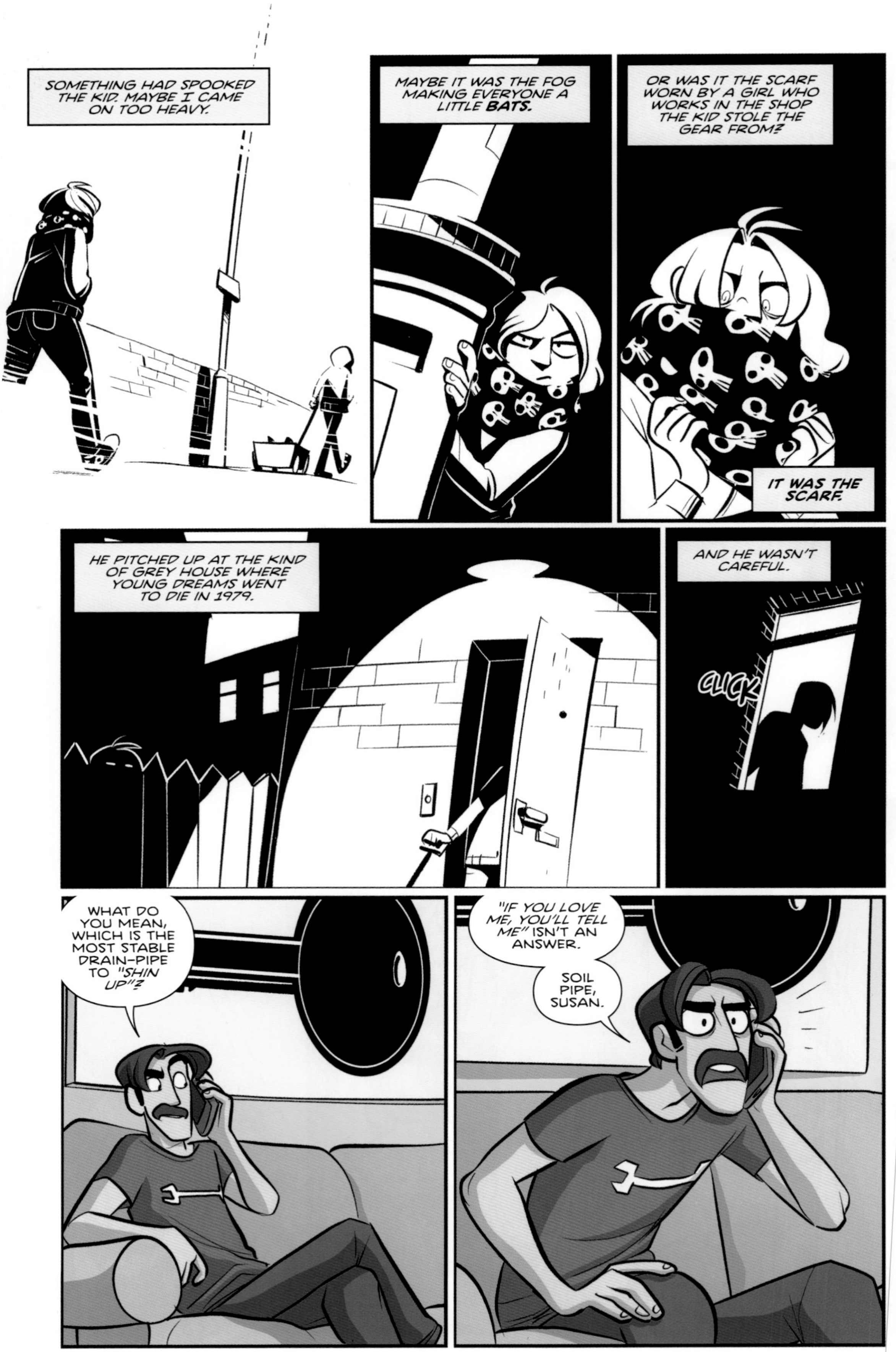
SOMETHING HAD SPOOKED THE KID. MAYBE I CAME ON TOO HEAVY.
MAYBE IT WAS THE FOG MAKING EVERYONE A LITTLE BATS.
OR WAS IT THE SCARF WORN BY A GIRL WHO WORKS IN THE SHOP THE KID STOLE THE GEAR FROM?
IT WAS THE SCARF.
HE PITCHED UP AT THE KIND OF GREY HOUSE WHERE YOUNG DREAMS WENT TO DIE IN 1979.
AND HE WASN'T CAREFUL.
CLICK
WHAT DO YOU MEAN, WHICH IS THE MOST STABLE DRAIN-PIPE TO "SHIN UP"?
"IF YOU LOVE ME, YOU'LL TELL ME" ISN'T AN ANSWER.
SOIL PIPE, SUSAN.

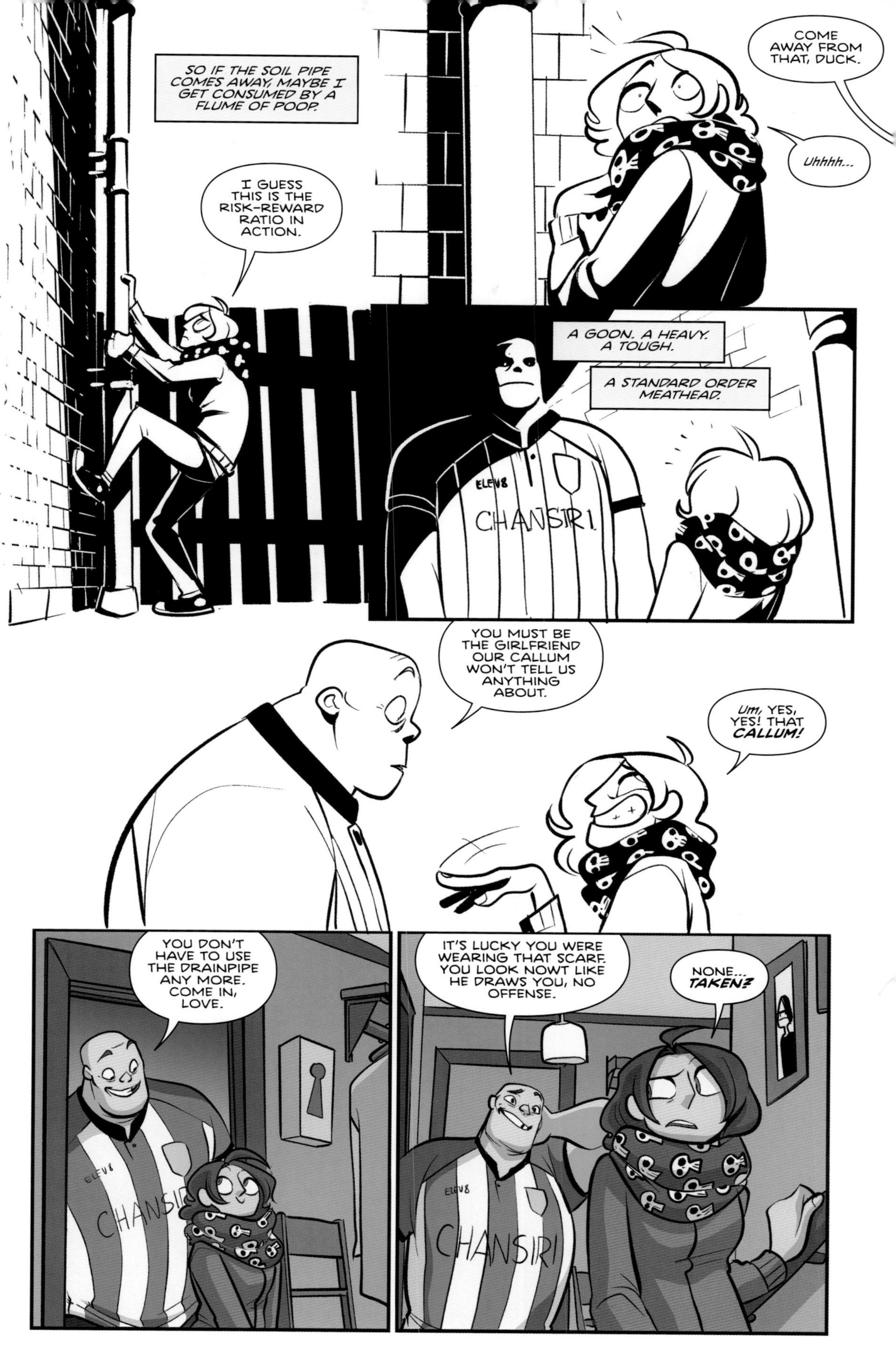
SO IF THE SOIL PIPE COMES AWAY, MAYBE I GET CONSUMED BY A FLUME OF POOP.
I GUESS THIS IS THE RISK-REWARD RATIO IN ACTION.
COME AWAY FROM THAT, DUCK.
Uhhhh...
A GOON. A HEAVY. A TOUGH.
A STANDARD ORDER MEATHEAD.
ELEV8
CHANSIRI
YOU MUST BE THE GIRLFRIEND OUR CALLUM WON'T TELL US ANYTHING ABOUT.
Um, YES, YES! THAT CALLUM!
YOU DON'T HAVE TO USE THE DRAINPIPE ANY MORE. COME IN, LOVE.
IT'S LUCKY YOU WERE WEARING THAT SCARF. YOU LOOK NOWT LIKE HE DRAWS YOU, NO OFFENSE.
NONE... TAKEN?

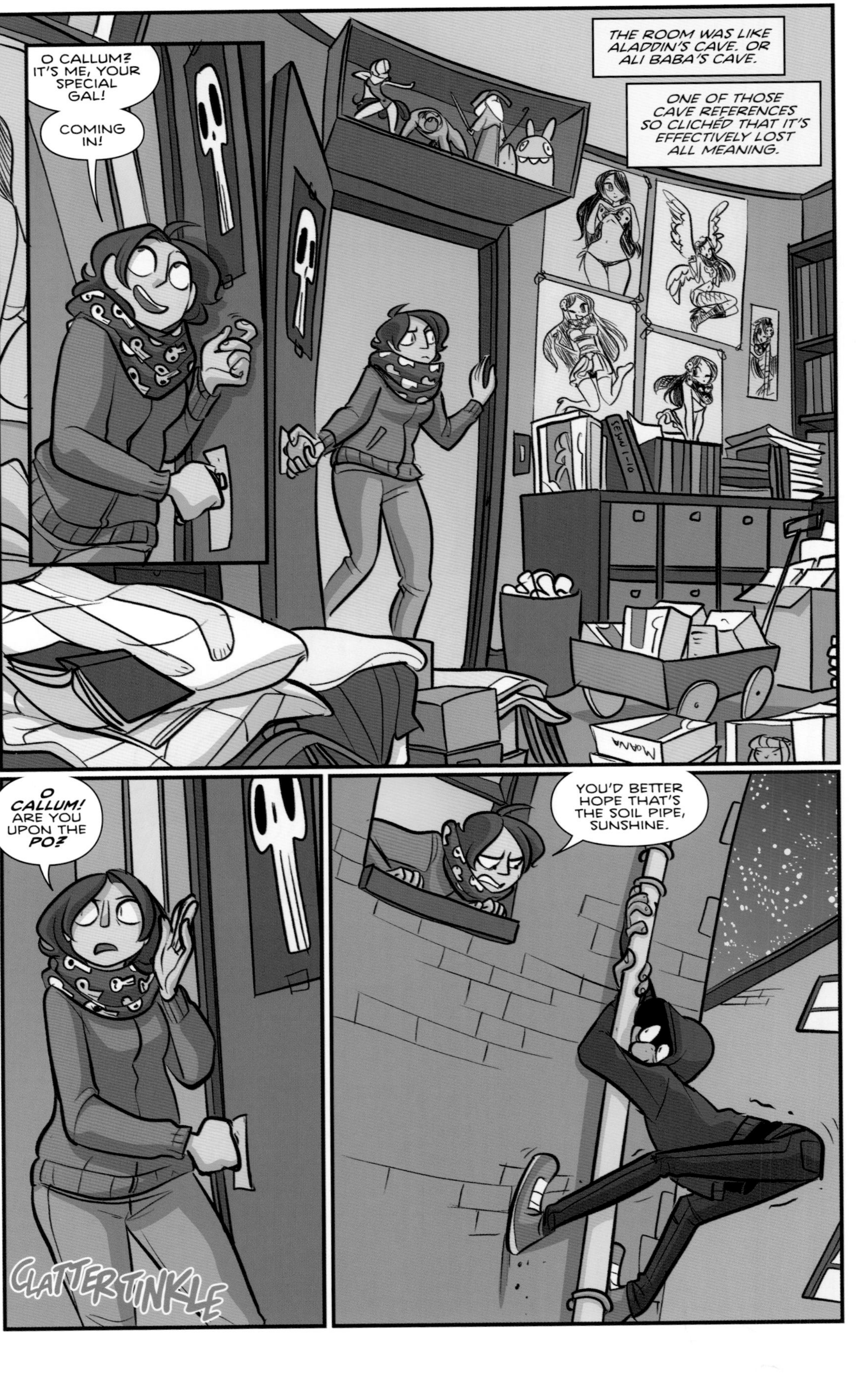
THE ROOM WAS LIKE ALADDIN'S CAVE. OR ALI BABA'S CAVE.
ONE OF THOSE CAVE REFERENCES SO CLICHÉD THAT IT'S EFFECTIVELY LOST ALL MEANING.
O CALLUM? IT'S ME, YOUR SPECIAL GAL!
COMING IN!
O CALLUM! ARE YOU UPON THE PO?
CLATTER TINKLE
YOU'D BETTER HOPE THAT'S THE SOIL PIPE, SUNSHINE.

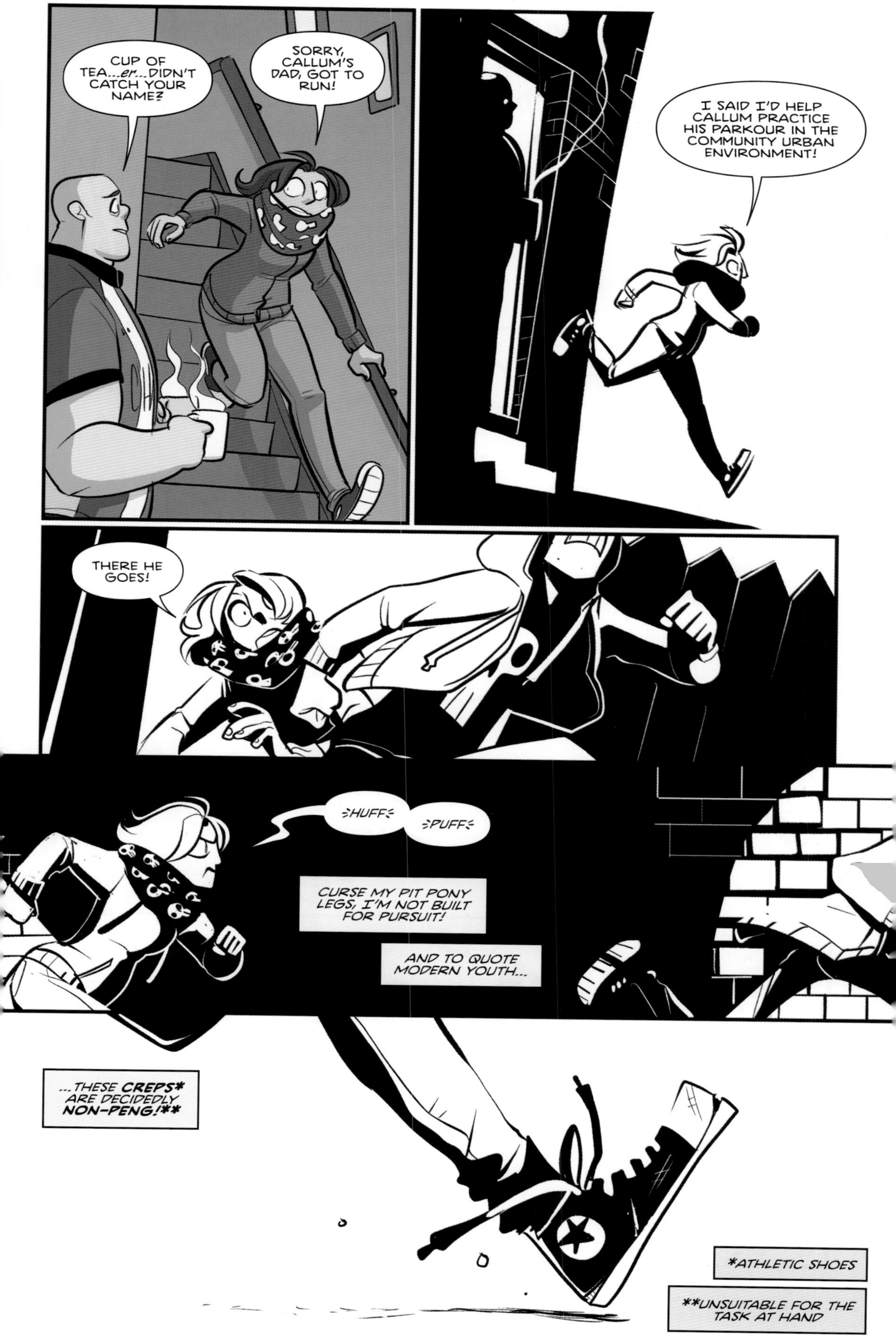
CUP OF TEA...er...DIDN'T CATCH YOUR NAME?
SORRY, CALLUM'S DAD, GOT TO RUN!
I SAID I'D HELP CALLUM PRACTICE HIS PARKOUR IN THE COMMUNITY URBAN ENVIRONMENT!
THERE HE GOES!
HUFF
PUFF
CURSE MY PIT PONY LEGS, I'M NOT BUILT FOR PURSUIT!
AND TO QUOTE MODERN YOUTH...
...THESE CREPS* ARE DECIDEDLY NON-PENG!**
*ATHLETIC SHOES
**UNSUITABLE FOR THE TASK AT HAND

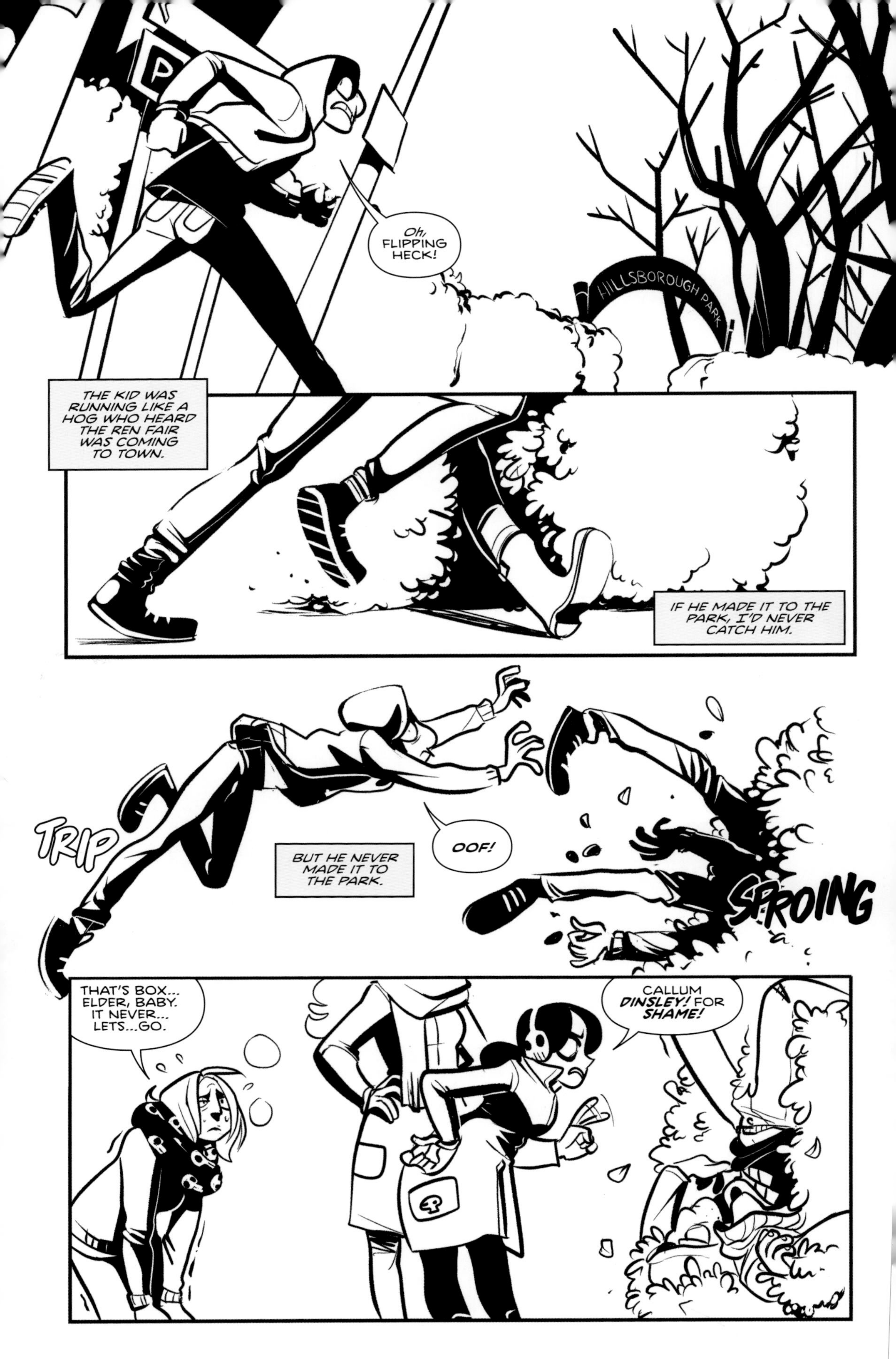
Oh, FLIPPING HECK!
HILLSBOROUGH PARK
THE KID WAS RUNNING LIKE A HOG WHO HEARD THE REN FAIR WAS COMING TO TOWN.
IF HE MADE IT TO THE PARK, I'D NEVER CATCH HIM.
TRIP
BUT HE NEVER MADE IT TO THE PARK.
OOF!
SPROING
THAT'S BOX... ELDER, BABY. IT NEVER... LETS...GO.
CALLUM DINSLEY! FOR SHAME!

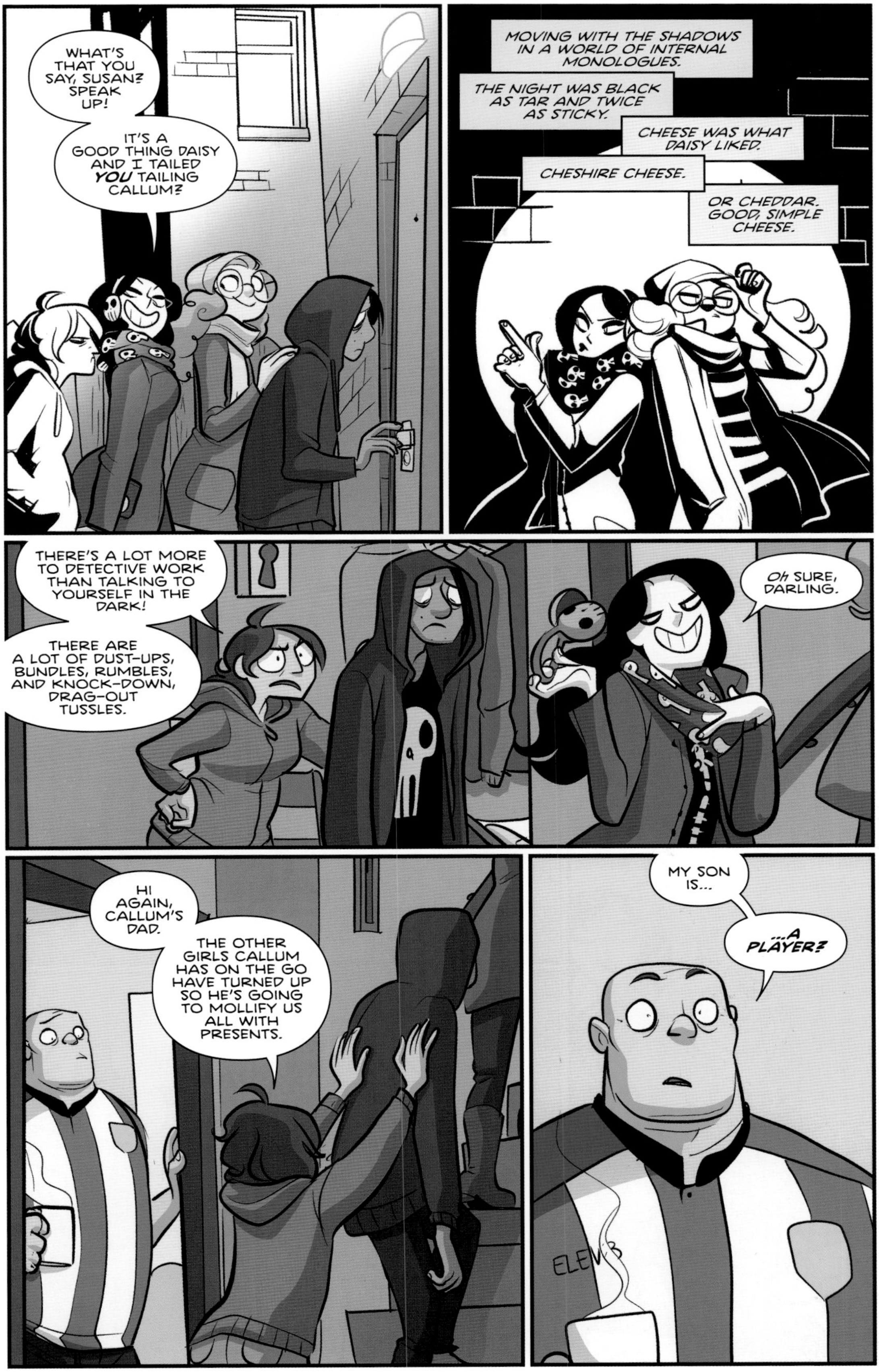
WHAT'S THAT YOU SAY, SUSAN? SPEAK UP!
IT'S A GOOD THING DAISY AND I TAILED *YOU* TAILING CALLUM?
MOVING WITH THE SHADOWS IN A WORLD OF INTERNAL MONOLOGUES.
THE NIGHT WAS BLACK AS TAR AND TWICE AS STICKY.
CHEESE WAS WHAT DAISY LIKED.
CHESHIRE CHEESE.
OR CHEDDAR. GOOD, SIMPLE CHEESE.
THERE'S A LOT MORE TO DETECTIVE WORK THAN TALKING TO YOURSELF IN THE DARK!
THERE ARE A LOT OF DUST-UPS, BUNDLES, RUMBLES, AND KNOCK-DOWN, DRAG-OUT TUSSLES.
Oh SURE, DARLING.
HI AGAIN, CALLUM'S DAD.
THE OTHER GIRLS CALLUM HAS ON THE GO HAVE TURNED UP SO HE'S GOING TO MOLLIFY US ALL WITH PRESENTS.
MY SON IS...
...A *PLAYER?*

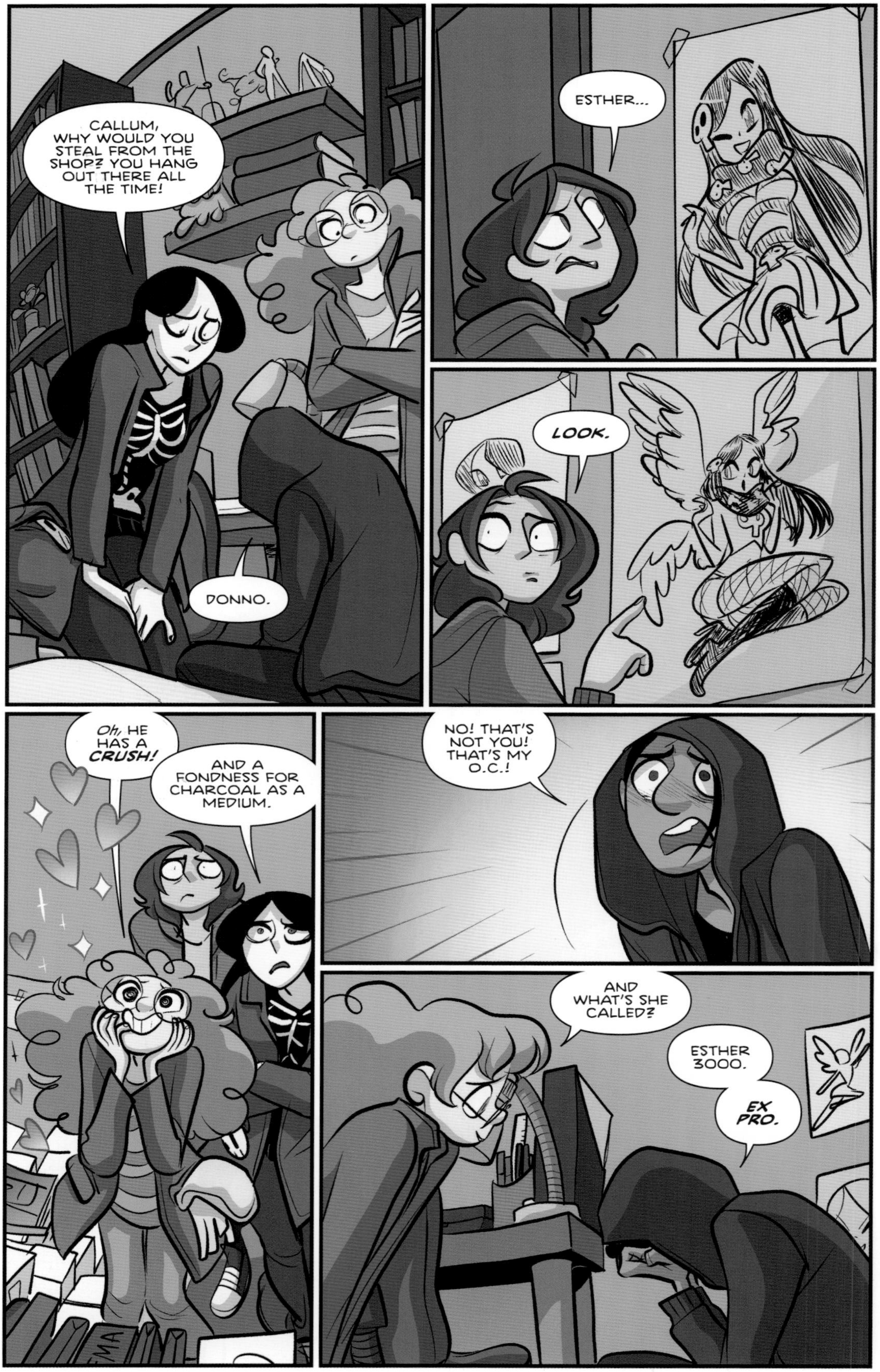

CALLUM, WHY WOULD YOU STEAL FROM THE SHOP? YOU HANG OUT THERE ALL THE TIME!
DONNO.
ESTHER...
LOOK.
Oh, HE HAS A CRUSH!
AND A FONDNESS FOR CHARCOAL AS A MEDIUM.
NO! THAT'S NOT YOU! THAT'S MY O.C.!
AND WHAT'S SHE CALLED?
ESTHER 3000.
EX PRO.

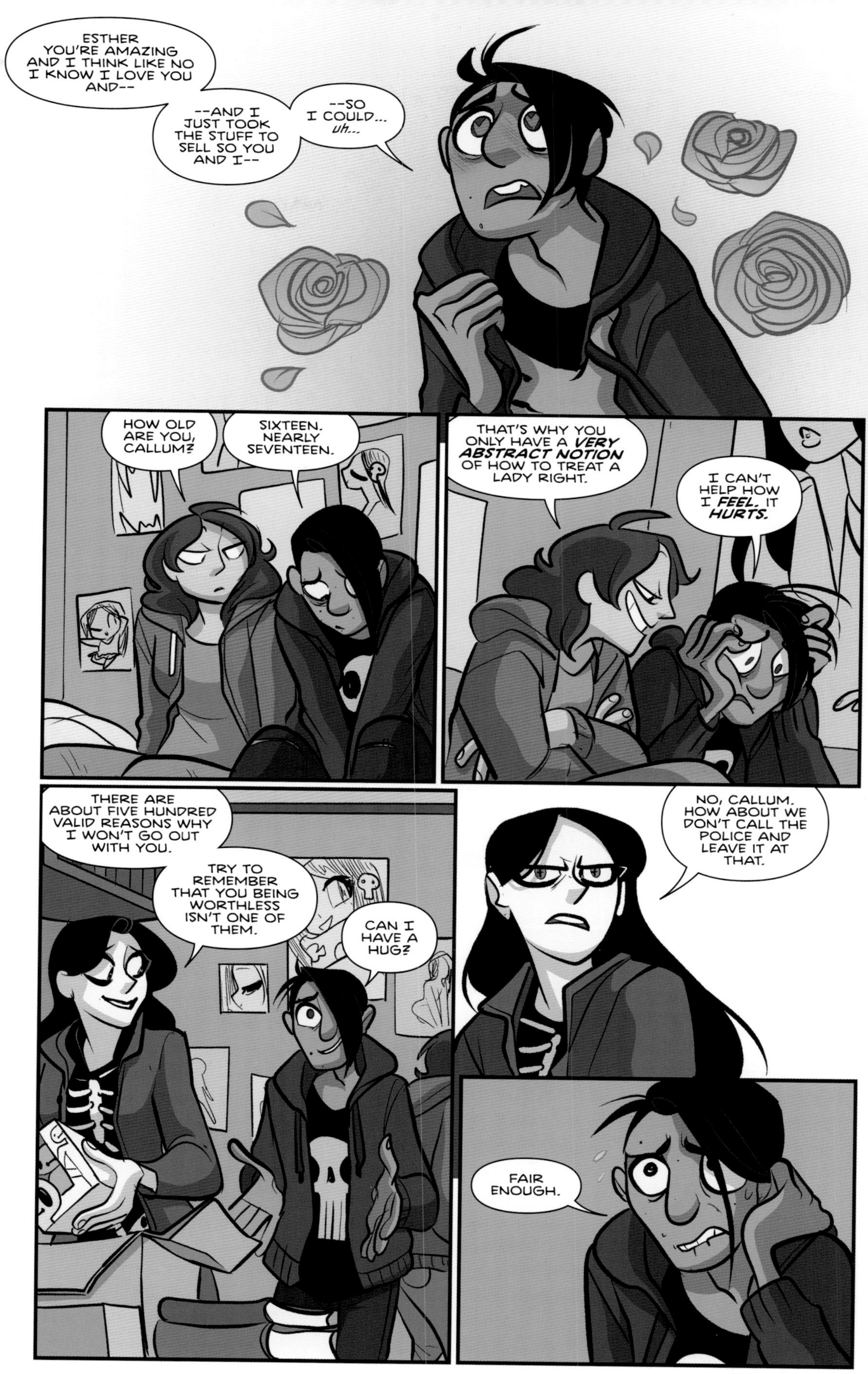
ESTHER YOU'RE AMAZING AND I THINK LIKE NO I KNOW I LOVE YOU AND--
--AND I JUST TOOK THE STUFF TO SELL SO YOU AND I--
--SO I COULD... *uh...*
HOW OLD ARE YOU, CALLUM?
SIXTEEN. NEARLY SEVENTEEN.
THAT'S WHY YOU ONLY HAVE A ***VERY ABSTRACT NOTION*** OF HOW TO TREAT A LADY RIGHT.
I CAN'T HELP HOW I ***FEEL.*** IT ***HURTS.***
THERE ARE ABOUT FIVE HUNDRED VALID REASONS WHY I WON'T GO OUT WITH YOU.
TRY TO REMEMBER THAT YOU BEING WORTHLESS ISN'T ONE OF THEM.
CAN I HAVE A HUG?
NO, CALLUM. HOW ABOUT WE DON'T CALL THE POLICE AND LEAVE IT AT THAT.
FAIR ENOUGH.

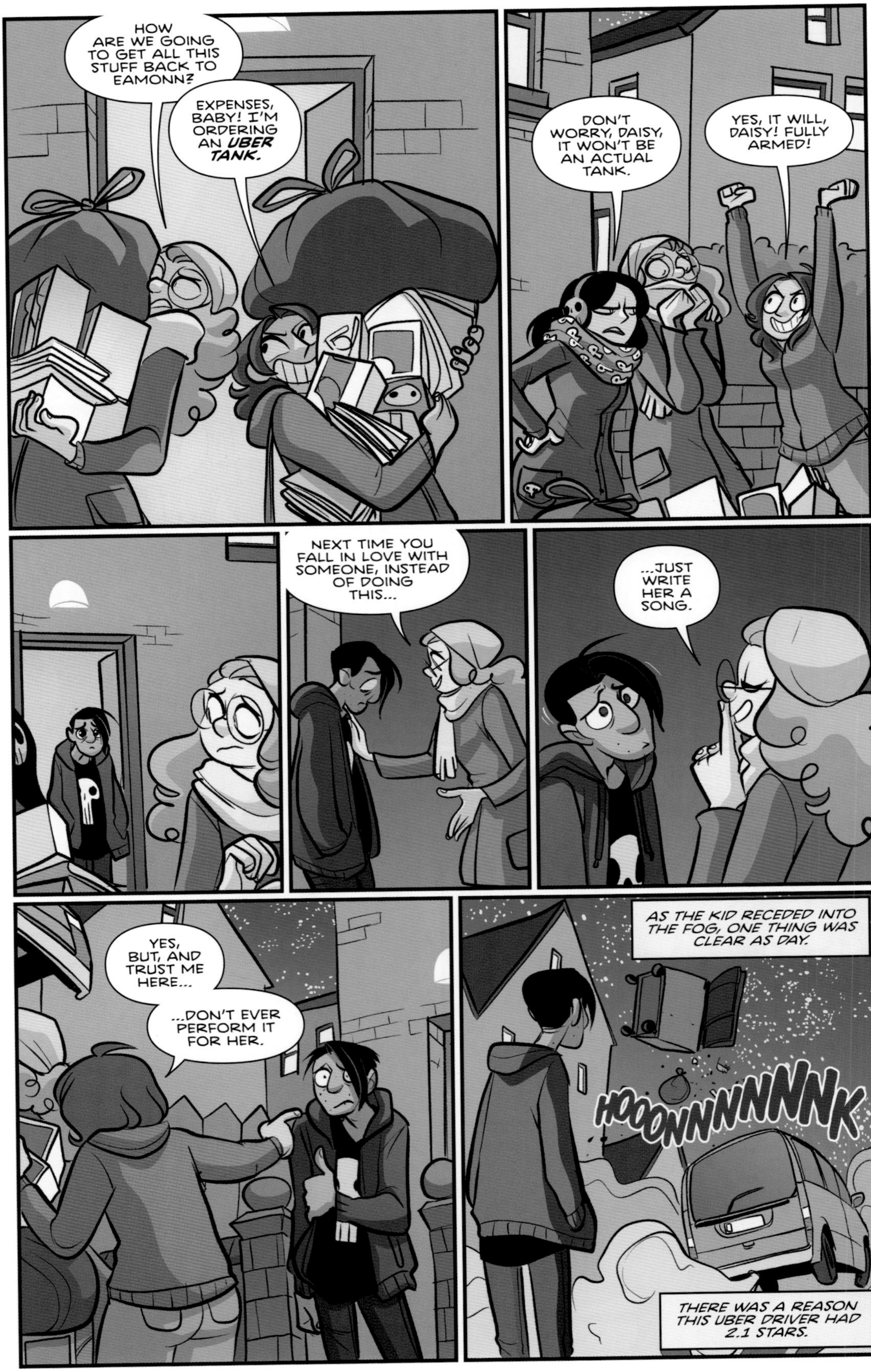
HOW ARE WE GOING TO GET ALL THIS STUFF BACK TO EAMONN?
EXPENSES, BABY! I'M ORDERING AN ***UBER TANK.***
DON'T WORRY, DAISY, IT WON'T BE AN ACTUAL TANK.
YES, IT WILL, DAISY! FULLY ARMED!
NEXT TIME YOU FALL IN LOVE WITH SOMEONE, INSTEAD OF DOING THIS...
...JUST WRITE HER A SONG.
YES, BUT, AND TRUST ME HERE...
...DON'T EVER PERFORM IT FOR HER.
AS THE KID RECEDED INTO THE FOG, ONE THING WAS CLEAR AS DAY.
HOOONNNNNNNK
THERE WAS A REASON THIS UBER DRIVER HAD 2.1 STARS.

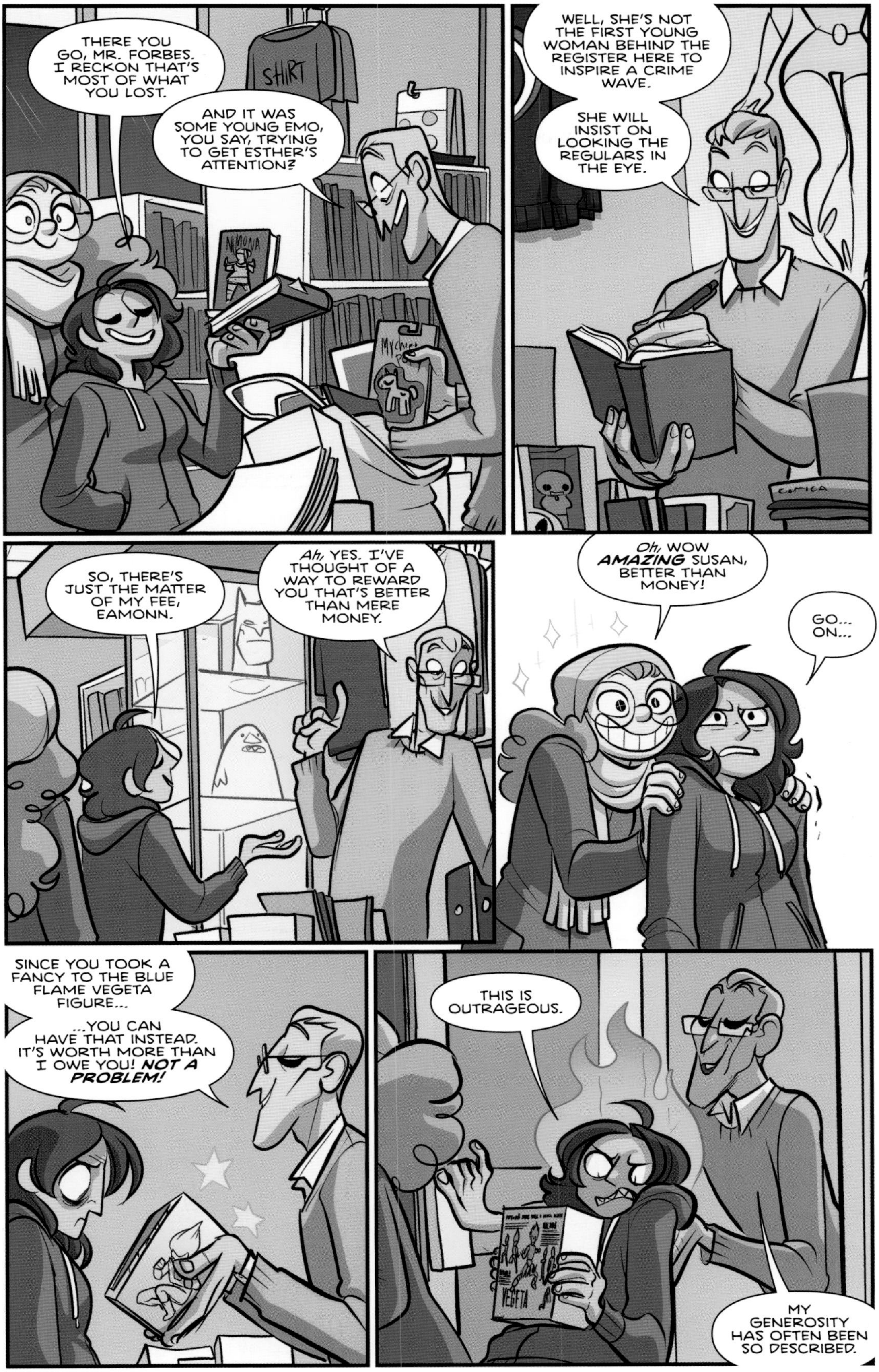
THERE YOU GO, MR. FORBES. I RECKON THAT'S MOST OF WHAT YOU LOST.
AND IT WAS SOME YOUNG EMO, YOU SAY, TRYING TO GET ESTHER'S ATTENTION?
SHIRT
NIMONA
WELL, SHE'S NOT THE FIRST YOUNG WOMAN BEHIND THE REGISTER HERE TO INSPIRE A CRIME WAVE.
SHE WILL INSIST ON LOOKING THE REGULARS IN THE EYE.
SO, THERE'S JUST THE MATTER OF MY FEE, EAMONN.
Ah, YES. I'VE THOUGHT OF A WAY TO REWARD YOU THAT'S BETTER THAN MERE MONEY.
Oh, WOW ***AMAZING*** SUSAN, BETTER THAN MONEY!
GO... ON...
SINCE YOU TOOK A FANCY TO THE BLUE FLAME VEGETA FIGURE...
...YOU CAN HAVE THAT INSTEAD. IT'S WORTH MORE THAN I OWE YOU! ***NOT A PROBLEM!***
THIS IS OUTRAGEOUS.
VEGETA
MY GENEROSITY HAS OFTEN BEEN SO DESCRIBED.

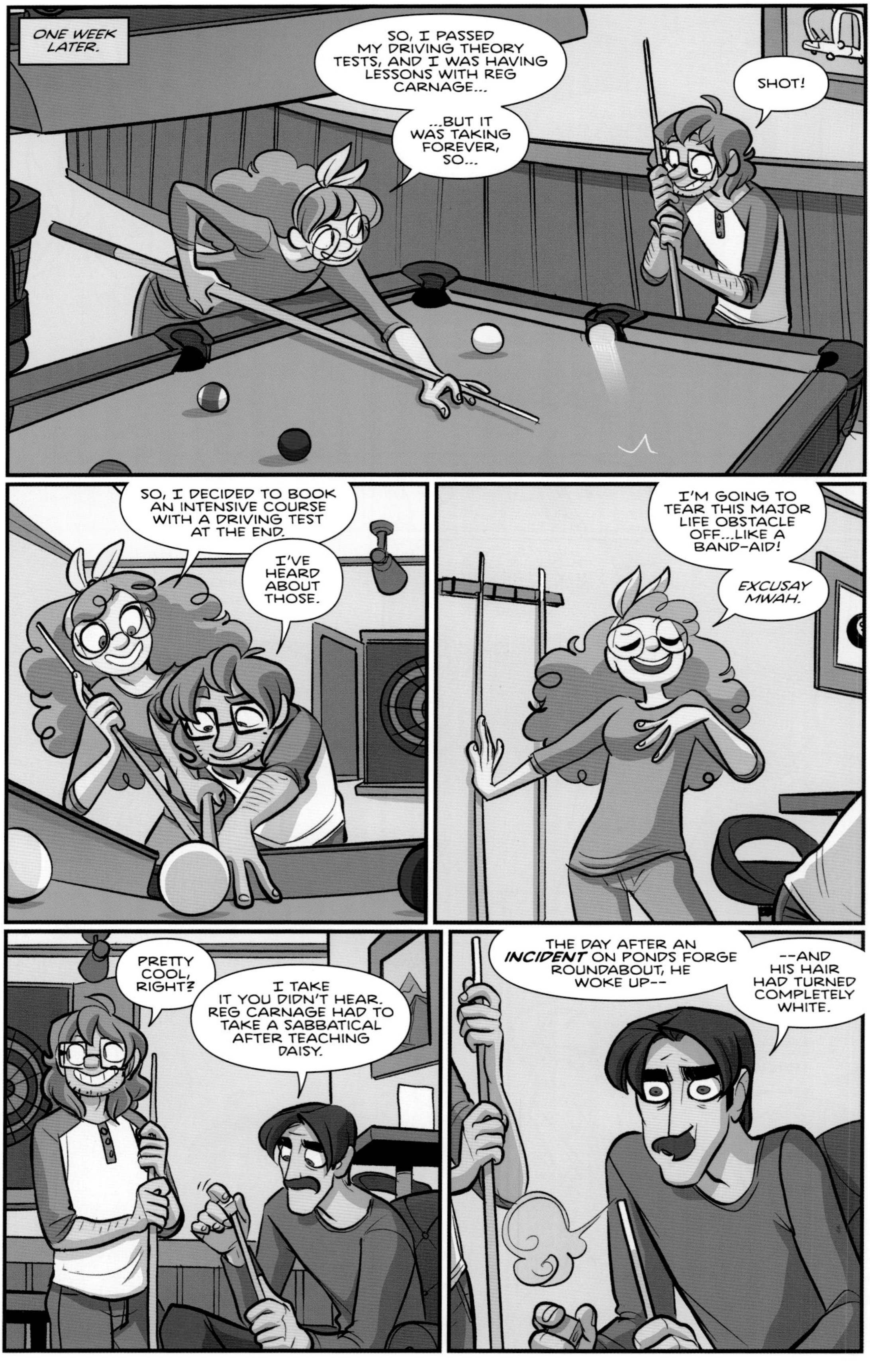
ONE WEEK LATER.
SO, I PASSED MY DRIVING THEORY TESTS, AND I WAS HAVING LESSONS WITH REG CARNAGE...
...BUT IT WAS TAKING FOREVER, SO...
SHOT!
SO, I DECIDED TO BOOK AN INTENSIVE COURSE WITH A DRIVING TEST AT THE END.
I'VE HEARD ABOUT THOSE.
I'M GOING TO TEAR THIS MAJOR LIFE OBSTACLE OFF...LIKE A BAND-AID!
EXCUSAY MWAH.
PRETTY COOL, RIGHT?
I TAKE IT YOU DIDN'T HEAR. REG CARNAGE HAD TO TAKE A SABBATICAL AFTER TEACHING DAISY.
THE DAY AFTER AN INCIDENT ON PONDS FORGE ROUNDABOUT, HE WOKE UP--
--AND HIS HAIR HAD TURNED COMPLETELY WHITE.

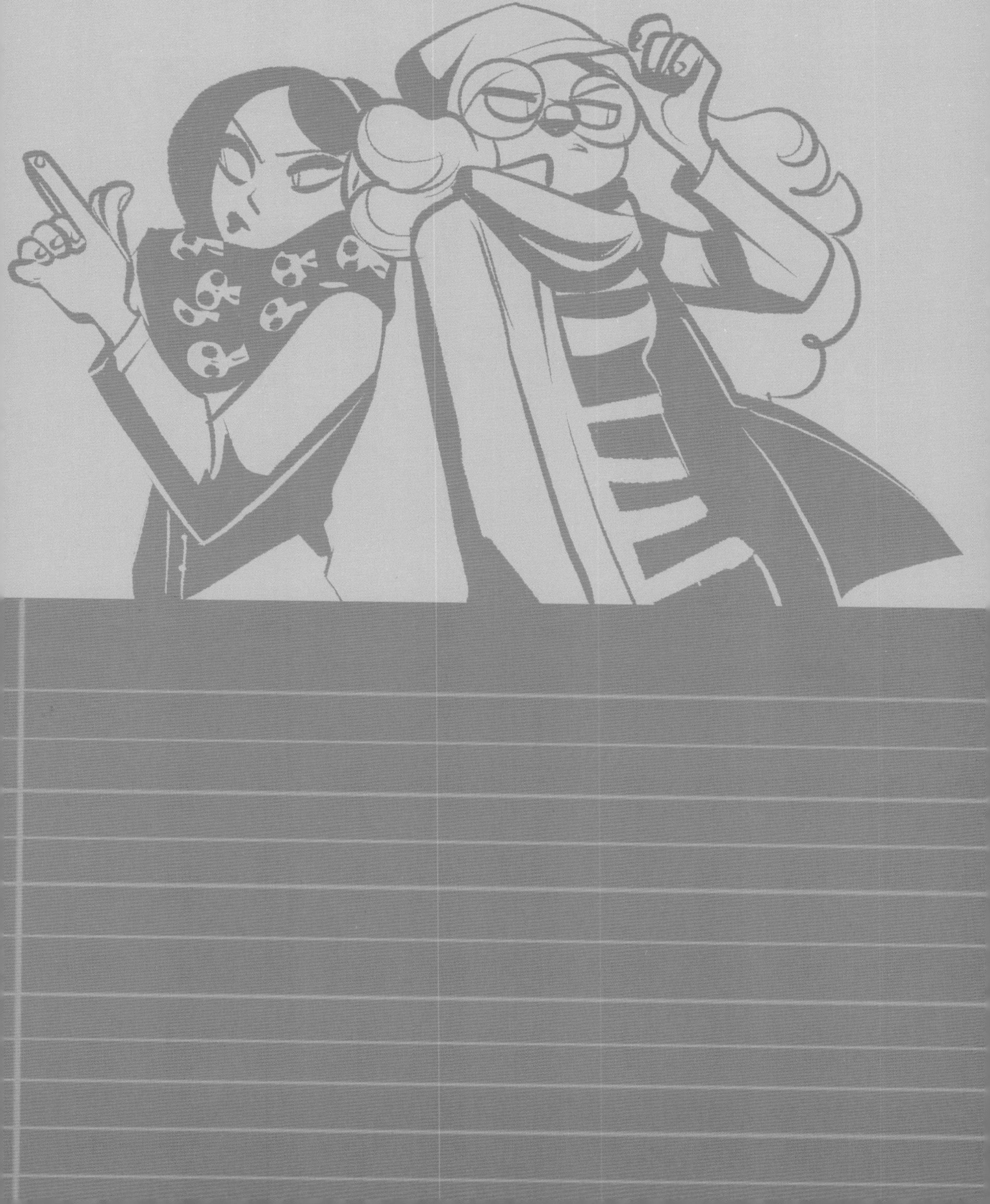

CHAPTER
FORTY-SEVEN

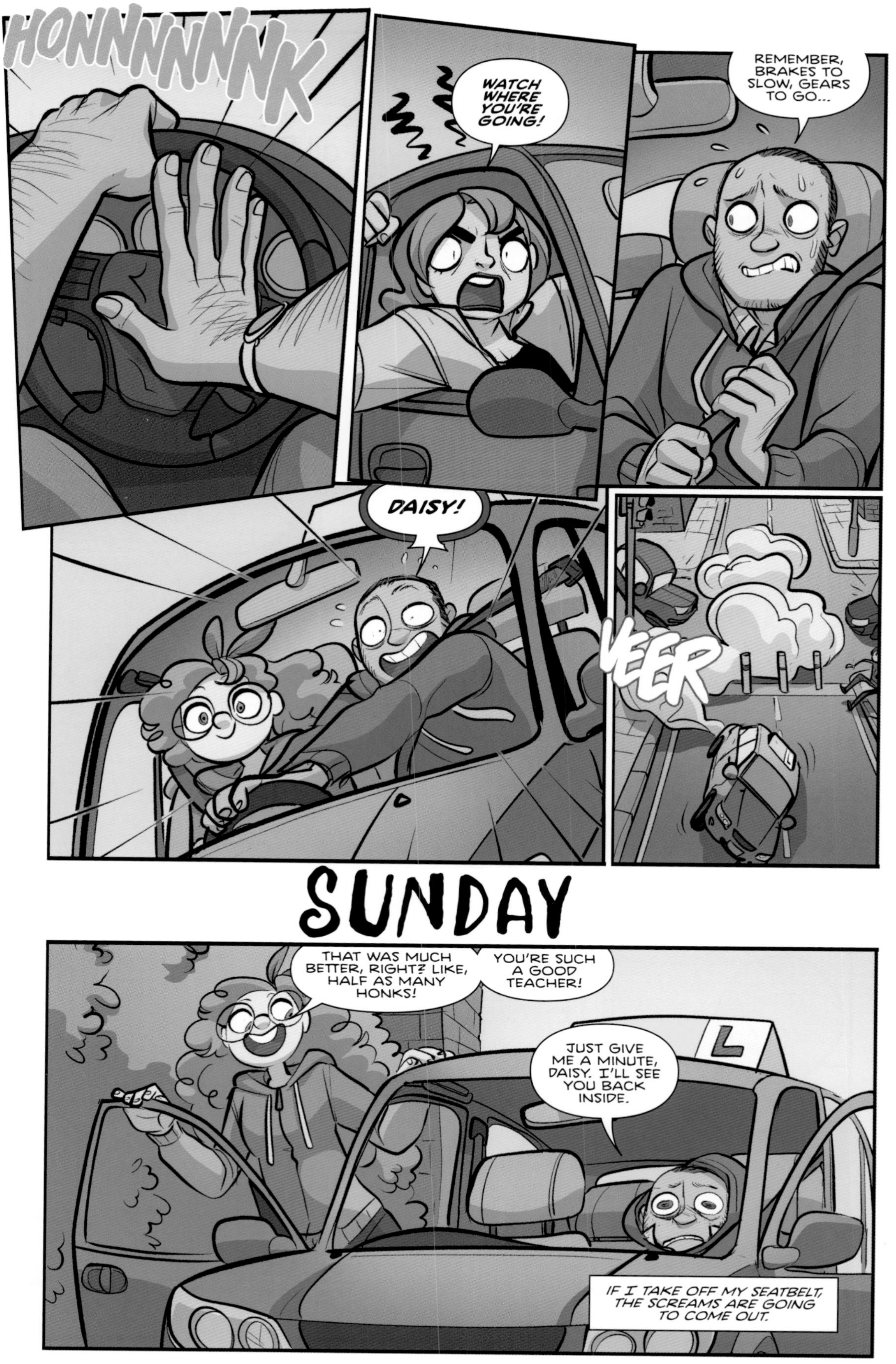
HONNNNNNK
WATCH WHERE YOU'RE GOING!
REMEMBER, BRAKES TO SLOW, GEARS TO GO...
DAISY!
VEER
SUNDAY
THAT WAS MUCH BETTER, RIGHT? LIKE, HALF AS MANY HONKS!
YOU'RE SUCH A GOOD TEACHER!
JUST GIVE ME A MINUTE, DAISY. I'LL SEE YOU BACK INSIDE.
L
IF I TAKE OFF MY SEATBELT, THE SCREAMS ARE GOING TO COME OUT.

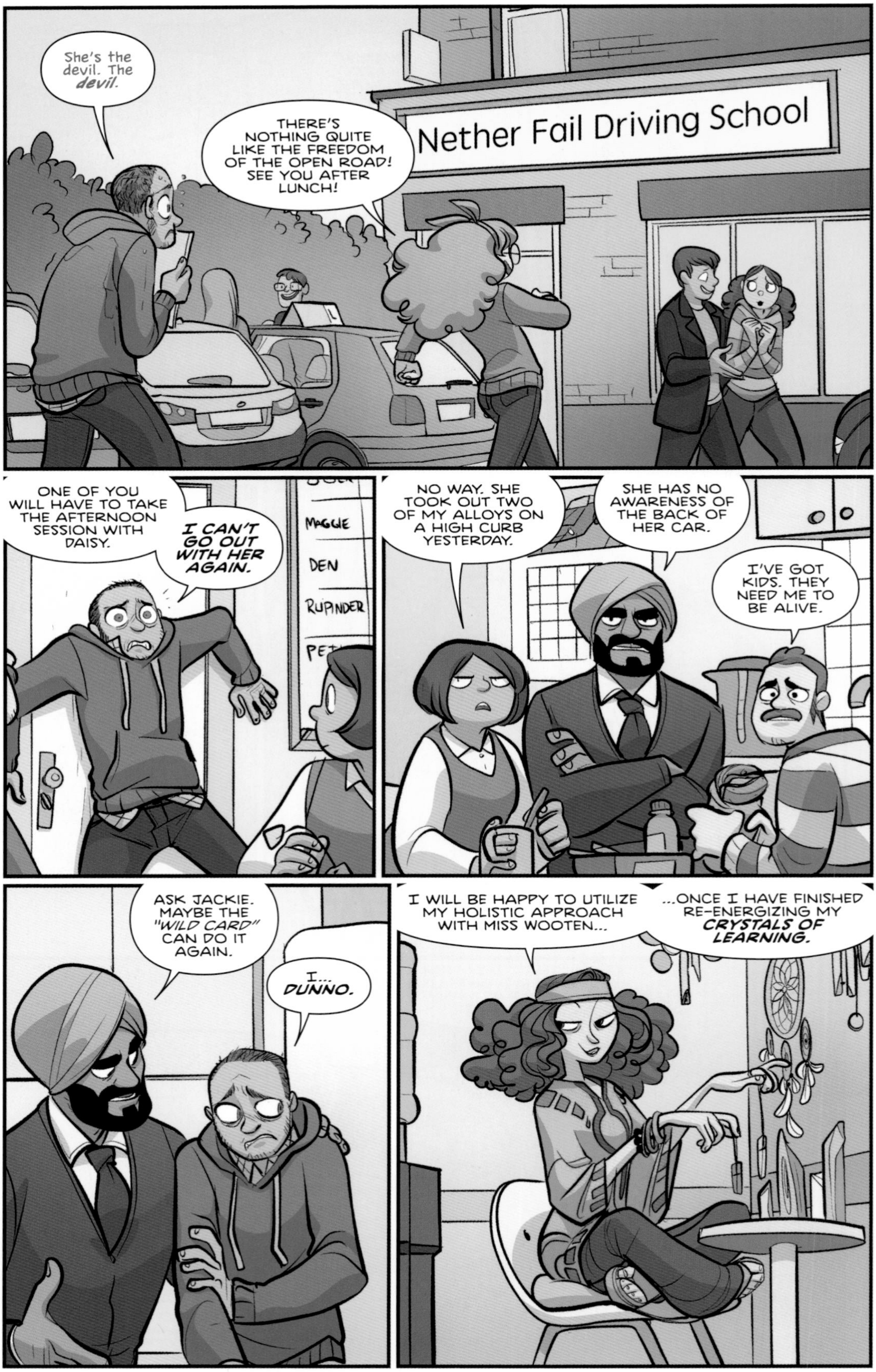
She's the devil. The *devil*.
Nether Fail Driving School
THERE'S NOTHING QUITE LIKE THE FREEDOM OF THE OPEN ROAD! SEE YOU AFTER LUNCH!
ONE OF YOU WILL HAVE TO TAKE THE AFTERNOON SESSION WITH DAISY.
I CAN'T GO OUT WITH HER AGAIN.
MAGGIE
DEN
RUPINDER
NO WAY. SHE TOOK OUT TWO OF MY ALLOYS ON A HIGH CURB YESTERDAY.
SHE HAS NO AWARENESS OF THE BACK OF HER CAR.
I'VE GOT KIDS. THEY NEED ME TO BE ALIVE.
ASK JACKIE. MAYBE THE "WILD CARD" CAN DO IT AGAIN.
I... DUNNO.
I WILL BE HAPPY TO UTILIZE MY HOLISTIC APPROACH WITH MISS WOOTEN...
...ONCE I HAVE FINISHED RE-ENERGIZING MY CRYSTALS OF LEARNING.

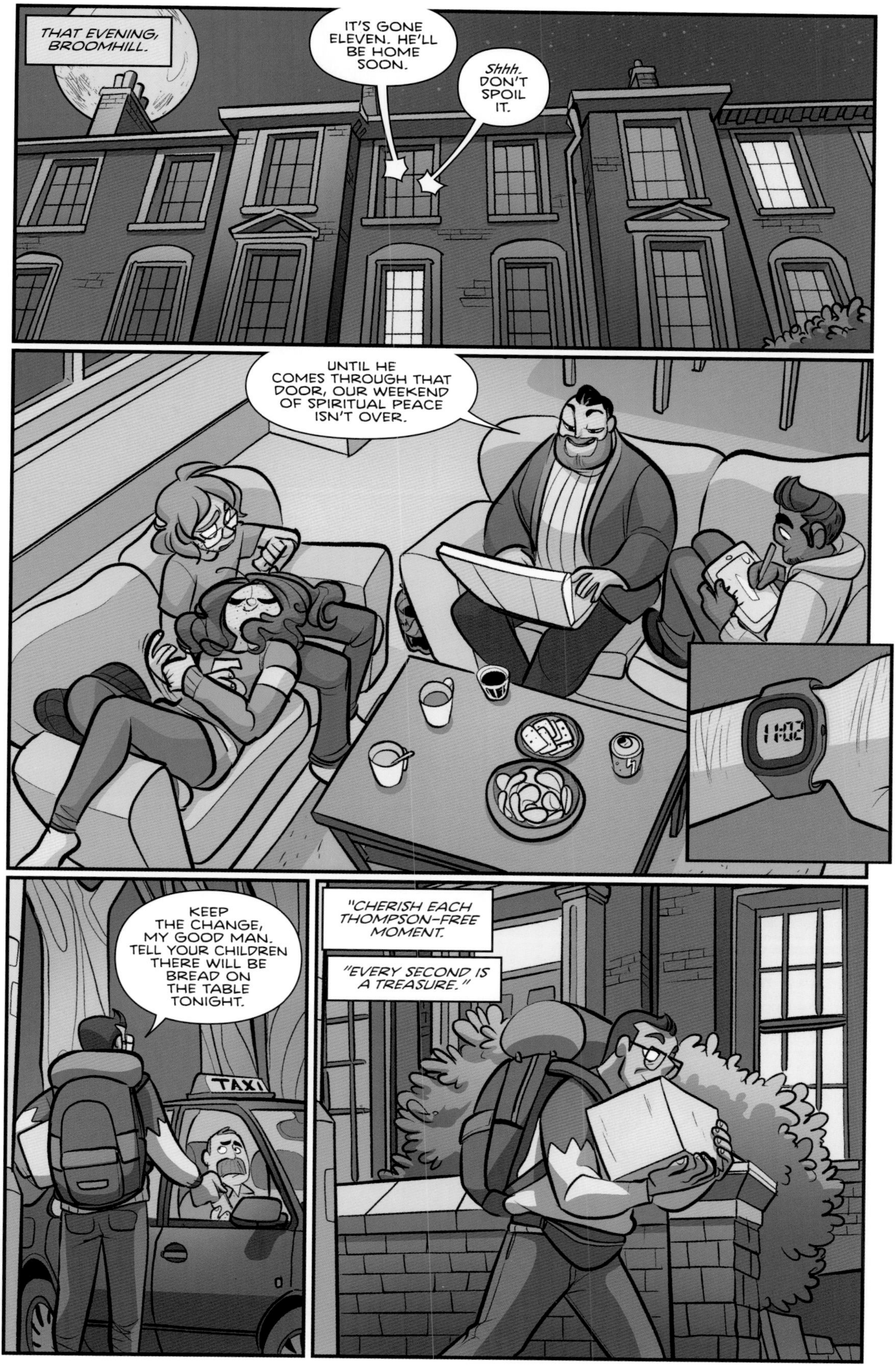
THAT EVENING, BROOMHILL.
IT'S GONE ELEVEN. HE'LL BE HOME SOON.
Shhh. DON'T SPOIL IT.
UNTIL HE COMES THROUGH THAT DOOR, OUR WEEKEND OF SPIRITUAL PEACE ISN'T OVER.
11:02
KEEP THE CHANGE, MY GOOD MAN. TELL YOUR CHILDREN THERE WILL BE BREAD ON THE TABLE TONIGHT.
TAXI
"CHERISH EACH THOMPSON-FREE MOMENT.
"EVERY SECOND IS A TREASURE."

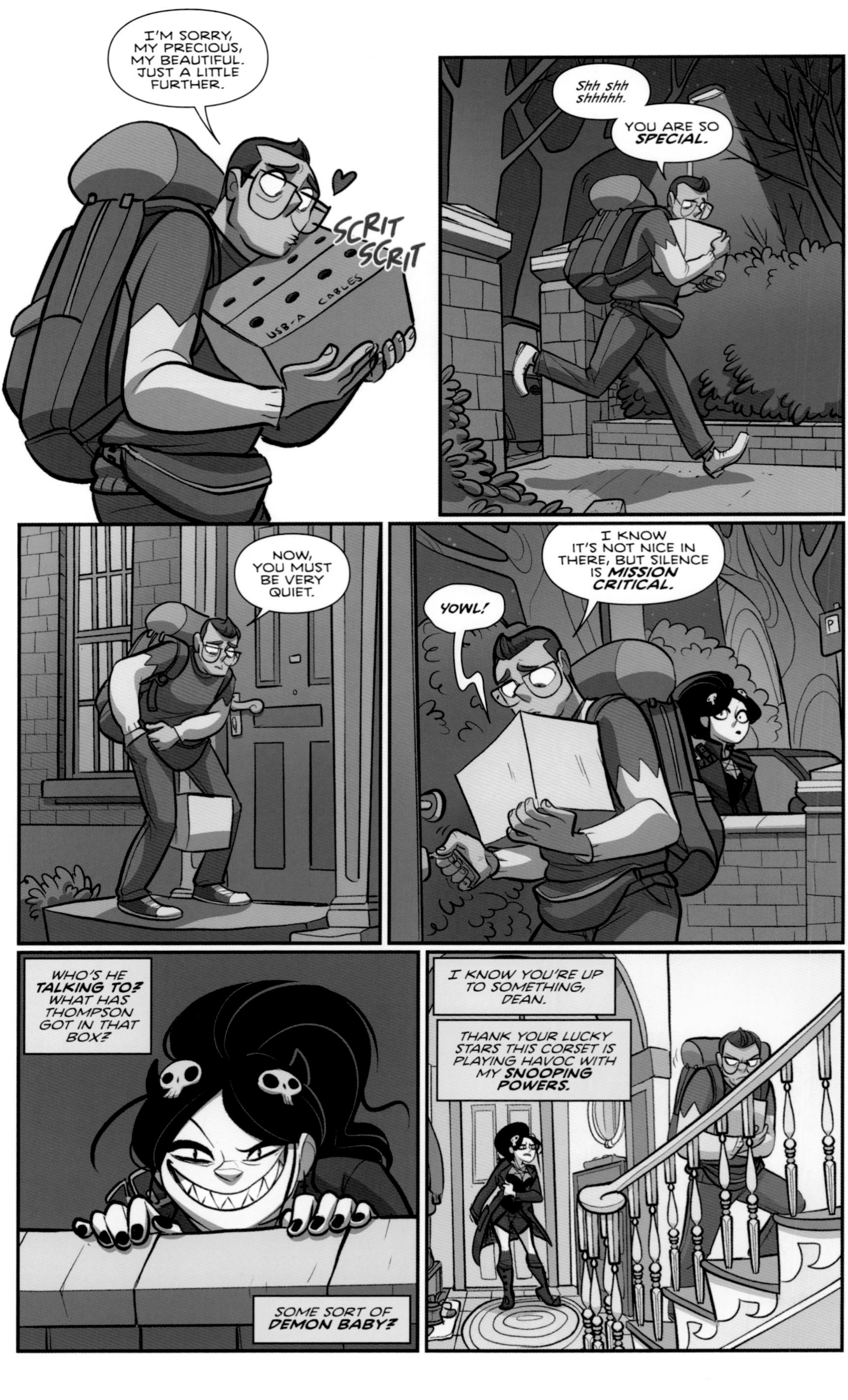

I'M SORRY, MY PRECIOUS, MY BEAUTIFUL. JUST A LITTLE FURTHER.
SCRIT SCRIT
USB-A CABLES
Shh shh shhhhh.
YOU ARE SO SPECIAL.
NOW, YOU MUST BE VERY QUIET.
I KNOW IT'S NOT NICE IN THERE, BUT SILENCE IS MISSION CRITICAL.
YOWL!
P
WHO'S HE TALKING TO? WHAT HAS THOMPSON GOT IN THAT BOX?
SOME SORT OF DEMON BABY?
I KNOW YOU'RE UP TO SOMETHING, DEAN.
THANK YOUR LUCKY STARS THIS CORSET IS PLAYING HAVOC WITH MY SNOOPING POWERS.

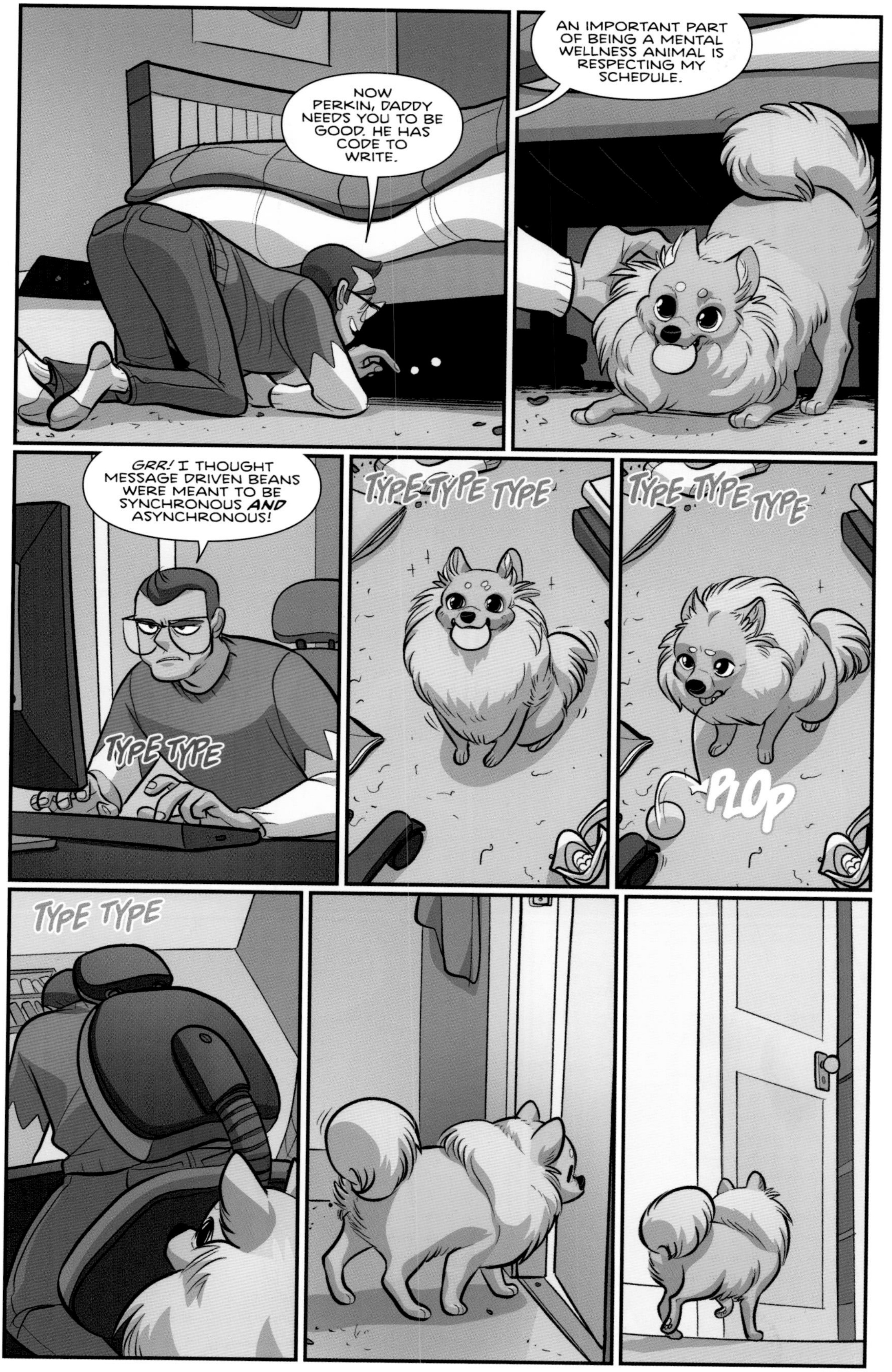
NOW PERKIN, DADDY NEEDS YOU TO BE GOOD. HE HAS CODE TO WRITE.
AN IMPORTANT PART OF BEING A MENTAL WELLNESS ANIMAL IS RESPECTING MY SCHEDULE.
GRR! I THOUGHT MESSAGE DRIVEN BEANS WERE MEANT TO BE SYNCHRONOUS AND ASYNCHRONOUS!
TYPE TYPE
TYPE TYPE TYPE
TYPE TYPE TYPE
PLOP
TYPE TYPE

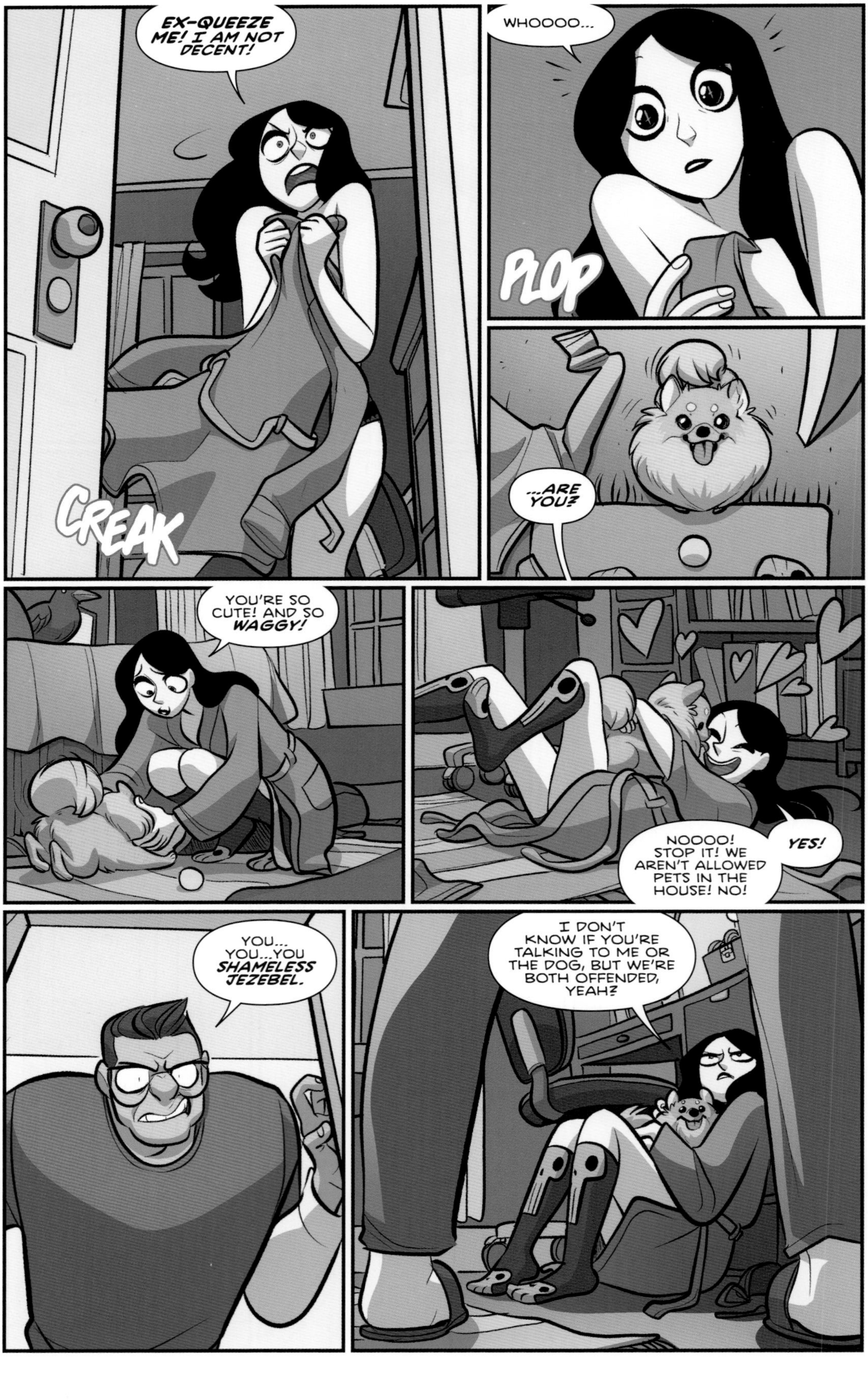
EX-QUEEZE ME! I AM NOT DECENT!
CREAK
WHOOOO...
PLOP
...ARE YOU?
YOU'RE SO CUTE! AND SO WAGGY!
NOOOO! STOP IT! WE AREN'T ALLOWED PETS IN THE HOUSE! NO!
YES!
YOU... YOU...YOU SHAMELESS JEZEBEL.
I DON'T KNOW IF YOU'RE TALKING TO ME OR THE DOG, BUT WE'RE BOTH OFFENDED, YEAH?

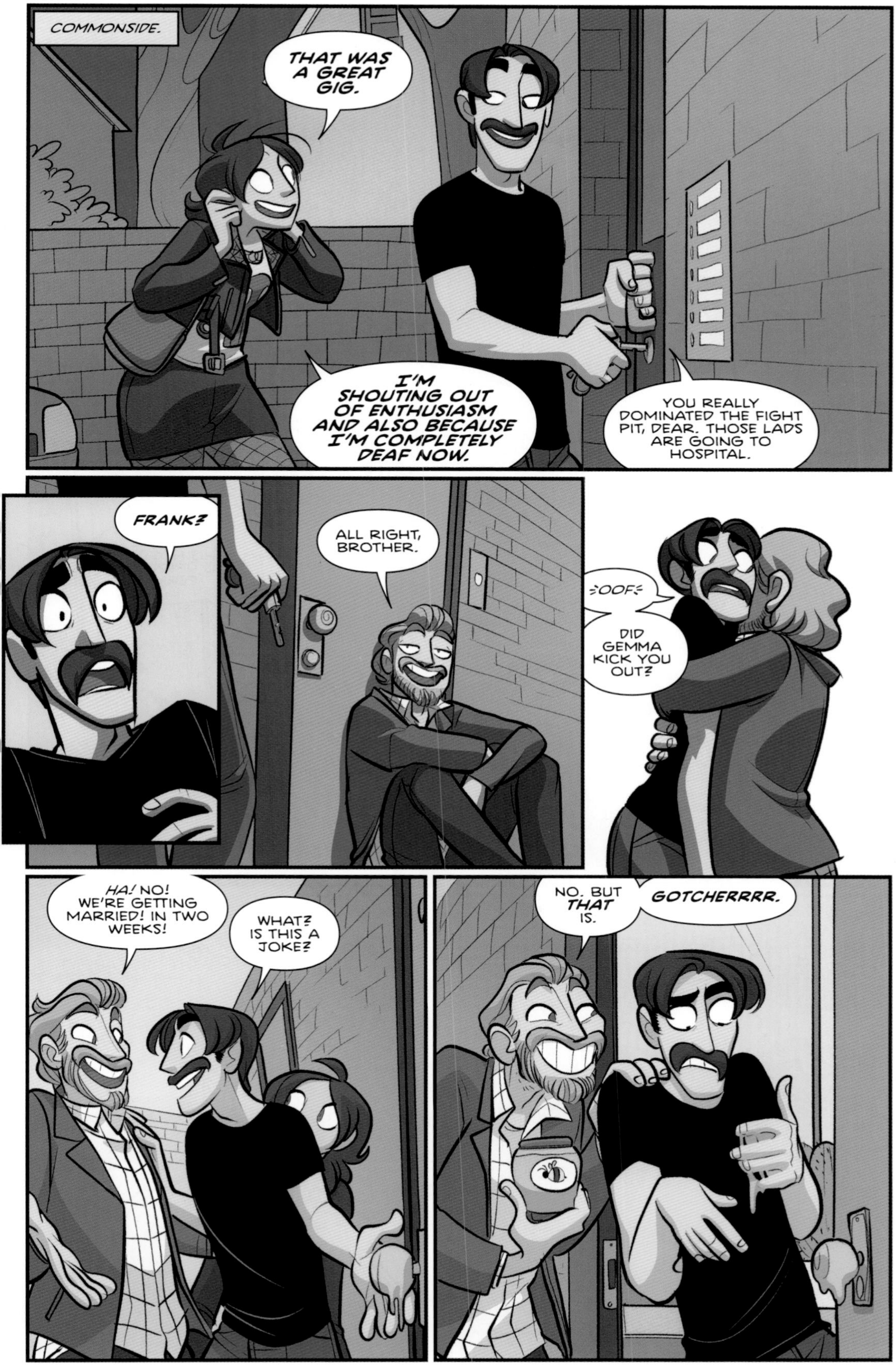
COMMONSIDE.
THAT WAS A GREAT GIG.
I'M SHOUTING OUT OF ENTHUSIASM AND ALSO BECAUSE I'M COMPLETELY DEAF NOW.
YOU REALLY DOMINATED THE FIGHT PIT, DEAR. THOSE LADS ARE GOING TO HOSPITAL.
FRANK?
ALL RIGHT, BROTHER.
OOF
DID GEMMA KICK YOU OUT?
HA! NO! WE'RE GETTING MARRIED! IN TWO WEEKS!
WHAT? IS THIS A JOKE?
NO. BUT THAT IS.
GOTCHERRRR.

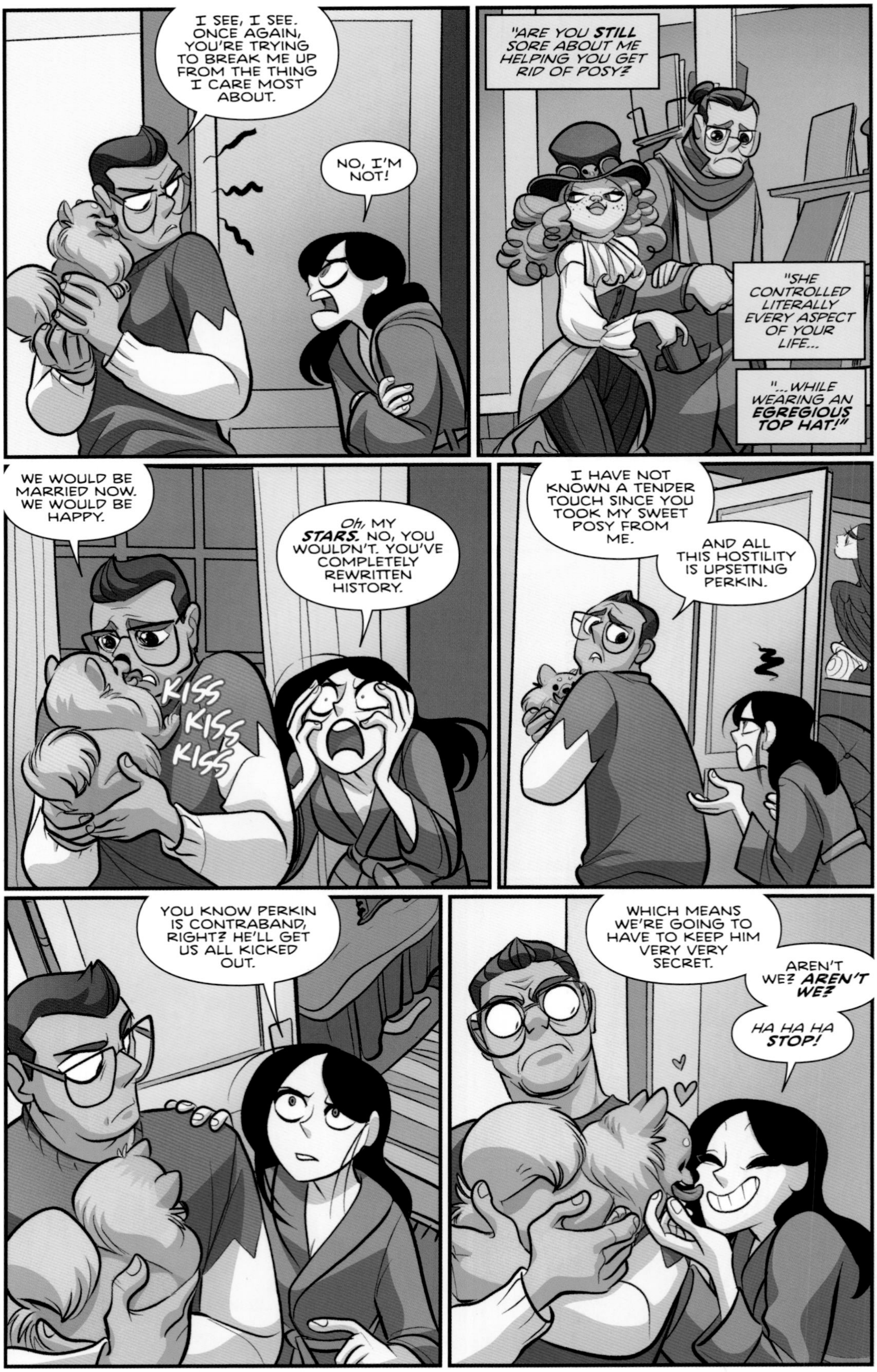
I SEE, I SEE. ONCE AGAIN, YOU'RE TRYING TO BREAK ME UP FROM THE THING I CARE MOST ABOUT.
NO, I'M NOT!
"ARE YOU **STILL** SORE ABOUT ME HELPING YOU GET RID OF POSY?
"SHE CONTROLLED LITERALLY EVERY ASPECT OF YOUR LIFE...
"...WHILE WEARING AN **EGREGIOUS TOP HAT!"**
WE WOULD BE MARRIED NOW. WE WOULD BE HAPPY.
Oh, MY **STARS.** NO, YOU WOULDN'T. YOU'VE COMPLETELY REWRITTEN HISTORY.
KISS KISS KISS
I HAVE NOT KNOWN A TENDER TOUCH SINCE YOU TOOK MY SWEET POSY FROM ME.
AND ALL THIS HOSTILITY IS UPSETTING PERKIN.
YOU KNOW PERKIN IS CONTRABAND, RIGHT? HE'LL GET US ALL KICKED OUT.
WHICH MEANS WE'RE GOING TO HAVE TO KEEP HIM VERY VERY SECRET.
AREN'T WE? ***AREN'T WE?***
HA HA HA ***STOP!***

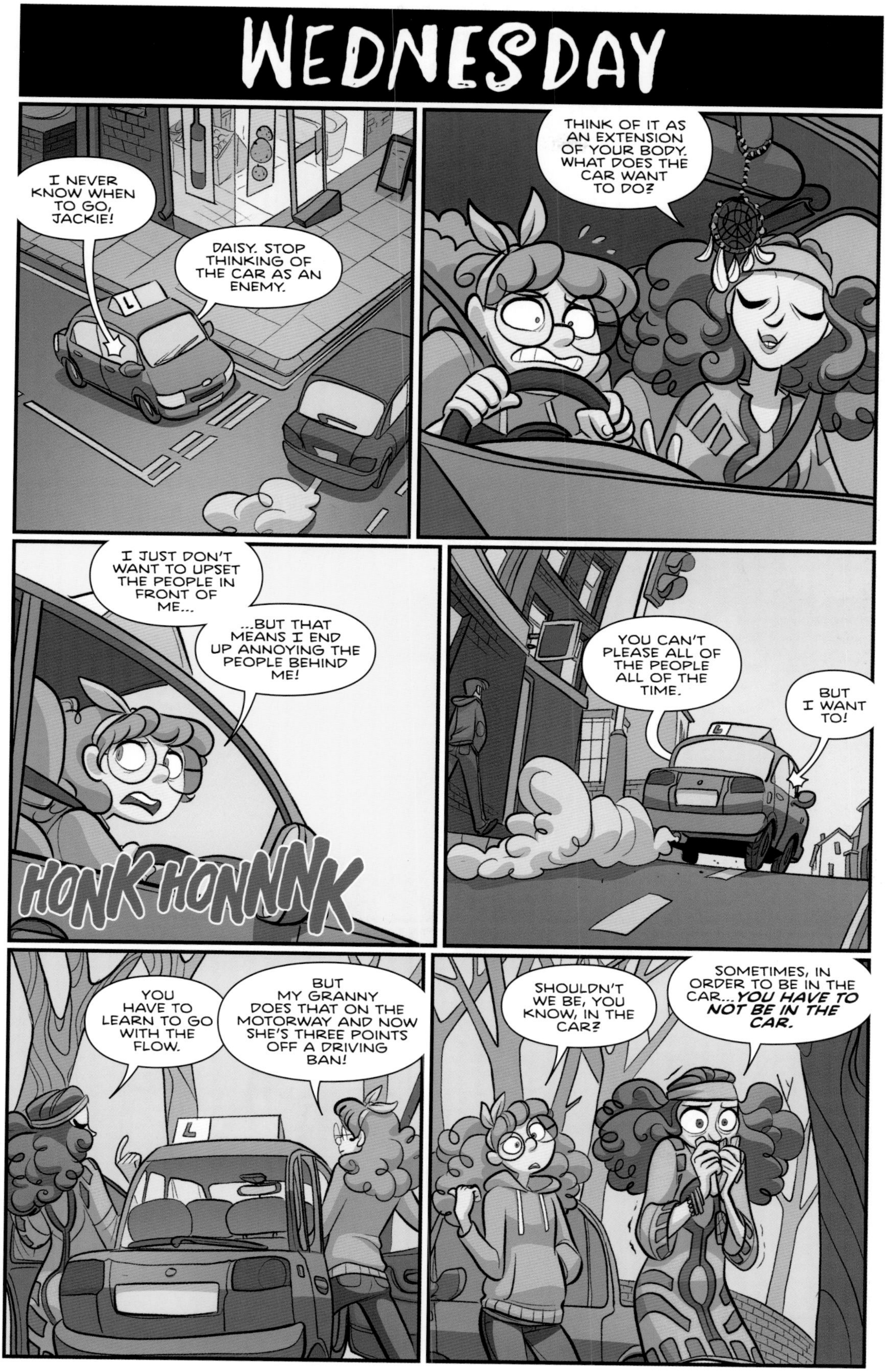
WEDNESDAY
I NEVER KNOW WHEN TO GO, JACKIE!
DAISY. STOP THINKING OF THE CAR AS AN ENEMY.
THINK OF IT AS AN EXTENSION OF YOUR BODY. WHAT DOES THE CAR WANT TO DO?
I JUST DON'T WANT TO UPSET THE PEOPLE IN FRONT OF ME...
...BUT THAT MEANS I END UP ANNOYING THE PEOPLE BEHIND ME!
HONK HONNNK
YOU CAN'T PLEASE ALL OF THE PEOPLE ALL OF THE TIME.
BUT I WANT TO!
YOU HAVE TO LEARN TO GO WITH THE FLOW.
BUT MY GRANNY DOES THAT ON THE MOTORWAY AND NOW SHE'S THREE POINTS OFF A DRIVING BAN!
SHOULDN'T WE BE, YOU KNOW, IN THE CAR?
SOMETIMES, IN ORDER TO BE IN THE CAR... ***YOU HAVE TO NOT BE IN THE CAR.***

THURSDAY

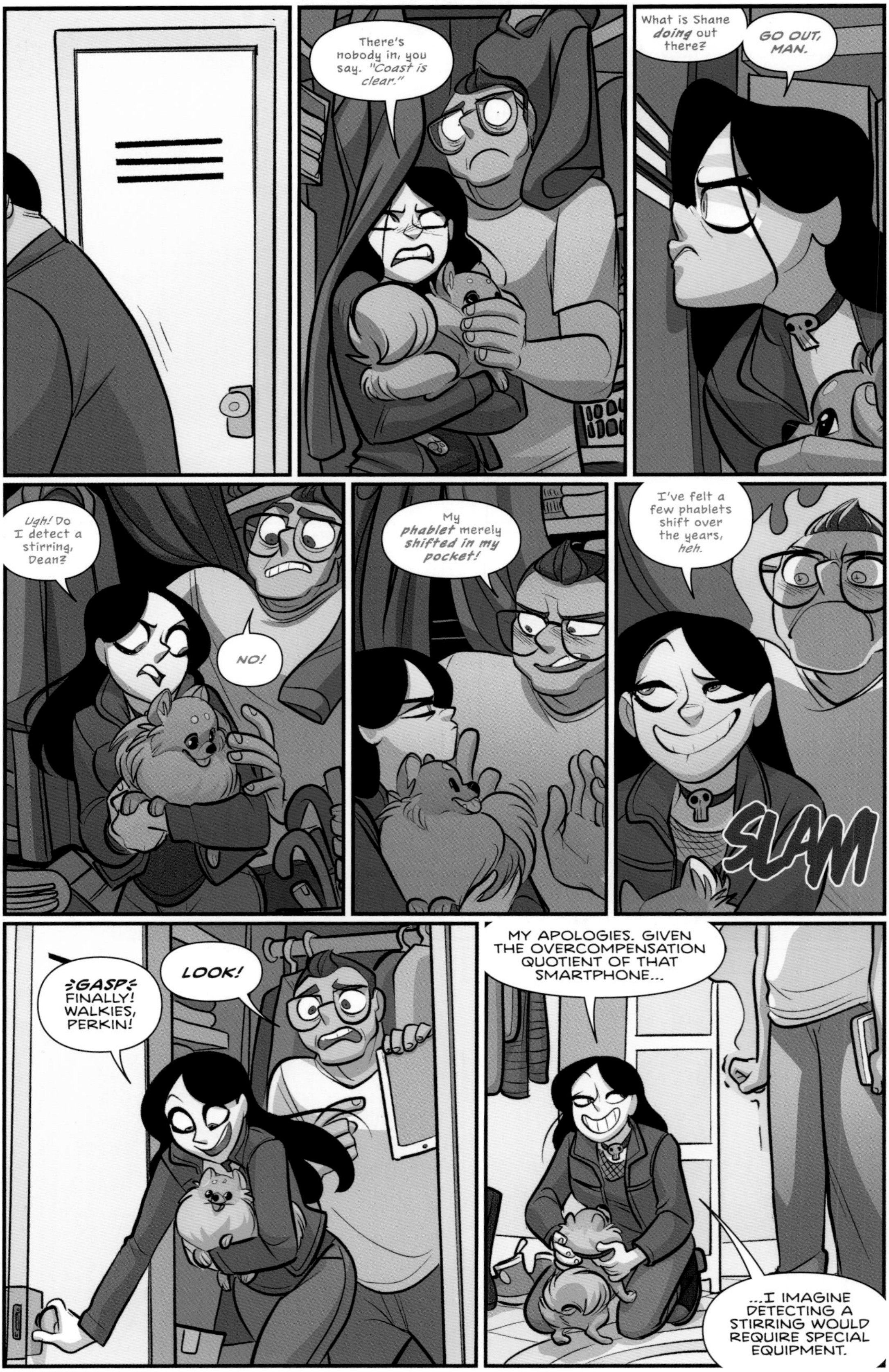
There's nobody in, you say. "Coast is clear."
What is Shane doing out there?
GO OUT, MAN.
Ugh! Do I detect a stirring, Dean?
NO!
My phablet merely shifted in my pocket!
I've felt a few phablets shift over the years, heh.
SLAM
GASP FINALLY! WALKIES, PERKIN!
LOOK!
MY APOLOGIES. GIVEN THE OVERCOMPENSATION QUOTIENT OF THAT SMARTPHONE...
...I IMAGINE DETECTING A STIRRING WOULD REQUIRE SPECIAL EQUIPMENT.

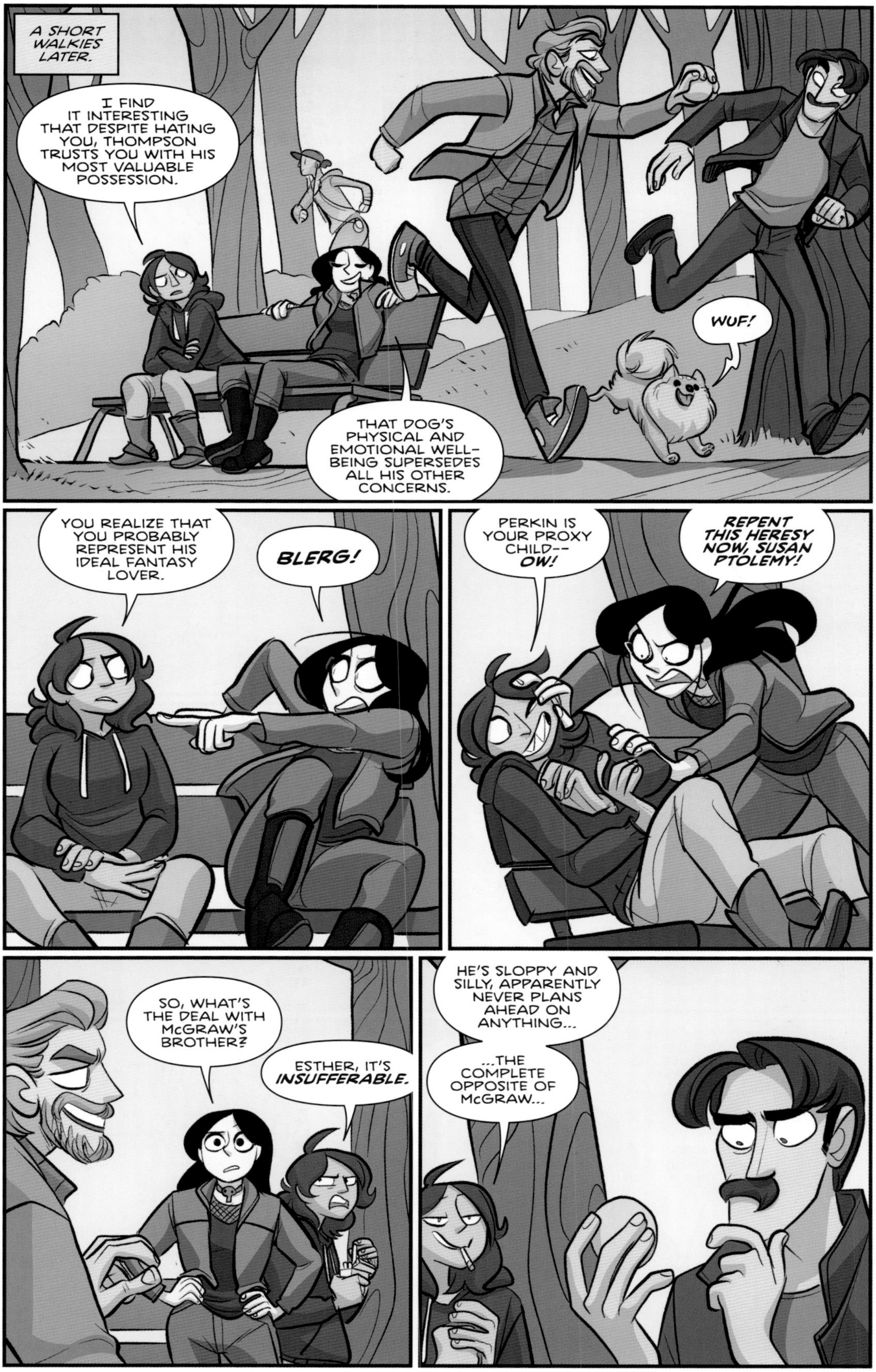
A SHORT WALKIES LATER.
I FIND IT INTERESTING THAT DESPITE HATING YOU, THOMPSON TRUSTS YOU WITH HIS MOST VALUABLE POSSESSION.
THAT DOG'S PHYSICAL AND EMOTIONAL WELL-BEING SUPERSEDES ALL HIS OTHER CONCERNS.
WUF!
YOU REALIZE THAT YOU PROBABLY REPRESENT HIS IDEAL FANTASY LOVER.
BLERG!
PERKIN IS YOUR PROXY CHILD-- OW!
REPENT THIS HERESY NOW, SUSAN PTOLEMY!
SO, WHAT'S THE DEAL WITH McGRAW'S BROTHER?
ESTHER, IT'S INSUFFERABLE.
HE'S SLOPPY AND SILLY, APPARENTLY NEVER PLANS AHEAD ON ANYTHING...
...THE COMPLETE OPPOSITE OF McGRAW...

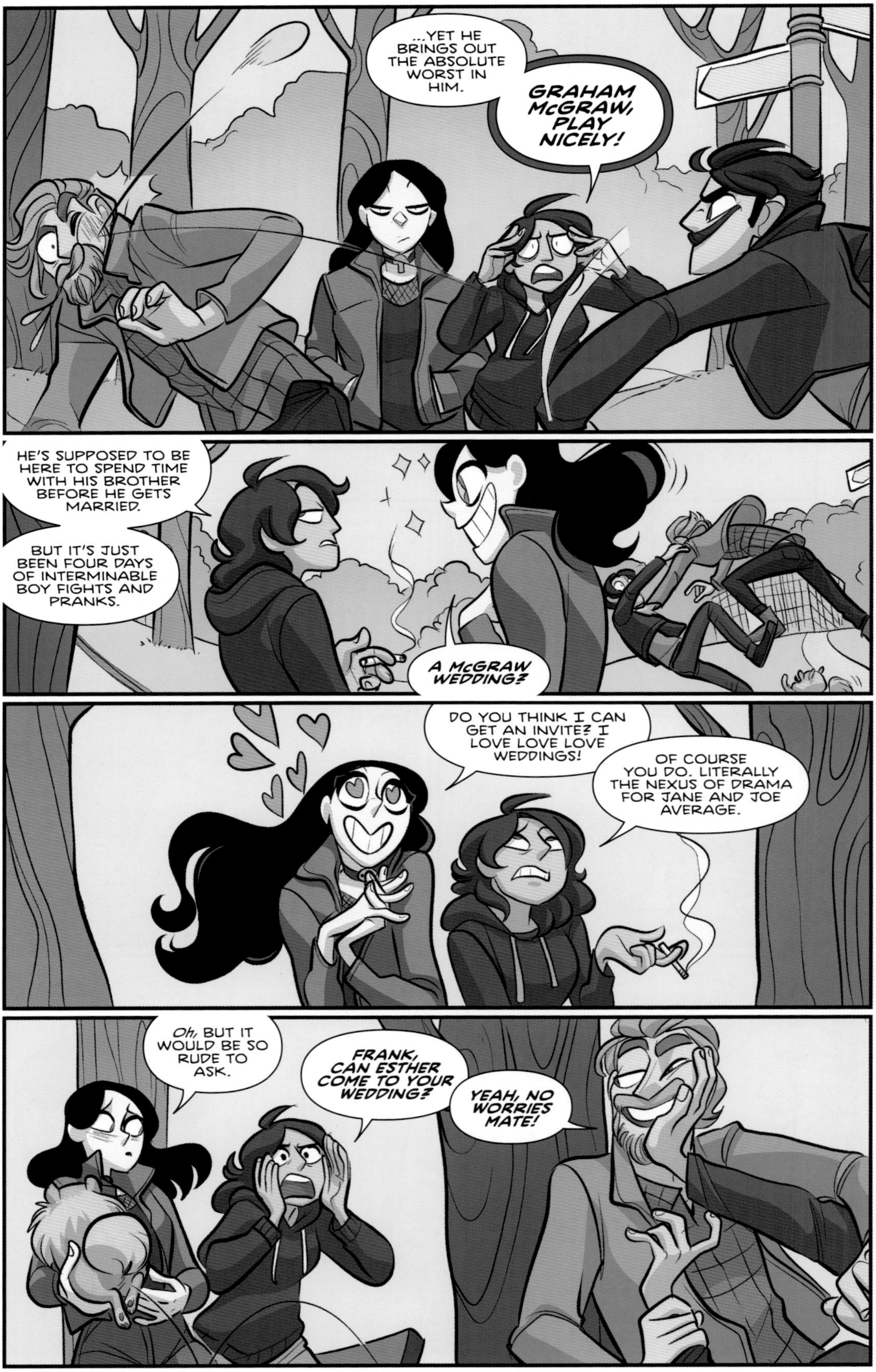
...YET HE BRINGS OUT THE ABSOLUTE WORST IN HIM.
GRAHAM McGRAW, PLAY NICELY!
HE'S SUPPOSED TO BE HERE TO SPEND TIME WITH HIS BROTHER BEFORE HE GETS MARRIED.
BUT IT'S JUST BEEN FOUR DAYS OF INTERMINABLE BOY FIGHTS AND PRANKS.
A McGRAW WEDDING?
DO YOU THINK I CAN GET AN INVITE? I LOVE LOVE LOVE WEDDINGS!
OF COURSE YOU DO. LITERALLY THE NEXUS OF DRAMA FOR JANE AND JOE AVERAGE.
Oh, BUT IT WOULD BE SO RUDE TO ASK.
FRANK, CAN ESTHER COME TO YOUR WEDDING?
YEAH, NO WORRIES MATE!

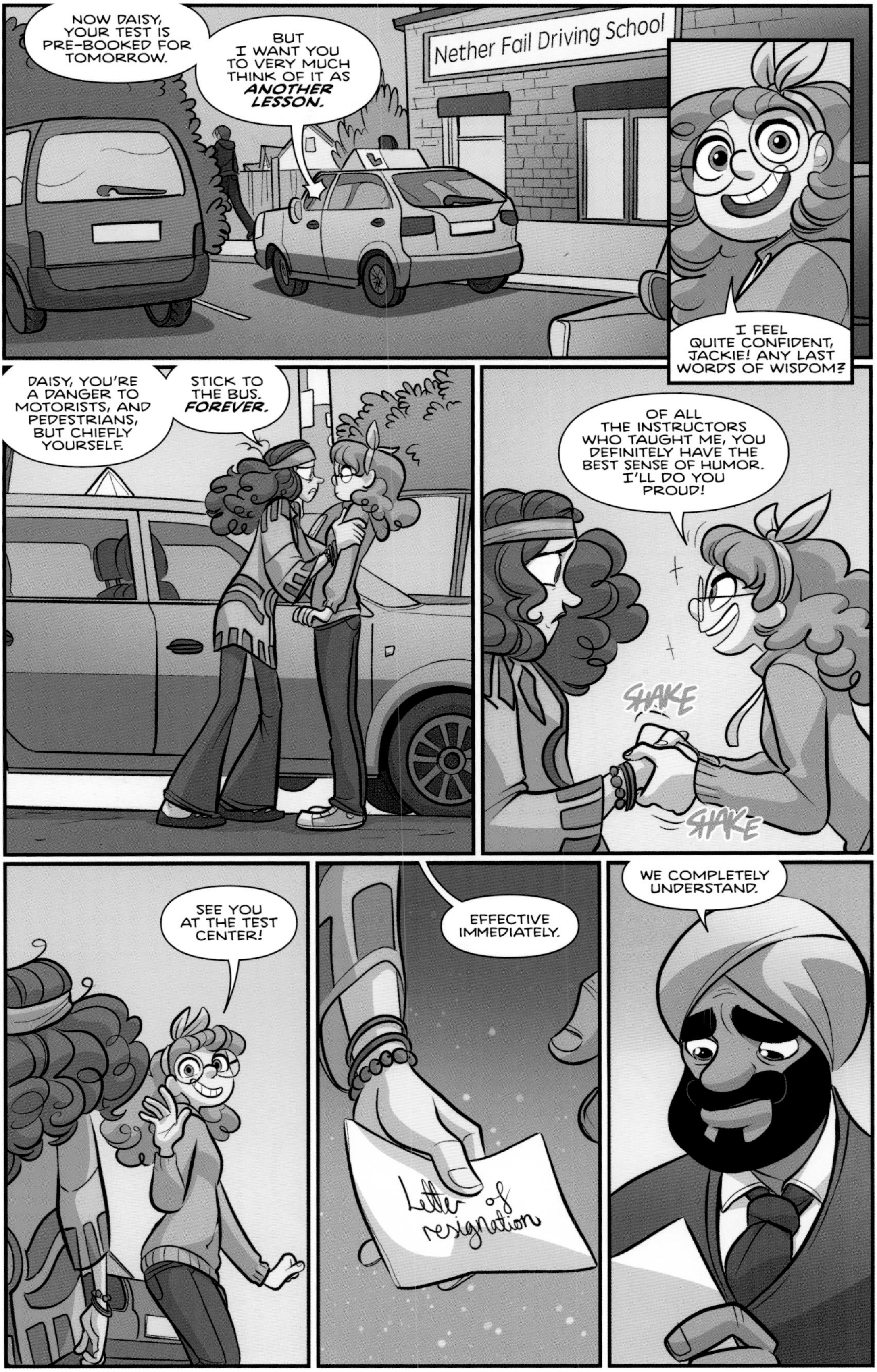
NOW DAISY, YOUR TEST IS PRE-BOOKED FOR TOMORROW.
BUT I WANT YOU TO VERY MUCH THINK OF IT AS ***ANOTHER LESSON.***
Nether Fail Driving School
I FEEL QUITE CONFIDENT, JACKIE! ANY LAST WORDS OF WISDOM?
DAISY, YOU'RE A DANGER TO MOTORISTS, AND PEDESTRIANS, BUT CHIEFLY YOURSELF.
STICK TO THE BUS. ***FOREVER.***
OF ALL THE INSTRUCTORS WHO TAUGHT ME, YOU DEFINITELY HAVE THE BEST SENSE OF HUMOR. I'LL DO YOU PROUD!
SHAKE
SHAKE
SEE YOU AT THE TEST CENTER!
EFFECTIVE IMMEDIATELY.
Letter of resignation
WE COMPLETELY UNDERSTAND.

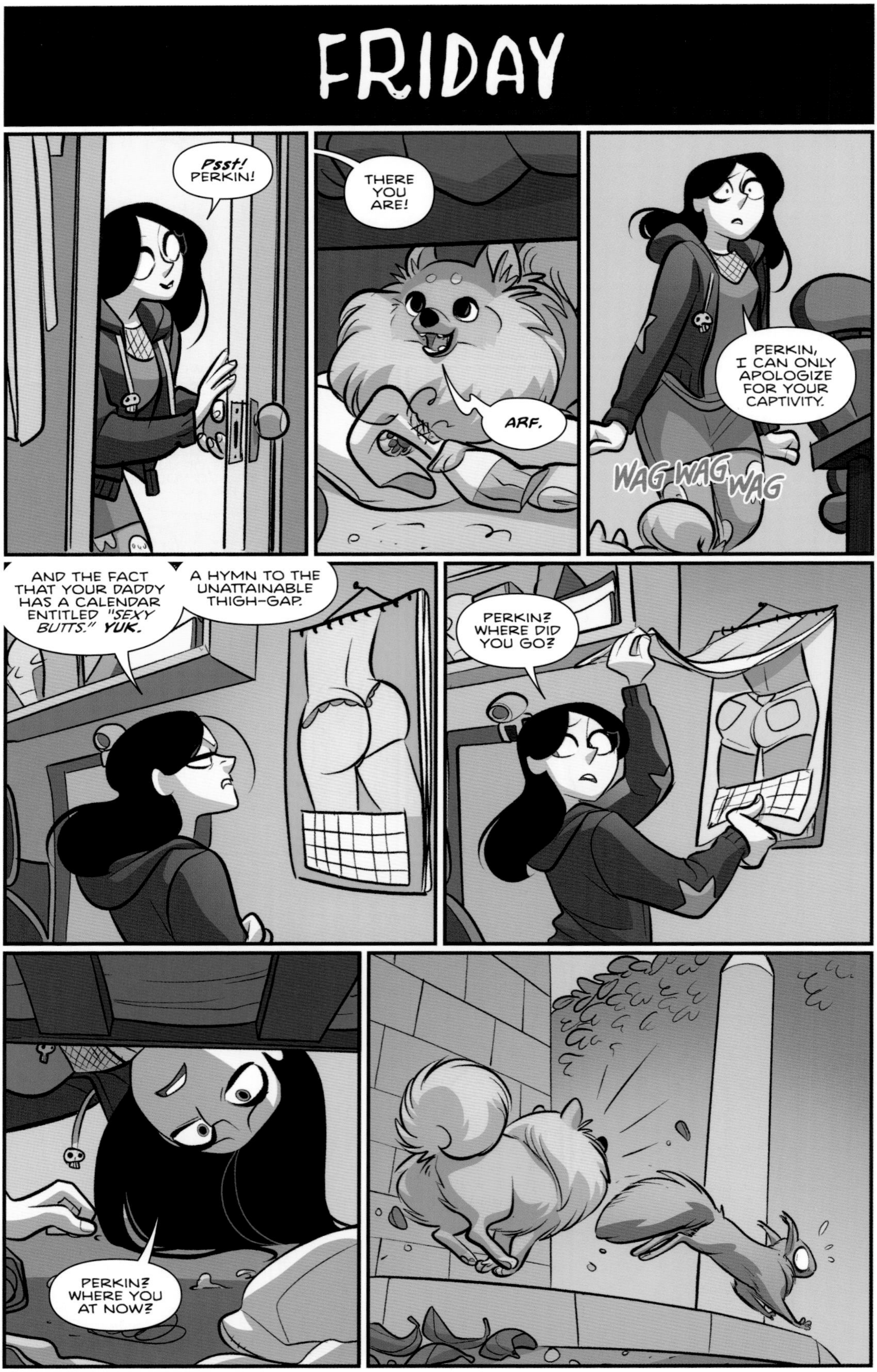
FRIDAY
Psst! PERKIN!
THERE YOU ARE!
ARF.
PERKIN, I CAN ONLY APOLOGIZE FOR YOUR CAPTIVITY.
WAG WAG WAG
AND THE FACT THAT YOUR DADDY HAS A CALENDAR ENTITLED "SEXY BUTTS." YUK.
A HYMN TO THE UNATTAINABLE THIGH-GAP.
PERKIN? WHERE DID YOU GO?
PERKIN? WHERE YOU AT NOW?

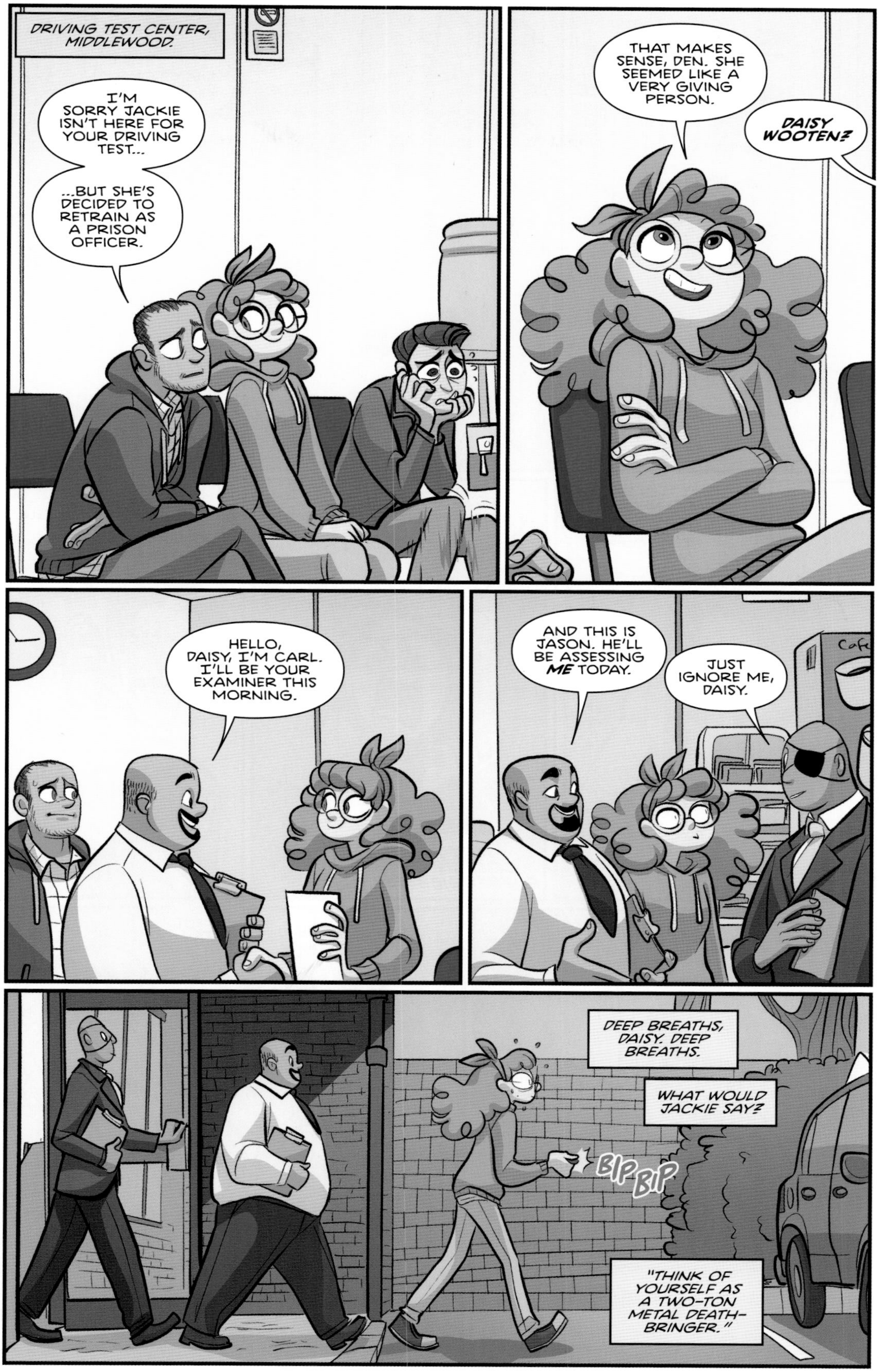
DRIVING TEST CENTER, MIDDLEWOOD.
I'M SORRY JACKIE ISN'T HERE FOR YOUR DRIVING TEST...
...BUT SHE'S DECIDED TO RETRAIN AS A PRISON OFFICER.
THAT MAKES SENSE, DEN. SHE SEEMED LIKE A VERY GIVING PERSON.
DAISY WOOTEN?
HELLO, DAISY, I'M CARL. I'LL BE YOUR EXAMINER THIS MORNING.
AND THIS IS JASON. HE'LL BE ASSESSING ME TODAY.
JUST IGNORE ME, DAISY.
DEEP BREATHS, DAISY. DEEP BREATHS.
WHAT WOULD JACKIE SAY?
BIP BIP
"THINK OF YOURSELF AS A TWO-TON METAL DEATH-BRINGER."

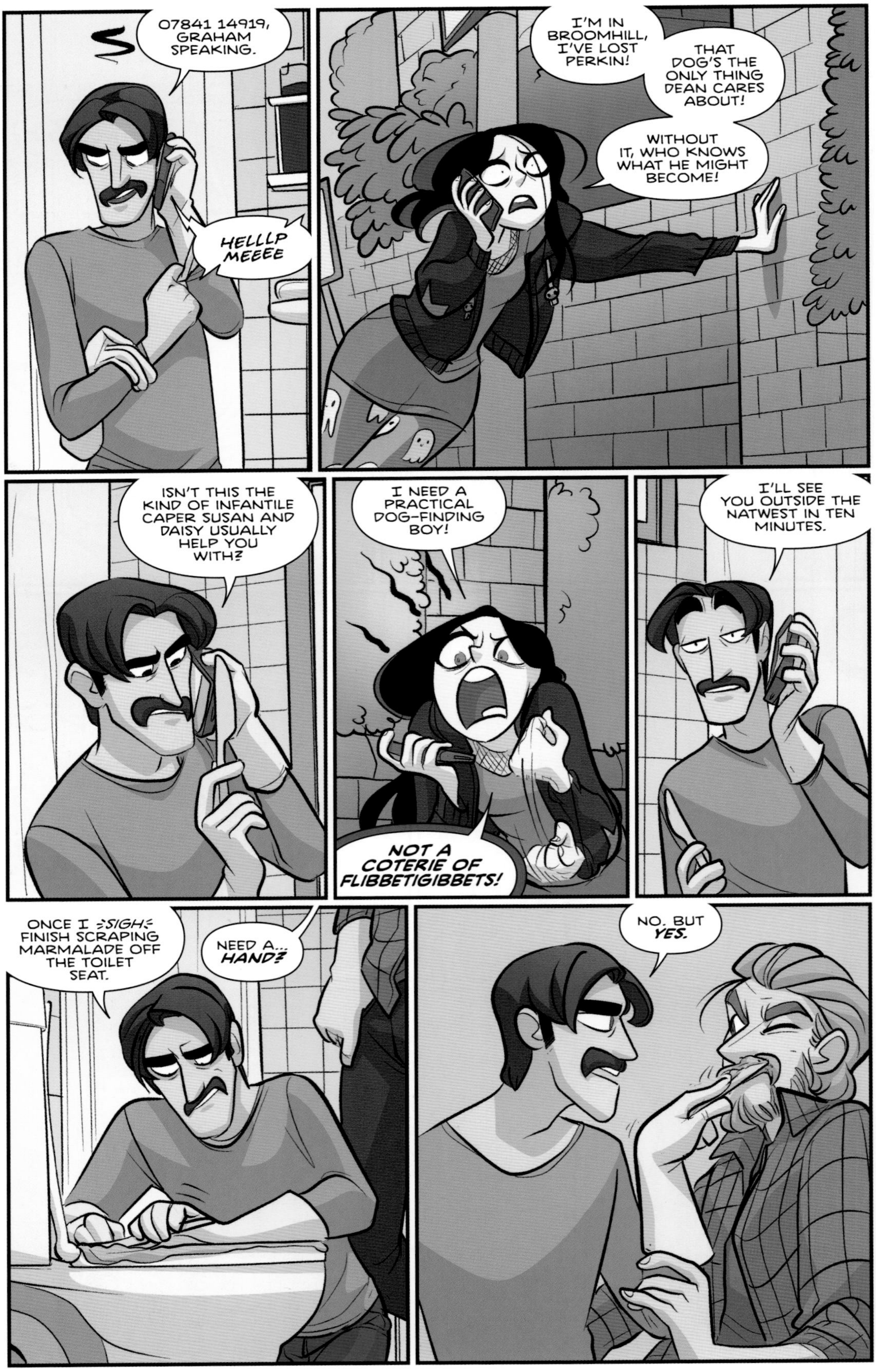
07841 14919, GRAHAM SPEAKING.
HELLLP MEEEE
I'M IN BROOMHILL, I'VE LOST PERKIN!
THAT DOG'S THE ONLY THING DEAN CARES ABOUT!
WITHOUT IT, WHO KNOWS WHAT HE MIGHT BECOME!
ISN'T THIS THE KIND OF INFANTILE CAPER SUSAN AND DAISY USUALLY HELP YOU WITH?
I NEED A PRACTICAL DOG-FINDING BOY!
NOT A COTERIE OF FLIBBETIGIBBETS!
I'LL SEE YOU OUTSIDE THE NATWEST IN TEN MINUTES.
ONCE I *SIGH* FINISH SCRAPING MARMALADE OFF THE TOILET SEAT.
NEED A... HAND?
NO. BUT YES.

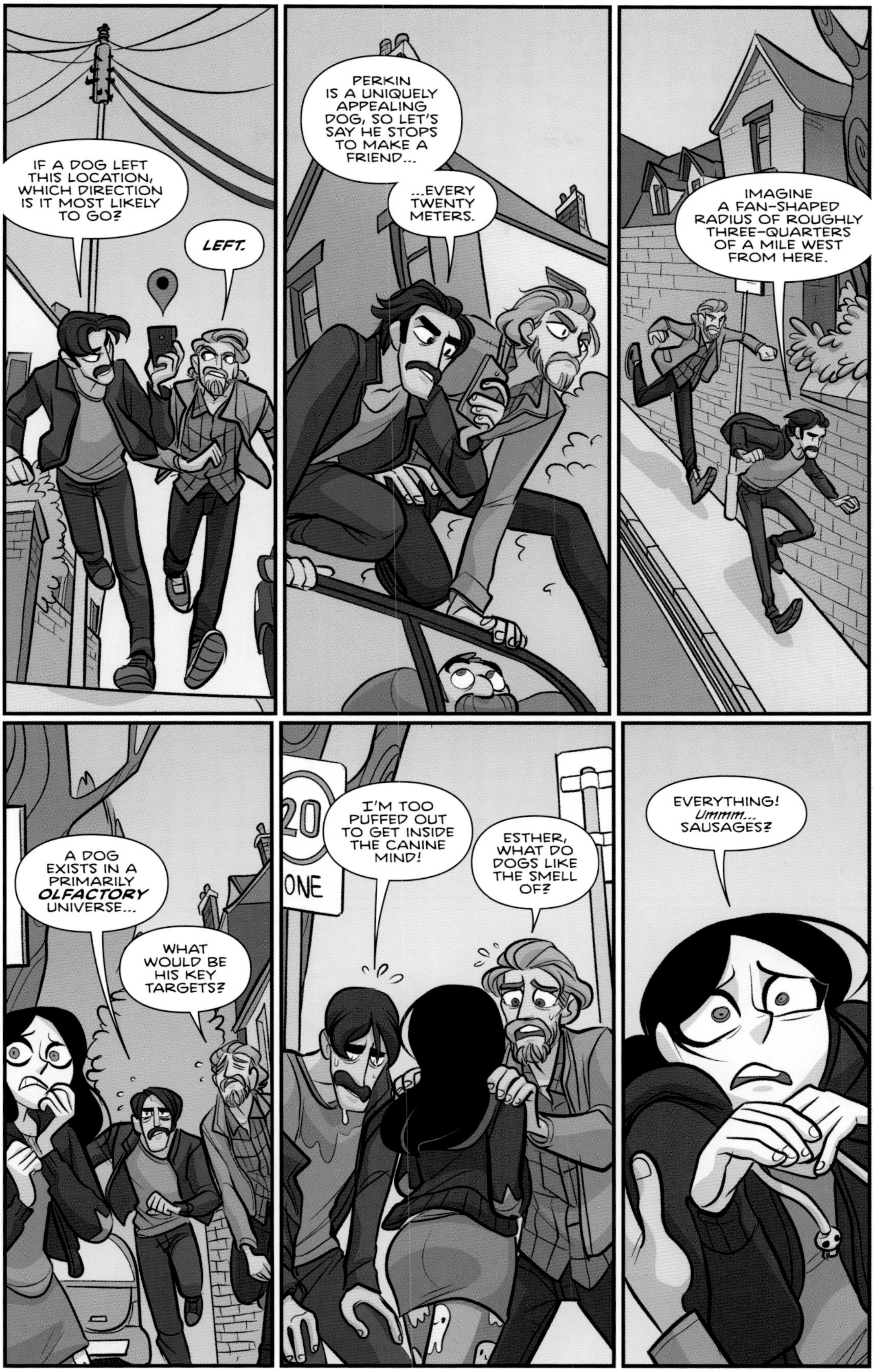
IF A DOG LEFT THIS LOCATION, WHICH DIRECTION IS IT MOST LIKELY TO GO?
LEFT.
PERKIN IS A UNIQUELY APPEALING DOG, SO LET'S SAY HE STOPS TO MAKE A FRIEND...
...EVERY TWENTY METERS.
IMAGINE A FAN-SHAPED RADIUS OF ROUGHLY THREE-QUARTERS OF A MILE WEST FROM HERE.
A DOG EXISTS IN A PRIMARILY OLFACTORY UNIVERSE...
WHAT WOULD BE HIS KEY TARGETS?
20
ONE
I'M TOO PUFFED OUT TO GET INSIDE THE CANINE MIND!
ESTHER, WHAT DO DOGS LIKE THE SMELL OF?
EVERYTHING! Ummm... SAUSAGES?

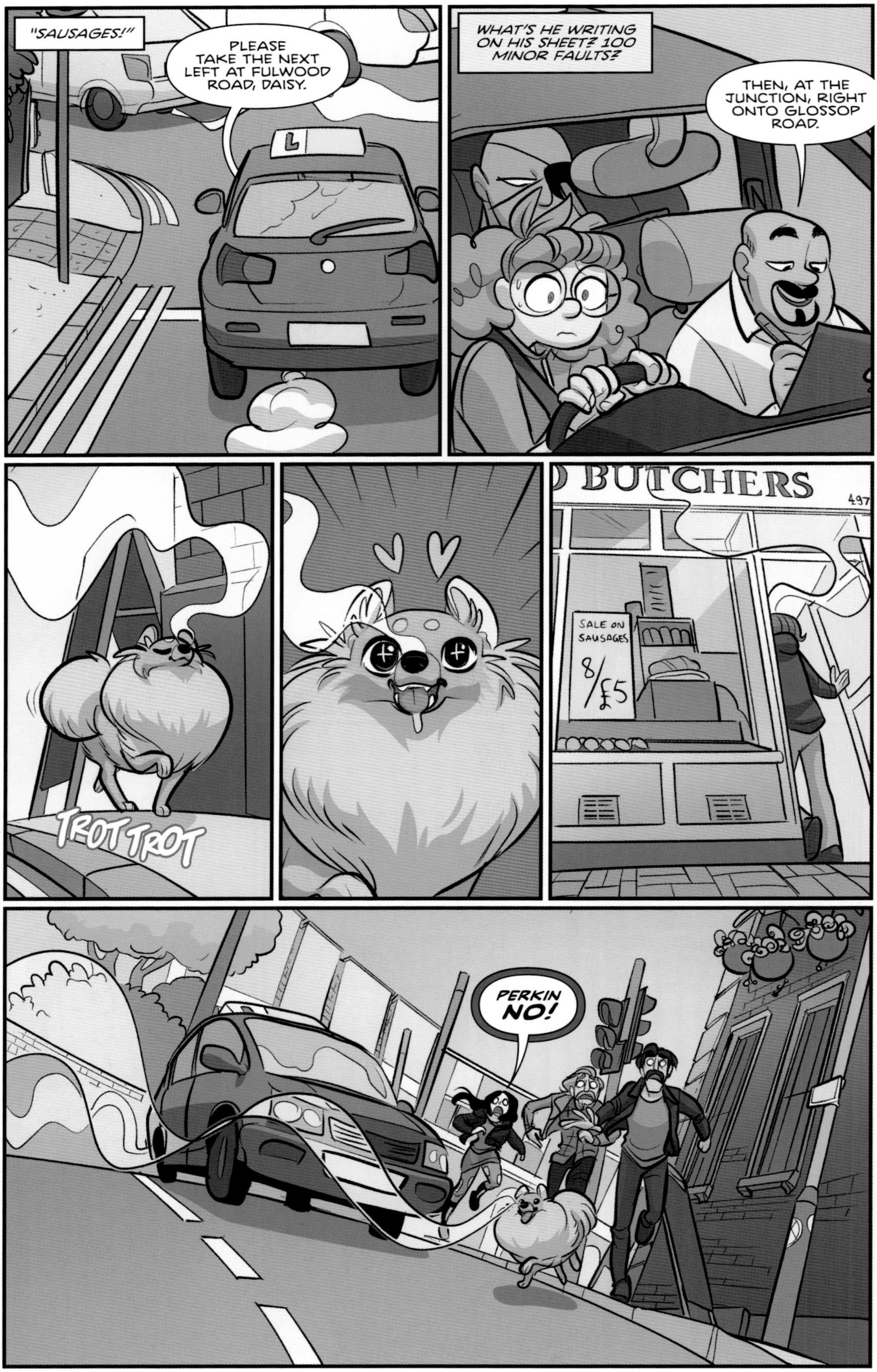
"SAUSAGES!"
PLEASE TAKE THE NEXT LEFT AT FULWOOD ROAD, DAISY.
WHAT'S HE WRITING ON HIS SHEET? 100 MINOR FAULTS?
THEN, AT THE JUNCTION, RIGHT ONTO GLOSSOP ROAD.
TROT TROT
D BUTCHERS
497
SALE ON SAUSAGES
8/£5
PERKIN NO!

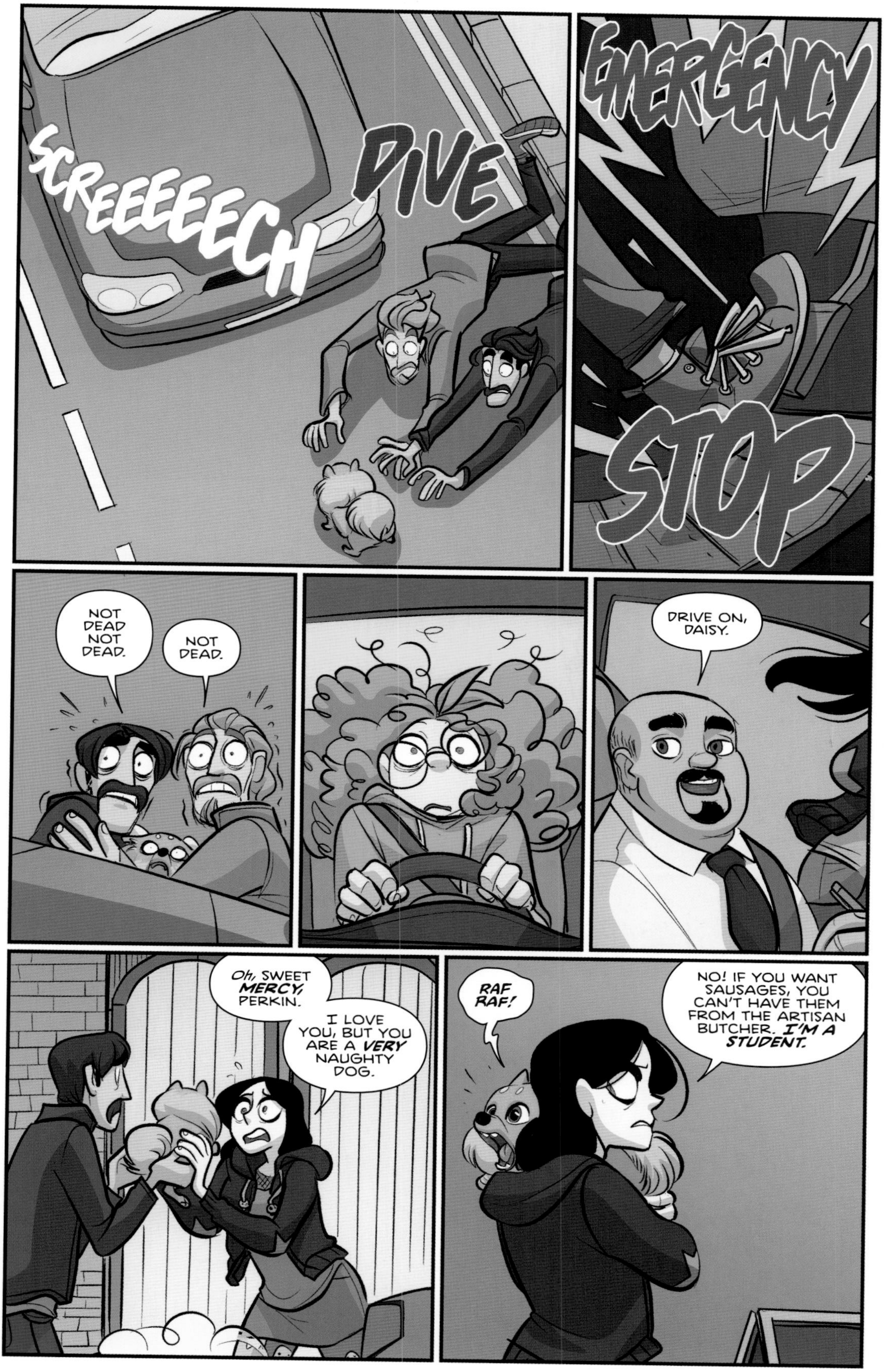
SCREEEEECH
DIVE
EMERGENCY
STOP
NOT DEAD NOT DEAD.
NOT DEAD.
DRIVE ON, DAISY.
Oh, SWEET MERCY, PERKIN.
I LOVE YOU, BUT YOU ARE A VERY NAUGHTY DOG.
RAF RAF!
NO! IF YOU WANT SAUSAGES, YOU CAN'T HAVE THEM FROM THE ARTISAN BUTCHER. I'M A STUDENT.

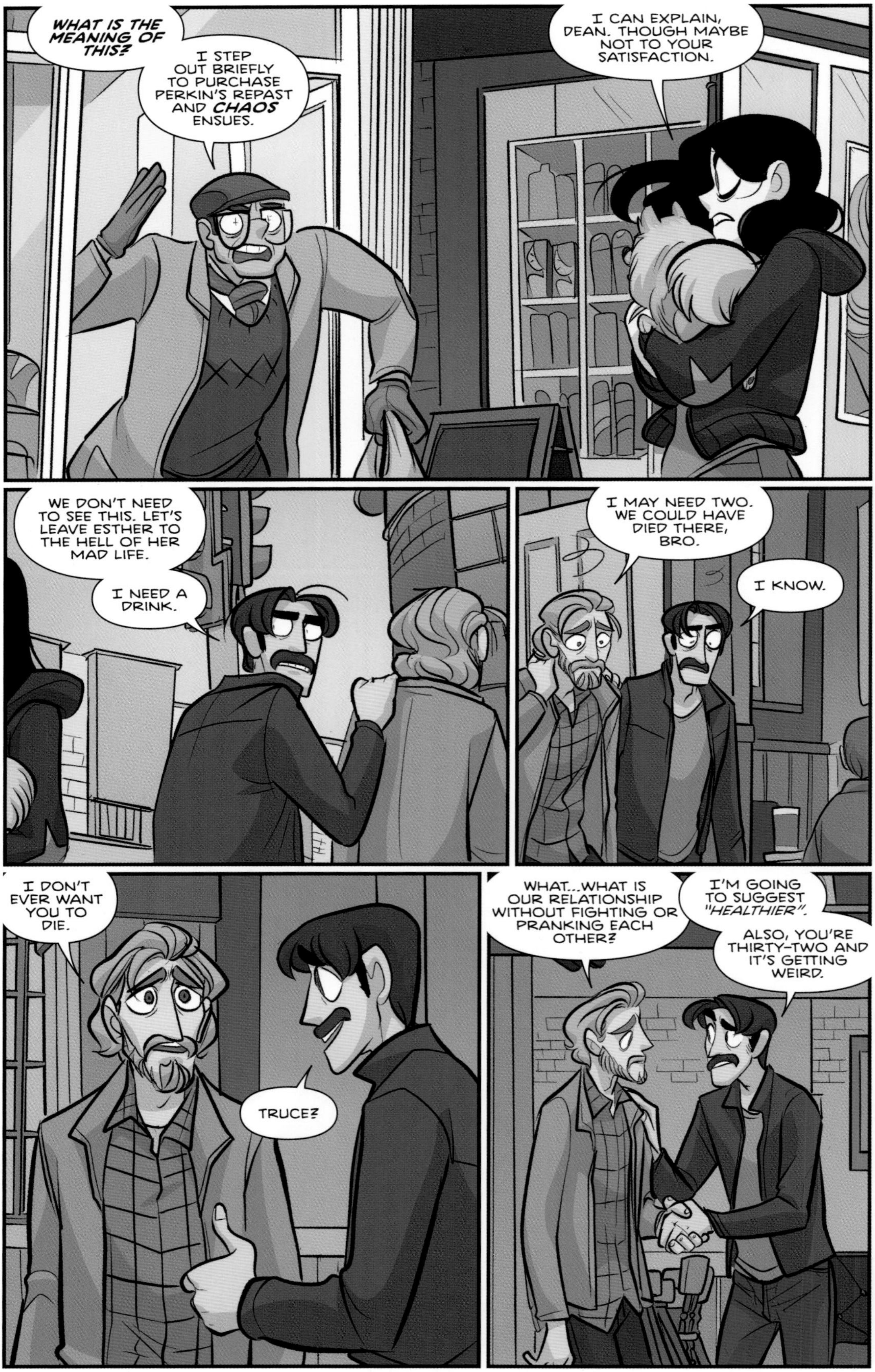
WHAT IS THE MEANING OF THIS?
I STEP OUT BRIEFLY TO PURCHASE PERKIN'S REPAST AND CHAOS ENSUES.
I CAN EXPLAIN, DEAN. THOUGH MAYBE NOT TO YOUR SATISFACTION.
WE DON'T NEED TO SEE THIS. LET'S LEAVE ESTHER TO THE HELL OF HER MAD LIFE.
I NEED A DRINK.
I MAY NEED TWO. WE COULD HAVE DIED THERE, BRO.
I KNOW.
I DON'T EVER WANT YOU TO DIE.
TRUCE?
WHAT...WHAT IS OUR RELATIONSHIP WITHOUT FIGHTING OR PRANKING EACH OTHER?
I'M GOING TO SUGGEST "HEALTHIER".
ALSO, YOU'RE THIRTY-TWO AND IT'S GETTING WEIRD.

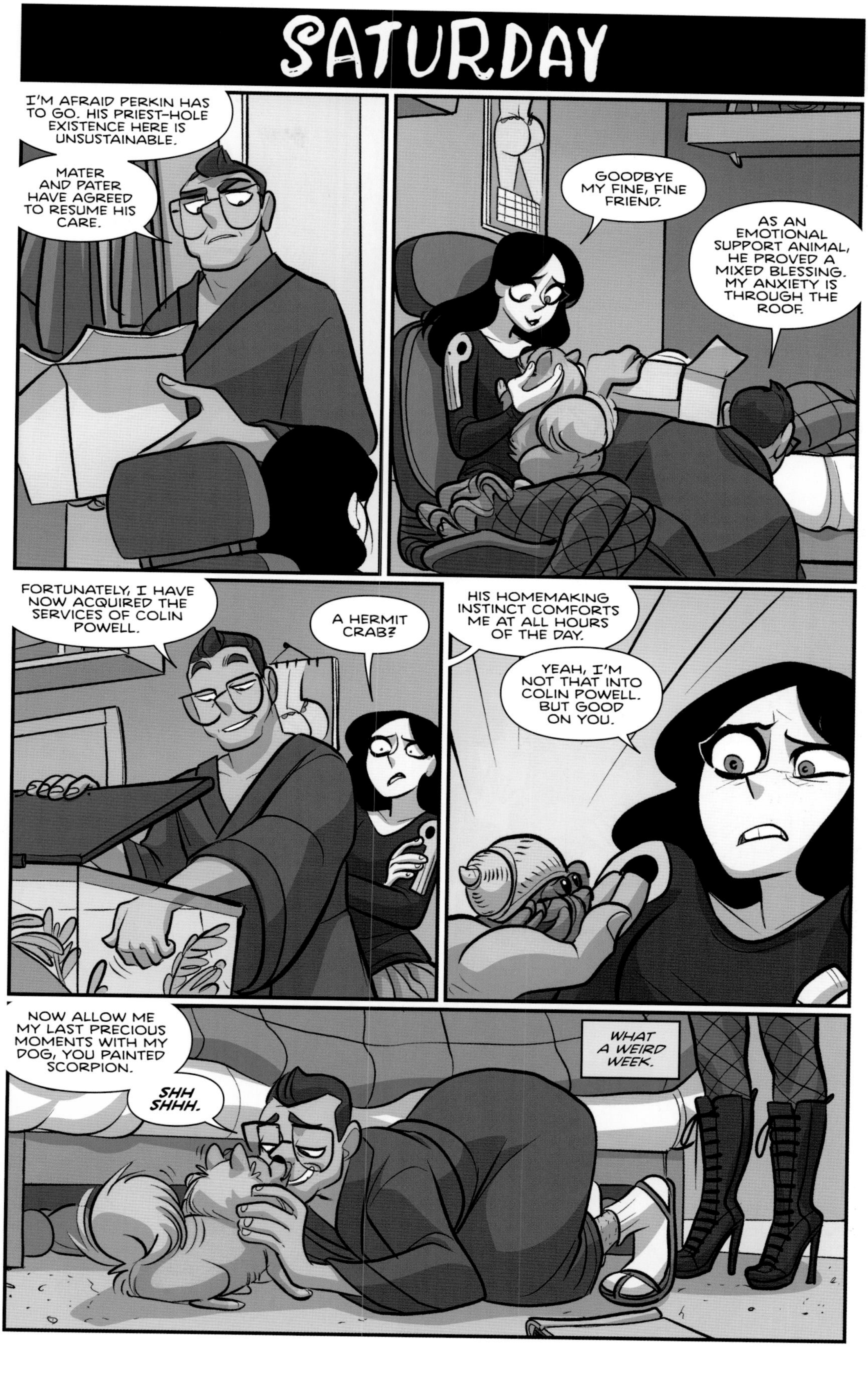
SATURDAY
I'M AFRAID PERKIN HAS TO GO. HIS PRIEST-HOLE EXISTENCE HERE IS UNSUSTAINABLE.
MATER AND PATER HAVE AGREED TO RESUME HIS CARE.
GOODBYE MY FINE, FINE FRIEND.
AS AN EMOTIONAL SUPPORT ANIMAL, HE PROVED A MIXED BLESSING. MY ANXIETY IS THROUGH THE ROOF.
FORTUNATELY, I HAVE NOW ACQUIRED THE SERVICES OF COLIN POWELL.
A HERMIT CRAB?
HIS HOMEMAKING INSTINCT COMFORTS ME AT ALL HOURS OF THE DAY.
YEAH, I'M NOT THAT INTO COLIN POWELL. BUT GOOD ON YOU.
NOW ALLOW ME MY LAST PRECIOUS MOMENTS WITH MY DOG, YOU PAINTED SCORPION.
SHH SHHH.
WHAT A WEIRD WEEK.

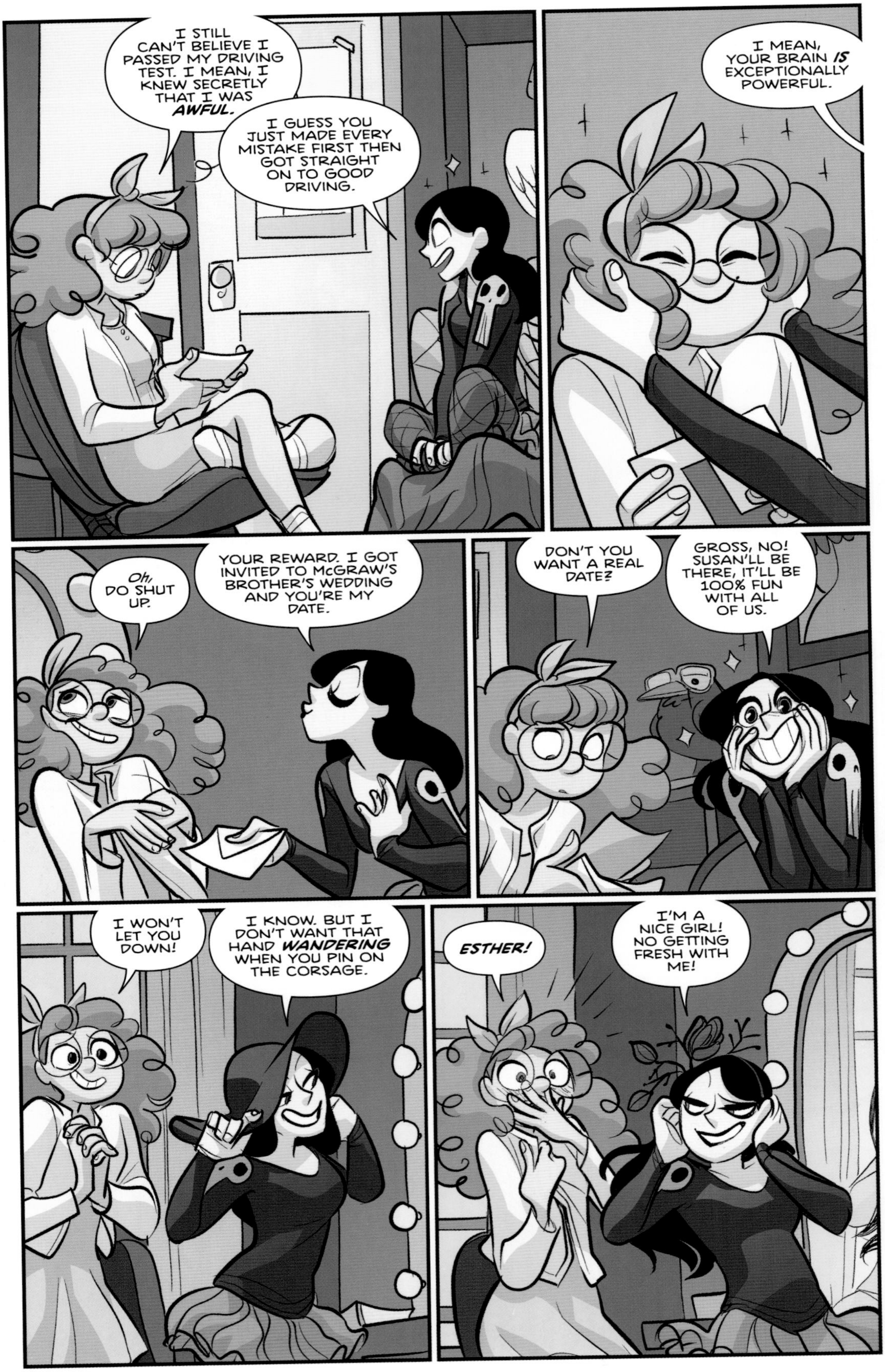
I STILL CAN'T BELIEVE I PASSED MY DRIVING TEST. I MEAN, I KNEW SECRETLY THAT I WAS AWFUL.
I GUESS YOU JUST MADE EVERY MISTAKE FIRST THEN GOT STRAIGHT ON TO GOOD DRIVING.
I MEAN, YOUR BRAIN IS EXCEPTIONALLY POWERFUL.
Oh, DO SHUT UP.
YOUR REWARD. I GOT INVITED TO McGRAW'S BROTHER'S WEDDING AND YOU'RE MY DATE.
DON'T YOU WANT A REAL DATE?
GROSS, NO! SUSAN'LL BE THERE, IT'LL BE 100% FUN WITH ALL OF US.
I WON'T LET YOU DOWN!
I KNOW. BUT I DON'T WANT THAT HAND WANDERING WHEN YOU PIN ON THE CORSAGE.
ESTHER!
I'M A NICE GIRL! NO GETTING FRESH WITH ME!

CHAPTER
FORTY-EIGHT

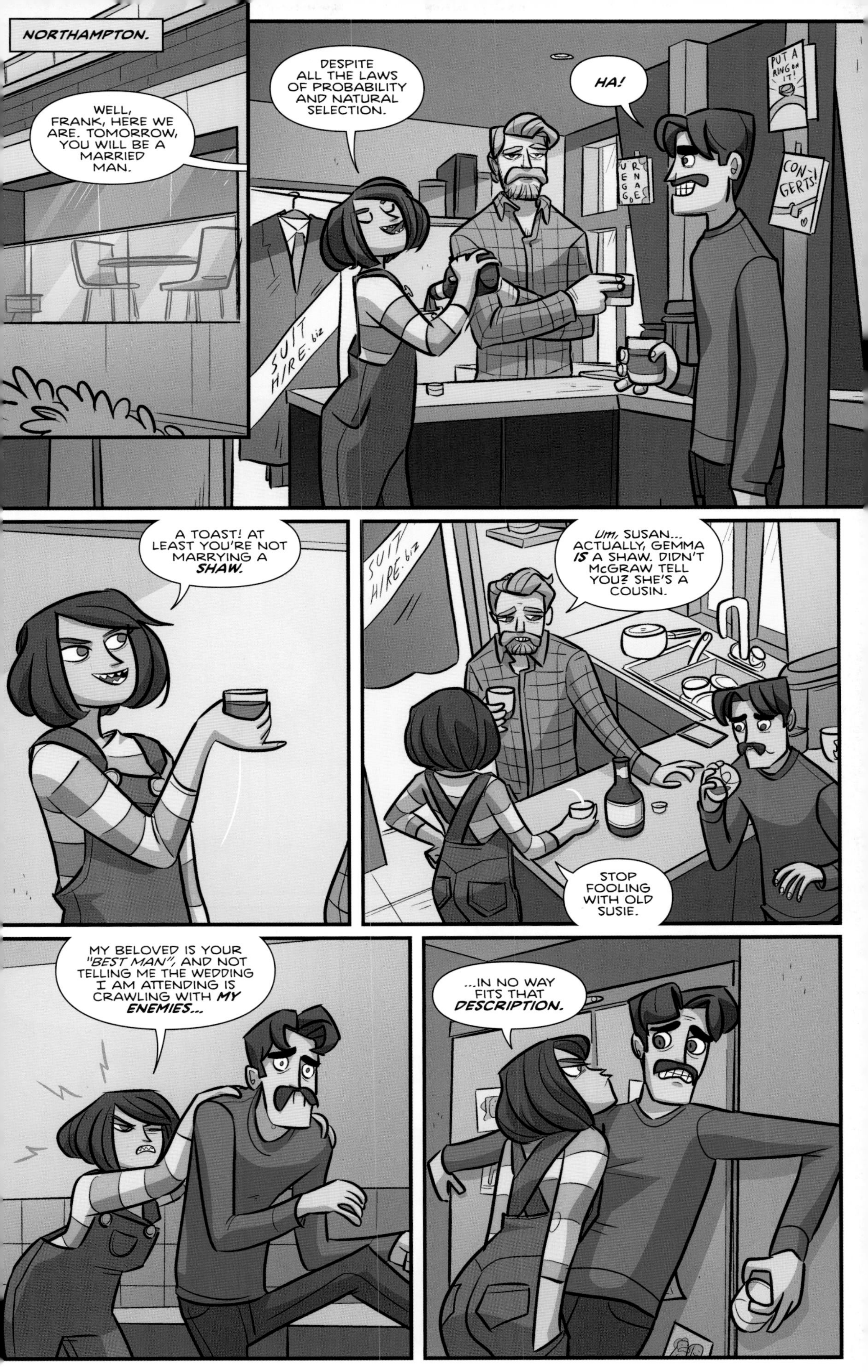
NORTHAMPTON.
WELL, FRANK, HERE WE ARE. TOMORROW, YOU WILL BE A MARRIED MAN.
DESPITE ALL THE LAWS OF PROBABILITY AND NATURAL SELECTION.
HA!
PUT A RING ON IT!
CON-GERTS!
SUIT HIRE.biz
A TOAST! AT LEAST YOU'RE NOT MARRYING A SHAW.
UM, SUSAN... ACTUALLY, GEMMA IS A SHAW. DIDN'T McGRAW TELL YOU? SHE'S A COUSIN.
STOP FOOLING WITH OLD SUSIE.
MY BELOVED IS YOUR "BEST MAN", AND NOT TELLING ME THE WEDDING I AM ATTENDING IS CRAWLING WITH MY ENEMIES...
...IN NO WAY FITS THAT DESCRIPTION.

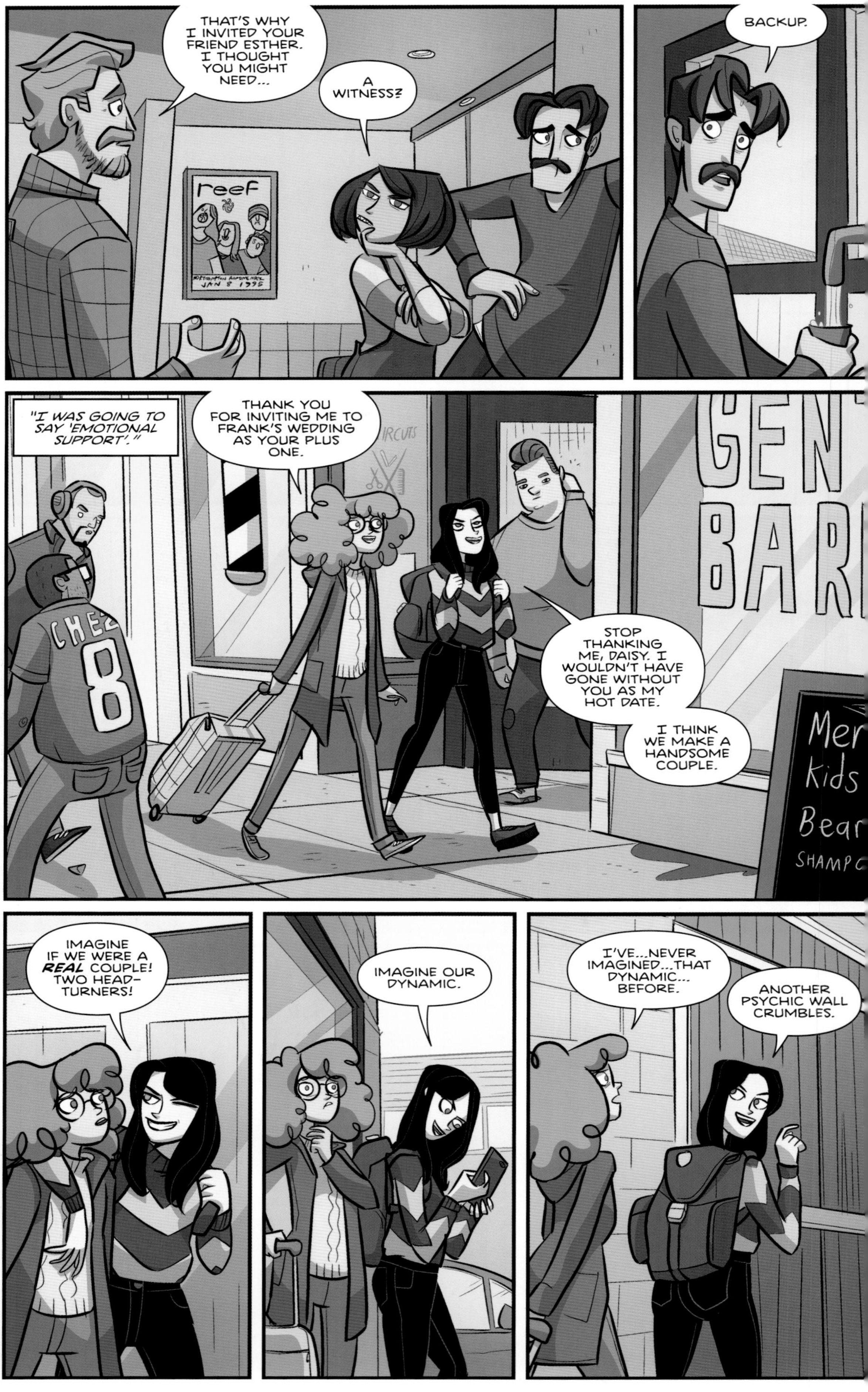
THAT'S WHY I INVITED YOUR FRIEND ESTHER. I THOUGHT YOU MIGHT NEED...
A WITNESS?
reef
JAN 8 1995
BACKUP.
"I WAS GOING TO SAY 'EMOTIONAL SUPPORT'."
THANK YOU FOR INVITING ME TO FRANK'S WEDDING AS YOUR PLUS ONE.
STOP THANKING ME, DAISY. I WOULDN'T HAVE GONE WITHOUT YOU AS MY HOT DATE.
I THINK WE MAKE A HANDSOME COUPLE.
IMAGINE IF WE WERE A *REAL* COUPLE! TWO HEAD-TURNERS!
IMAGINE OUR DYNAMIC.
I'VE...NEVER IMAGINED...THAT DYNAMIC... BEFORE.
ANOTHER PSYCHIC WALL CRUMBLES.

WELL, THIS IS MEANT TO BE IT. *FROG HALL.*

IS IT?

IT JUST APPEARS TO BE A DOOR IN A NONDESCRIPT WALL.

BZZZ

FRO
HALL

18

YES. IT'S BOUTIQUE! AND *QUIRKY!*

SO I GUESS THE FROGS ARE...A *THEME?*

YAH YAH, THE KIND OF ATTENTION TO DETAIL YOU DON'T USUALLY GET AT THIS PRICE POINT.

UMBRELLAS

REMIND ME, HOW MANY STARS DID THIS PLACE GET ON TRIPADVISOR?

AT THIS PRICE POINT, I PREFER TO LOOK AFTER I'VE STAYED...

...TO SEE IF I AGREE.

PING

TADPOL
SEASO

FROG

POND
WALK

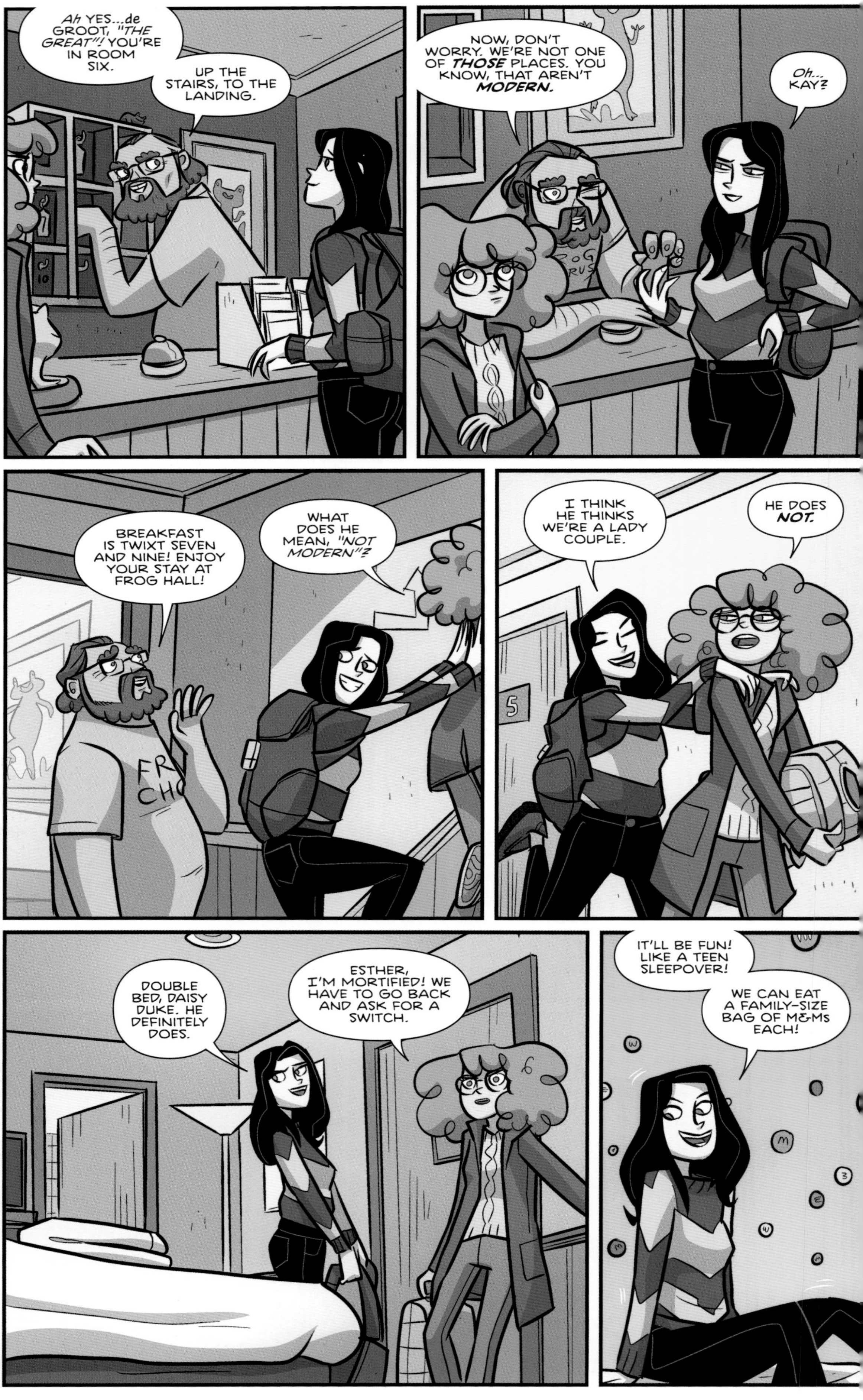
Ah YES...de GROOT, "THE GREAT"! YOU'RE IN ROOM SIX.
UP THE STAIRS, TO THE LANDING.
NOW, DON'T WORRY. WE'RE NOT ONE OF THOSE PLACES. YOU KNOW, THAT AREN'T MODERN.
Oh... KAY?
BREAKFAST IS TWIXT SEVEN AND NINE! ENJOY YOUR STAY AT FROG HALL!
WHAT DOES HE MEAN, "NOT MODERN"?
I THINK HE THINKS WE'RE A LADY COUPLE.
HE DOES NOT.
DOUBLE BED, DAISY DUKE. HE DEFINITELY DOES.
ESTHER, I'M MORTIFIED! WE HAVE TO GO BACK AND ASK FOR A SWITCH.
IT'LL BE FUN! LIKE A TEEN SLEEPOVER!
WE CAN EAT A FAMILY-SIZE BAG OF M&Ms EACH!

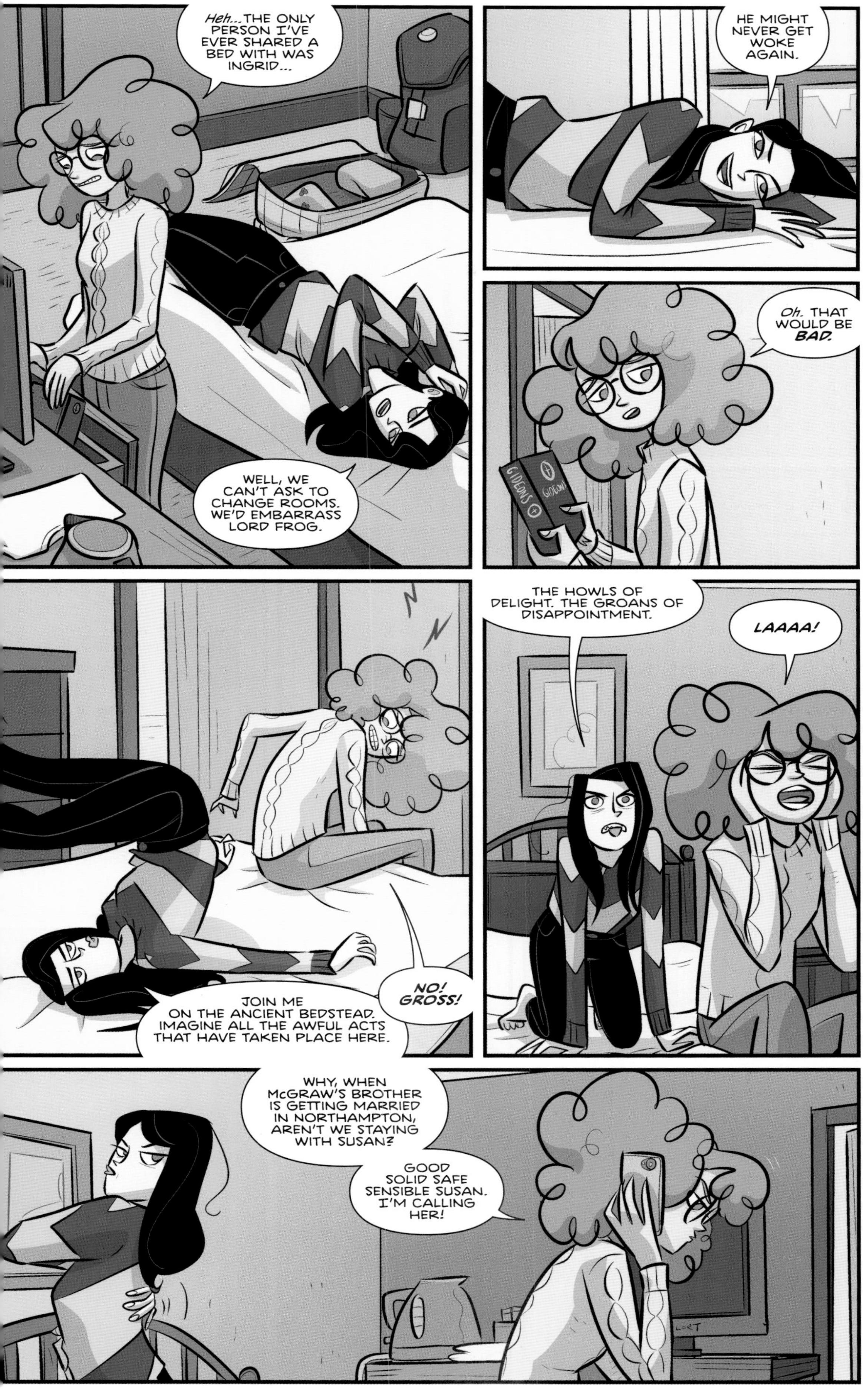

Heh... THE ONLY PERSON I'VE EVER SHARED A BED WITH WAS INGRID...
WELL, WE CAN'T ASK TO CHANGE ROOMS. WE'D EMBARRASS LORD FROG.
HE MIGHT NEVER GET WOKE AGAIN.
Oh. THAT WOULD BE ***BAD.***
JOIN ME ON THE ANCIENT BEDSTEAD. IMAGINE ALL THE AWFUL ACTS THAT HAVE TAKEN PLACE HERE.
NO! GROSS!
THE HOWLS OF DELIGHT. THE GROANS OF DISAPPOINTMENT.
LAAAA!
WHY, WHEN McGRAW'S BROTHER IS GETTING MARRIED IN NORTHAMPTON, AREN'T WE STAYING WITH SUSAN?
GOOD SOLID SAFE SENSIBLE SUSAN. I'M CALLING HER!

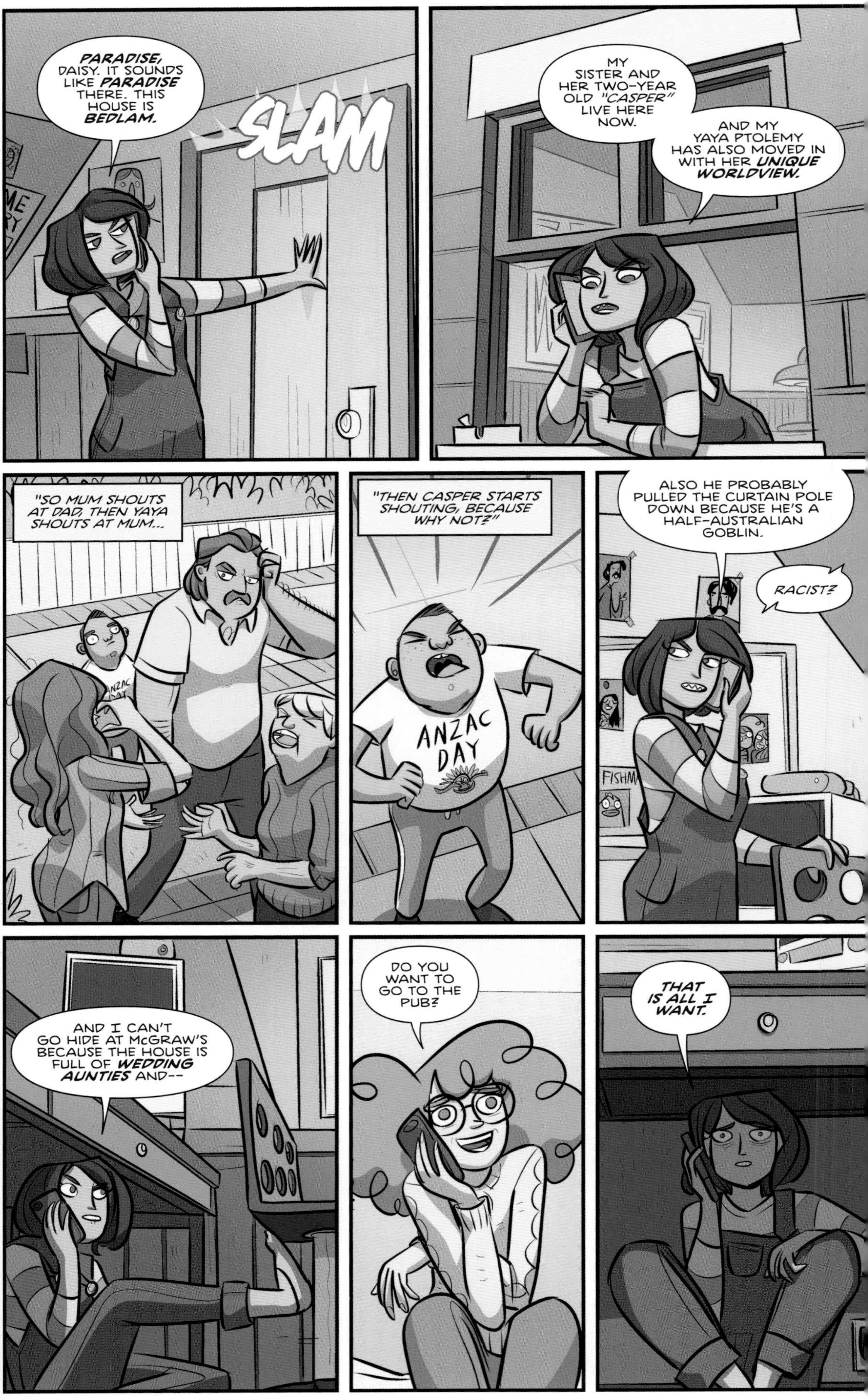
PARADISE, DAISY. IT SOUNDS LIKE PARADISE THERE. THIS HOUSE IS BEDLAM.
SLAM
MY SISTER AND HER TWO-YEAR OLD "CASPER" LIVE HERE NOW.
AND MY YAYA PTOLEMY HAS ALSO MOVED IN WITH HER UNIQUE WORLDVIEW.
"SO MUM SHOUTS AT DAD, THEN YAYA SHOUTS AT MUM...
"THEN CASPER STARTS SHOUTING, BECAUSE WHY NOT?"
ANZAC DAY
ALSO HE PROBABLY PULLED THE CURTAIN POLE DOWN BECAUSE HE'S A HALF-AUSTRALIAN GOBLIN.
RACIST?
AND I CAN'T GO HIDE AT McGRAW'S BECAUSE THE HOUSE IS FULL OF WEDDING AUNTIES AND--
DO YOU WANT TO GO TO THE PUB?
THAT IS ALL I WANT.

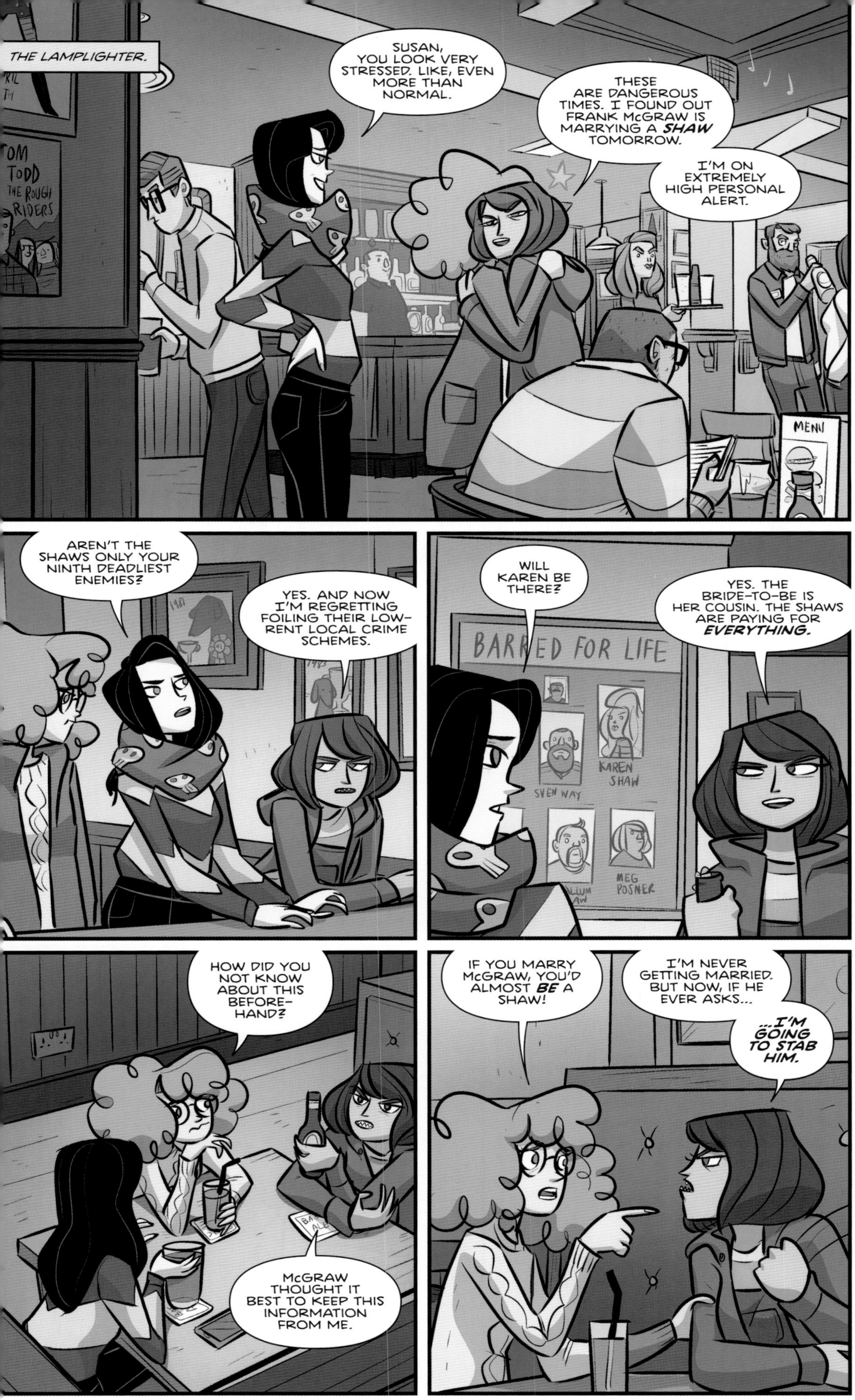
THE LAMPLIGHTER.
SUSAN, YOU LOOK VERY STRESSED. LIKE, EVEN MORE THAN NORMAL.
THESE ARE DANGEROUS TIMES. I FOUND OUT FRANK McGRAW IS MARRYING A SHAW TOMORROW.
I'M ON EXTREMELY HIGH PERSONAL ALERT.
MENU
AREN'T THE SHAWS ONLY YOUR NINTH DEADLIEST ENEMIES?
YES. AND NOW I'M REGRETTING FOILING THEIR LOW-RENT LOCAL CRIME SCHEMES.
WILL KAREN BE THERE?
YES. THE BRIDE-TO-BE IS HER COUSIN. THE SHAWS ARE PAYING FOR EVERYTHING.
BARRED FOR LIFE
SVEN WAY
KAREN SHAW
MEG POSNER
HOW DID YOU NOT KNOW ABOUT THIS BEFORE-HAND?
McGRAW THOUGHT IT BEST TO KEEP THIS INFORMATION FROM ME.
IF YOU MARRY McGRAW, YOU'D ALMOST BE A SHAW!
I'M NEVER GETTING MARRIED. BUT NOW, IF HE EVER ASKS...
...I'M GOING TO STAB HIM.

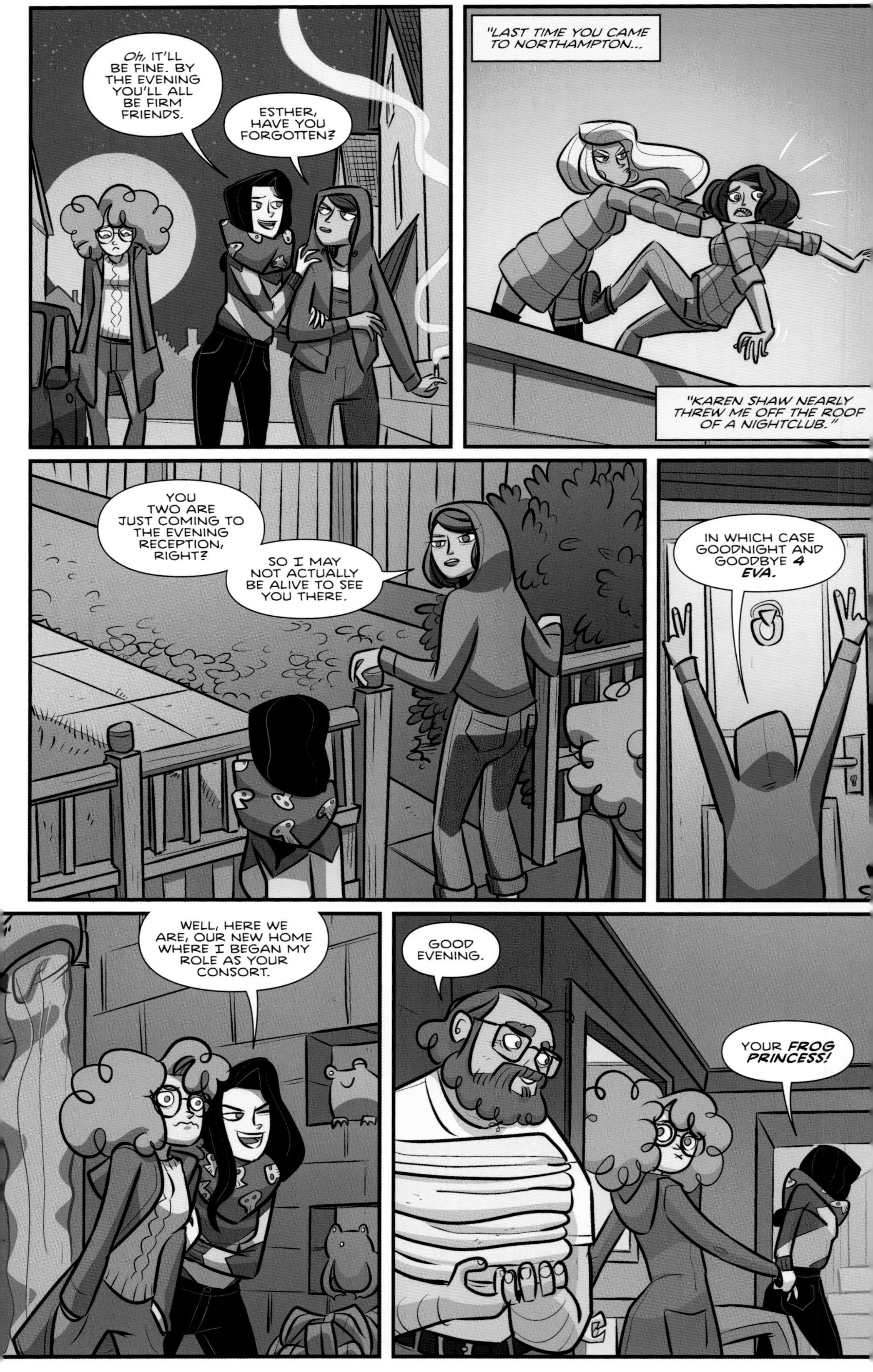
Oh, IT'LL BE FINE. BY THE EVENING YOU'LL ALL BE FIRM FRIENDS.
ESTHER, HAVE YOU FORGOTTEN?
"LAST TIME YOU CAME TO NORTHAMPTON...
"KAREN SHAW NEARLY THREW ME OFF THE ROOF OF A NIGHTCLUB."
YOU TWO ARE JUST COMING TO THE EVENING RECEPTION, RIGHT?
SO I MAY NOT ACTUALLY BE ALIVE TO SEE YOU THERE.
IN WHICH CASE GOODNIGHT AND GOODBYE 4 EVA.
WELL, HERE WE ARE, OUR NEW HOME WHERE I BEGAN MY ROLE AS YOUR CONSORT.
GOOD EVENING.
YOUR FROG PRINCESS!

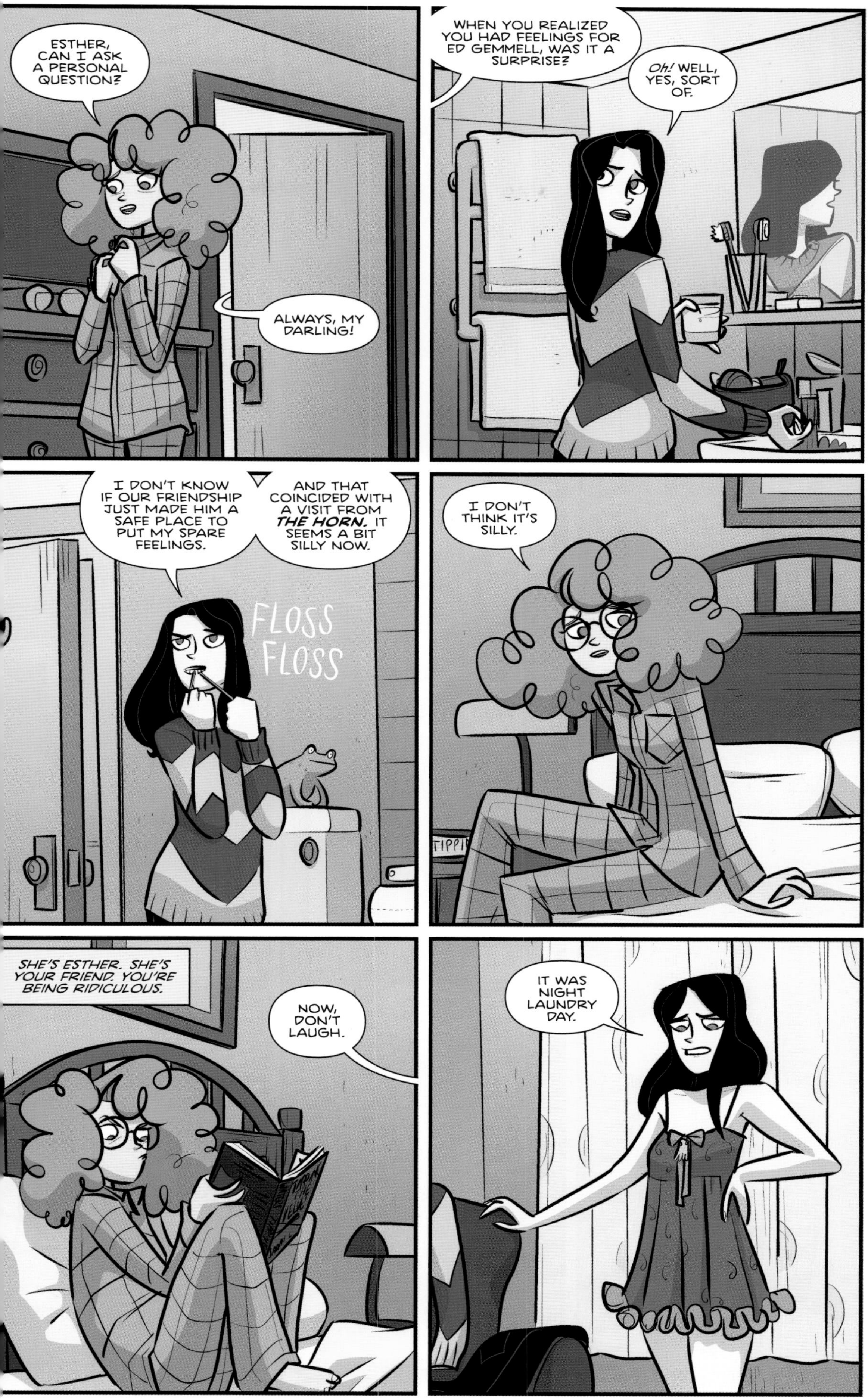
ESTHER, CAN I ASK A PERSONAL QUESTION?
ALWAYS, MY DARLING!
WHEN YOU REALIZED YOU HAD FEELINGS FOR ED GEMMELL, WAS IT A SURPRISE?
Oh! WELL, YES, SORT OF.
I DON'T KNOW IF OUR FRIENDSHIP JUST MADE HIM A SAFE PLACE TO PUT MY SPARE FEELINGS.
AND THAT COINCIDED WITH A VISIT FROM ***THE HORN.*** IT SEEMS A BIT SILLY NOW.
FLOSS FLOSS
I DON'T THINK IT'S SILLY.
SHE'S ESTHER. SHE'S YOUR FRIEND. YOU'RE BEING RIDICULOUS.
NOW, DON'T LAUGH.
IT WAS NIGHT LAUNDRY DAY.

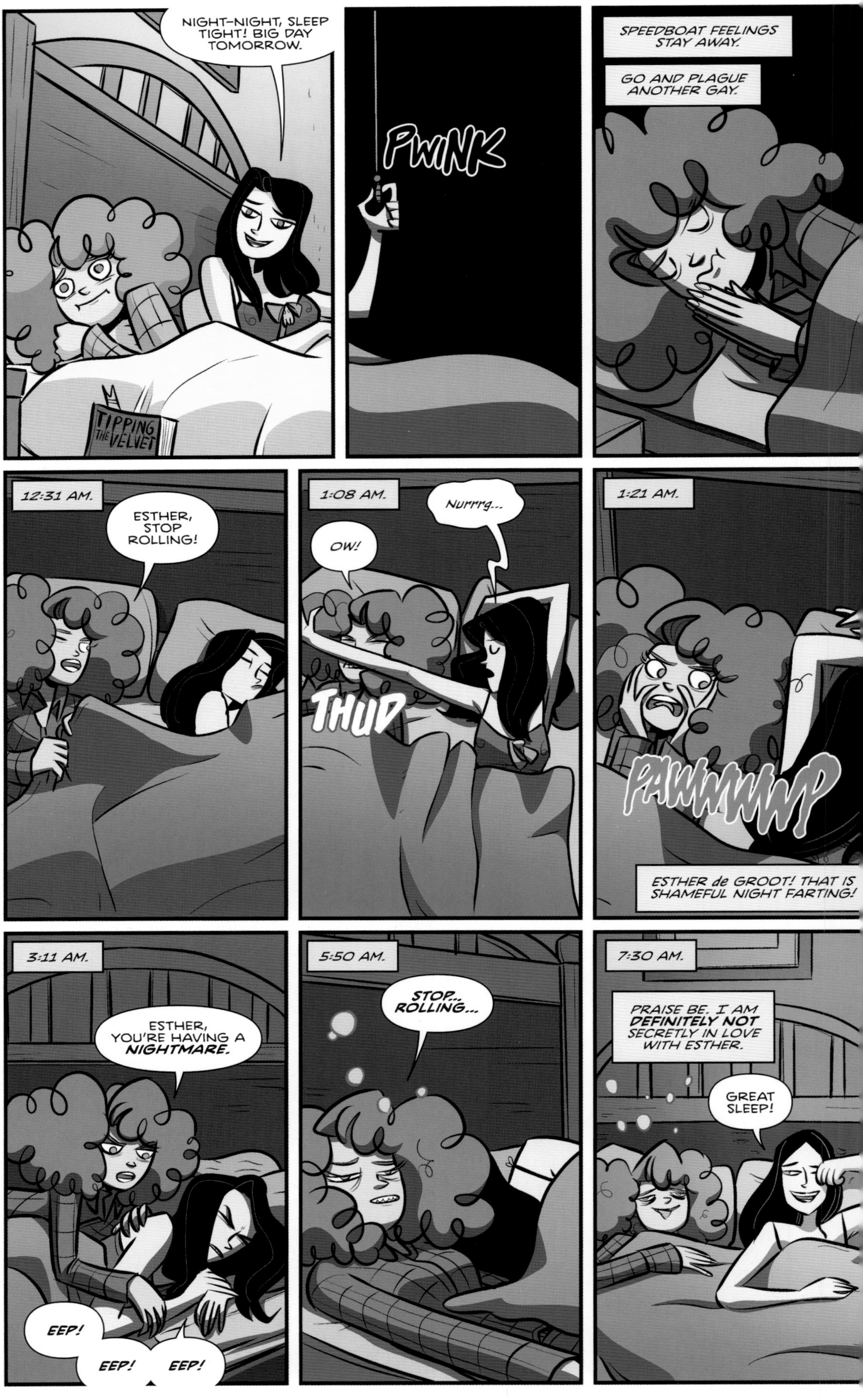
NIGHT-NIGHT, SLEEP TIGHT! BIG DAY TOMORROW.
TIPPING THE VELVET
PWINK
SPEEDBOAT FEELINGS STAY AWAY.
GO AND PLAGUE ANOTHER GAY.
12:31 AM.
ESTHER, STOP ROLLING!
1:08 AM.
Nurrrg...
OW!
THUD
1:21 AM.
PAWWWWP
ESTHER de GROOT! THAT IS SHAMEFUL NIGHT FARTING!
3:11 AM.
ESTHER, YOU'RE HAVING A NIGHTMARE.
EEP!
EEP!
EEP!
5:50 AM.
STOP... ROLLING...
7:30 AM.
PRAISE BE. I AM DEFINITELY NOT SECRETLY IN LOVE WITH ESTHER.
GREAT SLEEP!

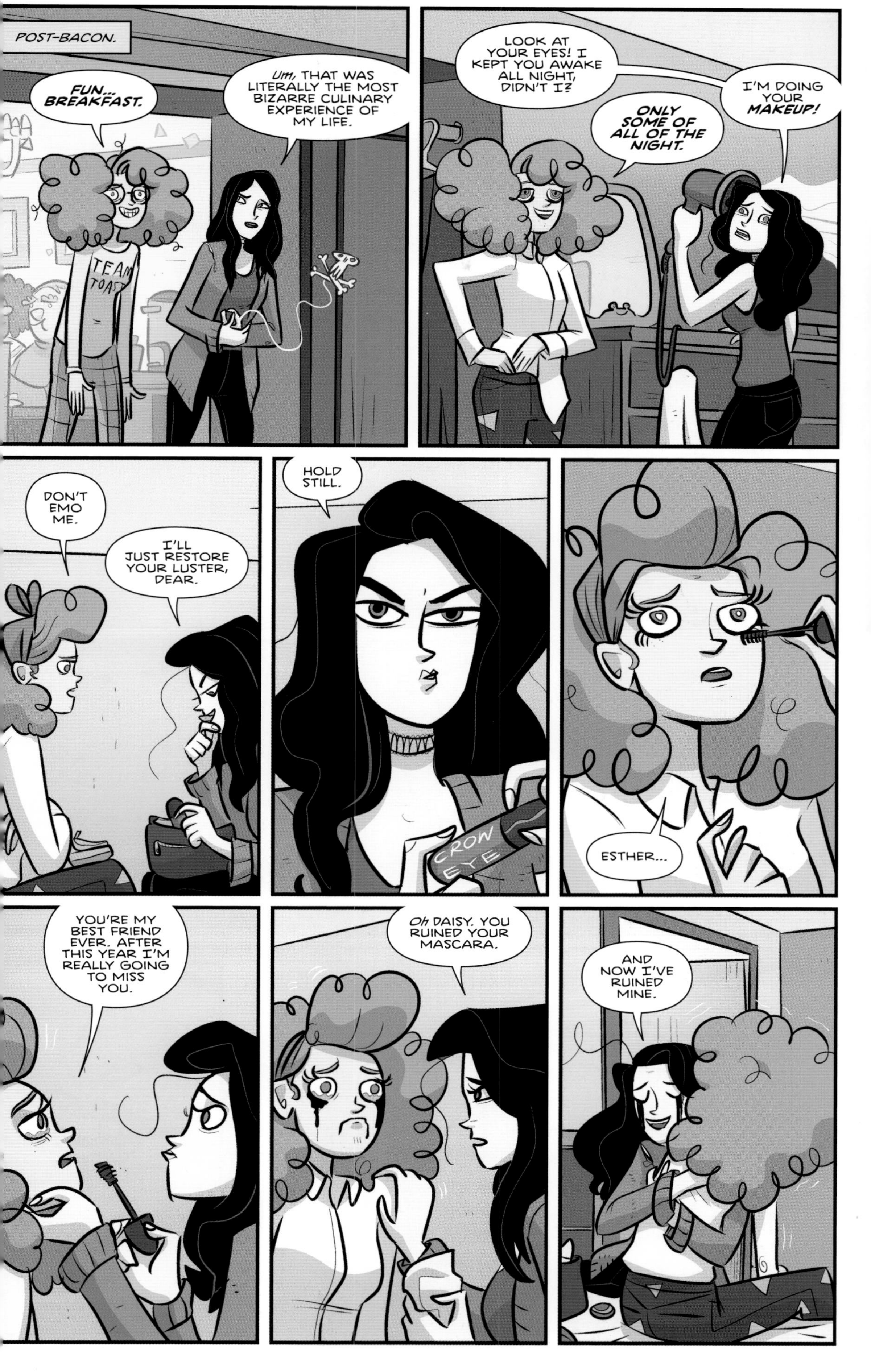
POST-BACON.
FUN... BREAKFAST.
Um, THAT WAS LITERALLY THE MOST BIZARRE CULINARY EXPERIENCE OF MY LIFE.
LOOK AT YOUR EYES! I KEPT YOU AWAKE ALL NIGHT, DIDN'T I?
ONLY SOME OF ALL OF THE NIGHT.
I'M DOING YOUR MAKEUP!
DON'T EMO ME.
I'LL JUST RESTORE YOUR LUSTER, DEAR.
HOLD STILL.
CROW EYE
ESTHER...
YOU'RE MY BEST FRIEND EVER. AFTER THIS YEAR I'M REALLY GOING TO MISS YOU.
Oh DAISY. YOU RUINED YOUR MASCARA.
AND NOW I'VE RUINED MINE.

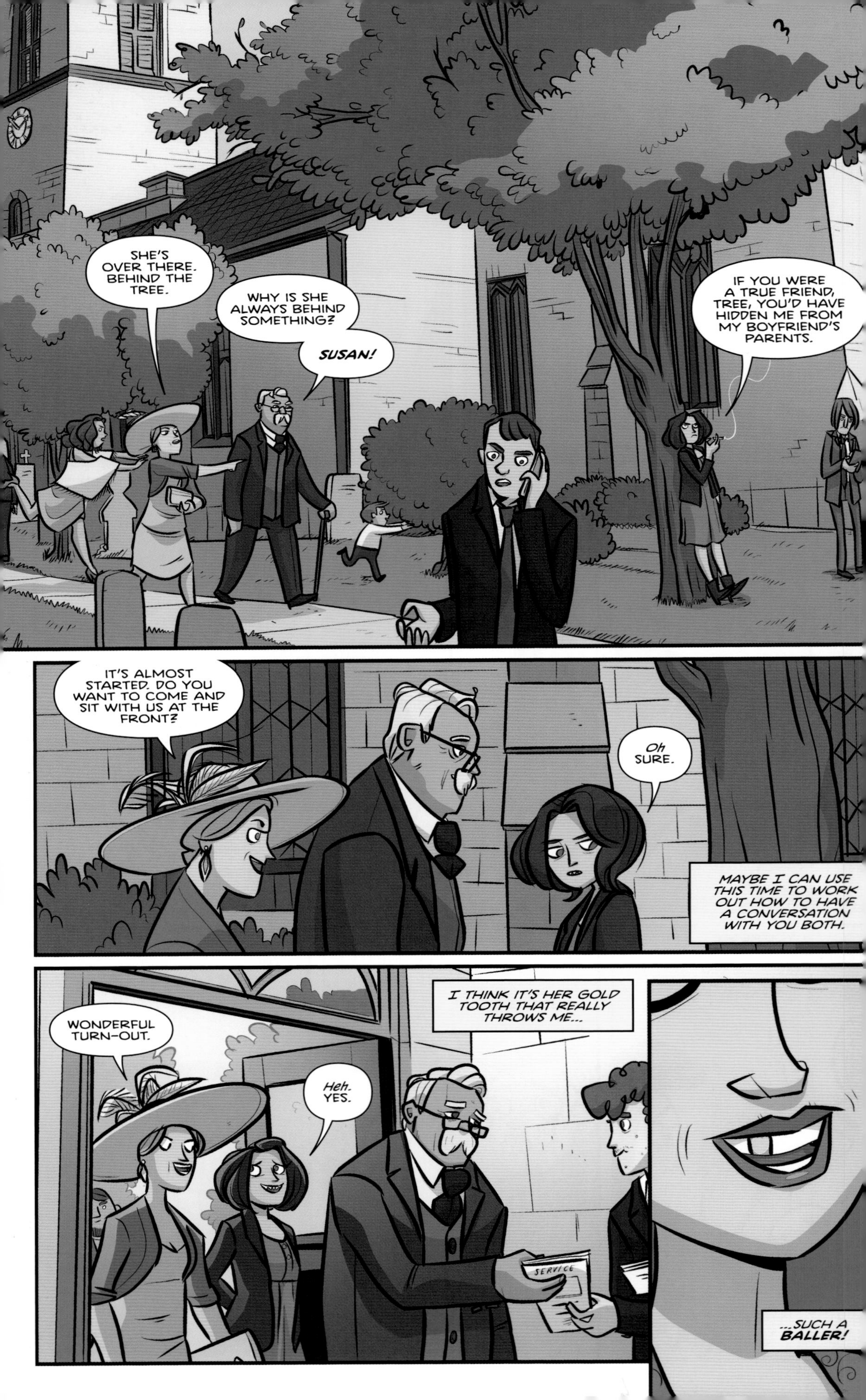
SHE'S OVER THERE. BEHIND THE TREE.
WHY IS SHE ALWAYS BEHIND SOMETHING?
SUSAN!
IF YOU WERE A TRUE FRIEND, TREE, YOU'D HAVE HIDDEN ME FROM MY BOYFRIEND'S PARENTS.
IT'S ALMOST STARTED. DO YOU WANT TO COME AND SIT WITH US AT THE FRONT?
Oh SURE.
MAYBE I CAN USE THIS TIME TO WORK OUT HOW TO HAVE A CONVERSATION WITH YOU BOTH.
WONDERFUL TURN-OUT.
Heh. YES.
I THINK IT'S HER GOLD TOOTH THAT REALLY THROWS ME...
SERVICE
...SUCH A BALLER!

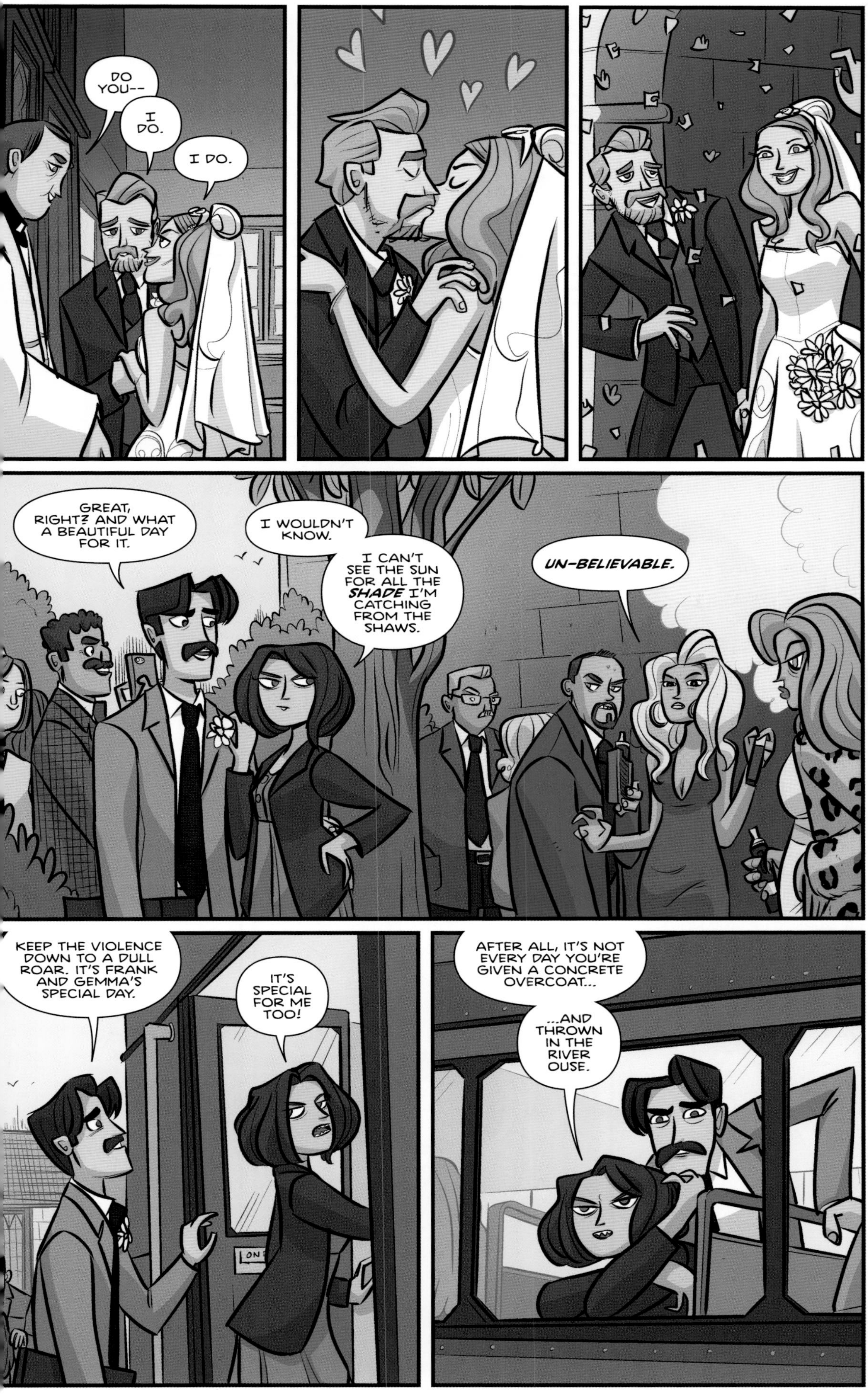
DO YOU--
I DO.
I DO.
GREAT, RIGHT? AND WHAT A BEAUTIFUL DAY FOR IT.
I WOULDN'T KNOW.
I CAN'T SEE THE SUN FOR ALL THE *SHADE* I'M CATCHING FROM THE SHAWS.
UN-BELIEVABLE.
KEEP THE VIOLENCE DOWN TO A DULL ROAR. IT'S FRANK AND GEMMA'S SPECIAL DAY.
IT'S SPECIAL FOR ME TOO!
AFTER ALL, IT'S NOT EVERY DAY YOU'RE GIVEN A CONCRETE OVERCOAT...
...AND THROWN IN THE RIVER OUSE.

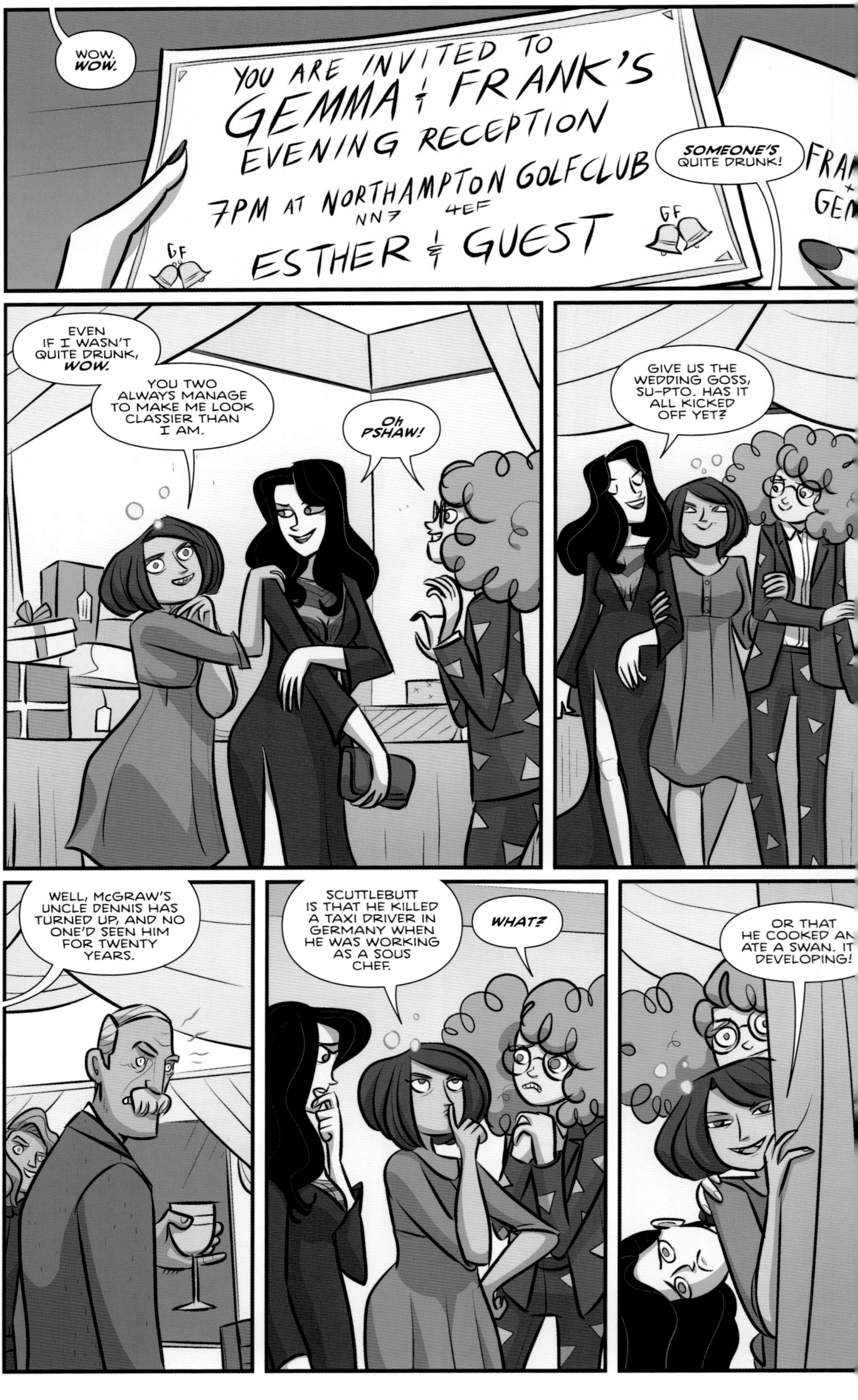
WOW. WOW.
YOU ARE INVITED TO GEMMA & FRANK'S EVENING RECEPTION
7PM AT NORTHAMPTON GOLFCLUB NN7 4EF
GF
ESTHER & GUEST
GF
SOMEONE'S QUITE DRUNK!
EVEN IF I WASN'T QUITE DRUNK, WOW.
YOU TWO ALWAYS MANAGE TO MAKE ME LOOK CLASSIER THAN I AM.
Oh PSHAW!
GIVE US THE WEDDING GOSS, SU-PTO. HAS IT ALL KICKED OFF YET?
WELL, McGRAW'S UNCLE DENNIS HAS TURNED UP, AND NO ONE'D SEEN HIM FOR TWENTY YEARS.
SCUTTLEBUTT IS THAT HE KILLED A TAXI DRIVER IN GERMANY WHEN HE WAS WORKING AS A SOUS CHEF.
WHAT?
OR THAT HE COOKED AN ATE A SWAN. IT DEVELOPING!

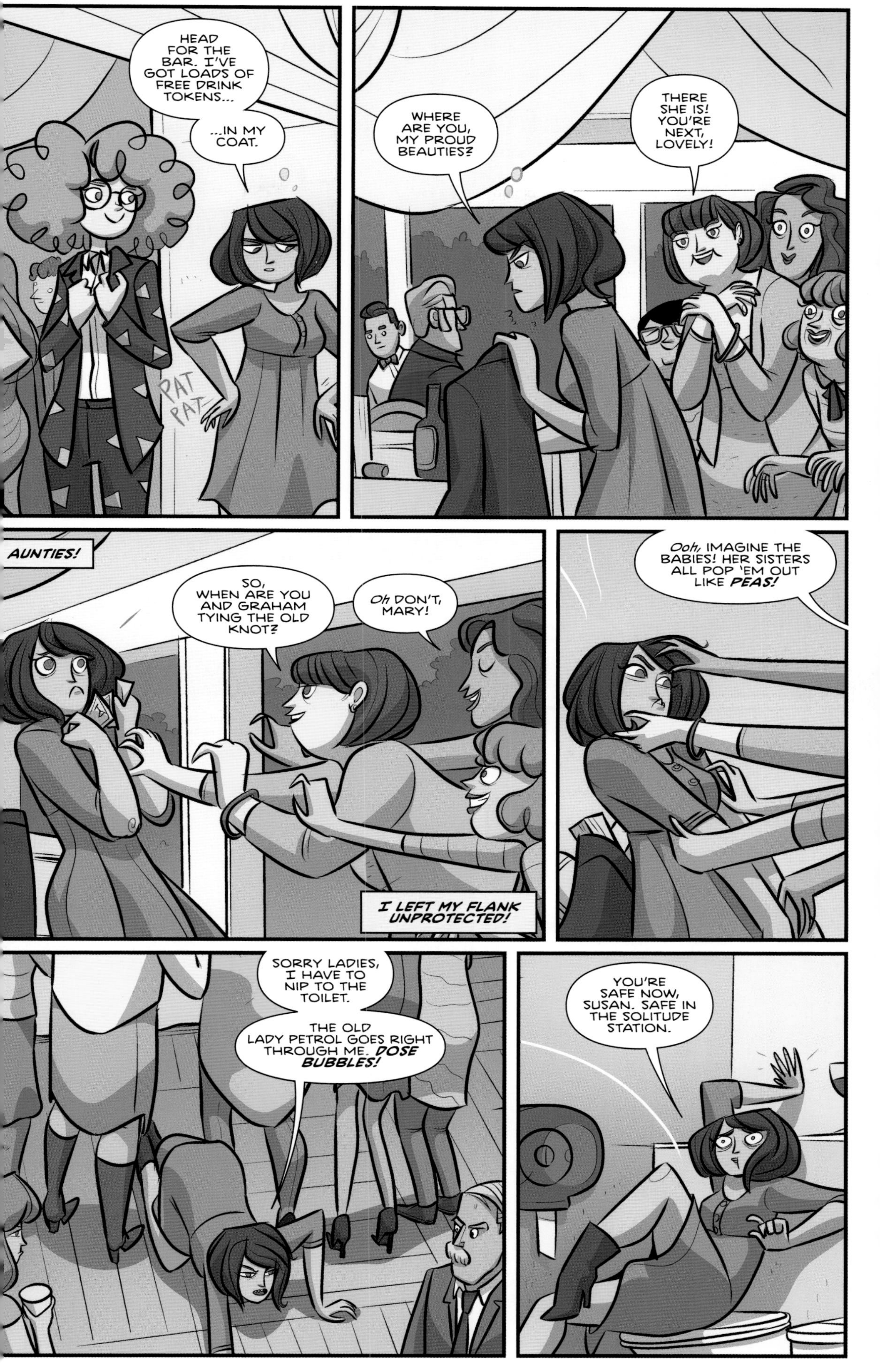
HEAD FOR THE BAR. I'VE GOT LOADS OF FREE DRINK TOKENS...
...IN MY COAT.
PAT PAT
WHERE ARE YOU, MY PROUD BEAUTIES?
THERE SHE IS! YOU'RE NEXT, LOVELY!
AUNTIES!
SO, WHEN ARE YOU AND GRAHAM TYING THE OLD KNOT?
Oh DON'T, MARY!
I LEFT MY FLANK UNPROTECTED!
Ooh, IMAGINE THE BABIES! HER SISTERS ALL POP 'EM OUT LIKE ***PEAS!***
SORRY LADIES, I HAVE TO NIP TO THE TOILET.
THE OLD LADY PETROL GOES RIGHT THROUGH ME. ***DOSE BUBBLES!***
YOU'RE SAFE NOW, SUSAN. SAFE IN THE SOLITUDE STATION.

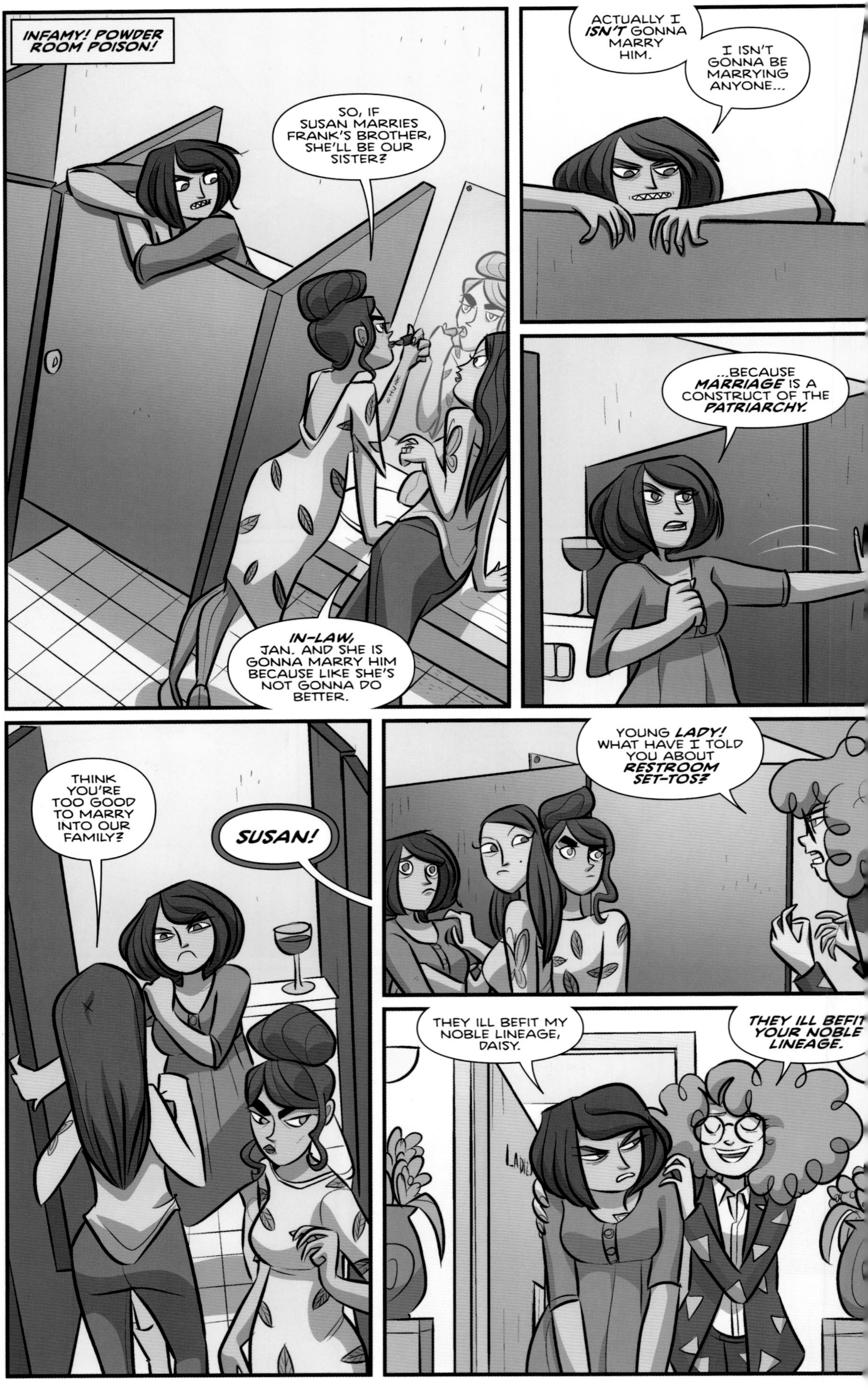
INFAMY! POWDER ROOM POISON!
SO, IF SUSAN MARRIES FRANK'S BROTHER, SHE'LL BE OUR SISTER?
IN-LAW, JAN. AND SHE IS GONNA MARRY HIM BECAUSE LIKE SHE'S NOT GONNA DO BETTER.
ACTUALLY I ISN'T GONNA MARRY HIM.
I ISN'T GONNA BE MARRYING ANYONE...
...BECAUSE MARRIAGE IS A CONSTRUCT OF THE PATRIARCHY.
THINK YOU'RE TOO GOOD TO MARRY INTO OUR FAMILY?
SUSAN!
YOUNG LADY! WHAT HAVE I TOLD YOU ABOUT RESTROOM SET-TOS?
THEY ILL BEFIT MY NOBLE LINEAGE, DAISY.
THEY ILL BEFIT YOUR NOBLE LINEAGE.

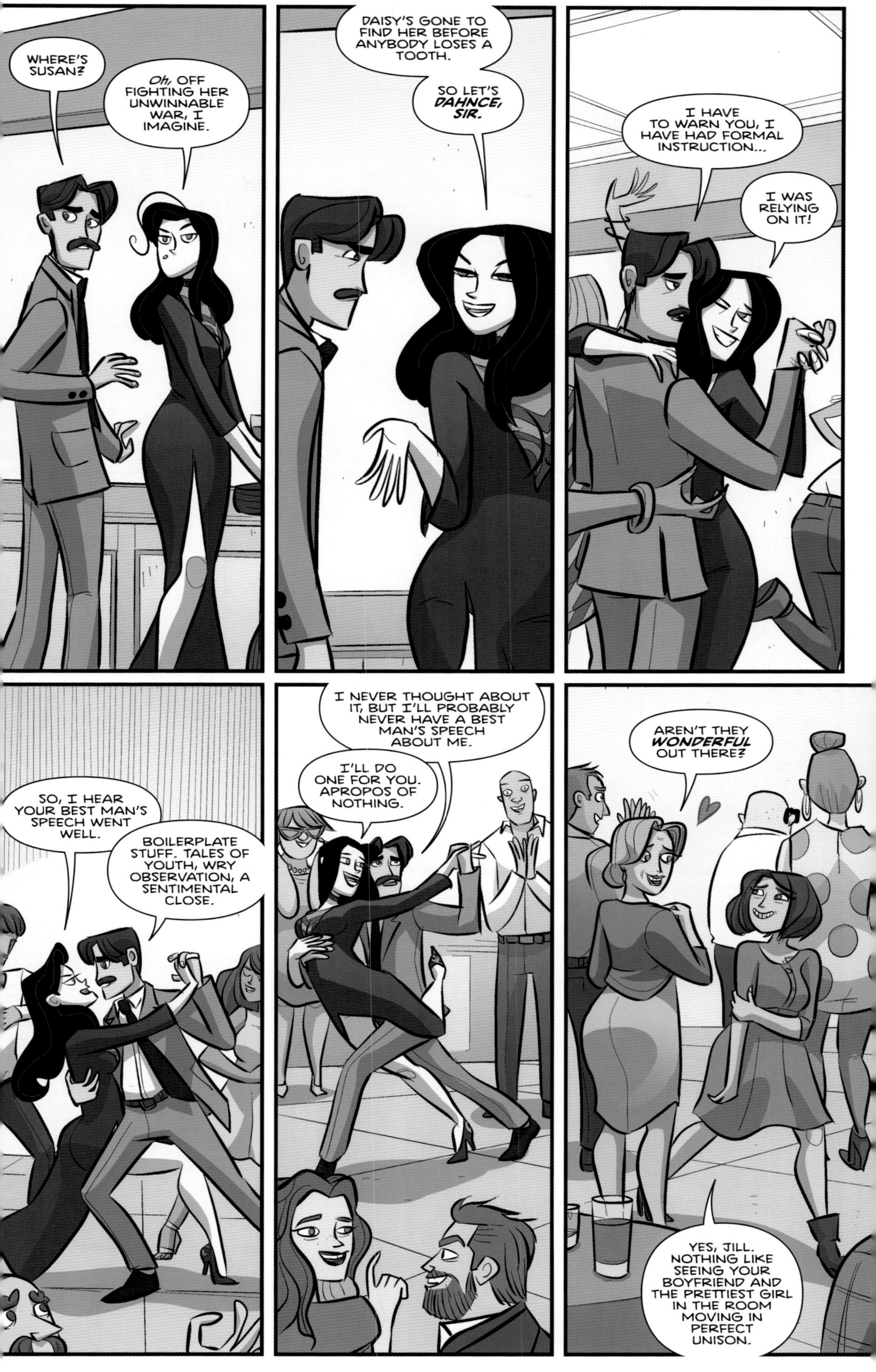
WHERE'S SUSAN?
Oh, OFF FIGHTING HER UNWINNABLE WAR, I IMAGINE.
DAISY'S GONE TO FIND HER BEFORE ANYBODY LOSES A TOOTH.
SO LET'S ***DAHNCE, SIR.***
I HAVE TO WARN YOU, I HAVE HAD FORMAL INSTRUCTION...
I WAS RELYING ON IT!
SO, I HEAR YOUR BEST MAN'S SPEECH WENT WELL.
BOILERPLATE STUFF. TALES OF YOUTH, WRY OBSERVATION, A SENTIMENTAL CLOSE.
I NEVER THOUGHT ABOUT IT, BUT I'LL PROBABLY NEVER HAVE A BEST MAN'S SPEECH ABOUT ME.
I'LL DO ONE FOR YOU. APROPOS OF NOTHING.
AREN'T THEY ***WONDERFUL*** OUT THERE?
YES, JILL. NOTHING LIKE SEEING YOUR BOYFRIEND AND THE PRETTIEST GIRL IN THE ROOM MOVING IN PERFECT UNISON.

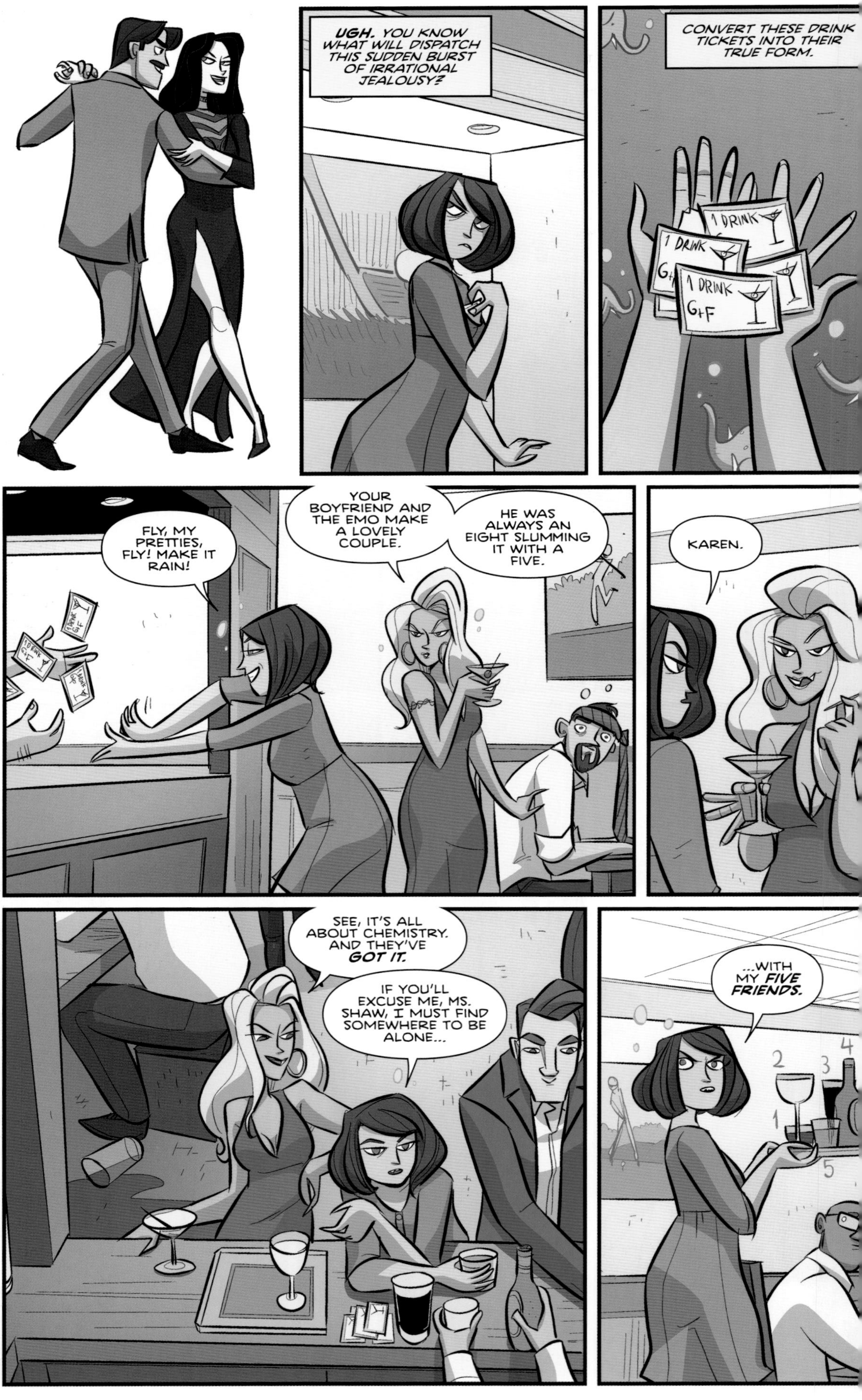
UGH. YOU KNOW WHAT WILL DISPATCH THIS SUDDEN BURST OF IRRATIONAL JEALOUSY?
CONVERT THESE DRINK TICKETS INTO THEIR TRUE FORM.
1 DRINK G+F
FLY, MY PRETTIES, FLY! MAKE IT RAIN!
YOUR BOYFRIEND AND THE EMO MAKE A LOVELY COUPLE.
HE WAS ALWAYS AN EIGHT SLUMMING IT WITH A FIVE.
KAREN.
SEE, IT'S ALL ABOUT CHEMISTRY. AND THEY'VE GOT IT.
IF YOU'LL EXCUSE ME, MS. SHAW, I MUST FIND SOMEWHERE TO BE ALONE...
...WITH MY FIVE FRIENDS.
1
2
3
4
5

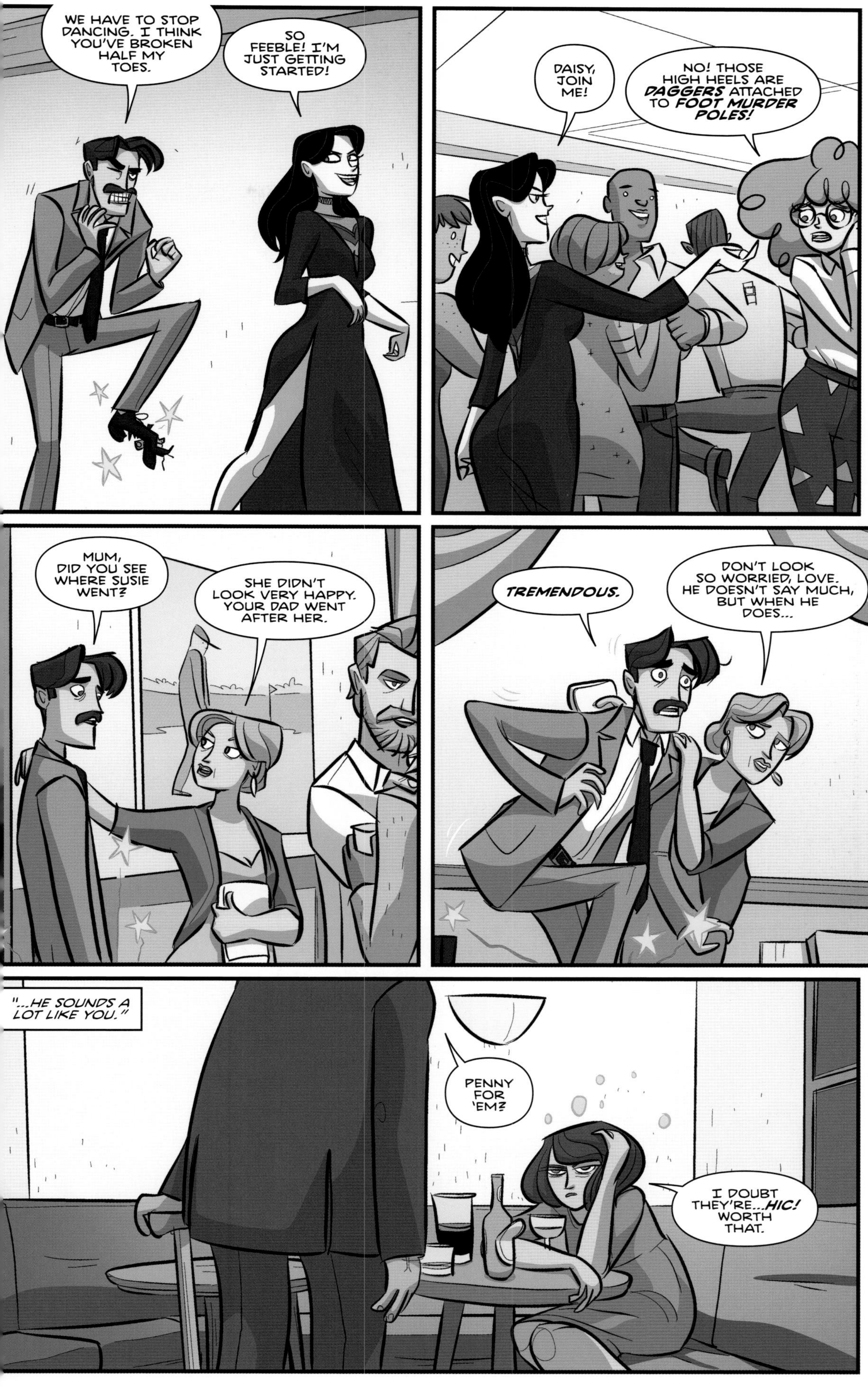
WE HAVE TO STOP DANCING. I THINK YOU'VE BROKEN HALF MY TOES.
SO FEEBLE! I'M JUST GETTING STARTED!
DAISY, JOIN ME!
NO! THOSE HIGH HEELS ARE DAGGERS ATTACHED TO FOOT MURDER POLES!
MUM, DID YOU SEE WHERE SUSIE WENT?
SHE DIDN'T LOOK VERY HAPPY. YOUR DAD WENT AFTER HER.
TREMENDOUS.
DON'T LOOK SO WORRIED, LOVE. HE DOESN'T SAY MUCH, BUT WHEN HE DOES...
"...HE SOUNDS A LOT LIKE YOU."
PENNY FOR 'EM?
I DOUBT THEY'RE...HIC! WORTH THAT.

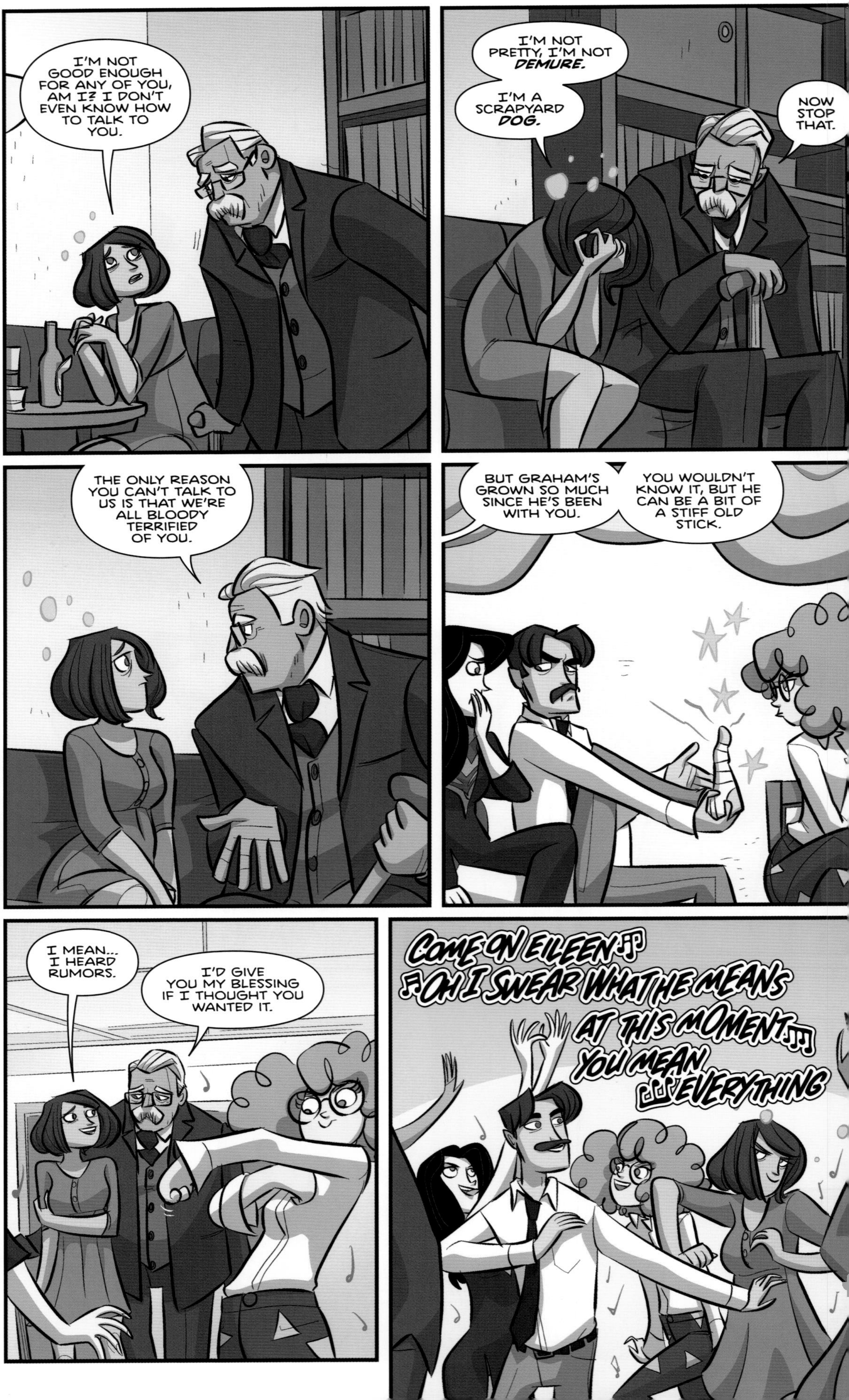
I'M NOT GOOD ENOUGH FOR ANY OF YOU, AM I? I DON'T EVEN KNOW HOW TO TALK TO YOU.
I'M NOT PRETTY, I'M NOT DEMURE.
I'M A SCRAPYARD DOG.
NOW STOP THAT.
THE ONLY REASON YOU CAN'T TALK TO US IS THAT WE'RE ALL BLOODY TERRIFIED OF YOU.
BUT GRAHAM'S GROWN SO MUCH SINCE HE'S BEEN WITH YOU.
YOU WOULDN'T KNOW IT, BUT HE CAN BE A BIT OF A STIFF OLD STICK.
I MEAN... I HEARD RUMORS.
I'D GIVE YOU MY BLESSING IF I THOUGHT YOU WANTED IT.
COME ON EILEEN
OH I SWEAR WHAT HE MEANS
AT THIS MOMENT
YOU MEAN
EVERYTHING

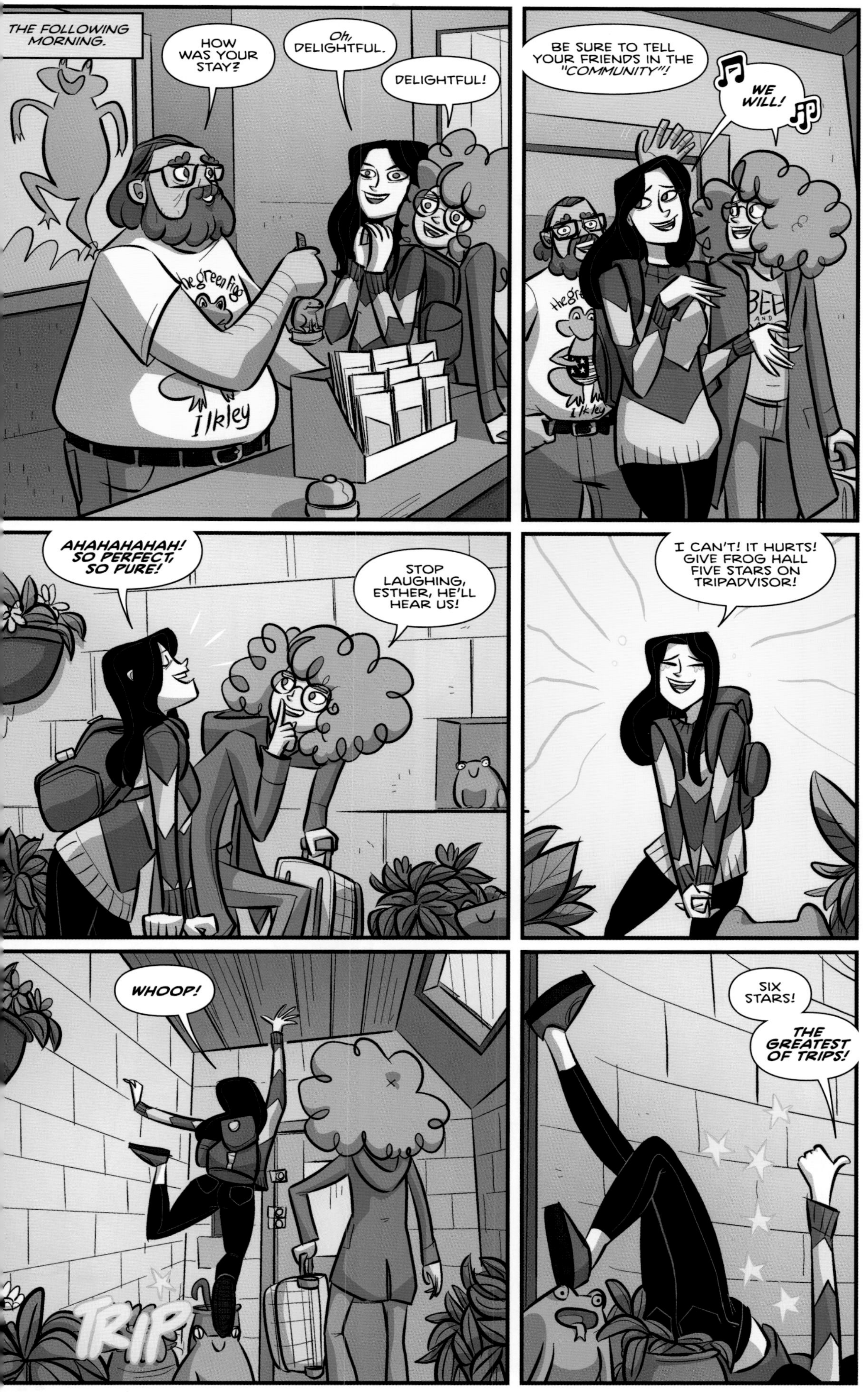
THE FOLLOWING MORNING.
HOW WAS YOUR STAY?
Oh, DELIGHTFUL.
DELIGHTFUL!
the green frog
Ilkley
BE SURE TO TELL YOUR FRIENDS IN THE "COMMUNITY"!
WE WILL!
AHAHAHAHAH! SO PERFECT, SO PURE!
STOP LAUGHING, ESTHER, HE'LL HEAR US!
I CAN'T! IT HURTS! GIVE FROG HALL FIVE STARS ON TRIPADVISOR!
WHOOP!
TRIP
SIX STARS!
THE GREATEST OF TRIPS!

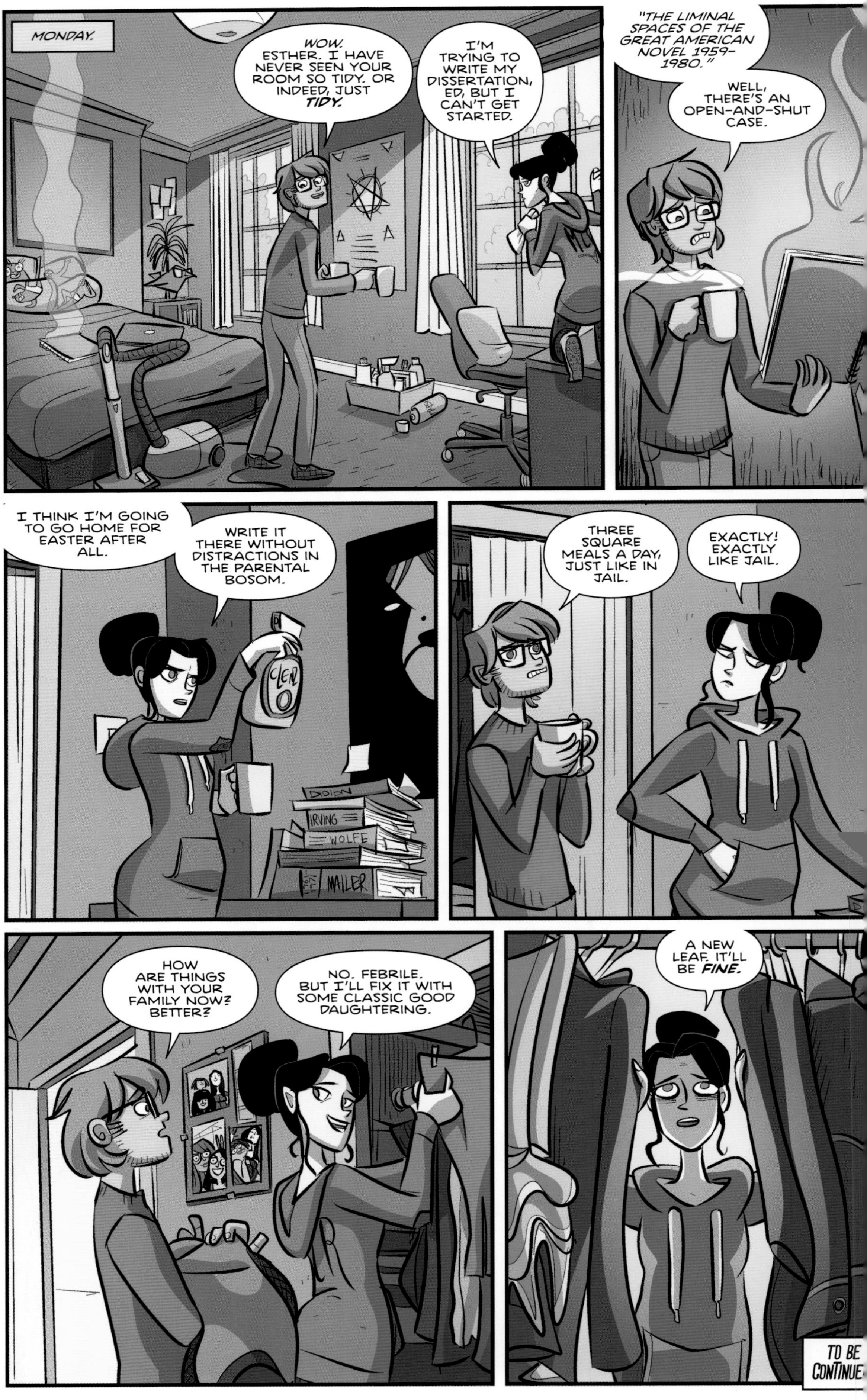
MONDAY.
WOW. ESTHER. I HAVE NEVER SEEN YOUR ROOM SO TIDY. OR INDEED, JUST TIDY.
I'M TRYING TO WRITE MY DISSERTATION, ED, BUT I CAN'T GET STARTED.
"THE LIMINAL SPACES OF THE GREAT AMERICAN NOVEL 1959–1980."
WELL, THERE'S AN OPEN-AND-SHUT CASE.
I THINK I'M GOING TO GO HOME FOR EASTER AFTER ALL.
WRITE IT THERE WITHOUT DISTRACTIONS IN THE PARENTAL BOSOM.
CLEAN
DIDION
IRVING
WOLFE
MAILER
THREE SQUARE MEALS A DAY, JUST LIKE IN JAIL.
EXACTLY! EXACTLY LIKE JAIL.
HOW ARE THINGS WITH YOUR FAMILY NOW? BETTER?
NO. FEBRILE. BUT I'LL FIX IT WITH SOME CLASSIC GOOD DAUGHTERING.
A NEW LEAF. IT'LL BE FINE.
TO BE CONTINUE

COVER
GALLERY

ISSUE #45 COVER
MAX SARIN

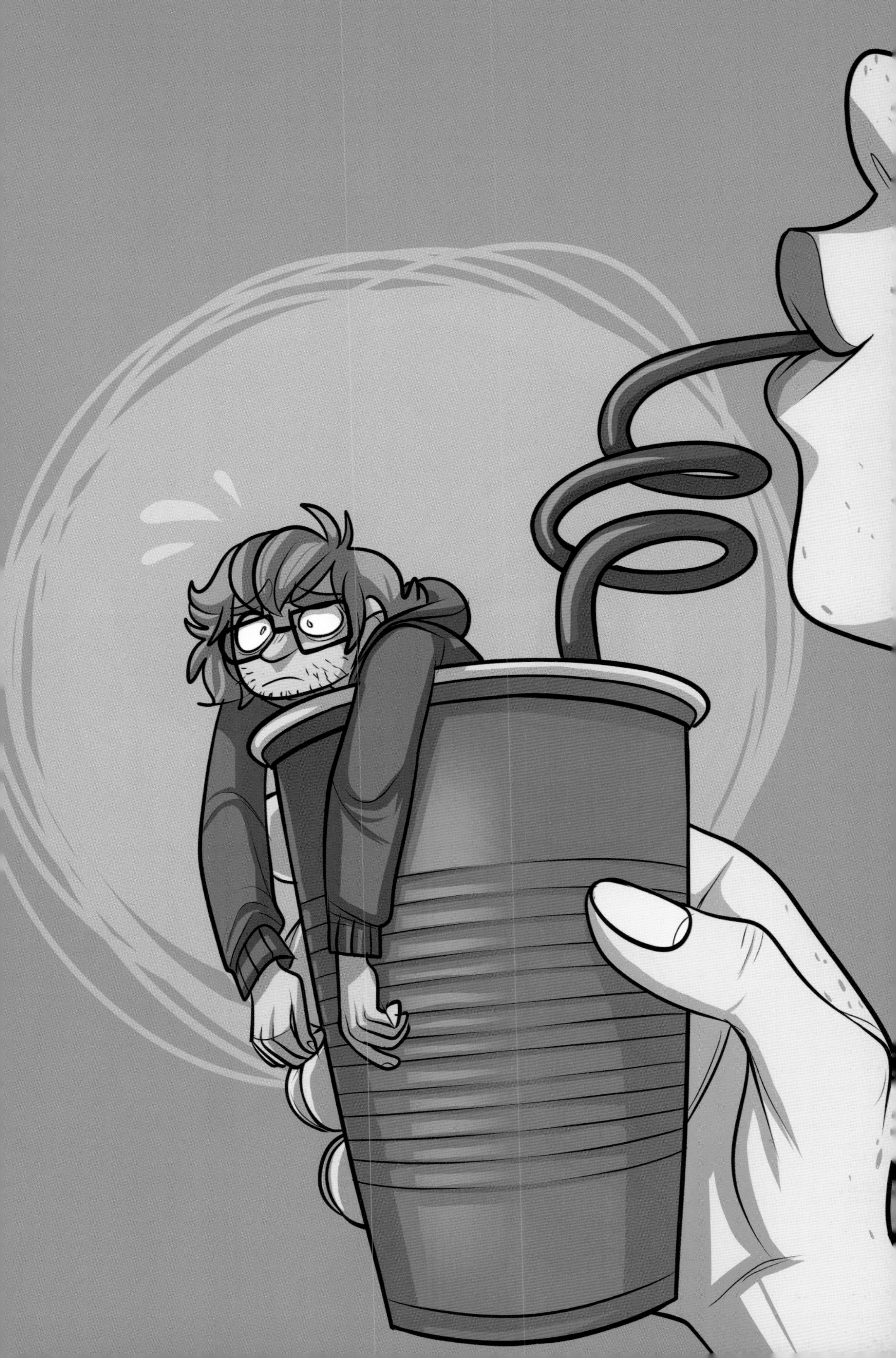

ISSUE #46 COVER

MAX SARIN

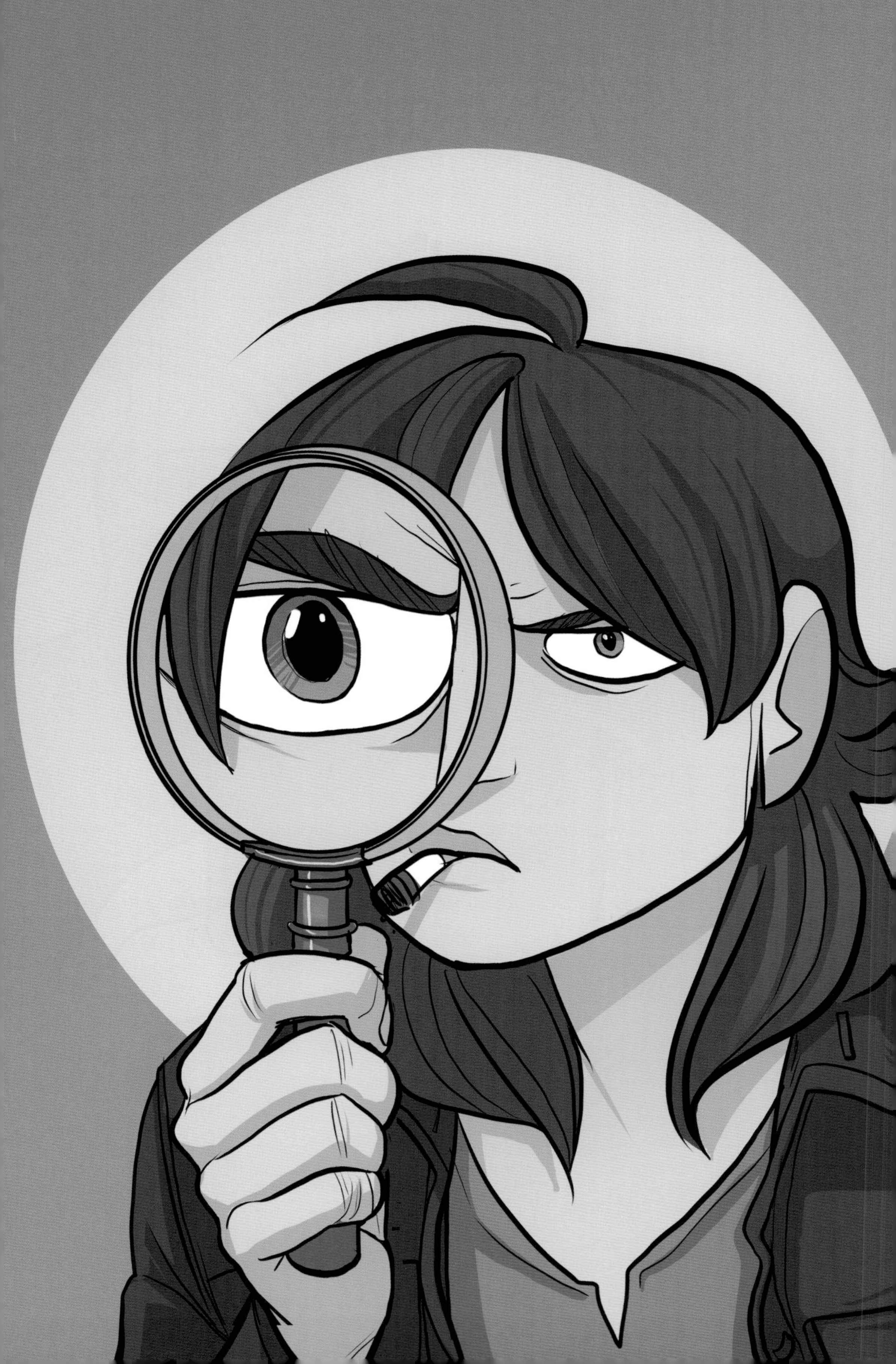

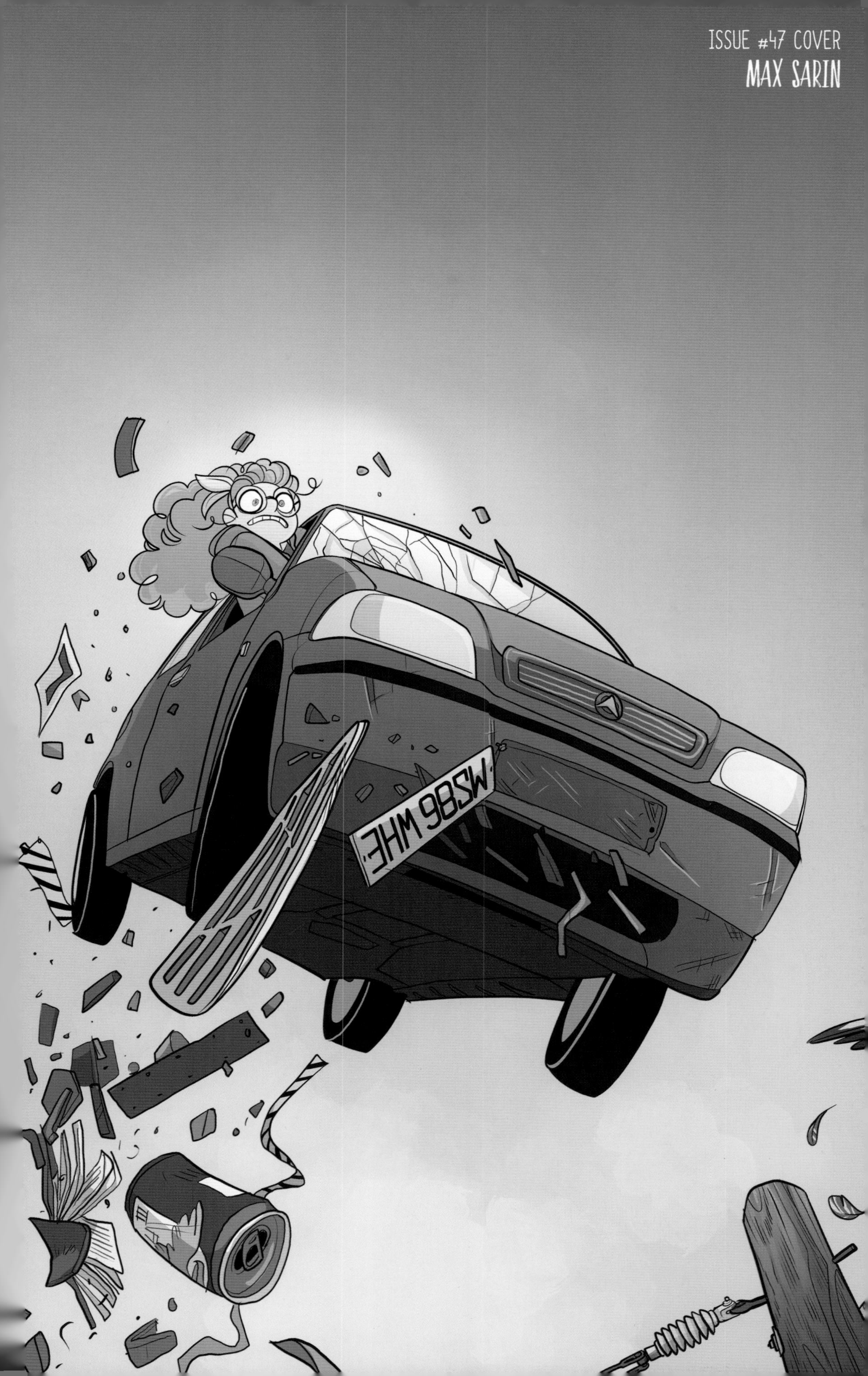

ISSUE #47 COVER
MAX SARIN

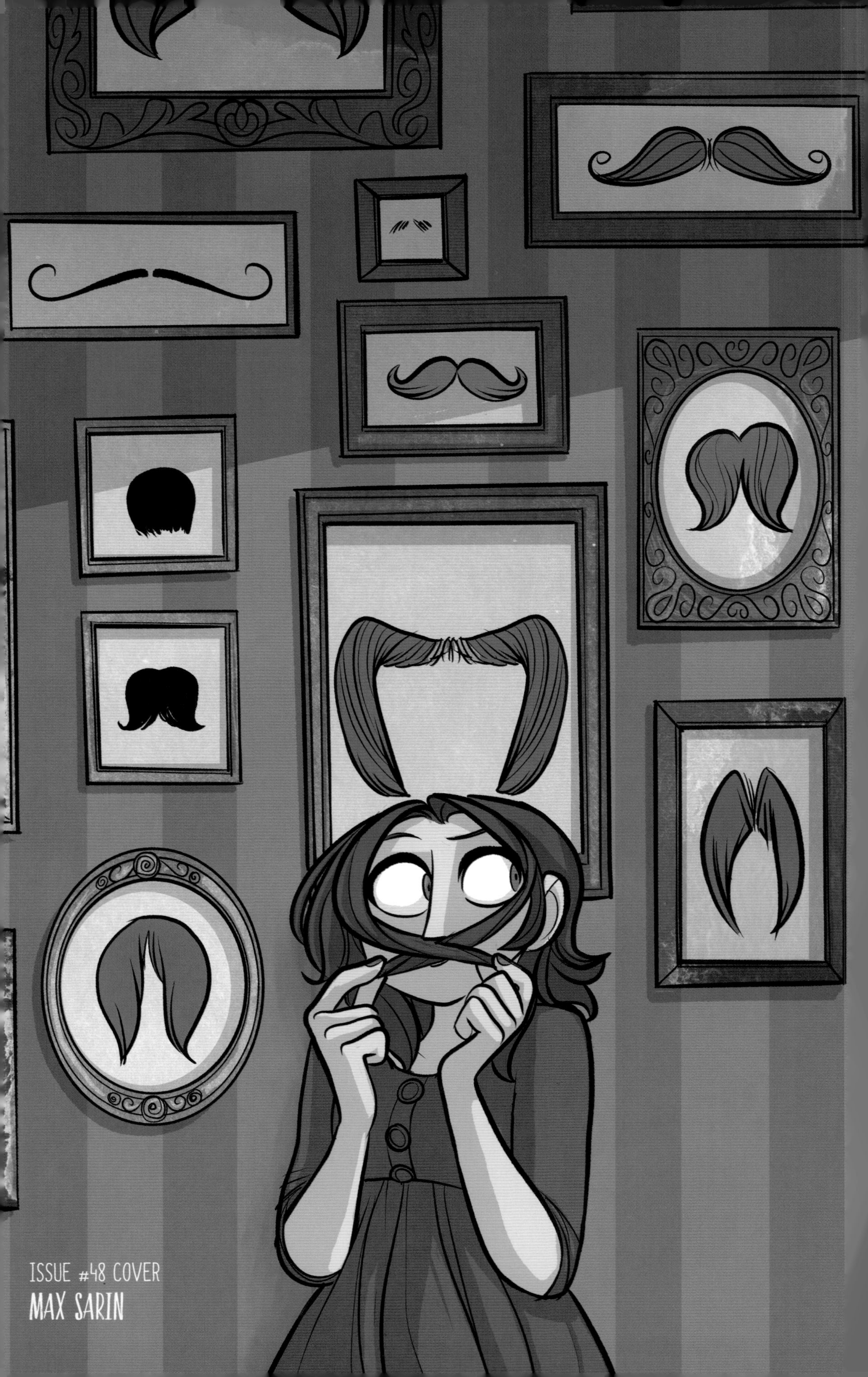
ISSUE #48 COVER
MAX SARIN

SKETCH GALLERY

SKETCHES AND DESIGNS BY MAX SARIN AND JOHN ALLISON

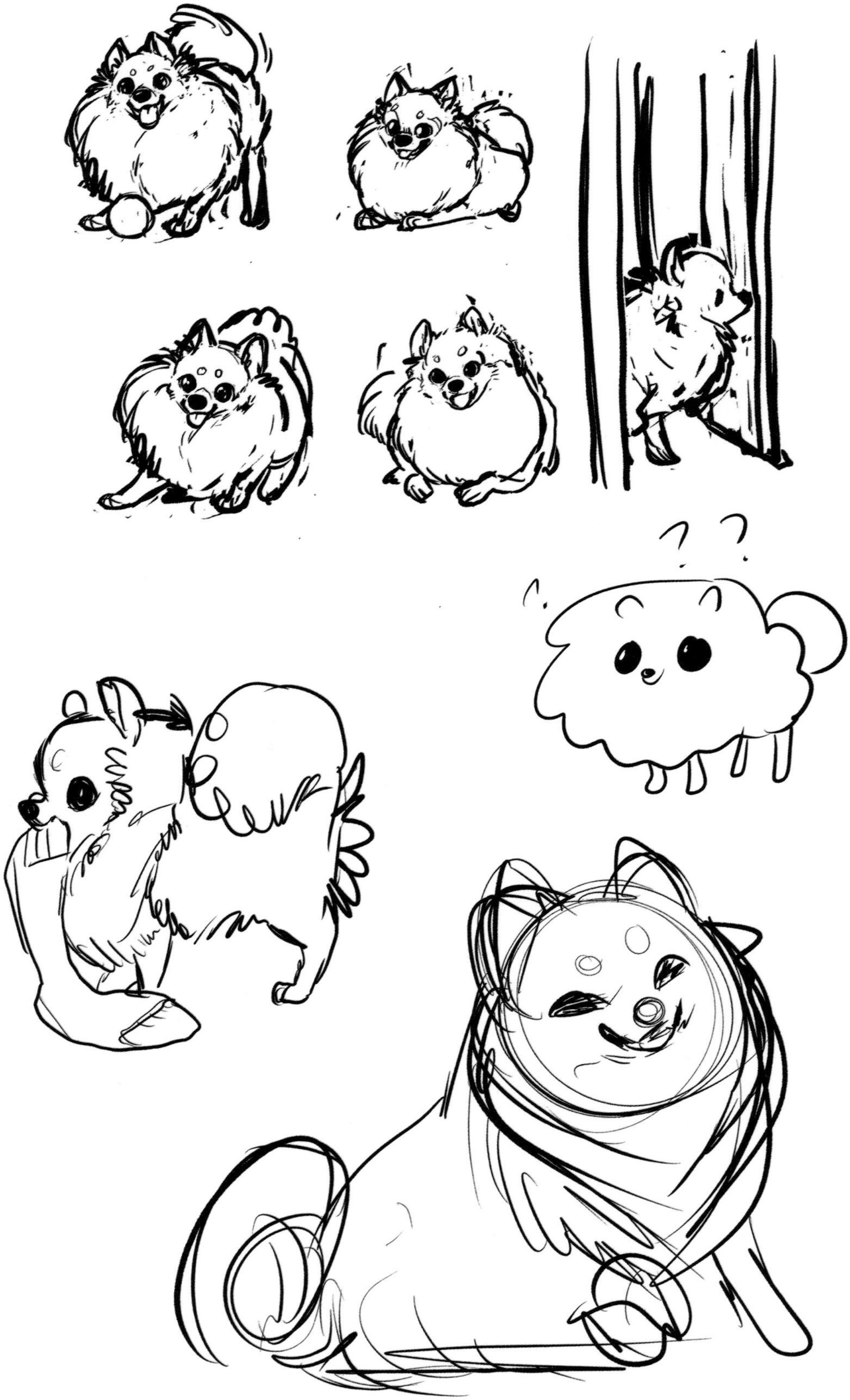
? ?

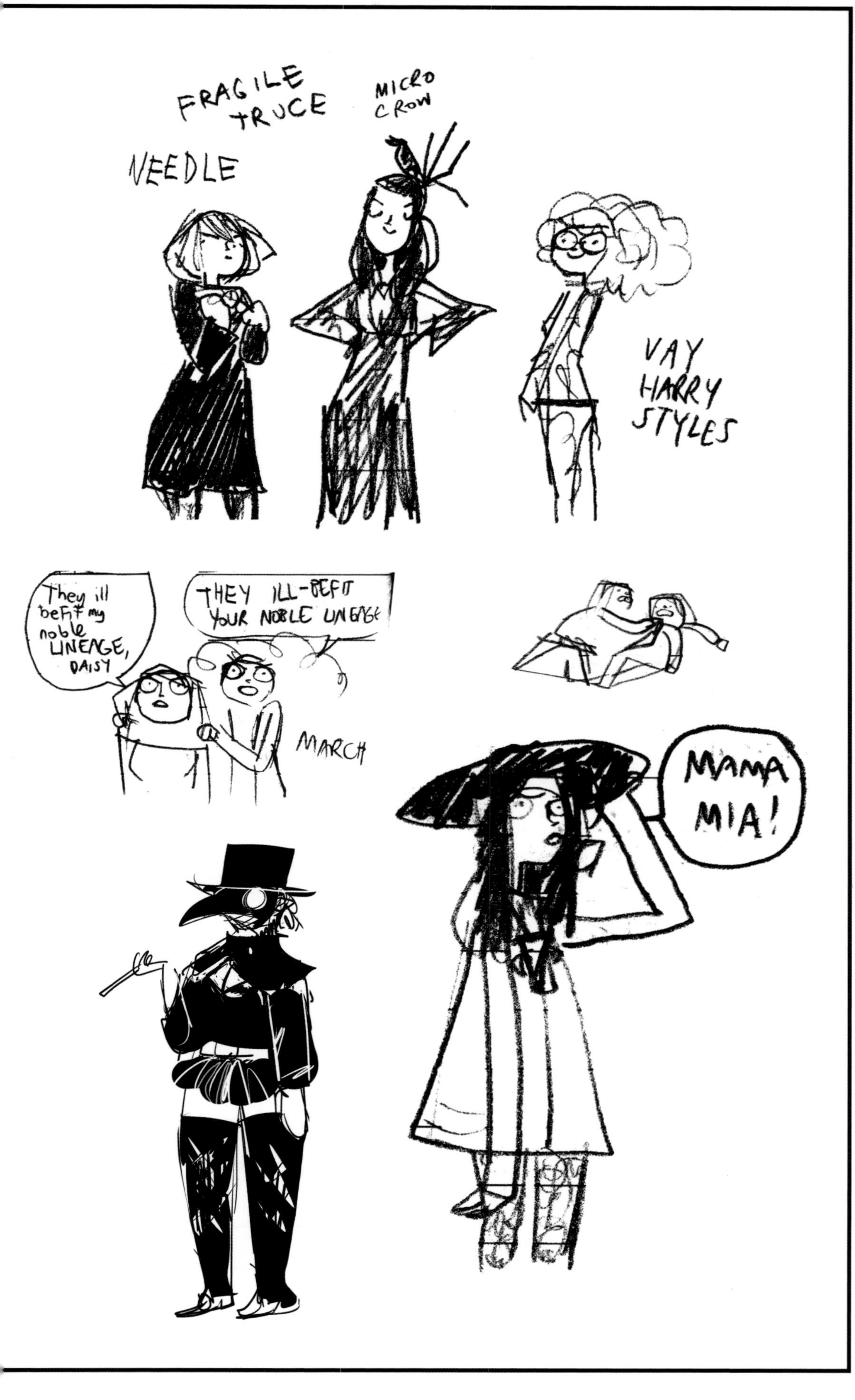
FRAGILE TRUCE
MICRO CROW
NEEDLE
VAY HARRY STYLES
They ill befit my noble LINEAGE, DAISY
THEY ILL-BEFIT YOUR NOBLE LINEAGE
MARCH
MAMA MIA!

PENCILS BY MAX SARIN

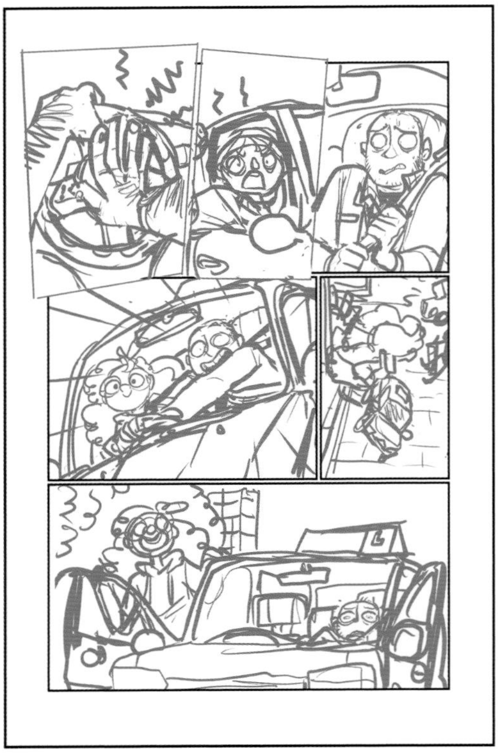

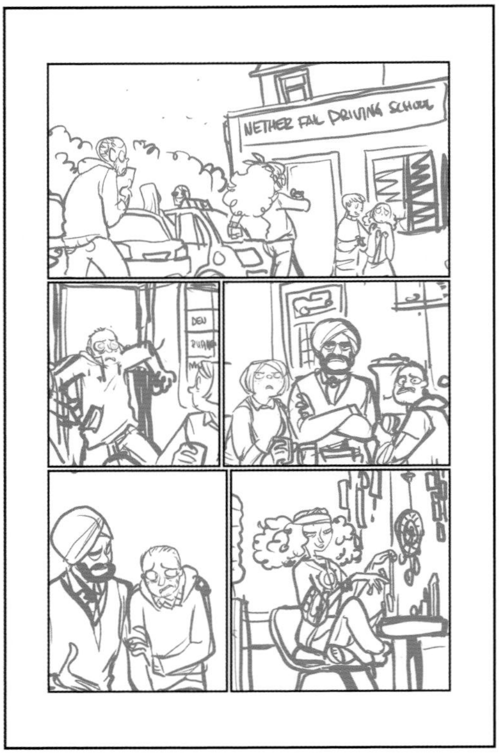
NETHER FAIL DRIVING SCHOOL

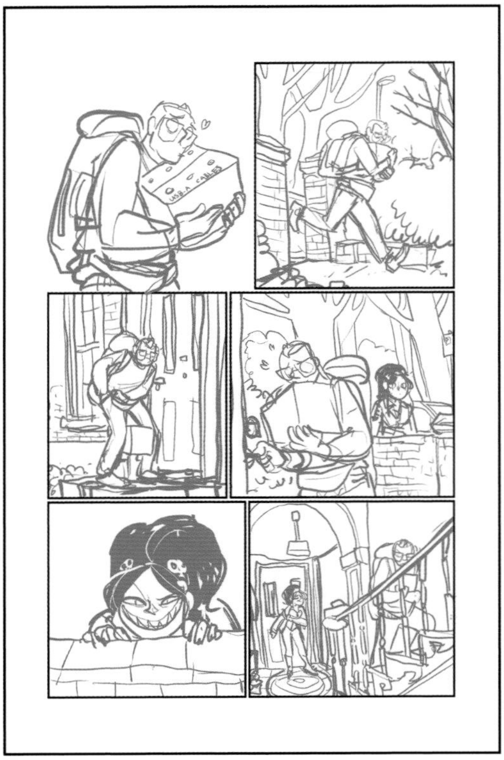

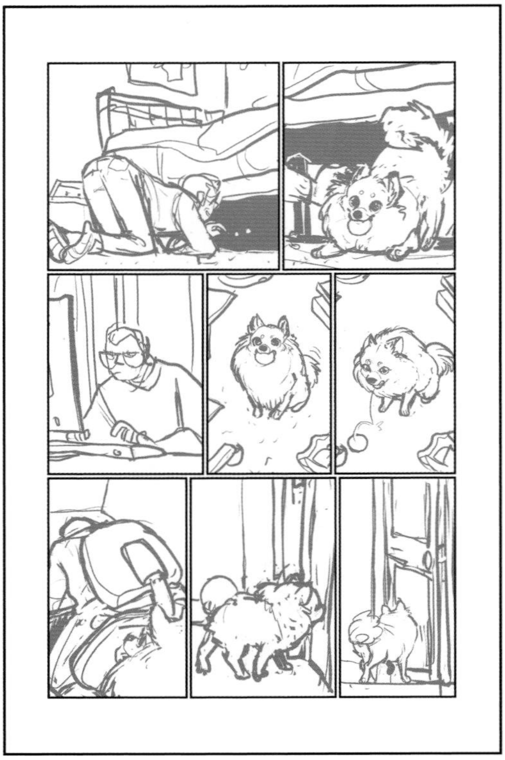

LAYOUTS BY JOHN ALLISON

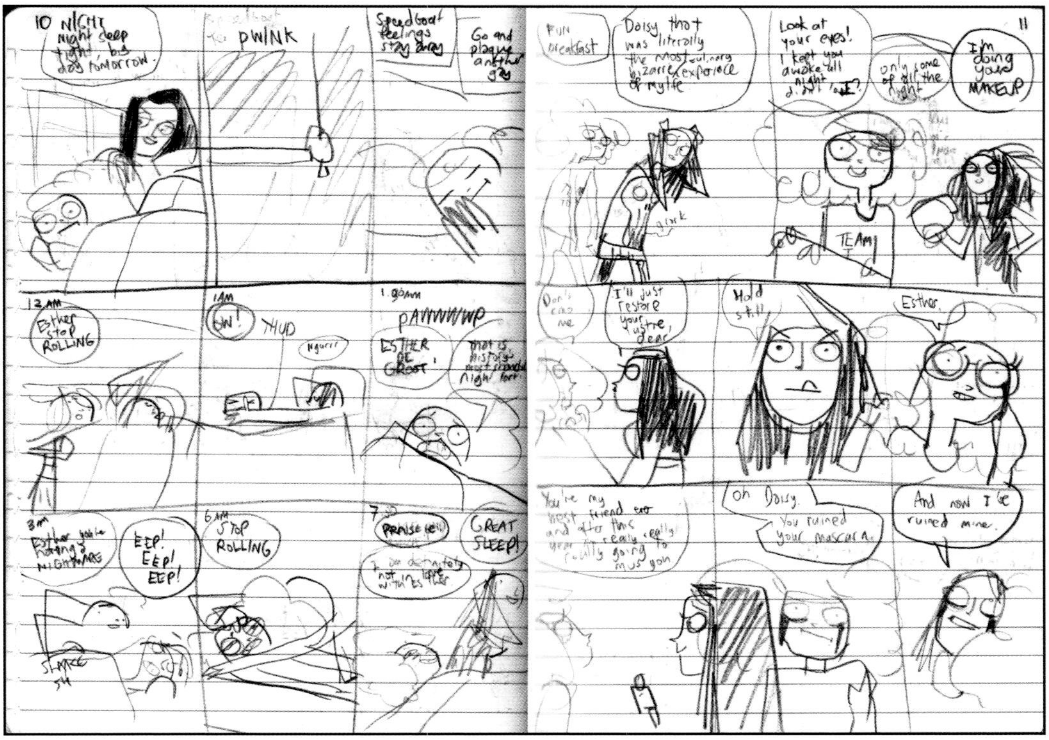
10
NIGHT night sleep tight, big day tomorrow.
PWINK
Speedboat feelings stay away
Go and plague another guy
FUN breakfast
Daisy that was literally the most extraordinary bizarre experience of my life
11
Look at your eyes! I kept you awake all night didn't I?
I'm doing your MAKEUP
TEAM
12 AM
Esther stop ROLLING
1AM
OW!
THUD
1.30AM
ESTHER DE GROOT!
I'll just restore your lustre, dear
Hold still
Esther.
3AM
EEP! EEP! EEP!
6AM
STOP ROLLING
GREAT SLEEP!
Oh Daisy. You ruined your mascara.
And now I've ruined mine.

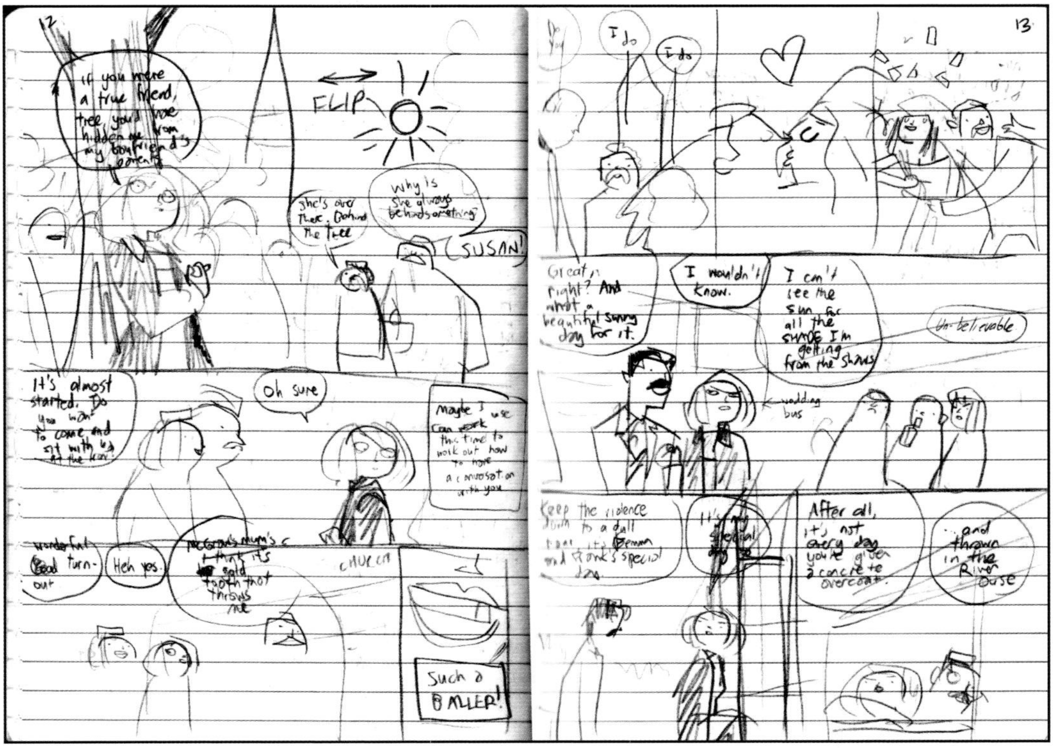
12
If you were a true friend, then you'd have hidden me from my boyfriend's parents
FLIP
She's over there. Behind the tree
Why is she always behind something
SUSAN!
It's almost started. Do you want to come and sit with us at the front?
Oh sure
Good turn-out
Heh yes.
Such a BALLER!
13
I do
I do
Great, right? And what a beautiful sunny day for it.
I wouldn't know.
I can't see the sun for all the SHADE I'm getting from the shades
Unbelievable
wedding bus
Keep the violence down to a dull roar, it's Denman and Frank's special day.
After all, it's not every day you're given a concrete overcoat
...and thrown in the River Ouse

DISCOVER
ALL THE HITS

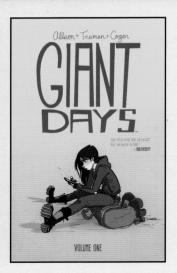

Lumberjanes
Noelle Stevenson, Shannon Watters, Grace Ellis, Brooklyn Allen, and Others
Volume 1: Beware the Kitten Holy
ISBN: 978-1-60886-687-8 | $14.99 US
Volume 2: Friendship to the Max
ISBN: 978-1-60886-737-0 | $14.99 US
Volume 3: A Terrible Plan
ISBN: 978-1-60886-803-2 | $14.99 US
Volume 4: Out of Time
ISBN: 978-1-60886-860-5 | $14.99 US
Volume 5: Band Together
ISBN: 978-1-60886-919-0 | $14.99 US

Giant Days
John Allison, Lissa Treiman, Max Sarin
Volume 1
ISBN: 978-1-60886-789-9 | $9.99 US
Volume 2
ISBN: 978-1-60886-804-9 | $14.99 US
Volume 3
ISBN: 978-1-60886-851-3 | $14.99 US

Jonesy
Sam Humphries, Caitlin Rose Boyle
Volume 1
ISBN: 978-1-60886-883-4 | $9.99 US
Volume 2
ISBN: 978-1-60886-999-2 | $14.99 US

Slam!
Pamela Ribon, Veronica Fish, Brittany Peer
Volume 1
ISBN: 978-1-68415-004-5 | $14.99 US

Goldie Vance
Hope Larson, Brittney Williams
Volume 1
ISBN: 978-1-60886-898-8 | $9.99 US
Volume 2
ISBN: 978-1-60886-974-9 | $14.99 US

The Backstagers
James Tynion IV, Rian Sygh
Volume 1
ISBN: 978-1-60886-993-0 | $14.99 US

Tyson Hesse's Diesel: Ignition
Tyson Hesse
ISBN: 978-1-60886-907-7 | $14.99 US

Coady & The Creepies
Liz Prince, Amanda Kirk, Hannah Fisher
ISBN: 978-1-68415-029-8 | $14.99 US